At Least Once

A Novel

D. M. Cuffie

Cover Design by Kerry G. Johnson **www.kerrygjohnsonDRAWS.com**
Author's Photo by Andre Dunston of Epic Photography

This book was printed in the United States of America.

ISBN: 1511938803
ISBN 13: 9781511938808
Library of Congress Control Number: 2015906943
CreateSpace Independent Publishing Platform
North Charleston, South Carolina

Dedication

To my mom, Mary Cuffie, for all of her love, all of her laughter, all of her wisdom, and my favorite facial feature.

Acknowledgements

First, I praise and thank God for placing the core message of this book in my heart. Thank you for allowing this book to encourage me, as I pray these words will encourage others...and provide a much needed laugh.

Giving so much thanks for my dad, George Cuffie, for just being a great dad! I praise my Heavenly Father that you are my earthly daddy!

Thank you O.A. Vicks for enjoying my emails so much, that it inspired me to write 10 years ago, being among my first set of eyes, and holding me accountable to get this book finished.

I am extremely thankful for P. Albert, D. Duren-Jones, O. A. Vicks, M. Hines, and R. Pompey for 20+ years of amazing friendship.

Thank you K. Cornish, K. Yarborough-Grissom, and M. Hines for being my first set of eyes.

A special thanks to C. Matthews of 'Jazz It Up' Studios & T. Thomas of 'A Thing of Beauty' for making me pretty and ready for my close up! N. Bastfield for my editing. M. Cornish for my first set of pics.

Thanks to my awesome Aunt M. Owens and my late Great Aunt L. M. Moore, for that special level of sass and to the rest of my family and friends for your love, support, good times and yes, Pokeno.

Thanks to my travel partner-in-crime Aunt E. Johnson for filling in the Bowie State University blanks and to her cohort S. Jones for the Wednesday night laughs. My La Fontaine Bleue (Retro) and Temple Hills Elks Lodge line dance family for 3+miles of guaranteed hip shakin' and good times.

Thank you D. Love, P. Styles, R. Carter, R. Mann, and T. Gordon for answering my questionnaire and/or shedding some light on the male perspective.

Thank you A. Terell for your thoughts, encouragement, and red pen.

Thanks to the employees at the Hagerstown Waffle House for the great service and letting me spend quality time writing in my favorite chair.

Thanks to my awesome 'Buck Club' for exposing me to some of the best books on the planet.

Thank you L. Lough, J. Fields, D. Smith, and especially D. Lawrence for all of your literary advice, expertise, feedback, and support.

Thanks to G. Tyler from the Top Shape Fitness Center for reminding me to "Stop being anonymous. Stand up and be counted." I will never will forget that advice.

Heavenly thanks to Bro. Fred Powell for reminding me to "make that man a plate."

Great thanks to my favorite teachers: J. Jackson, M. Morris, D. Elshafei, and Cliff Becker. And a sweet thanks to the sweetest advisor: M. Chaykovsky.

1

The Tea Party

"What did I smoke to get myself involved in this mess?" she sighed witnessing the spectacle before her. A burley older security guard dressed in an ill-fitting uniform with a stained tee shirt screaming to be washed, peered in her car window, and asked for her name and destination. She provided the requested information, while he checked his list.

"Gotcha right cheeah," he said tapping his clipboard and provided brief directions. "Are you a bridesmaid, li'l missah?"

"Yes sir, I am," she said smiling politely.

"Good. Give a sangle man like me sumptin' else ta look at outtah dan da couple in question." Before she could thank him for directions, he continued. "Yeah. You gotta fellah, dahlin'?"

"No sir, I don't," she said nervously looking at the queue forming behind her. "Well, thank--"

"You gotta date fo' dis weddin', pretty ladah?"

"At the moment no, but--"

"Mr. Fellows is always availahbah," he said proudly. "Yeah…weddins', bar mitzvahs, maybe a Christenin', and dat occasional funeral in case you need yo' hand held," he said smiling with his stained summer teeth. "Well, lemme let you go 'cause a line is formin'. You tell dat fine Mrs. Knight to send meh ovah a plate wit summah dat pound cake. Bettah yet, can ya brang it to meh?"

"I sure will," she said graciously. "I will keep your offer in mind and thank you." Breeze finally drove off to relieve the not-so-patient passengers behind her.

Despite the flirtatious security guard, it being a Saturday before school started, and being a bridesmaid to what Breeze describes as two of the vilest self-centered human beings that God has ever made, the landscaping was worth the trip to too-darn-far Virginia. Beautifully groomed lawns with oak and magnolia trees, deeply rooted in history, swayed in the rare August breeze. Flowers of every color of the rainbow pompously graced each lawn, street, and roundabout.

Amazed with the preciseness of the directions, it did not take her long to reach her destination. The modern ranch style home was nestled proudly on a well-manicured lawn with magnolia trees providing a welcoming canopy of shade.

She parked across the street and touched up her hair and lipstick. Saying a quick prayer for grace, she removed her purse and baked goods from the car, adjusted her pencil skirt and appropriately fitted top, and made her way across the street. "*Oh, can you make those wonderful homemade petite cheesecakes I like and bring them to my party, please?*" Tuesday asked with cavity causing sweetness before ending the voice mail of her impromptu invite. "*It's a tea party not a pot luck,*" she recalled as she carried a container full of her "homemade" confection up the three-car-deep driveway.

Strategically placed purple impatiens, hydrangeas, and rhododendrons said their hellos as she knocked on the door. A well-seasoned version of the bride-to-be with a smile as wide as Texas answered. "You must be Breeze," Mrs. Knight said welcoming her in.

"Yes ma'am," she answered as she walked in the door.

"I know, because my Tuesday said you would be the only one with enough manners to bring a dish. When you come to someone's home, you bring something other than your appetite," she laughed, hugged, and relieved her of the carrying tray.

"Aren't you just lovely?" she commented walking towards the household chatter. "Smile, figure, and not a blemish on that cream-in-your-coffee complexion of yours. And just which side of your family did you get that lovely head of hair from?" she asked temporarily placing the tray on an already crowded dessert table.

"Aww, thank you, Mrs. Knight," she said graciously. "I got it from my mama."

"Dahlin', you can't even buy it that pretty," she giggled. "According to my daughter, a tea party to welcome the bridal party was your idea," she stated fetching another silver tray for her desserts.

"Somewhat," she answered while helping transport the dessert from the carrier to the tray. "The tea party has been sort of a tradition among my circle of friends. I mentioned the idea to one of the teachers getting married and I think Tuesday was really sold on the idea. It's just a nice way to get together, and meet and greet."

"I hope the arrangement meets your expertise. I just had to add some items to the table or I would have some hungry folk in my house."

A plethora of tea party essentials covered the buffet table. Watercress and cucumber, ham, cream cheese, and egg salad sandwiches were perfectly arranged on an extremely polished silver platter. Four sweating silver pitchers of cold tea were strategically placed on matching round woven coasters. Crudités and five varieties of salad were placed on matching silver serving trays and bowls to complement the arrangement. *This woman has excellent taste,* Breeze thought surveying the items on the table.

"Let's get you introduced to my family."

A sea of adults with various shades of brown skin were scattered all over The Great Room. Women admiring artifacts and pictures, laughing as stories were told. A sight in the center of the room was all too familiar to Breeze: advice giving women. The older ladies gathered around the bride-to-be offering their do's, don'ts, will's, won'ts, and bet' not's. Ladies all too happy to share wisdom with a touch of sass, placed their hands on the roll of their hip, pointin' their hussy red polished finger, with their salt-n-pepper curls bouncin'.

"Sisters, this is Breeze, one of Tuesday's bridesmaids."

An assortment of nice-to-meet you, smiles, and extended hands came from the circle.

"Jus' look at Miss Thang with all that pretty 'grease and water' hair!"

"Grease and water? Chile, dats sto' bought!"

"Nah it ain't, dat's hers! And I hope she wears it down like that for the weddin'."

"Hold on ladies," Tuesday interrupted. "I haven't decided yet as to how my girls will wear their hair. However, the dress I chose will work either way."

"Well, you and your hair are absolutely lovely," one of the quieter aunts said finally. "Now, let's get back to the subject at hand, which is giving Tuesday the real deal on married life."

"She should be writin' all dis' wisdom down, Opal. You know how Tuesday fo'gets er'rythang," another sister said also wanting to go back to the conversation. She was indeed one of the main sisters pointing and shaking.

Tuesday's mother coaxed her to get pen and paper from the buffet to pacify her sister named Ruby.

"Mom, I was supposed to do the introductions," Tuesday whined.

Mrs. Knight flashed a look and Tuesday immediately did what she was told. Breeze secretly enjoyed that display. She came back with pen and paper and resumed her seat among her circle of aunts.

"Someone is finally giving that chile the attention she craves," Mrs. Knight said exhaustedly. "I don't know what I'm going to do for the next 10 months with her asking me 'bout various shades of yellow," she laughed. "Breeze, dahlin' the color of your skirt looks absolutely lovely against your skin tone. What is it? Coral?" Before Breeze could respond, she continued. "Maybe I can persuade that chile to change the color of y'all's dresses. I wish you could see the color she wants to put *me* in!"

"*Is this chick gonna put me in a yellow dress?*" Breeze thought to herself. "*We do like the mama, though.*"

"Come, let's introduce you to the masters of the barbecue pit," she said leading Breeze through the patio doors. "Now, I must warn you. Some of the men out here are married. But when they see you, their weddin' rings may find their way in somebody's pocket." Breeze offered a polite laugh. "Yeah, pretty young thing with a head full of curly hair with some meat on her bones will have dem boys drooling over more than that barbecue."

Mrs. Knight brought her to the backyard where the men were allowed to be men. Bald, curly, gray, good, and bad haired men gathered to admire the newly installed hot tub. A few others swarmed around the grill, as Mr. Knight held court.

"Now, whatchu need to do...oh hey Bunny," he said giving his wife a peck on the cheek.

"Shine, this is Breeze."

"Ah, yes, nice tah finally meet 'chu," he extended one hand while the other never left the grill tongs.

"Nice to meet you, too, Mr. Knight. I've heard so much about you," she said shaking his hand.

"Yeah, I heard much about 'chu," he said. "And I'm wonderin' why you are still a bridesmaid?" he mumbled.

Breeze smiled graciously in lieu of a snappy comeback.

"Shine, stop foolin' around with the chicken and finish cookin' so we can eat, please," Mrs. Knight ordered, giving him a love swat on his bottom and introduced her to the rest of the nearby men.

And Mrs. Knight did not exaggerate. The men were extremely friendly, especially when the simple handshake would not do. However, Breeze hoped no one noticed her change in demeanor, when *he* joined the group.

"It's about time you showed up! I do believe the invitation said, '*two*'," Spencer announced.

"Man, is you crazy?" asked one of the men. "This right here was worth the wait!"

Breeze slightly blushed, thanked the handsome admirer, and addressed Spencer's remark. "I must have missed the formal invitation, because my *voice mail message* said, '*three*.'"

He smiled and extended a hug, "It's good to see you, too, Breeze."

"I think I could have waited for another life time," she laughed and received the hug. "*Oh, he smells so good*," she thought. The welcoming embrace made her briefly recall as to why she tried to hang on to their relationship.

Her thought was interrupted and quickly realized the reason for the years' worth of chaos when he whispered, "Don't embarrass me."

"Then don't even think about giving me a reason to," she shot back.

She released him. He gave her a fake sweet truce look. She mirrored it back.

"Now that you're here, we can eat. Tuesday wanted everyone here before the food was served and a brothah is starvin'." He extended his arm, which she reluctantly took, walking back to the house as masters of their own personal charade she knew she was going to regret.

Tuesday snatched away her fiancé from their linked arms as he walked in, snuggled up to him, and assumed her position at the focal point of The Great Room. It was her turn to hold court, clinking her glass.

"Everyone, before we eat, I would like to thank everyone for coming and sharing this moment with us. Now, most of us are family, but I think that we should introduce ourselves and--"

The masses had other plans. "Chile," someone interrupted. "The hot food's gettin' cold and the cold food's gettin' hot! Let's get some grub on our plates and then you can bring on the speech!" The crowd agreed with, 'Amens and Mmm hmms.'

"Okay, all right," Tuesday said yieldingly. "Daddy, can you bless the food, please?"

Once her father said the blessing, the crowd made a bee-line for the grilled items, ready to throw down. By the looks of their plates, finger foods were considered side dishes. With the amount of food on their plates, Breeze thought it would be best to get in line. She had to admit she was ready to eat, but was concerned about what to eat. She had not seen the bridesmaid dress yet and dealing with the lack of sizes will not be on the agenda, this go round. *"Not for this bride at least,"* she thought to herself looking over the table.

"Is that all you goin' to put on yo' plate, chile?" asked an aunt that was introduced as Jade.

"I better watch what I eat before I won't be able to fit into any of the dress samples," Breeze responded.

"Chile please! Order a size up, get a seamstress to tuck it in, and let someone else watch that thick, pretty figure of yours," Jade commanded, consorting with the lady behind her.

"Yeah, just as long as it's not my husband. That's how mine found me!"

Breeze giggled and graciously obeyed. Once served, she took her seat on the sofa, sitting next to a young lady that could not have been any more than 15. She had a timid, yet hungry-for-some-attention look on her face, looking out of place.

"Hi, I'm Breeze" she said as she sat down.

"I'm Tuesday's cousin, Wednesday," she smiled nervously. "So you're the other bridesmaid."

"Yes. Wait, what do you mean *other* bridesmaid? How many people are in the bridal party?"

"Five on the bride side if you count the junior bridesmaid, flower girl, you, me, and our other cousin Monday." She nodded her head to the direction of a taller version of Tuesday who appeared bored and intentionally unconcerned. "Monday is the maid of honor. None of us are sure as to why." Breeze was intrigued and anxious to get to the bottom of the sentiment when Tuesday requested attention on the floor again.

"By the looks of the members of my bridal party, it's time for some introductions and ice breakers. If you would all be so kind as to say your name, your relationship with either me or my handsome groom, and your role in the wedding."

"Um, I'll start," Wednesday said as she stood up. "My name is Wednesday. I'm a cousin of the bride, a bridesmaid, and glad to be a part of their special day." She ticked off the points with her fingers as she walked towards the remaining items on the barbecued buffet and helped herself.

Guests of the Knight's introduced themselves throughout The Great Room. Warm sentiments, brief toasts, and words of wisdom from both sides of the family were showered over the happy couple. They were both beaming and a little teary eyed.

"Good evening all. I'm Breeze Monsoon, Tuesday's co-worker, and a bridesmaid. To Tuesday and Spence: I honestly believe that you both truly deserve each other's love," she said smiling as the guests 'awed.'

"She's also the reason why we are here today," Tuesday added. "If it wasn't for Breeze, we probably would not have met." The family smiled, 'oh'd,' and raised their glasses of whatever to Breeze.

As Breeze took her seat, she noticed a petite, mahogany, weathered skinned woman whose face hid behind spiral curls, shaking her head while peering at her. Her lips formed, as if she was trying to remove a piece of leftover food from her teeth. Breeze smiled nervously, listening to the remainder of the introductions.

Once they were done, the guests quickly went back to their meal and conversation. Wednesday finally returned to her seat on the sofa, balanced her plate on her lap, and proceeded to reveal the 'Monday mystery.' Breeze interrupted her. "Was I supposed to make myself known to the woman over there that looks like she needs a toothpick?"

Wednesday chuckled, however, Mrs. Knight responded. "That would be Spencer's mother," she said plopping herself on the couch between the bridesmaids for a moment of rest. "She asked about you as soon as you walked in. I had to apologize for not introducing you to her. Come to think of it, I don't recall her saying anything during the ice breaker. I could get you two acquainted, if you wish?"

"No ma'am, I'm fine. I'm sure we will meet soon enough."

"Good, 'cause I'm hungry," she said nibbling off of Wednesday's plate.

"The secret to my slimness," Wednesday said pointing to the fingers that were not hers on her plate.

Tuesday clinked her glass again. Her guests, even Spencer, turned towards her looking annoyed at yet another interruption from the food.

"Excuse me, one more thing. These are your informational handouts designed especially for your role in the wedding."

"Good golly, girl! That ain't a handout, it's a handbook," Mrs. Knight remarked.

"Mom, this is my day and I want everything to be perfect. Absolutely no stone left unturned!"

"Lemme see dat thang," Mrs. Knight sighed.

Breeze handed her the large overflowing three ringed binder and leaned over her shoulder, as Mrs. Knight wiped her fingers on Wednesday's napkin, ready to thumb through the small text book of Tuesday's expectations and demands. The binder was divided into bridesmaid attire including swatches, the dress, shoes, suggested hairstyles, shower preparations, and assignments. An 11 month calendar with pre-scribbled appointments, in addition to hotel accommodations, prices, and assigned homes selected to perform tasks.

"You even have the nerve to include the order of service and a timeline?"

Breeze froze when she saw not one, but two names listed for the processional. "Did I miss Branford? Is he here this evening?"

"No, he had another event to attend *with his wife*. And just how do you know Branford, anyway?"

"Tuesday, I am very much aware that Branford is married. I was at the wedding--"

"What, you weren't *in* the wedding?"

"No, just a guest," she said mustering up a pleasant smile from her reserve stock. "I was a friend of the groom, not necessarily the bride."

"I'm surprised." Tuesday turned her head to the newly forming audience. "Breeze has been in...like...20 weddings?"

"Nine, actually."

"Nine?" the chorus of curly headed women questioned. "You should have hung up your bouquet at five," said an aunt introduced as Pearl. Before Breeze could respond, the ladies fired the dreaded questions, comments, and assumptions.

"You one a dem independent gals, ain't cha?"

"Is you one of dem, whatchu call 'em, *lesbians*?"

"Heifah, jus' cause she ain't married don't make her no lesbian." She looked at Breeze sideways. "Is ya?"

"No ma'am, I'm not."

"Well, you must doin' sumptin' wrong, dahlin'. The bettah question is, whatchu brangin' to da table besides all dat pretty hair and a smile?"

"Ma'am, I bring plenty to the table. However, I have a disagreement with the men I date: I need them to treat me with love, decency, and respect...they all disagreed."

They all laughed, nodding their heads in agreement, while Tuesday gloated, "Well, I'm so glad those days are over for me!"

"You ain't married yet, chile," said Ruby.

"Maybe you weren't meant ta git married," hissed Spencer's mother, wanting a piece of the conversation. "Not every gal is marriage material. Did jah evah thank a dat?"

"Actually, with the past choices and what's left at this point, I am very much aware that marriage may not be in His plans for me. And the good news is, I'm okay with that. Did *you* ever think of that," Breeze shot back. Realizing this conversation was taking an ugly turn, she excused herself, and walked off to the patio for some air.

2

Airing Out

Breeze found a shady spot outside and took a seat on a soft cushioned, bold floral printed, swinging loveseat. *"Maybe Willow was right. I should have said, 'no,'"* she thought throwing her head back taking in the evening air.

Unfortunately, Spencer came out to confirm her thought. "'We deserve each other's love'," he said sarcastically. "And just what was that supposed to mean?"

"Exactly what I said. You two deserve each other. There was no hidden meaning. It was simple, true, and to the point."

Before Spencer could answer, Tuesday sidled up to her groom. "There you are. You left in a heated huff before I could get a few things corrected," she said waving her clipboard. "We'll need to have your real name for the program."

"'Breeze' is my real name."

She laced her arm with his, "Spencer wants full names for the program."

"I assume you need a full legal name for an official document. That would be Monday's job. I am just a bridesmaid, my name should be fine for the program."

"Well, if you won't give us your real name, then you cannot be in the wedding."

"Oh, okay." Breeze shot up and walked back to the house. "Mrs. Knight, may I have my carrying tray, please?"

"You leaving so soon? We haven't even served dessert yet," she said concerned, springing from the sofa. "And you need a piece of my pound cake after all this," she said shaking the handout.

"I'm no longer in the wedding. So, at this point--"

"What do you mean you're no longer in the...Tuesday, what is going on?"

"Mom, we need first names not nicknames on the program."

"Chile, is 'Breeze' somewhere on your birth certificate?"

"Yes ma'am. But that's okay. Your daughter has plenty of time and friends willing to fill my shoes." Breeze said looking for her tray. "As a matter of fact, you may want to ask Britt. She'll do anything, especially for you."

Spencer pulled away from Tuesday in attempts to get Breeze to stop. "Hold on, hold on, we will use 'Breeze' in the program."

"I'm glad somebody acts like they got some sense around here! You two, go inside with your guests. Breeze, come sit a spell with me. We both can use some air."

Mrs. Knight sighed heavily, as she sat on the bench. "I have no idea what to say about my daughter. And I apologize for what she has said, done, and what she is going to do. What is your real name anyway? I promise I won't tell 'em."

"'Breeze' is my middle name. I just choose to keep my first name private."

"Gotcha. You know I'm intrigued." She laughed again. "Let's take a look at that big 'ol book of action items."

The two snatched a piece of chicken from the grill and proceeded to soak up the evening air, laughing as Mrs. Knight reminisced about her wedding.

"Bunny, baby? I hate ta interrupt. A few of our guests are ready ta go," said Mr. Knight.

Mrs. Knight excused herself and followed her husband inside to say 'good night' to their guests. Breeze decided to stay outside a little bit more. The lush green grass felt cool under her feet, as she inhaled the smoky aroma still lingering from the grill. She took a little comfort knowing there were a few stones that were indeed left unturned and smiled to the star filled sky. The cool breeze and humorous thought made her feel like she could stay out here forever, until...

"I want ta apolahgize if I came 'cross rude," said Mrs. Lyte. "It's jus dat mah son got ovah a bad break up right befo' meetin' Tuesday. And guhls dees days jus' ain't dah marryin' kin' no mo'."

"Apology accepted...I guess. But I hardly think it's fair to include me in that category without knowing me."

"Well, weren't you mah son's guhlfrien'?"

"No, we went out a few times, hung out. That was it."

"Mmm hmm. So you don't know who dis las' gurl was, huh?"

"No ma'am, I don't. But you said Spence was hurt by his *last girlfriend*? I didn't think he was capable."

"Capable of what? Whatchu mean by 'dat?"

"Not one thing." She rose from the swing. "Come. I smell strawber-ries. Let's have some dessert."

Breeze escorted Mrs. Lyte back into the house. The Knights were saying their good byes, while the sisters were doling out the desserts and wrapping up plates to take home. "This will help give a man somethin' ta squeeze," whispered one of the aunts as she handed her a generous piece of pound cake.

"Got plenty for him to squeeze already. Just need the squeezer," she laughed. She winced shortly after making that last statement. She did not need a man, nor did she particularly want one, especially after Spencer. She sampled the confection. The moment it hit her lips, she knew she tasted heaven. Breeze closed her eyes and savored the next morsel.

Nirvana was interrupted when Spencer hissed, "Why must you make everything so difficult?"

"Why do you insist on talking with your mouth full?" she asked wiping a spittle size piece of cheesecake from her ear. "And for your information, it's because you take me there! You are so determined to find out my first name. If it was that big of a deal, you should have asked Branford. Just let it go!"

"It ain't even about that, so calm your nerves. Besides, he still refuses to tell me. Anyway, all I want to do is make my bride's day special."

"Mmm hmm. Why am I a bridesmaid, Spence? Seriously, why am I here?"

"First of all, isn't it an honor to be asked to be a part of somebody's wedding?"

"Under normal circumstances. This mess right here ain't normal."

"You agreed when my bride asked. You had the option to say 'no.'"

"Dude, *you* had the option of sayin'--"

"Listen, 90 percent of this is Tuesday's doing, aw'ight? And I will agree to anything my bride wants, to make our day special. She insists that we met because of you. And in some strange way, it's true. She likes you and for some reason, she looks up to you at work."

"What on earth do you mean, *for some reason*?"

"Put your guns on safety, poor choice of words," he said while stuffing another piece of cheesecake in his mouth.

"So what was the last 10 percent?"

Spencer paused for a moment before answering. "'Cuz you're good people, Breeze," he finally said without looking at her. "I realized that after our last conversation. Allowing you to be a part of our special day is my way of showing you that I'm not a total monster."

"I would've settled for a gift certificate as a 'thank you' for all of this happiness."

"Look, just do whatever a bridesmaid is supposed to do to make my bride happy, okay?" he sighed. "By the way, you and Sara Lee put a hurtin' on the cheesecake," he winked and left to find his love.

Breeze no longer needed air; she needed an escape before her words got her into any more trouble and instinctively made a beeline for her car.

"Do you have a man ta go home to my dear?" Mr. Knight asked intercepting her path.

"No sir, I don't."

"You mean you won't be seeing no man when you get home?"

"Shine, please," Mrs. Knight playfully nudged.

"I will be seeing my dad and a good friend of mine, eventually. But no significant other is waiting for me."

"Okay, just remember when you do, make sure you make that man a plate to take home. Better still, go make your father and that, um, *friend* a plate."

"Oh, wait! I promised to take the security guard a plate."

"Already taken care of," said Ruby walking out with a plate of goodies in her hand. She also handed her the serving tray and a plate of food for Breeze to take home. "He should be off by now and if you don't mind, I will be deliverin' dis to Mr. Fellah's villa personally," she whispered.

"No, not at all. And I am sure he will appreciate the gesture. Have a wonderful evening everyone and behave yourself, Ms. Ruby," she said finally making her way for the car.

"I'm so glad Tuesday picked you to be one of her bridesmaids," said Mrs. Knight while walking her to her car. "You drive a Beetle?" She peered in the car. "Oh, mama drives a stick?" Mrs. Knight giggled and started bragging like a school girl. "Shine picked me up for our first date in his 1974 lime green Super Beetle convertible. We were going to the movies, but ended up riding all over town that night. I didn't want that beautiful night to end," she said with a dreamy look in her eyes.

"Mind you, when he arrived, my hair was fierce! *Ev-ver-ry* curl was in place! When I came home, my brothers took one look at me and started for the door with a baseball bat," she said laughing. "We would put the top down at the drop of a hat, even in the winter! Some of our best moments were in that car..." She giggled and looked up before finishing her last thought.

"I know we all gave you some food for thought tonight. But don't dwell on it too much, baby. You'll find him, just like Tuesday found Spencer."

Breeze simply smiled. Finding *him* was not her main concern, especially anyone like Spencer. Her focus was getting through this circus of a wedding without using four letter words unbecoming of a human being.

She hugged and thanked Mrs. Knight for being a gracious hostess and placed her purse, serving tray, and big book of bridal demands in the trunk. This was an evening to drop the top, pin up the hair, and let the air blow through her brains. There were too many emotions, thoughts, and feelings going on in her head to keep the top closed.

"Okay, you have to promise you'll take me for a spin," she said admiring the convertible's transformation and waving her goodbyes. "See you next month."

She waved back and started off. As soon as she was out of sight, she stopped the car, sighed, and rested her head against the steering wheel. Almost on cue, her phone rang. Normally, she would have answered it right away. But she was in no mood to rehash today's events with others. She started the car, selected her cool-down CD, and headed home.

However, her thought was interrupted again from a persistent caller. She finally answered, "Do you mind if I give you a call when I get home?"

"Yeah, I mind! We want to know what happened."

"Willow, I really don't want to talk at the moment. I just want to get across this highway, run to Bun Penny for a sandwich, catch the last of *Are You Being Served*, take a long hot shower, and hide under the covers for the rest of the night."

"You are so full of it. Meet me at DSW in an hour."

"What? No, I am goin'--"

"To DSW. You need cheering up. I need shoes...and a good burger. See ya in an hour." Click.

Ah, the magic word: shoes. Her spirits lifted with the mere thought of trying on what this season's collection had to offer. She just hoped her budget could stand it. This time, she turned her phone off and placed it in the glove compartment to avoid additional interruptions. It was time to be alone with her thoughts and salvage the rest of the evening.

3

Guard Not Hide

Her destination was reached in record speed. Unfortunately, so did Willow, leaving no time to put on an *'everything's-fine'* face.

"Bun Penny and Britcoms on a Saturday night, I can't wait to hear this," she said hugging her friend of 34 years. The statuesque half African-American, half Filipino with her unruly hair-band mane piled high in a ponytail, looking quite comfortable wearing faded jeans, a white fitted V-neck tee, and white slim flip flops steered her friend in the direction of the store.

"You're gonna wait. It's shoe time," Breeze said looking for Willow's three year old twins. "Hey, where are my godsons?"

"Home, with Reach. Its boy's night-in, especially when I told him what you were doing today. He told me to bring home details and some onion rings."

They walked in and took the escalator upstairs. It never ceased to amaze Breeze the sea of shoes that would meet her gaze, as she ascended to the upstairs floor. The endless options and sale prices were waiting anxiously for her arrival. Willow started to pursue the conversation, but stopped when she noticed the gleam in Breeze's eye.

"I'll be over in the sensible, but stylish section. Don't be long, 'cause this sistah is starvin'!"

Breeze savored each aisle, accessing which function and outfit would go with whatever shoe she fancied. She allowed herself to get lost in deep thought, admiring her toes in one shoe, and her ankles in the other. Any sign of pump fat was grounds for immediate dismal. If the shoe made her legs look even more irresistible, they were in her bag before she could blink. Slipping on her fifth pair, this time a fuchsia, Steve Madden sandal, Willow interrupted her.

"Why is Liddy-Bee blowin' up my phone?" she asked handing the phone to Breeze. She shrugged her shoulders, and accepted the phone while posing in the mirror at all angles.

"*Breezy-Bee, where is your phone and why ain't you in the house by now? Don't even think about buyin' another shoe--*"

"Sorry, I left my phone in the car. How'd you get Willow's number, anyway?" She really did not feel like hearing yet another lecture on her spending habits, especially from those who had nothing to do with her pockets.

"*I have my ways, dahlin'. Now, step away from that shoe and tell me if you saw anythang interestin' at the party.*"

"Of course not on both counts. The only thing interesting this evening, are these tan leather heels I'm about to try on."

"*Breezy, put the shoe down and talk to me. I am beyond concerned with your thinkin' skills. Acceptin' yet another invitation to be a bridesmaid...to an ex's weddin'?*"

"Liddy-Bee," she sighed, "he was not my ex--"

"*Don't interrupt me! I didn't get a chance to write down what I want to say, so let me get this out. It's high time you start movin' on. Get a fresh start. You got a good job, a beautiful home, plenty 'a friends. You come from a good, fun, yet kinda Christian family. You're cute as a button, look nice in your clothes, and got plenty to offer. It's high time you go find yourself some happiness and remove that dark cloud hangin' over your head.*"

She turned to Willow for any sort of support. "I agree with everything Liddy-Bee has to say," Willow said not looking up from Breeze's shopping bag. "We had a nice little chat before I came over."

"You two had a chat about me?" she asked on the phone and to her friend. "The Word says for us to *learn* to be content. Did it ever occur to either of you that I have a Ph.D. in contentment? I *am* happy, especially in these tan Mia heels!"

"Nah you ain't," the two said in unison. *"You might be content, but you ain't happy, baby."* Breeze could hear her aunt shaking her head over the phone.

"Look, both of you. There are plenty of women who are single at my age or older, and they are doing just fine. Why should I be any different?"

"Because there's a lid for every pot! Even the cracked ones."

"I give up," Breeze sighed. "I'll just slap a sign on my chest saying 'available to anyone with a Y chromosome.'"

"Good idea. Make sure that sign doesn't cover one of your best features. You gotta show those off a little and add a little glitter to 'em. I don't know where you got those from; but you certainly didn't get them from our side of the family."

"I'm hanging up now," she said laughing at her aunt's directness.

"Breezy, think about what I said. And let me know if I can help you in any way. For starters, how 'bout battin' your eyes at--"

"Bye Liddy-Bee!" Breeze disconnected the call before another suggestion was given and handed the phone back to Willow. She snatched her shopping bag of shoes from Willow's grip and stormed off to another section.

"That bad, huh?" A voice came from the other side of the aisle. Breeze was so into the flirty black Nine West sling back to notice the woman smiling at her. "Bad break up?" This time the woman placed her hand on Breeze's wrist, as she reached to admire another shoe on display.

"Uh, no. Just in need of some new shoes," she said nervously as she pulled back her hand. She quickly glanced to see if her watch was still on her arm.

"Mmm hmm. I recognize shoe therapy when I see it. If you need to talk about it, come see me." She handed her a flyer. "I offer a course in relationship repair. And I am sure your budget will thank me," she said nodding to Breeze's overflowing shopping bags.

"Certainly not with the prices you charge," she said glancing at the thick pretty pink paper. "Besides, I'm not in a relationship."

"My dear, you are indeed in a relationship. And for half the price of your bags of shoes, with much more lasting effects, my course may be just the thing you need."

"What I need right now is a size 10 in this pink sling back. But I thank you for the offer." Arguing with a stranger was not on the menu tonight.

The woman extended her hand, "Zenobia."

"Breeze," she shook her hand.

"Breeze, here is your pink size 10. I hope to see you soon." She waved and headed for the escalator. Her white linen outfit with matching duster jacket, made her float away.

She looked at the flyer one more time. "'While we wait for what?'" she mumbled disgustedly at title, folded and stuffed it away deep in her shoe bag. She believed in people peddling their services, just not during her shoe time. "Why is everyone so concerned that I'm single 'cept me? What I need to do is go home and be alone with me. And another footie."

"Oh, I know you' kiddin'," Willow said with her hands on her hips. "Six pairs of shoes? At least put back three!"

"They're all on sale and I have a coupon, so step away from the bag."

"You are putting back three!" Willow reached into the bag, choosing the returns. "Keep. Nope. Nope. Oh this is too cute, I can borrow this one, so we keep. Wait, how much is this shoe? Girl, you dun fell and bumped yo' head. Absolutely not! Okay, keep this and the ones on your feet, and let's go!"

Breeze stood up in her soon-to-be new wedged heel and placed her hands akimbo. "Okay, we need to get you some food because apparently you dun lost yo' mind! If you even dream of puttin' anythang back, you and I are gonna dance right here, in dis shoe sto'!"

"Get your hands off your imagination and come on, please. The store's closing. And I ain't droppin' nothing!"

She started to turn, when Breeze reached out and grabbed a fistful of Willow's hair. "Drop the shoes and no one gets hurt," she growled.

"Oww...too late," Willow wailed. "Let go of my hair."

"Wench, drop the shoes or you will miss the clump of hair that is in my hand!"

"Dang it," she said struggling. "Listen...to me...the only way you can...justify this price tag is...if you were datin' a millionaire...with a shoe fetish. And with that...let him pay for it! OUCH! Friends don't let friends...buy two months' rent worth...of shoes," Willow struggled. "Will you let go, please?"

"I *said* they were on sale. Now-let-them-go!"

"Uh, Ladies? Is everything okay here?" A young, short, curly headed man with slight traces of peach fuzz and pimples in a DSW uniform, peered gingerly at the spectacle.

"Yes, everything here is fine. I just need you to take the shoes out of this lady's hands, and the ones stacked on the floor and have them ready for purchasing." Breeze still had a handful of Willow's ponytail. The sleepy eyed young man with incredibly long eyelashes started for the shoes on the floor.

"There's a 10 in it for you, if you take that bag and these shoes back to where they came from," Willow said struggling. "Ouch! We'll take the rest." The young man quickly followed instructions, grabbed the shoes from Willow, and scooted away.

Breeze finally let go of her hair. "Hateful, heifah," she spat, plopping herself on the nearest bench, and placed her head in her hands. "I have had a very trying day with *five* different emotions going on inside my head. You are taking away the only thing that is giving me joy at this moment. I look good in those shoes! *And they were on sale!*"

"Dahlin'," she said sweetly, "Get over it. Get the shoes that are on your feet, and the ones I left in your bag, get up from that bench, cease with your pity party, and let's go!"

"I will be the only single woman in the faculty lounge," she bellowed. "I have to look my best."

"Please, and go broke in the process?" Willow asked flippantly. "And since when did you ever give a kitty what those chicks in cheap shoes think, in the first place?"

Breeze defeatedly picked up her shoes and what was left of her dignity, and made her way for the escalator. On the ride down, Breeze met the eyes of the young man who had an odd smile on his face, like he had just finished telling a juicy story. "Don't forget to pay him," she said nodding in his direction. She made her way to the checkout counter and was thankful the lines were short.

"Oh, Ms. Monsoon? We have a special today," the cheery teenaged sales clerk offered. "You could save an additional 25% if you--"

"Stop," Willow interrupted. "What she has, with this coupon, is enough."

Finished with their purchases, they made their way to the car in silence. She opened up her trunk and before she could load the car, Willow stopped her. "Why did you bring this year's teacher's manual to the tea?"

"That is Tuesday's bridal party packet of the duties and responsibilities customized according to your role in the wedding."

"A packet," Willow snapped. "Darling, this no packet. That's a--"

"Tuesday's mother called it a handbook."

"Oh, I gotta see this." She looked at her friend's reaction. "Better still..." She reached in the trunk and pulled it out so that Breeze could finally put her purchases away.

"Must I rehash the past four hours of my life and gander at what's expected of me for the next nine *months*? I really want to enjoy my meal," Breeze pleaded.

"Sorry darlin'. This will add fuel to tonight's fiery dinner conversation. By the way, get your phone... and please turn it back *on*." She closed the trunk, while Breeze grabbed the phone from the glove compartment. "It will be all right," Willow said walking her towards the restaurant.

Coaxing Breeze out of her mental fortress was Willow's specialty. The first day they met in nursery school, it was Breeze who brought her out of her shell. Willow, clinging to her father's pant leg, was crying, refusing to enter the classroom doors of Singer Learning Center. Breeze grew tired of the scene, took Willow by her dry hand, and escorted her inside. The tears stopped and the smiles started. The pair have been as thick as thieves and the tables have been turned ever since. Different villages in Columbia kept them apart for the rest of their school career. However, birthday parties, sleepovers, bullies, boys, and secrets kept them close. From dolls to shoe fights, they were inseparable sisters.

"Did I tell you that I saw Stealth on the way to the Knight's?" Breeze asked excitedly.

"Did you get the digits?" questioned Willow.

"How? He was two cars back in standstill traffic."

"I'm sure your 5 o'clock dulce la leche crush was a welcomed sight. Bother me about it *once* you get his digits."

They arrived at Hamburger Hamlet, ready to order. Mentally, Breeze was not hungry. But her stomach told her, and those around her, otherwise, as she was unable to enjoy the meal at the Knight's house after the inquisition ensued. The pencil thin hostess with mousy brown hair, clothed in a basic black ensemble, escorted them to their seats.

"Hey girl, good to see you. How you doin'?" Breeze asked the ladies sitting at a nearby table. They, in turn, responded uneasily, yet politely.

"Girl, do you know everybody in this state?" asked Willow. "Whom on earth is that?"

"Have no idea," she said dismissively. "But if you are gonna stare the brown off of me, you might as well speak."

Moments later, an overly cheery, thick, dark haired man introduced himself, ready to provide drinks. They smiled and placed their full order instead. He wrote down their request and scooted off.

"Let's take a gander at this," Willow said eagerly as she pulled out the packet. Breeze grunted, waving the notion away. "It's a shame that you didn't spend your last Saturday of freedom at Kings Dominion. Why don't you and Elliott go tomorrow?"

"For starters, I have to serve during early morning service. Then, Elliott and I are spending the rest of the day downtown. The Orioles are playing the Rangers and we got great bleacher seats." Her mood suddenly perked up. "Then to J. Paul's for some steamed shrimp, a side salad, and pretzels with spicy mustard." Almost on cue again, her phone rings.

"'S going on," she answered smiling.

"Are we still on for tomorrow?" Elliott asked.

"Can't wait. We were just talking about it," she said still smiling.

"Tell Willow I said hello. But, I have one request."

"What's that?"

"Can we not talk about the inane details of yet another wedding that you're in?"

"See, this is why you are my friend." They laughed and ended the call.

"Elliott," Willow sang.

Breeze chose to ignore the teasing, hoping to move away from the predictable discussion, "Mmm hmm, he said hello."

"When are you going to finally sample some of that?"

"Some of what?" she asked feigning innocence.

"You have been friends for entirely too long--"

"The operative word here is *friends*. Besides, I'm not his type."

"Which is?"

"Swan-like waif, artsy, patchouli wearin', preferably second generation American. My okra and cornbread fed behind ain't it," she chuckled. "His last girlfriend was a total earth cookie. He even turned vegetarian for a good five days until he attended Birdie Bee's Pokeno party. He took one look at the spread and it was curtains!"

"Who broke up with whom?"

"It was mutual, actually. She found out that he was back to eating meat and couldn't take the betrayal. He wasn't too heartbroken, though. He said the only thing they did have in common was great sex."

"In some temporary cases, that could be enough."

"I guess, but he said he was looking for more. He was intrigued by her passion. It's what she was passionate about that got old and boring." Breeze sighed, "Can we change the subject?"

"Not yet--" She was interrupted by the waiter serving the iced teas. "Are you interested in him?"

"I told you, I'm not his type." Breeze said reaching for the sweetener packets.

"You didn't answer my question."

"Why would I be, if he isn't interested in me?"

"'Cause your feelings count, too," Willow snapped back.

"The bottom line is I have a tendency to change my plans to accommodate his. Unfortunately, I am not granted that same courtesy. The feeling of being taken for granted gets old after a while."

"What are you going to do about that?"

"Continue to smile as if nothing is wrong."

"We need to find you a clinic for that noise," she said pulling out a familiar pretty pink paper. "And speaking of which..." Willow loved teasing her friend about Elliott, but apparently she had other plans tonight. It was the flyer the stylishly dressed stranger handed to Breeze in the shoe store. "Take out your calendar and fit this course into your schedule."

"How did you get a copy of that? Didn't she see the shiny boulder sitting on your finger?"

"She asked me to keep a copy for you. She said you look like you easily dismiss things you need."

"That's so wrong."

"Where's your copy?"

"Hopefully, stuffed in one of the bags of shoes you sent back!"

"On that note, the defense rests. *You* will be taking *this* course."

"Willow, I can't afford this," she sighed treating the flyer like a coaster.

"Oh, but you can afford a pair of $245 shoes on a teacher's salary?" she asked moving the glass elsewhere and air drying the flyer.

"*IT WAS 50% OFF!*"

"Yeah, and add that cost to five other pairs of shoes." To end the discussion, Willow reached for the thick book and ignored her friend's looks.

Breeze tasted her tea. The bitter bite begged her to add another packet. She stirred in the granules, while Willow studied the book. Her head was aching from disagreements coming at her from all sides. She had enough of dodging subjects, trying to win losing arguments, not knowing which subject to mentally dwell on first.

"Is this chick for real? She must have planned this day since she learned how to cut and paste," she said trying to lighten the mood. Breeze made her signature look of disgust and continued to play with her tea rather than meet her friend's answer searching gaze.

She pondered the questions of the day: Why did she agree to be a bridesmaid? What did she smoke to let things get this far? Why didn't she just say, 'no'? Maybe she felt sorry for Tuesday, but just could not understand why. Tuesday had her circle of friends at work. She also noticed none of them were at the tea.

She finally accepted that she just liked being a bridesmaid. A pretty dress, a trip down the aisle escorted by a handsome man, *hopefully*, and her own floral souvenir without humiliating herself in the bouquet toss to all of the single ladies. Tuesday will probably insist on that antiquated ritual most self-respecting single women dread and avoid. Standing there anticipating any source of chance to come her way, clinging on to the big fat myth that she will be next.

It was the garter toss that Breeze feared the most. Not the leg showing, though. She always welcomed an opportunity to show off her gams. She ended up with a date after one wedding reception because of them. However, he wanted to see, touch, and unfortunately, lick more during their first and only date.

Her fear, though, was what if the group of single men did not want to catch the garter? What if they did not like the looks of the lucky gal that caught the bouquet and the garter landed on the floor like a used tissue?

And now Breeze was facing yet another class capitalizing on the phenomenon facing single African American women 35 and over with zero or negative prospects. *"How on earth were these classes supposed to help?"* She felt they were only designed to remind you of what some call silence and loneliness. Breeze called it peace and quiet. The church environment did not help matters. If He felt it was not good for man to be alone, then He should have made courting and loving easier. *"What they really need are classes for those saints and ain'ts on how to keep their unsolicited, venom laced opinions to themselves."*

"...Girl this dress is ugly," Willow said looking up. "Earth to Breeze," said Willow snapping her fingers to get her friend's attention.

"Hmm?"

"You've been stirring that iced tea for the past 10 minutes. Where were you anyway?" Before Breeze could answer, "Never mind, what color is this: cheese? Y'all are gonna look like three deranged school buses rolling down that aisle," Willow laughed with tears in her eyes. "Breezy dahlin', you endure this here train wreck for a friend, not some chick in your office that you don't even like.

"And this girl takes meticulous to a whole new sickening level. She has your duties, a theme, what to bring, and what and where to purchase. And that's just the shower! She has your spring break hemmed up with preparations."

"That won't happen! Dad and I have plans for Niagara Falls Sunday through Tuesday; Elliott and I go to Las Vegas, Thursday through Sunday."

"Speaking of which, it appears that Elliott will not be attending or any other 'plus one' you may have had in mind."

"What do you mean?"

"She indicated here how many guests, including you: One! This page probably serves as your wedding invitation." Willow turned the packet towards Breeze.

She was not surprised that Tuesday would pull something like this. She also knew Elliott would be thrilled to miss it. She looked at the page. "Why didn't I just say no," she whined.

"This noise ain't etched in stone."

"It might be. Turn to page 25," she said with her head still in her hands.

"Her program is printed already?"

"No, just the order of service."

"Omigoodness! You're walking down with Branford? Not the Branford from college? Your 'Oh-where's-Breeze-she's-out-with-Branford', Branford," Willow said with a teasing smile. "The man you should have married, too sweet and innocent to close the deal, Branford? And why is your *first* name and his *last* name on this program?"

"First of all, I think you mean my friend from college, Branford. Yes, that would be the one. He wasn't there, neither was his *daughter*. Tuesday did, however, start her mess when she found out I knew him."

"How do you mean?"

"She *informed* me of his marital status in her own special way."

"You corrected her, right?"

"Of course. But that was just enough ammo to get the party started--"
She was interrupted when the food finally came. Breeze's hunger senses
awakened when she smelled her burger with the side order of peppercorn
buttered broccoli. They blessed the food and started their meal. Willow
took a bite of her mushroom burger, while Breeze savored one of the
florets.

After a few nibbles of her food, Breeze shared the ugly turning
point of the tea party. Willow made her start from the beginning. Breeze
thought about the setup, the discussion, seeing Spencer again, finally
meeting his mama, and proceeded to tell her friend everything.

"*Don't embarrass me*, huh? I see that chocolate hazel eyed booger hasn't
changed. What did he think you would do when you saw him anyway?"

"Who knows?" Breeze said dismissively and started on her meal again.

"I'm trying to understand. He really did a number on you. And he,
in his sick sort of way, admits it. His fiancé asks you to be in the wedding just because she looks up to you? It doesn't make sense. Why would
a woman knowingly want her man's ex *in her* wedding? Maybe I can see at
the wedding, but not in it. There is more to this story than what has been
said. And if you decide to stay on this jacked up assignment, you better
keep *your* first name *and home address* private!"

She shrugged her shoulders and kept at her meal. She noticed that
it was starting to get cold and considered boxing up the rest. Willow was
still firing questions, Breeze did not feel like answering. In her eyes, all
will be revealed, hopefully before she spends money on a cheese colored
dress.

"Breeze, are you listening to me?"

"Yeah, I'm listening. I just need to take it one day at a time. I have
other issues to deal with."

"Such as?" Willow was interrupted by the waiter asking the ladies for
anything else. "Could you bring us the hot fudge cake and two spoons,
two 'to-go' boxes and...oh and an order of onion rings to go, please?"

Willow watched the waiter move away and turned back to her friend for answers.

"For starters, I can't even swing a cat in my classroom. How am I supposed to teach 35 kids who don't want to be there for an hour and change, in that tiny classroom? I have to figure out how to provide air, air freshener, and algebraic equations all at the same time. And when I do get a break, I know I'm going to have to face Tuesday and her flaky friends on Monday flaunting her happiness all over the school." Breeze winced once the words fell out of her mouth. She was by no means in love with Spencer. She just did not want to be the last single girl standing.

"I knew you felt some kind of way about this! I knew it, knew it, knew it! That's why you should take the course. Take the time to find yourself. Put Spencer, what he did to you, and I do believe unresolved bitterness behind you," Willow said with sincerity. "Then you'll be free to find somebody new."

"Listen, as a single Christian girl, I'm supposed to guard my heart. That is what I'm doing. And I do believe I am doing just fine. When I finally let my guard down even for a minute, my heart was handed back to me with crap covered all over it. When He feels that He is ready for *him* to find *me*, He'll work it out."

"The Word says to guard, not *hide*," hissed Willow. "And how is He supposed to work it out when you're sittin' at home plannin' out your evenings by the cable guide, watchin' reruns of *Law & Order* throughout the week, Britcoms on Saturday, and DVDs of the *Golden Girls* on Sunday?"

"And football season will officially start, shortly," Breeze added. "Look, I can be a better friend, an awesome godmother, a good daughter, and a tremendous teacher *without* the drama." She recognized the pleading in Willow's voice, but she was getting frustrated, too. What did she need to do to make everyone that cared for her understand that everything is not okay, but she was dealing with it...her way. She was also not as confident in her statement about Him. She understood nothing was impossible with God. But her situation, and the time it is taking, probably has Him stumped.

They sat in silence as the waiter brought the cake, boxes, and onion rings. "Anything else, ladies?" They shook their heads, as a reply. He placed the check on the table and started off.

"Excuse me..." Willow said motioning for the waiter. "I'll take care of this now." Breeze reached in her purse for her wallet. "No, this one is on Reach." She did not say another word as she started on the cake. She noticed her friend was not eating when she said, "Breeze, you know I love you dearly. But I refuse to believe everything is fine. You can be all that you are and still be in love with a great man at the same time. And yes, without the drama."

"Willow--"

"If you will not talk to me, then take the course and talk to this Zenobia person," she continued. "Something is wrong. And whatever *it* is, it's hindering your personal relational growth. But first, pick up the spoon and help me eat this cake."

Breeze sat there looking at her friend and decided she did not want to pick up her spoon. What would this Zenobia have to say that she has not already heard: *'you'll find 'em baby,' 'you need to put on some lipstick,' 'wear some color, chile,'* and *'smile?'* She could write her own book loaded with advice. Too bad it would be a book of endless advice with no success stories. The scent of the cold, creamy vanilla rounds with an avalanche of fudge cascading from all sides reeled her in. She finally gave in and picked up the spoon. She still was not taking the course.

The girls finished their dessert and headed out to their cars. The night air that greeted them was still and warm. The clear night sky showed every possible star in the universe. The faint piped in music became louder with the stillness. The crickets were singing their songs, too.

Willow gave the book back to her friend. "You can stay mad at me as long as you want to. But, you know I'm right," she said attempting to end the evening on a positive note.

"I'll think about it," said Breeze.

"The course or me?"

"Staying mad at you. By the way, did you pay that kid at the shoe store?"

"No, he paid *me* for the cat fight, sight. How'd you think you got that extra discount?"

"Okay, that's bizarre. Anyway, just so you know, I am not mad. I'm just tired of having to constantly explain myself. My situation will work itself out without any extraneous roots in my equation."

"I'm not liking that answer. Not even quite sure I understand it. But, I love you no less," she said hugging her friend.

"At a quarter to twelve, that's the answer you're going to get. Love you, too." Breeze hugged her friend back.

"Ring the phone when you get home," they said in unison while climbing into their cars.

4

Summer Sum Up

"Did you fall and bump your head over the summer?" A thick, brown skinned gentleman with a neatly trimmed goatee, and well managed dreadlocks just missing the top of the doorway, entered the classroom. His pearly white, gapped teeth smile lit up the room.

"Thaddeus" Breeze cheered excitedly. "Where have you been all summer?" she asked greeting him with a warm hug.

The neatly dressed man suited in jeans, a sandy brown blazer with matching colored Bucks, smelling like sandalwood and vanilla was labeled by others as Breeze's work husband. She just called him a good friend. "I had some things to take care of. We'll get to that later. I just heard Tuesday is getting married to what's-his-face and that you are in their wedding. Are you crazy? Can't she ask one of her minions to do the dishonor?"

"I tried to decline, but Tuesday wouldn't hear of it. Can we not talk about this? I want to hear what kept you away from me for an entire summer. I got no phone calls, emails, mental telepathy, nothin'!"

"I told you, I had some things to work out."

"Such as?"

"I'll tell you over dinner. What are you doing tomorrow night? Let's go to Gladys'."

"'Got plans. Liddy Bee and Willow are taking me to a back-to-school dinner tomorrow night. Anyway, the fact that you are withholding information has me intrigued. Did you do what I think you did this summer?" she asked inquisitively.

Thaddeus was in a wonderfully committed, loving relationship. She wondered if they made their union official without her; and if so, she was going to be livid. Unfortunately, their budding conversation was interrupted before he could respond.

"What kind of drugs are you taking? Because anything that would cause you to say 'yes' to this potential mess, I want some," said another teacher friend.

"Secret! Come in and join the party."

"I knew Thaddeus would be here, so I brought provisions to ease your self-inflicted suffering," she said setting down three mutant sized glazed doughnuts.

"Self-inflicted?"

"You could have just said, 'no!' Just tell me I'm not on the guest list."

"*You* could just say, 'no.'"

"And miss this circus? Please! Now, take a bite first."

"Fine, pull up a chair while I tell you the sordid details of that horrible afternoon. Picture it: A cute, chubby brown skinned girl with cascading dark brown natural ringlets receives a call from a self-absorbed she-monster."

"Breeze, will you please take a bite of the doughnut? You have a tendency to be forgetful when you are hungry. Inquiring minds want to know the *entire* story!"

While noshing on their doughnuts, Breeze continued to tell her teacher friends the whole summer story. Her audience had facial expressions of disbelief and annoyance, as she rehashed the events.

"At least her mama seems all right," Secret interjected. "Scared of his mama, though. I still cannot understand why you didn't let either mama know the real deal between you and Spencer, as your ticket out."

"Breezy, does Tuesday know about you and Spencer?" asked Thaddeus.

"She probably feels that it's a friend introducing another friend to a new possibility," she shrugged.

"Y'all were *never* friends! She said so herself when her sorry behind asked if she could start seeing him."

"What do you mean?" he asked.

"I told you, Thaddeus. Two days after my last run in with Spence, she busted in my classroom asking if it was okay with me if she could start seeing him."

"And get this," Secret interrupted. "She had the nerve to say 'it's not like we're friends or anything,'" she mocked. "Then why'd you ask?" Secret tried to regain her composure. "Breeze, put a stop to this before this noise gets out of hand! I bet the only reason why she asked you to be a bridesmaid is because you were in my weddin' and know how to throw a shower. My family is still talking about it."

"Girl, that was two years ago," Breeze laughed. "And, I do believe it was the *bachelorette party* that is still on everyone's lips, mind, digital camera, and in my closet. Now *that* was a party...that I did not throw."

"Yeah, but not everyone went, especially Tuesday and her henchmen. Only a chosen few ladies from this place were privy to join the elite sorority of scandalous bachelorettes!"

"To this day, I am still wondering why Breeze has not said anything or shared any pictures. I mean she tells me just about everything, and all I got from her was, 'I had a good time.'"

"And I intend to keep it that way," she said still laughing. "Back to the subject at hand. Tuesday gave me a laundry list of reasons as to why I should be in their wedding. Spence finally agreed that in some way, I managed to bring the two together. If it wasn't for me, they would have never fallen in love."

"The yenta strikes again."

"Yeah, but they could have just sent a fruit arrangement for her successful matchmaking skills."

"I knew this room was the source of the classical music. It's heavenly," Tuesday said interrupting the frivolity. "Breeze, I think you should pick out a classical piece for my wedding. I don't want to walk down to that played out, 'Here Comes the Bride' or some of that hip-hop nonsense that *my* Spencer suggested.

"You both are aware that our Breeze here is one of my bridesmaids when I get married this summer. Spencer and I intend to put all of her past experience...as a bridesmaid, to good use." Secret flashed Breeze a 'see what I mean' look. "By the way, you two, I will be asking for your addresses later this year, that is if your names make the cut. No inquiries."

"No problem," both responded in unison.

Tuesday just smiled while hopping on the desk. "Yes, Breeze, you--," she stopped abruptly noticing Breeze's facial expression and hopped right back off. "I need you to add 'choosing the musical selection' to your list of bridesmaid responsibilities. I can't wait to hear what you decide. Come to think of it, add 'gathering addresses of the coworkers' to your list, as well," she commanded and left the room before any other objection could be made.

"How about Handel's *Arrival of the Queen of Sheba*?" she mumbled.

"Actually Breeze, that's not a bad piece," said Thaddeus.

"Is there a piece called the 'Exit' of the Queen?" asked Secret.

"Speaking of exits, we have a new administrator to meet," said Thaddeus cleaning up. "Did anyone find out if he was single?"

"Down boy," said Secret.

"Oh no, trust and believe, I'm cool. This is all about Breeze. It's time to end her career as a bridesmaid."

Breeze flashed him a look. He gently pulled her back and whispered, "Seriously, when was the last time you were on a date? What happened to your smile? You deserve to be happy."

"Thaddeus, I am happy."

"Please! You may be 'content' with the status quo, but you ain't happy. Now what do we need to do to make that happen?"

"Find me a man, but not from your team. I already have male friends that I don't sleep with."

"Are you talking about that blue eyed Elliott? That all could change if you stop being so stingy with it."

"You know what…"

5

Mexican & Meltdowns

Willow and Liddy Bee picked up Breeze for her special 'back-to-school' dinner. Despite the stares, questions, and expressions of 'still single' sympathy during the work day, Breeze could not wait for her mini Mexican fiesta with her girls. Their dinner choice was hard to believe, since the two have expressed repeatedly they could not stand Mexican food. But it was her night and she felt honored to be celebrated. As they traveled down the road, Breeze entertained them with a recap of yesterday's events.

"Let me find out old man Jarvis is your new administrator. How on earth did he react when he saw you?" Willow asked with disbelief.

"He was happy to see me, actually. Considering the split was far from amicable."

"The man was too old for you any way," Liddy Bee said dismissively. "You should have introduced him to me. Is he still available?"

"I think that's why he was glad to see me. He put 'us' behind him, found a younger, prettier Hispanic chick, married her, and pumped out two more children."

"Takes care of that," Liddy spat.

Willow shook her head in disbelief and announced that she needed to make a stop to drop off documents for one of Reach's clients. Breeze continued her recap of the reunion with her partial pun intended, old flame, but Willow needed her to come in. She obliged and walked in the one story cookie cutter red brick office building with black trim and large tinted windows. The lobby was busy with ladies looking slightly perplexed, some holding a sheet of pretty pink paper. Breeze shrugged it off and asked her friend if she would be long. She was hungry and was anticipating spending quality time with some tortilla chips and salsa. Willow reassured her and proceeded to the table at the end of the lobby.

She took the pretty pink piece of paper out of her purse and handed it to the young woman manning the table. Suddenly, Breeze felt sick. She prayed that her eyes were deceiving her...the thick pretty pink paper and the looks of bewilderment. She put two and two together a little too quickly, and dizzily stormed out.

"Hey, wait," Willow shouted from the office doorway and ran after her friend.

"I cannot believe you would do this to me!" Breeze's eyes were filled with anger and tears as she shouted at her friend. "I specifically said that I did not want to waste any of my time and money on this class! And to dangle food in front of my face?"

"It's not all Willow's fault, baby." Liddy Bee waddled out the car hearing the one-sided shouting match. "When she called me that night from the shoe store, I told her to sign you up immediately, no matter the cost. She argued with me that you wouldn't go. And I know it's wrong to deceive you like this, but you need to do something that would bring back your hopes and dreams that devil in a cheap linen suit, stole from your life. You are not the same niece my sister raised you to be, Breezy Bee.

"You don't talk to us. You sit at home and hide your life away. I promised your mother to take care of you and that's what I'm doing right now. You say you are content. We know better. You are complacent! You ain't living, you're existing! The Word says to stir up the gifts. I think this class will let you do just that.

"So, don't be mad at Willow. I give you permission to be mad at me for a little while. And before you object, I'm not saying some man will bring you happiness. You are responsible for your own happiness. Take the course. See what it has to offer. If you don't like it, don't go no more. Just don't let me know, 'cause your heart and my money are terrible things to waste, heah?"

"Then you shouldn't have signed me up for something I did not want to take!"

"Breeze, you need to receive some clarity for His plans for your life. You know we are here for you, but you need to be with like-minded people. Just go in, see what this class is all about and make a decision from there, okay?" Willow reached in her purse for some tissues and wiped the tears from Breeze's eyes.

"What is it going to take to convince y'all that I'm really okay with my season?" she pleaded swatting Willow's hand away.

"This course," they said in unison.

Liddy Bee gave Breeze a big hug and a kiss on her plump cheek and got back in the car. "Go on baby, it will be all right." Willow gently coaxed Breeze back to the office where the lobby had thinned out. The helpful lady Breeze saw in the shoe store greeted her with a warm, reassuring smile and ushered her in the conference room.

— ◆ —

There were two empty high back leathers chairs sitting around an oval, cherry oak table in the hint-of-mint colored conference room. Breeze quietly chose one nearest the door for the possibility of a quick getaway. Her head and face were kept down to avoid meeting the gaze and stares of the women already in the room.

"She asked that we choose seats nearest the front," said someone.

"Yep, there's a seat right here waiting for ya," said another.

Breeze sighed and did what she was told, not looking up to see who made her move.

"You know the answer to your question is probably not on the floor." Someone attempted to lighten Breeze's mood, but she was not to be pacified. She was hurt, deceived, and still hungry.

"Good evening, ladies." Breeze looked up reluctantly from her chosen seat. She finally noticed the lady from the shoe store had on another white linen suit.

"She must be trying to get the last bit of wear before the end of the season," she thought resting her elbow on the table, propping her head up with her fist.

"My name is Zenobia Zee and welcome to my class, 'While We Wait'. For the next 20 to 30 minutes, I will inform everyone what this class is and what it is not. I want all minds clear and understood before we embark on this journey.

"I am not here to tell you that some of you may not be getting married. Why pay to hear such trash and add more negativity to your thinking? I do not believe in speaking death to what He may have placed on your heart or your heart's desire.

"However, this course is not 'How-to-Find-Me-a-Husband 101,' either. My job is to speak life and encourage you during your season of singleness and to properly prepare you for what He has in store for you. I want you to discover how amazing it is to walk in the blessing of complete freedom *and preparation*.

"Ladies, I designed this course to show each of you what to do after you have prayed, fasted, cried, begged, touched, and agreed with like-minded individuals for Him to bring you the man of your dreams. What do you do when nothing happens or the options you thought you had are taken away? For starters, you live. You experience what He and life has to offer. Believe me ladies he is out there. Your past experiences are hindering his efforts to find you. Hiding, keeping your heart on lock down, and refusing to fellowship with others will not bring him to you.

"There is a lot of disgruntled, disgraced, displaced, discontented, dismissive, disenchanted, disheveled, disinterested, and just plain dissed faces, hearts, and minds in this room. We will examine and discuss whatever dis-ease you are feeling. But ladies, we will not stay here. I want you to learn and grow from your past, not just run away from it.

"Now, some of you have given up finding him. Some of you are tired of waiting for him to find you. But each of you, in some way, is hiding His best. And that is unacceptable. I am not here to show or tell you what you are doing wrong. I want to enhance what you are doing right.

"Ladies, according to your bios you got it going on: properties, careers, side hustles, and exotic trips. You are in situations of prosperity your parents did not dream of doing by themselves. Each of you has never been married and have no children. All of you are over 35, except for one. Your faith and trust is somewhat strong in Him and are quite active in your place of worship. You have a strong foundation of support from your family and friends, which love and care for you deeply.

"However, for some reason, you are letting your heart and mind dwell in an extremely dark place. We will spend the next eight months getting you out of that dark place and let your light shine bright even if you find yourself *visiting* that dark place again.

"Ladies, if you do not want to stay, are not willing to stay or cannot stay, you are welcome to leave. And yes, I will give you your money back, tonight. But I would love for you to stay, share with me, and grow with your sisters. I will leave the room to allow you to think it over." She smiled while her white line ensemble made her float out of the room.

"How did Zenobia know all of this?" Even though Breeze knew that she was in a dark place, she felt quite comfortable, *safe*. She also realized that to her family and friends that safe, dark place excuse was getting old. *"Eight months? I really don't have that kind of time. Maybe if I get the refund, I can think about that dark place all day at Lynn's Day Spa."*

"My cousin took this course last year and is getting married next year," said one of the ladies interrupting Breeze's exit strategy.

"I thought she said this wasn't a 'husband-finding' course?"

"It's not. But whatever it is, this course will allow Him to help him, find you," the interrupter replied. "And he found her in the strangest way. Besides, this course sounds deeper than any singles course I've ever taken, especially with all women."

"Yeah, but for eight months?"

"Why not nine?"

"Please, and give her the opportunity to say 'you are about to give birth to a new creation'?"

"If that comes out her mouth, I'm outta here and I will be getting my money back," Breeze chimed in. "Besides, I too, have taken a few single's classes: 'Single and Satisfied', 'Pray, Sit, and Wait for him,' 'How to Please him Without Compromising Your Virtue'..."

"What kind of class is that?"

"You don't want to know," Breeze assured.

"I could *teach* the single and satisfied course. Though, I must admit I am quite intrigued with that virtue course."

"Well, I don't know what else to do. When the engagement of my ex-boyfriend was announced during church service, I ran out in tears. Before I could reach the door, someone stopped me and told me about this course."

"*I* shouldn't be here. For the first time in five years, I am having a good time being by myself."

"I'm sorry, ladies. I'm single, but I am not satisfied. And in some capacity no one here is satisfied with your single life. That is why we are all here."

"Have any of you experienced the overwhelming feeling that you are being left behind? Don't get me wrong, you are indeed genuinely happy for your friends and family that do find someone special, get married, and have families of their own. But, when you see your crushes, the kids you used to babysit, and in overwhelming cases: your parent's friends, or anyone in your office younger than you announcing their engagement, how do you feel? What do you do?"

"You call your most trusted girlfriends."

"You call your most trusted travel agent."

"Make a mean martini."

"Flirt shamelessly at the bartender making you that mean martini."

"Walk around the house naked and be glad that you can."

"But don't forget to pray. Because you know He will work it out."

"Yeah, but in His time. That could be a lifetime. I want to move on to the next emotion, now."

"Ladies, when was the last time someone asked you what you wanted, and actually listened without judgment, pity or offered joy stealing opinions? Everyone should have this opportunity to say and express what's on our heart without sounding like we are complaining, at least once. Actually, every woman, especially in this room, should experience the love of their lives, at least once."

"Eight months' worth is a lot of expression."

"Yeah, I feel you. But even Esther went through 12 months of beauty treatments before meeting her king."

"Then it's agreed. We all stay."

"Are you our spokesperson?"

"No, but the look on our faces scream something is clearly wrong. And maybe this course will reveal to us what He wants us to fix."

"Have we made the decision to stay?" Zenobia asked peering into her conference room. Eight women reluctantly nodded their heads in agreement. "Splendid. Each of you are about to look at your singleness in a whole new light," she said darting back out of the room.

"Girl, I was about to get up," said Breeze.

"We know. We all looked at you."

6

Zenobia's Garden

Zenobia came back with her assistant carrying two boxes filled with binders. Without being asked, her assistant distributed a pretty pink slim binder, matching the color of Zenobia's flyer, and a new, clear black ink pen to each person at the table. The ladies attempted to open the binder, but Zenobia made a gesture not to.

"Ladies, before we begin, you will be given the name of a flower. This way, you can speak freely, share openly, and be completely transparent. I do not want you to hold back whatever is on your heart in fear of being found out, hurting someone's feelings, or cause a beat down after class, because this is indeed, a very small world. Once you receive your name, please write it on the first page in your binder."

Her diligent assistant brought Zenobia a small pink box. She shook it and pulled out the first name. "Rose." Her assistant busily wrote down the assigned names on a clipboard, careful not to reveal the real names of the students. She distributed names such as Tulip, Daisy, and Lily. When Zenobia reached Breeze's seat she smiled and said, "I hear you are a fan of British comedies, and quite the persnickety party planner. So this name will suit you: 'Hyacinth'. Breeze opened her binder to find a 'Welcome to the Garden' certificate.

Zenobia continued to dole out more names like Violet and Iris. "I am reluctant to use this name," she said reaching her last student.

"What is it, Stinkweed?"

"No, Petunia."

"Even Petunia had *Porky the Pig*. Maybe there's some hope in that name for me."

"Now we can begin," she said smiling and patting Petunia on the shoulder. "As I said before, each of you are wallowing in a dark place. I want us to examine that place for the evening. Again, we will not stay here. I will only allow you to dwell in this place for one night and do a little man hating for a couple of sessions. If all you want to do is bash the men in your life, you can do that at home with your girlfriends, for free.

"You see, the problem is not with men. The root of the problem is the choice of men you decide to let in your life. I want you to look at the options available to you in a different way and ultimately, His way. As like-minded individuals, you know your choices and thoughts must first be pleasing to Him. Trust and believe, I know firsthand how hard it is to put Him first, especially when the results are not coming quick enough. Or the ones He places in your life do not meet your standards...your superficial standards."

"What! Are we supposed to just accept anybody?" asked Violet. "I mean this girl must have her standards."

"You know men have *their* standards and they will not accept just any ol body," Iris chimed in.

"How do you know he's the one anyway?" Lily asked with a soft yet strained voice. "Am I supposed to hear some booming voice?"

"I have, what The Word says, 'delighted myself' in Him," said Daisy. "And I have been waiting entirely too long for the desires of my heart to come to pass."

"Ah my dear, for starters The Word does say *He* will *give* you the desires of your heart," said Zenobia with a relieved look on her face. "Your accomplishments come from Him. And remember a few verses later The

Word says for us to be still and wait patiently. He is interested in what you do during your season of waiting and not necessarily, lack.

"We will get to all of this in later sessions. I want us to focus on you. As I said, there is a lot of bitterness, anger, impatience, and isolation in this room. I want us to examine these dark places first. So, here is what I need you to do: In three words or less, I want you to describe your love life," she said passing out 8x10 poster cards and a black marker. "If your love life was a book, what would be the title?"

Some of the ladies looked at each other. Some rested their heads in their hands. Breeze sighed and stared at her blank card. She hated exercises that made her think about her feelings. She was with them long enough and did not feel like expressing them this early in the game.

"If you are having difficulty, think of some of the reasons why your last relationship did not work. Or, maybe what you think is holding you back from receiving His best."

"That announcement didn't help," Breeze thought staring at the blank card. She saw other ladies taking out scraps of paper, scribbling and scratching things out. She thought about why a lot of her relationships never progressed. When she went through her mental laundry list of reasons, one thing held true and neatly placed her answer on the poster card.

"Will anyone need more time?" Zenobia asked as she looked around the room. She took her seat at the middle of the table. "Just so you know, refreshments will be provided after this exercise. I needed you to do a mini fast, so that you can dig deep. When the exercise is over, we all can dig in. Okay? Who will be first?"

Violet confidently raised her hand. She raised her card with her long, slim, neatly French manicured claw like fingers to reveal: '**ALL ABOUT ME**.' "I am trying to figure out since when did confidence and having it goin' on become such a turn off? As far as I'm concerned, I am, just like each of you in this room are and should be considered as 'number one draft picks.'"

"I'm sorry," said Breeze. "I don't mean to interrupt. But I wouldn't want to be the *number one* draft pick. That means I'm going to the worst team in the league. Who here has time for all that build up, train up, and tightening up?"

"Yeah, for some other team to eventually *snatch up*," added the Flower named Petunia.

"Ah, ladies the team may be the worst in the league, *last year*. However, this overlooked team has great potential," Zenobia responded. "This team player is willing to conform, aiming to please, and offering the most, thereby getting you and the team to the ring and the 'super bowl' of parties a lot faster."

"Point taken," said Breeze and Petunia in unison.

"Well, I am still having 'number one draft pick' stitched on my Chicago Bears jersey," she said proudly. "Anyway, I've never had a problem dating or men finding me. I feel that I am doing what I'm supposed to do: gathering information. Therefore, I am fully equipped knowing what I want and don't want in a guy.

"Unfortunately, the choices of men that we can *court* are extremely limited. The pickins' aren't necessarily slim, because indeed, there are single men out there. But as Believers, we should only date other Believers. Have you looked at the choices at your church?

"One service, my pastor had all the single men stand up. I mentally took inventory and said, 'dated that one, he had chronic bad breath, way too young, too weird, too creepy, too holier than thou, all he wanted was the booty, not enough money, quite impressed with himself.' The list went on and on. And the more I listed, the more depressed I got. I couldn't wait for them to sit down. I don't know what's taught during men's Bible study, but it ain't how to be a suitable suitor."

"Maybe they are teaching the Bible," Lily interjected.

"I'm sure. But aren't there seminars during their conferences for single men that believe in Him, and are looking for us? And they are certainly not participating in the single's ministry. It's hard to find a man who is a Believer, who will wait until marriage, doesn't have children, or a past that would make the hair on the back of your neck stand up. I'm thinking of taking this party outside the faith. Maybe I can convert a few. Hey, I know

I've done my duty when I can lead someone to Him or at least have dude speaking in tongues."

Zenobia chuckled while making some final notes and thanked Violet for being the first to share. "There is nothing wrong with confidence and having it going on. It is how you use that information that you gathered. But hold that thought, I want to hear some other stories first before we get into the subject. Who is next?"

Iris meekly raised her hand. Zenobia nodded her acknowledgment. She brushed her blonde highlighted spiral curl from her face and revealed: '**MISSED OPPORTUNITY**.' "My pastor did the same thing, one Sunday while I was away for the weekend. I always miss opportunities like that. And no one seems to get a copy of the DVD for me to review.

"One day my gym class instructor told us to stop being anonymous, to stand up and be counted. I'm not sure if I know how to do that anymore. I can't let myself get hurt again. I'm frightened of the possibility of putting myself out there. And with my timing? Every time I get an ounce of nerve to make myself available, he's already unavailable, physically or emotionally. If He wants me to get married, He needs to put him in front of my face with a sign, holding a bag of Mary Jane candies, because otherwise I will have missed him."

"Ms. Zenobia, if you don't mind, I would like to go next," Tulip said politely.

"Very well. Before you begin, Tulip, Iris are you finished?"

"In more ways than one," Iris sighed. "Yes, I'm done."

"My dear, you are not even close to being done. Do keep a mindset of 'just getting started'," Zenobia responded motioning for Tulip to share.

Tulip held her card in front of her, almost hugging it: '**DATE PROOF**.' "I have never been on a date. I have a great social life. I go out, travel, score great seats to the best shows. But I never bring a date, never talk about going on a date, or speak about someone that I'm seeing. I've spent hundreds of dollars on online dating and match making services. I even mustered up the courage to ask my friends to hook me up. They claim they don't have any single male friends. And if they do, their husbands don't want their wives to interfere.

"One of my coworkers heard of this class and signed me up. But what if the right guy was to come into my life? I wouldn't know what to do with him."

"Sweetie, none of us in here would know what to do with him. That's why we're here," a woman given the named 'Daisy' interjected.

Tulip smiled displaying incredibly deep dimples. "I've learned to live my life without romantic love," she finally said quickly losing the dimply display. "Now this class has me facing my lack of possibilities again. Is it too late to drop the course?"

"Knowing what to do is partially why you are here and no, it is never too late to drop the course. Unfortunately, you will not be able to get your money back." Zenobia smiled reassuringly. "Your situation will soon change, my dear."

Daisy decided to go next without an invitation. She held up her card with a hint of attitude: '**HE'S NOT LISTENING**.' "I do not believe 'old as Methuselah' was placed anywhere on my prayer list. But I always seem to attract the very much older, yet well put together, that 'wants-him-a-young-gal-but-don't-want-no-mo'-chur'n', kind of gentleman. Doesn't this same man realize that young gals may actually want children? Despite our age difference, we would have a great deal in common. However, our goals are never on the same page. Among other things, he just wants the companionship with me doing the listening and encouraging. All the time. I need the encouragement and dream sharing reciprocated."

"Wait," said Violet. "Among *other* things?"

"Yeah, get this. The last straw landed when one guy joked the last time he was finally able *and* ready to use a condom, he couldn't remember where he put 'em! I need *both* brains to work! I am a 39 year old virgin and the moment I say 'I do', take the snapshots, cut the cake, dance the first dance, slide the Electric Slide, and make our rounds to greet family and friends, he and I are getting it on! He would need to find some pills, props, rope, anything for him to be ready! Why would I need someone to spend the rest of my life with who couldn't, you know, perform, can't find it, or won't put all that practicing to good use? I can be sexless by myself! I'm sexless now. I know that is not the only part of marriage. Dude may *want* the companionship, but I *need* the *benefits*...after we get married of course."

"Please Daisy, I'm not making light of your situation...," Zenobia lost her composure and her train of thought. "Actually, we will get to that issue in the next few months. Everyone, keep in mind there is medication for the latter part of your concern. So ladies, do not block your blessings because of it. Now, if he does not want to take them, feel free to keep things moving. Oh my! Who is next? Rose?"

"Okay, how am I supposed to follow that?" Rose asked still laughing. "My story is a little different..." She sighed, ran her hand over her cropped curly hair, and held up her card: '**DISRESPECTED & DONE.**' "Now, I know I did wrong by shacking up. Our arrangement was a means of convenience. He needed a place to stay. I didn't want to be lonely. We enjoyed each other's company. We had a nice thing going...for five years.

"Then one evening, my family had a little gathering for my cousin getting married. She was casually discussing her plans and I whispered to him, 'when are we getting married?' He gave me the side eye and said, 'Aww, don't start that sugar-honey-ice-tea, tonight.'

"Unfortunately, my brothers overheard and were ready to take some corrective action. But I saved face and snuggled up to him. To make sure there wouldn't be any violence erupting in my momma's house, I got up for a moment. This knucklehead had the nerve to ask me to fix him a sandwich.

"I graciously nodded and went into the kitchen with my brothers trailing me. As soon as my toe hit the threshold, they asked me if they should take care of the matter, startin' with his sandwich. I assured them that everything will be all right. I came back serving him a sandwich with pickles, chips, a glass of ice tea, and nice sweet smile.

"When we got home, I got me some really good lovin'. I made him a full breakfast the following morning, fixed his lunch, gave him some more lovin', and sent him on his way whistlin'.

"Now, here's why I think my cousin signed me up for this class, against my will. Once that door was closed, I called in sick. Then, I called the locksmith to change every lock I could think of to my house. I changed the code on my garage door opener. I even got new house alarm remotes. Next, I proceeded to pack up his stuff in cheap flimsy trash bags. Normally you need to give the person 30 days' notice before throwing them out. But he made two mistakes, which allowed me to throw his dusty behind out the door at *my* will, since it was *my* house!

"I gathered up everything that belonged to him. He was entitled to his stuff and I no longer wanted his mess in my house. I called him up and whispered some sexy things, just to make sure he was still at work. Once everything was changed and packed, I set the trash bags outside.

"I went across the street to a neighbor's house to watch the festivities through some binoculars. He finally came home. He had this bewildered look on his face, since it wasn't trash day and the grass was already cut. He tried his key, but it didn't work. He started pounding on the door. He called me and asked what was going on. I told him not to start that 'sugar-honey-ice-tea' and that this is what he gets for embarrassing me in front of my family...for the last time! He asked where he was supposed to go, I suggested his momma's house.

"After a few expletives, he finally asked if we could work things out. I said if we are not getting married there was nothing left to work out. It was way past time for this dude to go. We watched that fool trying to haul his stuff, and what was left of his dignity, to and 'fro. And we just laughed.

"I know that you don't disrespect your man in front of people. However, men need to know, realize, and understand that you don't disrespect your woman either. There is nothing Biblical that says they have the right to treat a woman this way. This wasn't the first time he did this. But it was the last time.

"He calls me every week to see if my feelings have changed. He even suggested couples therapy. I told him if I see him again, he will need *physical therapy* after I'm finished with him. I know that shacking up is not in His plans and was something we never should have done. But this experience has really caused me to harden my heart. And for the past year, I have refused to let anyone in."

"Wow," sighed Zenobia. "Ladies, just so that we are clear and on one accord, shackin' up is not beneficial; and this arrangement does not line up with His Word. However, I am not here to pass judgment on anyone. Rose, I truly appreciate your transparency. Now, let us see what we can do about letting someone into your heart, and not necessarily your house." Zenobia smiled. "Lily, this would be a good time to share with us, please."

Lily looked nervous and frail behind her long hot-combed pressed, stringy curls. She looked up sheepishly and reluctantly picked up her card: '**BROKEN PROMISES.**' "As I said, my ex-boyfriend is marrying a member of my church. When I brought him to church with me for the first time, I had to momentarily fill in for a greeter. I seated him and saved a seat for myself when my time was done.

"It was time for the visitors to stand and be greeted, which is our cue to be seated. As I made my way back to my seat, I noticed this petite woman with a determined look on her face, get up, make her way from the front of the church, hook a left, step over a crawling baby, almost knocking down one of the senior saints all just to shake my boyfriend's hand. I quickly took my seat next to him, said hello to her, and to introduce him as my boyfriend. I thought the subject was closed. I thought wrong.

"After service was over, I introduced him to more people and here comes this woman, again. She had the nerve to lace her arms with his and flashed me this great big toothy smile and ask 'where have I been hiding this man', Well, to make a long sad drawn out story short, *they* are getting married.

"Although he never asked, we made plans to be married. We even took the marriage counseling course to ensure we stayed on the correct path. We were going to honeymoon in Israel and be baptized together. We had plans to build a strong, wonderful Christian life together. I found the one who would make my dreams come true and provide an amazing testimony of my faith. Only to have it snatched away." Lily started to cry. "What did I do wrong? What prayer did I not pray? Was I not humble enough? And as an additional slap in my face, I have been invited to the bridal shower and was instructed to bring a *gift card and a dish*."

"Why do you have to bring a dish?" Breeze asked giving her a tissue. "It's a bridal shower not a pot luck."

"That's what it said on the invite," Lily said dabbing her eyes. "No matter! Although the hostess is encouraging ladies from various ministries to attend, I'm not going. This woman is getting married to someone I thought He had for me."

The Flowers handed Lily more tissues. The room was silent with all eyes on her, with no one having a clue as to what to say. Zenobia attempted to make some notes but had to let out a huge sigh after the recent story.

Zenobia finally said, "You are going to that bridal shower with a great big smile, your head held high, and the best dish those unsuspecting women ever tasted! That man you thought you were in love with was clearly not for you, and he was certainly not your king! Just bring a camera to the shower to appear supportive. Speaking of jokers, do you want to share your story about yours, Hyacinth?"

"Maybe at a later time," Breeze said politely. "Here's what I've learned," she said flipping over her card: '**DRAMA FREE**.' "I am fine with being single. Why can't my family and friends understand this? I enjoy my own company. I have plenty of time for my family, friends, and my students. I'm on a happy merry-go-round instead of riding an emotional roller coaster. I'm fine with the idea of living by myself, going to the movies by myself, traveling by myself, just being by myself. Just because I don't have him, has not stopped me from living. I think adding him into the equation would just complicate matters. I can honestly say that I am absolutely fine with being single.

"My family thinks that I would be happy if I had a man in my life. Have they forgotten the hell I went through going out with that controlling, conniving monster that I mistakenly let creep in and trample my good, stable life? At that point in my life, I was *not* happy! Why in the world would I need to let someone else in my life like that again? The last guy *was* the last guy. I refuse to let anyone even attempt to get that close to me again." She turned to Zenobia and hissed, "So are you up for the challenge to change me?"

"I am not here to change you," Zenobia said calmly. "However, are you up for the challenge to let Him change your heart?" she asked with a smile. "Last but not least, Petunia."

Petunia attempted to sigh but her full plum stained lips got in the way, making a jalopy motor like noise. She reluctantly lifted the card with her matching plum nail polished hands to reveal: '**THEIRS, NOT MINE.**' "You know, Ms. Zenobia talks about this light that we are supposed to shine. I have a tendency to only shine it for married, engaged, questionably straight or even emotionally unavailable men. The dates are fun, but this is getting old. The good news is, I do see married men that truly love their wives and are willing to make it work. It is comforting to know that there are men out there that still love and are in love with their first wives. It's just disconcerting that there is no one available for me."

"Not to make light, but I want to hear about the crush on the questionably straight guy," Tulip interrupted. There was a lot of 'me, too's' going around the table.

"It's funny though, none of us want to know about the emotionally unavailable," Daisy interjected.

"No, 'cause that's all that's left," spat Iris.

"Let's face it, the choices are limited. And there is nothing we can do about it," Violet said defeatedly.

"Ladies," Zenobia pleaded. "I want our focus to be on us. I have to admit I would not want to be a young single woman today. However, the one He made especially for you is out there. I believe in my heart that if a woman desires to be married, then she should have her glorious day down the aisle. If this is indeed your desire, you need to be smart about one of the biggest decisions you will ever make in your life. Because this is not about the dress, the ring, the shower, the bridesmaids you choose or the actual wedding day. It is about the marriage and the rest of your life.

"Before we get into our preparation, I want you to examine your dark place as your homework assignment for this week. I want you to write down every negative thought that comes in to your head and comes out of your mouth this week. Write them all down. There is a tablet in your binder, portable enough so that you can keep it handy. Make sure that you transfer your notes on to your master list.

"And, let me forewarn each of you now. The Word says for us to shine our light before others, because it glorifies Him. Therefore, satan will be on his job, while you are finding and shining your light. Your doubts, deflating self-confidence, not being prepared when opportunity presents itself, and harsh words coming at angles you never knew existed, will come about. This, however, should actually make you stronger and shine a little brighter. It will be a must keeping His Words and promises close to your heart and mind. Because you are aware that He is ultimately in control.

"On that note, let us close with grace and prayer and I will see everyone here, the same time next week." She ended her session with a quick blessing of the food and a closing prayer. The Flowers closed their binders, packing up their belongings in silence. Her assistant broke the silence bringing in pretty pink boxed lunches for everyone. The air in the room finally perked up as soon as they sampled what the box had to offer.

"Ms. Zenobia, do you mind if I eat in here?" Lily asked.

"Be my guest."

Each of them decided to stay, and dine on their meals. The box contained a turkey sandwich on wheat Kaiser Roll, a bag of UTZ plain potato chips, and two oatmeal cranberry cookies. Various hot and cold beverages were neatly arranged on the back wall.

"So Hyacinth, what's your football team?" asked Petunia grabbing a bottled water.

"The Bal-ti-more Ra-vens," she cheered proudly while opening her chips. "What about you?"

"I occasionally get a hold of some Washington tickets, but I love me some Colts."

"Baltimore or Indianapolis?"

"Indianapolis," she clarified. "I remember the day they arrived. My dad was so happy."

"I remember the day they left," said Breeze. "The entire state was in an uproar."

"Forget about the football teams, tell us about that, 'How to Keep Your Dude Happy while Keeping Your Legs Closed' class, Hyacinth," Violet said savoring one of the chips.

"Yeah," Daisy said chiming in while opening a canned iced tea. "As an intellectual, I am willing to go to a class to learn how to be a good freak...for my husband, of course."

Breeze and anyone within earshot lost it. "Maybe one day," Breeze said still laughing. "What I can say is that I have some colorful friends that do some colorful things. Albeit strange, it was a lot of fun."

The ladies finished their meals with light conversation, packed up their things again, said their goodbyes, and headed for their cars. Breeze searched for her ride and spotted Liddy Bee's jiggly arms waving her in. During her brief walk, she decided to harden her face. She was still beyond vexed they would do this to her. But after the stories she heard tonight, the next eight months should be interesting, if not entertaining. She had to fight the smile forming on her face when she thought about Daisy's remarks.

"Girl, it's almost 10:30! What on earth did y'all have to say that kept you for three and a half hours?" asked Willow. Breeze did not answer. She opened the back door, placed her belongings on the floor and plopped herself in the open seat. She hoped her silence would indicate to drive her home.

"Are you hungry, baby?"

She was still giving them the silent treatment and stared out into the darkness of I-295 North.

"Breezy Bee, answer me!"

"I am not hungry," she said stifling a burp.

She thought about the daunting task of visiting those places in her head and heart that were neatly and conveniently tucked away...for eight agonizing months. Sharing them with eight total strangers made the thought absolutely overwhelming. As far as Breeze was concerned, relationships were grossly overrated. However, she realized the key word of her last thought is 'were.' *"Maybe it is time to change my point of view."*

Liddy Bee pulled into Breeze's driveway. Breeze quickly got out only to have Willow follow and stop her at the door.

"Dahlin', you need this course. You wouldn't have come if we didn't con you into going. And here's a little something to put that smile that we love back on your face and to let you know that we love you and are behind you every step of the way." Willow gave her a small DSW shoe bag, containing the shoes she and Breeze argued over. She could not help but crack a smile.

"Was the guy still there?"

"Yeah, he gave me a discount if I promised to take a picture of your legs in those shoes."

"And the word of the day is: Creepy," she said looking in the box. "But oh so worth it," she said hugging her friend and leaned in the car to kiss her aunt good night. "But know this: y'all are still on my list!"

7

Doughnuts & Deal Breakers

"I know you didn't think you were gonna dance past this office and not say hello," said the office administrator with her hands on her ample hips. The petite, roly poly, tightly curled woman with 1960's cat eyeglasses greeted Breeze with a great big smile and a bigger box of donuts.

"That was the goal when I spotted that box," Breeze said and gave her a big hug.

"Stop trying to watch that weight, girl! I got your favorite," she said temptingly while opening the box of glazed doughnuts. Breeze could not resist. Given the opportunity she would eat the entire contents.

"Thanks, Mrs. Tingle. You're too mean."

"Ms. Monsoon has nine months to stay away from unnecessary carbs and watch that waistline," someone hissed in the background. Breeze knew the voice all too well. She reluctantly spun towards the source of the comment and saw one of Tuesday's henchmen strolling towards them.

"Nine months? And just what did we do over the summer," Mrs. Tingle said while disapprovingly peering over her glasses. "I don't see no ring on no finger," she said taking Breeze's left hand. "And I know you ain't pregnant."

"No, *she* is not the one getting married," said Tuesday's friend. "As usual," she mumbled. "I ain't sure 'bout the pregnant part, though."

Tuesday had a posse of 'stuff starters' she hoped would all be in the teacher's lounge ogling at her ring. She thought this one probably escaped. Mrs. Connor was a dark brown skinned Amazon, with blond, curly ringlets cascading everywhere. Her fire engine red lipstick, painfully tight blue jeans, flesh showing canary yellow blouse with matching shoes reminded Breeze of a melted banana split.

Breeze sighed and confessed to the ladies that she was indeed pregnant. A huge brown and red "O" formed, consuming the ladies faces. "Just kidding, I'm a bridesmaid again," she said. "I'm sure Mrs. Connor will be more than happy to fill you in on the wonderful details, as I have to get to my classroom and prepare my 'back-to-school' speech." She took another doughnut and left the ladies where they stood.

As she walked down the royal blue locker lined hall, determined to get to her classroom, Breeze was cornered by the rest of Tuesday's cohorts. "We understand that you are planning the bachelorette party *and* the co-worker bridal shower for Tuesday."

"And a good morning to you too, ladies," she said with the brightest smile she could muster. "Correction! I am planning the work bridal shower, but I will leave any bachelorette party planning to the ones who know her best, such as yourselves. Because of the significance, we'll probably hold the event in the party room of Hunan Manor. Then, if you so choose, swing around to Silver Shadows."

"In Columbia?" asked cohort number three. "Why so dag gone far?"

"If the distance is that big of a deal, then I suggest you carpool, preferably with someone who hasn't used up her allotted miles on their brand new *leased* Mercedes. Now, if you will excuse me--"

Cohort number three just sucked her teeth in response.

"Hold on," cohort number four stopped her with a dip and a hand on the roll of her hip. "Tuesday said *you* were gonna do both!"

"She also told me she wanted strippers," said cohort number two.

"She can have strippers at her bachelorette party that I am sure each of you will do a fine job hosting...without me."

"What, you too good of a Christian that *you* can't hire a strippah?"

"Yep and quite frankly, if you have to pay a man to get naked, you are clearly doing something wrong. Anyway, the wedding is nine months away. There's no need to hash this out now. I'm sure Tuesday will keep those closest posted on the specifics. Have a good morning, ladies." Breeze stormed straight ahead instead of side stepping, breaking the circle.

"Why she Tuesday's bridesmaid, anyway?" snorted cohort number three. Breeze felt their eyes still staring at her as she walked away wondering the same thing.

— —

"Good evening my beautiful garden. I trust everyone had a blessed week. Ladies, I just want to reiterate that this course is designed to repair your relationships. Some of you informed me that you were not in a relationship. But yes, each of you are, indeed, in a relationship. In some cases a very jacked up, verbally and/or mentally abusive relationship... with yourselves.

"For your homework assignment, I wanted you to write down every negative thought, idea or words spoken throughout the week. Please take out that list," she said floating to the back of the room. "I am sure each of you could write a book of your negative thoughts," she said carrying a portable shredder back to her seat. The Flowers handed in their lists as Zenobia turned on the shredder. "This is your former way of thinking," she said holding up the pile. "There is no need to think this way, ever again," she said shredding the lists.

"This is your season for preparation. I want you to be properly prepared for what God has in store for you. You need to be mentally, physically, intimately, spiritually, financially, socially, and domestically prepared for the love of your life. During these next eight months, we will be tackling each in great detail. Because right now, he is not ready for you, and you are not ready for him. If you are not ready, He will not be ready to grant the desires of your heart. So, let us get to work."

Almost on cue, her assistant came in the classroom with several small white boxes with a pretty pink satin ribbon. Without being told, she distributed the boxes tied in Zenobia signature pretty pink ribbon to each member of the class. Breeze could not tell if it was the color or the element of surprise that brightened everyone's faces. Curiosity of the box's contents got the best of everyone as they started to undo the ribbon.

"Now ladies, please do not open your gifts just yet."

After her assistant distributed the boxes and saw that everyone was served, she immediately left the room.

"Okay, now you can peek!"

The ladies pulled out a pretty pink rhinestone mirror and two black cosmetic bags with the initials "H" and "E" etched in pink. Some of the ladies looked at each other, while the others checked their makeup, stray hairs, teeth, and potential wrinkles.

"This course is faith based. As Christian women, you should be familiar with God's Word and His promises. And we will go into other scriptures that will uplift and support what is being said in the class. However, there are two scriptures that you need to focus on and have in your heart. Ephesians 2:10 because you 'are God's masterpiece' and Psalm 139:14, as each of you are 'fearfully and wonderfully made.' The first scripture I want you to say to yourself every morning and before bed time. Look in the mirror and recite the second scripture when the world says and you think, otherwise.

"Allow me to explain the concept behind the two small bags. Again, you *will* be prepared when he walks into your life. The 'H' represents 'Hope.' The 'E' stands for 'Expectancy.' I designed this course to rediscover hope and expectancy. Everyone in this room needs their hope restored and expect good things out of their current situation. Keep one bag in your car and one at work. As the divas that you are, I am sure you already have several cosmetic bags. I want to make sure that you do. In it, I want you to include the following: gum or mints, lip balm or tinted lip gloss, a spare pair of earrings, knee high's, two bobby pins, three safety pins, and $7."

"After all that, why $7?" asked Lily.

"You never know when you fall short on cash or forget your wallet. You can get a nourishing lunch for seven bucks. It may not be the healthiest, but you will not go hungry. Or you will have enough to share if you order something from a dollar menu. Now, as for our ice breaker--"

"Wait," Petunia interrupted. "Why three safety pins?"

"A temporary fix for a missing button or an overly eager open blouse. Choose to add anything you want that will make you look your best in a hurry. And please, do not forget the pen, paper, and business cards that you do not mind giving out to total strangers.

"Ladies, our ice breaker for tonight--"

"I could have used this bag when I went to the gym last week," said Iris. "I exercise five times a week; three of those days are done in the afternoon. I like the noon class because I can focus on me and my form. There is no one to impress because most of the men in the class are married, so I can go in, looking any 'ol kind of way: legs ashy and bristly, nonmatching outfit, hair thrown in a ponytail, earrings optional. I usually see this cute guy during the weekend class. But oh, no, he decides to show up at my noon class.

"So, I ran to the car, used the remains of my melted lip balm, and searched for some earrings. I had a pair of small gold hoops and some silver dangles. Of course, I couldn't wear the dangles. That would look silly. The gold ones would have to do. But, I was wearing a silver necklace and I didn't want him to think that I mixed metals. However, desperate measures kicked in. I took off the necklace, put on the hoops and walked back in. My prime spot was gone and I had to go to the back. The good news is I got to check out his rear view...very nice. The bad news is, my instructor threw me out of my comfort zone, introduced us, and stated that I wanted to meet him."

"Did sparks fly?" asked Daisy.

"Uh, one, I'm in this class. Two, not only was I not prepared, I think he wiped his hands on his shorts after we shook hands. I don't know about his, but my palms weren't sweaty."

"Are you still interested?" asked Rose.

"Extremely. Something about this guy I really like."

"Okay, ladies: Exhibit A." Zenobia gestured like a show girl towards Iris. "A key thought: he is most likely going to find you while you are doing your normal activities like shopping at Target, being involved in your church, gym class, or where ever you naturally shine bright. I need you to be ready. And if anything else, when you look your best, you feel it, especially when no one is watching.

"However, Iris' interest reminds me of the topic I want you to think about later this evening. However, before we get into that, let us proceed to the ice breaker. In a few words or less, what is your ultimate deal breaker?"

"Chapped Lips and Bad Teeth," Daisy said with her hand on her hip. "Do folks not have a dental plan included in their benefit package? Lip balm only cost $1.00. Find some. Brush your lips when you brush your teeth. That's assuming that he does. The first thing I notice about a guy is his smile. If I am going to spend the rest of my life putting a smile on his face, I want to at least like the look of it."

"I'll see your Chapped Lips and Bad Teeth," laughed Iris. "And raise you 'Bad Breath.' I always keep gum handy, in my purse, in the car, in my gym bag, or at work. When I'm on my annual cruise, I always keep a few pieces in my wristlet, especially during the 2:30 AM concerts."

"Wait," said Petunia. "I've been on cruises before. A club may be open, but a concert?"

"This, ladies, is a cruise like no other! Anyway, I was at the late night concert and this guy strikes up a conversation. Girl, his breath formed a hand that grabbed my lips, made a fist, and contorted my face! He did at least ask if I was okay, but I was struggling to get to my gum.

"I gave him *three* pieces and he tells me, 'good looking out,' places one in his mouth and proceeds to talk to another chick. I was like, 'am I not worthy of fresh breath?' The good news is she rejected him. And, I noticed he proceeded to put the other two pieces in his mouth, and kept it movin'. Now, whenever we see each other on the cruise, he asks for some gum. I'm like you really need to skip a year and take that money to see a dentist."

After the laughter subsided, Violet spoke next. "Y'all I cannot stand 'Cheap Men.' Dude receives the first strike if he uses a coupon on the first date. Strike two, if he asks if I still carry my student I.D. before purchasing a movie ticket. If dude has McCormick and Schmick's tastes but Long John Silver pockets, I can meet him halfway with some Red Lobster. And with that, a coupon can be used.

"If your funds are temporarily low, at least make the date creative. There are so many places in this state and the surrounding ones to make a date fun and affordable. Plan it out so I won't have to go in my purse or show me how cheap you can be. However, when he is no longer financially embarrassed, please allow me to supersize. And furthermore, what is he saving his money for: bills, a car, house, or a better date...with somebody else? I guess I should have asked that question instead of blowing him off. I could have been married now, with my two sets of twins.

"Anyway, I love how this one guy tries to date me in church. Any time the church provides food, he's there making sure I have everything I need while chatting me up in the process."

"Maybe he's trying to get to know you before spending his hard earned money," Lily said.

"For two years? If you haven't made up your mind, don't bother. At first, the gesture was nice, but after a while it makes me bitter and turns me off to talking to men in church. You have to reach back to date the seriously unsaved with good teeth," she pointed to Daisy, "to go to a concert, see a comedy show, or just go to a party. *Then* you reel him in."

"Speaking of men in the church, I'm a little...scratch that! If a man talk about 'submitting,' I'm running," Lily said. "I made the mistake of not running from that numbskull I almost married. I was happy that I was going to have my Christian relationship. However, he quickly established 'order' within the relationship. Looking back, he forgot to treat me like the prize that I am, his potential wife. I was more his child or for that matter, a doormat. It was always *my* role, *my* place, and always, always know who was running things. He became agitated when I made decisions on my own. And the last time I checked, we ain't married and my parents taught me common sense!"

"Not to cut you off," Violet interrupted. "Let's talk about that nasty little word, 'submit'. I've noticed men are taking that word just a bit too far. He may have the final say, but as a grown woman, *we will* discuss the issue and my feelings, thoughts had better be considered when making that final decision. And if you mess things up, especially my money, I promise I won't nag or even say I told you so. However, it will be hard to trust him with decisions again."

"Okay, you want to talk about submissive? How about another nasty little word: 'Let'!"

"Ladies," Zenobia said interrupting the brewing discussion. "We will discuss submission in greater detail in a later class. I would like to get through the ice breaker first because we have two very important assignments to do tonight. Now, who would like to go next, Tulip?"

"Sure. 'Laziness' is at the top of my list. Not just not wanting to work, because we all agree that a man needs to get up at least five days a week doing something to earn a paycheck, support himself, and have enough left for a decent date.

"The ones who engage in no extra activities grate on my nerves. No movies, vacations, parties, job functions, going out to dinner, nothing. Just stay at home, wait for me to cook and serve him his dinner while watching my cable, complaining that I don't have the sports package. My expectations of a boyfriend should enhance those things, not add dead weight. And what happens when you marry that dead weight? I can't take that on a cruise!"

"Good news, you won't have to because he won't go," said Rose.

"Hold it, if you knew what you were getting into, why would you even consider marrying dead weight dude?" Breeze asked.

"Good point," said Tulip. "All I'm saying is, for those chicks who don't want to do nothing, too scared to do nothing, or just plain refuse to do *anything* that involves your hair getting messed up, need to seek out the brothers who don't want to do nothing. Better still, start an on-line dating service: let-grass-grow-under-my-feet.com. Specializing in finding that lazy someone to be a couch potato with."

"I'm just a hair appointment away from signing up for that dating service," laughed Iris.

"My deal breaker would have to be a 'Dallas Cowboy' fan," said Petunia. "As a football lover and my access to free tickets, football season is when I meet the most men with common interests. I can hold my own during a conversation with the best of them. Then here comes the Cowboys' fan gloatin' when they win. If I see that blue and silver star coming my way, I'm runnin' the other way, especially if I'm wearing my burgundy and gold."

"Um, that seems rather petty," said Lily.

"Mmm, not petty," said Breeze. "I'm the same way with the Indianapolis Colts, honorable mention: the Pittsburgh Steelers. We still can't believe they had the gall to take the name and team colors. Now, that dishy Tony Dungy has my heart. But how can I bring home a guy with 'Yay, Indianapolis Colts' on this breath? Now I've embraced my Baltimore Ravens and I look quite fetching in my purple and black football jersey. And a guy could score some serious points if he has season tickets. But the bitterness still lingers."

"Let's circle back to Tony Dungy and The Battle of the Black Coaches," said Iris. "Now *that* was, indeed, a Super Bowl!"

"Who you tellin'," added Daisy wanting a piece of conversation. "I'm not a football fan, but I watched that game with a few friends imagining what Coach Dungy and that chocolate cutie pie Coach Lovie Smith were like in college. Like, you were in love with Tony because he was fine, light skinned and those freckles and bitable ears added fuel to the fire. You dated Lovie, because not only was he cute, he treated you right, and was willing to please."

"Yeah, like bringing you cheese sticks and/or milkshakes from the late dining hall and he didn't care about the calories you consumed at such an hour," Breeze said laughing.

"Late night dining?" asked Daisy. "Where did you go to school?"

"College Park. Go Terps!"

"Petunia, be careful who you talk to," said Zenobia. "I am a long time Cowboys fan and yes, I look quite fetching in my dark blue, silver and white hat, and jersey combo. Ladies, you may want to rethink about opposing teams as deal breakers and make them your conversation starters.

"My first husband was a Steeler's fan. I lost a bet and nine months later my third son was born. Maybe that was not the best example for my impressionable Flowers, but you get the gist. I think we have two more left or was the Colts your deal breaker, Hyacinth?"

"No, but along the lines of appearing petty, I actually had to stop a date when he claimed roller coasters killed brain cells. I told him that he's dining with a walking vegetable because I can't get enough of them. There are only a few things that I want and expect for my birthday: dinner with my dad, a few phone calls and cards from my friends, and jewelry from my mom. And since she is no longer here, I get that myself.

"I need to experience an amusement park with more than five thrill rides, during the birthday week. Some of the best conversations I've had involved a walk around the amusement park. And during this perfect day, you get to see if he's fearless riding in the front car, overly cautious riding in the 'let's get this over with' seat in the middle, or his walk on the wild side in the 'crack of the whip' seat in the back."

"So, you can put up with all of those things we talked about, but if he is a roller coaster lover he's in there?" asked Violet.

"The bottom line is it's the simple things that really matter. If he can't pay attention to what I want and act upon it, what would be the point? Besides, a good roller coaster rider incorporates most of what we've discussed tonight. First, an amusement park is *not cheap*. I will respect the brother if he uses discount coupons or tickets. That shows me he is a good steward of his finances and there will be more to spend on me. And, he can use my guest pass if he drives. Second, he needs to be a *fan* of the coaster. It's all about the coaster and a few thrill rides. And he, wait, add 'arrogant' to my list."

"You can't have two," laughed Daisy.

"Ms. Zenobia said deal *breakers*. Anyway, he can't be so *arrogant* that he is not able to appreciate the simple joy that loops, dips, hills, and funnel cake can bring. Just good clean, thrilling fun even a super Christian could appreciate. And, we will be there until it closes, so he cannot be lazy and has to have some *staying power.* He will need to chew some *gum* to control the hunger pangs because I really do not eat during my coaster time. And to top it all off, let's hope the brother has a *pretty smile* for the pictures."

"You forgot one, Hyacinth," said Rose. "You didn't mention argumentative."

"Oh, the only thing we will be arguing about is which coaster to go on next. He won't be messin' up my day with intense fellowship."

"Try messin' up the past five years of your *life* with intense fellowship," said Rose. "Knucklehead loved to start fights. The only good part was the makeup sex. Maybe that's the reason why he kept startin' stuff. Anyway, when I do date, which is pretty rare and there is an argument brewing, I will order dessert, box it up with the leftovers, pay for my share of the meal, and roll out!"

"Wow, I see we have a lot of concerns on the table," said Zenobia. "I cannot wait to hear how you respond to today's topic. Let us take a break, first. A mini fast will not be necessary to complete the next tasks, as I see everyone is in the mood to talk."

8

Fried Rice & Fears

"I hope everyone likes Chinese," Zenobia's assistant, Lourdes, said setting the food on the back wall credenza. When she finished arranging the dinner choices to her liking, she moved to the opposite end of the room to refresh the beverage table. "Enjoy, ladies," she said floating out the room once finished.

"I do insist that we eat healthy, so there are dishes with lots of seafood and vegetables. But, I need my egg rolls," Zenobia said while reaching for one.

The Flowers eagerly rose from their seats to sample the Chinese buffet. Everyone served themselves, with their full plates indicating the ladies were hungry. Eating in silence was also an indication.

"Did I also mention he can't have nappy chest hair?" asked Daisy, breaking the silence. "All that taco meat peeking through his shirt can be a real turn off."

"Darlin', that can be fixed," Rose said laughing.

Some of the ladies agreed with Rose. The others were still laughing.

"Daisy, you are absolutely too much," laughed Zenobia. "Ladies, due to time, let us make this a working dinner. I want to begin discussing the one common topic on our minds: marriage. So quite frankly, how many of you actually *want* to get married?" The number of hands startled Zenobia. Two hands belonging to Daisy and Lily proudly shot up, while the others looked on. "Okay," Zenobia said uneasily. "How many of you do *not* want to get married?" Rose raised her hand proudly with a hint of attitude.

"There are five of you that are unsure?"

"Try scared to death," said Tulip.

"Of getting married?"

"Actually, admitting that I want to," Tulip replied. "You make an attempt to put yourself out there. When you let folks know that you are interested, the flood gates of criticism get thrown wide open. 'Aw, you still can't find a man? Well, you know...' and they start quotin' stats and adding their own stink to the situation."

"Like, point out that you're not wearing enough color."

"Or unkindly point out that you're too fat."

"'You're too thin.'"

"'How you gonna keep a man when you can't cook?'"

"'Yo' problem is dat you too picky. You got a lot of pickiness in ya, girl!'"

"Personally, I just don't see the benefits," said Petunia. "I know marriage is a lot of work. But is anyone happy in their relationship, or at least look like it?"

"I agree," Lily chimed in. "Even though I want to get married, the look on the faces of married folks has a tendency to scare me. You would think they would be happy because they found the love of their lives."

"The struggles of life are branded on their faces and advertised through their actions," added Tulip. "More books, seminars, retreats, and support groups are designed for married couples. Somebody should be happy while making it work."

"I just zone out when the pastor starts preaching about issues mostly related to married folk," said Violet. "He'll go on preaching a wonderful topic, but steers it towards married life. While we singles need to smile, shut up, take notes, and dig them out *if* the time comes."

"Please, my pastor did a series about sex and only a footnote's worth of information was directed towards single folk," said Tulip.

"Yeah, like if you are single, don't have sex, period, end of discussion," said Lily.

"Mmm hmm," added Daisy. "Why should I frantically take notes when the message won't apply to me?"

"It may apply to you eventually," Lily said.

"And it may not."

"Speaking of which, you would think these married couples would have a happier disposition, because they are or should be getting regular sex. Right?" asked Daisy.

"One would think," said Tulip. "But some married couples are experiencing the same drought as some of us single folk."

"My challenge is once you get married, you have to think about someone else besides you," said Breeze. "As an only child, that's a foreign concept. And then factor kids into the equation..."

"I don't see the benefits in them either," said Petunia.

"Girl, please," spat Violet. "Children are a nicety, not a necessity."

"But what I'm afraid of is marrying a real jerk," said Iris. "You may get the representative. He may bring you flowers, say sweet things, and listen attentively. Then once you say 'I do,' he turns out to be a real monster."

"I agree. My cousin married one and I'm like, 'did you realize he was a *beep* before you married him?'" said Tulip. "Pardon me, Ms. Zenobia, for the language. There was no other way to describe him."

"That is why we are in this setting instead of a church. A course of this nature, peppered expletives may come out," Zenobia said smiling reassuringly. "Let us just keep them to a minimum."

"I want to go back to that nasty six letter expletive, *submit*," said Violet. "I know as future wives, The Word commands us to submit to our husbands. But a few of these knuckleheads want this particular benefit way before we say 'I do.' If I hear that word during the sermon or a discussion, I zone out."

"I *tune in* to make sure I hear what the pastor is saying to these Christian men we have to work with," said Lily.

"Whoever is teaching or preaching the subject needs to let them know The Word also says for them to *love* their wives," said Petunia.

"Show me love and I'll show you submit," said Daisy.

"And what is going on with this 'let' mess?" asked Iris. "I asked a friend to attend a function and she stood erect, stared blankly and said, 'I-don't-know-if-my-husband-would—let-me.' Now, I understand there is a courtesy thing where you see if you and hubby had plans. But *let*? To give someone that much power and control over you can be quite scary."

"All right, you have 'submit,' 'let,' and here's mine: 'We'll see,'" said Breeze. "As a single chick going to work every day, paying her own bills, and making her own way, if there is something I want to do and I would like for him to come along, I bet'not hear him say, 'we'll see!' We'll see what? We'll see me leaving his sorry rump at home.

"My 'whatever' pulled that 'we'll see' mess. My favorite artist was coming for his supposedly last concert, and I asked if he wanted to see it. He said, 'we'll see.' I let him think that was the end of it. Since I'm a member of the artist's fan club, I get tickets in advance. Two of my church members stated they wanted tickets. I didn't bother with homeboy because I knew the meaning behind 'we'll see.'

"Suddenly, an opportunity presented itself, so I tried to contact homeboy. He wouldn't return my calls. So, I went to the concert and had a great time. That acoustic guitar segment took his music to a whole new level. As I was leaving, I saw homeboy walking out with some 20-something stick figure wearing a skirt the size of a tissue, thanking him for the tickets. I kindly approached the two of them, asked politely if they enjoyed the show, told him that it was good seeing him, and headed for the Metro. The look on his face was priceless and so was the story I had waiting for my girls.

"Was this the end of the issue you ask? Oh no! He calls and asks me why I had tickets. Then, he accuses me of not trusting him. And the last straw was him accusing me of blowing up his phone. I told him I was not going to place my favorite singer's *last performance* in the hands of 'we'll see,' especially with no updates. And besides, I was calling him about the concert for the next day. Apparently, they added another show due to popular demand. I was messing around on my phone, accidently called a radio station and ended up being caller 19 for two front row tickets for the show the next day. Then he says, 'oh, when are you picking me up?' I told him 'we'll see.'"

"Hyacinth, please tell me you didn't take him?"

"I had the good sense to take somebody else."

"Did you ever see him again?"

"That's a whole 'nother story. Let's just say I thought it was over when I wished him a 'happy mother's day.'"

"Personally, I just wish He would remove the desire to be married if He's not going to grant it," Iris sighed as the laughter subsided. "Why does this aspect of my life have to be so mysterious? If I'm not worthy enough to be in a loving relationship, tell me. I don't want to waste my time on this earth, when I can pray for something else worthwhile and obtainable...like that new Volkswagen. I do not want drama. I do not want him to rule over me. And I certainly do not want to change who I am for him."

"So, why are y'all in this class?" Lily said exhaustedly.

"You know, that's the question I've been asking myself ever since I got conned into coming to this class," said Breeze.

"You should not change for him or anyone for that matter, Iris," said Zenobia while shooting Breeze a look. "Just as men do not want you changing them, he should not have the need to change you. However, lasting relationships require compromise and growth. When you find that right person...and I am speaking from experience, ladies. When the right man appears, you will want to *submit* to each other. You can call it change, but it should not be viewed as a negative.

"This class is for every stage of your love life: wondering, hoping, praying for your heart's desire, or wishing it would go away. The two of you that want to be married are in the right place, because you are going to be prepared to receive. As for the rest of you, your mindset needs a different focus. It is good that you are noticing the potentially ugly and lonely side of marriage. And yes, sermons are designed to uplift the married, because all married folk need help...*daily*. And the available support strengthens relationships and in most cases encourages the making of other little Christians," she said giggling as she rose from the table.

"Ms. Zenobia, did you have to go through all of this back in your day?" asked Violet. "I mean you have to admit, the situation is completely out of control. I'm sure it was not always like this."

"The pickings, as you call it, were slim during my day, too. However, my dating years were not as bad. Going to a black college made it easier to get your M.R.S. degree. If a man liked what he saw, especially on campus, he went after it. That was the difference between then and now.

"I met this tall, pretty, cream-in-your coffee skinned, naturally wavy haired track star. We fell in love, married, and made four pretty baby boys. He was also the meanest son-of-a gun to drag his knuckles across the earth. Although I was in love, I got caught up in what I was supposed to do: finish high school, go to college, find a husband, and make babies.

"When he passed away, I genuinely grieved because I did love the man. However, I was able to be Zenobia for the first time in my life and able to do what I wanted. In the process of discovering me, the love of my life found me. We knew each other in college, but never really received the chance to connect, especially if my first husband had anything to say about it. Not only was he mean, but extremely possessive, which I mistook as love and devotion.

"Then, one lovely homecoming at Bowie State University, I had the pleasure of reconnecting with my Linden. Our conversation started at a tailgate party and lasted all the way to 5th Quarter. He was not my type in college. Come to think of it, he's not my type now. But, I have never laughed and loved as much until I met Linden. Twenty years later, the very thought of him still gives me goose bumps," she said with a bright, sly smile painted on her face. "Uh, ladies, this would be a good time to take another break," she said still smiling as she signaled her assistant to serve the dessert. She started to excuse herself as one of the Flowers had one more thing to add.

"Ladies, after listening to our concerns and fears, is it just me or is God letting us know that we are acting as if we don't need Him anymore?" challenged Tulip. "And not bringing him is His way of getting us to talk to Him? All of us have the material dreams we prayed for. Do we act like there is no more need for prayer?"

"Tulip, I can see your point, but I still need Him in my life," said Iris. "The situation has come to a head so much so, that it will take nothing less than an act of God to find someone we want. The need and want for a connection with the opposite sex is Biblical. And since it is, why does it have to be this difficult?"

"Yeah, even He has to admit the situation, especially among His children, is completely out of control," said Daisy. "And when did it start falling apart, anyway?"

"Personally, I think so many of us being single is His way of letting us know that we are out of order," confessed Lily. "Refusing to submit, viewing children as options, being picky and petty. In the process of school, work, and obtaining possessions we lost our focus."

"What on earth do you mean by that?" spat Petunia. "Are you saying He's *punishing* us for having opinions and minds of our own? It's *your statement* that is out of order!"

"Petunia..." Zenobia interrupted trying to calm her and the rest of the class down. Words were not spoken but every Flower's facial expressions spoke volumes. "Ladies..."

"Wait a minute, Ms. Zenobia," said Rose. "Lily, are we supposed to accept anyone, be treated any old kind of way, and accept anything that comes out of a man's mouth? Are we supposed to sit around and *wait* for him to get a house, get the car, get a life, *and then* add me and stir?"

"Okay, everyone just stop and fix your faces! I have not seen this many shades of red on brown faces since I visited the makeup counter at Fashion Fair!" After the laughter lightened the air in the room, Zenobia continued.

"First and foremost, do not think for one second that any of you are out of order. Not putting Him first, not trusting Him, and not doing what He asks you to do *is* out of order. Living your life, acquiring the things that you work hard for, and being the person you want to be is in line with what He wants for His children. You are building careers, relationships with your family and friends, doing what you are supposed to do during your season of singleness. And quite frankly, God does not punish. He gives you choices. If you make the so called wrong choice, He will *correct* His children. He never punishes.

"Your parents have done a fine job of raising strong, independent, wealth creating young ladies. You listened to the advice of keeping your heads and eyes in the books, and for the most part, your legs closed. Now, they want grandchildren and cannot understand what is taking you so long. I just wish there was discussion as to how to have and maintain a healthy relationship. In some cases, their own relationships were not healthy. So, on behalf of mothers who did not, I apologize."

"Ms. Zenobia, why are you apologizing? You didn't have girls."

"I raised the boys who will be marring the girls I am apologizing to. Actually, there is one more left. Three of my boys are already married."

"I'm not blaming my mother," said Petunia. "And Ms. Zenobia should not have to apologize if she raised her boys' right."

"I just wished my mama stopped feeding me with so many 'you ain't's or bet'nots,'" said Daisy. "I don't need to know everything about her past relationships. Personally, I don't *want* to know. But at least let me know *why* I shouldn't."

"I want to know what my dad did do to woo my mom," said Violet. "What did he see in her that said, 'I think she's the one I want to spend the rest of my life with?' Was it her cooking, the way she wore her hair, her attributes?"

"Well, my father wasn't around so that would be hard for me to ask," said Rose. "I do want to know why my mom chose him and did she ever figure out why he left. And if so, what would she have done differently."

"My parents went through a painful divorce," said Breeze. "And my mom and I were having a random conversation about me getting married. And I said, 'with all you and dad went through, why would you possibly want me to go through that?' She simply said, 'everyone should experience marriage, at least once.'"

Zenobia rose from her seat. The room became quiet as they searched her face. Breeze noticed the look of concern with a hint of a smile. "Your parents have lived and are still living their lives. This is now, your moment. And you are taking this class to ensure this moment is lived to the fullest, whether he finds you or not.

"So, your homework assignment tonight is to go home and ask mom and/or dad these exact questions. Take them to lunch or cook them dinner. Do whatever needs to be done to have an open and heartfelt conversation about their love life and what they expect and want from you. Get their views out on the table if you feel it is hindering you from truly moving on.

"In addition, your fasting assignment is no television until we meet again. I want you to feed your mind with something other than the media's standard of love, relationships, intimacy, and an ideal mate.

"Let us close with prayer, but let me say this. Every opinion expressed in this class is welcomed. Everyone has a right to be heard. We are not to be judgmental. We also need to be able to handle what has been said. This environment is designed for you to be open, candid, raw, and extremely transparent. By the way, do not forget to take the cookies with you. Now, shall we close?"

A few Flowers looked at Lily with a hint of attitude, while the others looked with understanding. Breeze noticed that Lily did shrink back a little, but her head was still held high. She admired that, even though she too, felt her statement was ridiculous. Lily was the last to join the group for the closing prayer. After the 'Amens' were said, the ladies gathered their items in silence. Breeze picked up a couple of still warm chocolate cookies and walked out mentally planning a date with her dad.

9

Lipstick & Line Brawls

"Breeze Monsoon," announced the petite sales consultant with golden spiral dreadlocks.

"Blue!" she exclaimed hugging her friend.

"Ladies, this is one of my favorite clients, Ms. Monsoon. She will be joining The Knight party this afternoon. Come, they're waiting."

While escorting her friend/client through a sea of white satin, lace, tulle, and faux flowers with eager sales consultants, dreamy eyed brides, giddy mothers, and not-so-thrilled wedding attendants bustling about, Blue decided to have a little chat. "Good grief, how many weddings have we outfitted?"

"I think six."

"When I heard you were coming in, I took the liberty of helping you out. That dress she picked for you would have your girls dragging on the floor by the end of the night! And that color will have you looking like Big Bird's stunt double. Listen, I recommended some changes based on her theme, so just look surprised. And by the way, the next time you come in here, make sure that you are the bride. I have just the perfect dress and I want you to try it on."

"Blue, dahlin', this day ain't about me."

"Just try it on, and let me know what you think," she smiled waiting for the green light.

"Slip it into my dressing room," she sighed. "You know my size."

"Consider it done."

"There she is," Tuesday said excitedly. "Now the fun can begin." Tuesday shot up from the crowd of female family members wanting to get a peek of what would be walking down the aisle of their niece's special day. Tuesday did not waste any time doling out the chosen dresses. "Breeze, this will be your dress," she said handing her a V-neck sheath with cummerbund middle. "Wednesday, this is yours. I figured you could get away with a strapless style. And Monday, we thought you could do a lot better with spaghetti straps."

"What? I thought that was my dress," Monday whined pointing to Breeze's dress.

"Well, we made a few changes to properly accommodate everyone's shape."

"Tuesday, didn't you say every decision etched in that book of yours was final?"

"Monday, darling, you have too much backyard for that dress and that chest of Breeze's would be sliding out before the end of the Electric Slide," Mrs. Knight interjected. "And with no unattached men at the reception, the spectacle would be pointless. Now please stop whining and go try on the dress."

"Oh, by the way ladies, there will be no Electric Sliding or line dancing of any kind at my reception."

"I know you kiddin'," spat Ruby.

"Spencer and I agreed since the majority attending are couples, y'all can dance together."

"So what are your single folks without a 'plus one' supposed to do? Sit around and watch?"

Tuesday shrugged her shoulders feigning innocence...poorly.

"And who says I want to dance with my husband?" asked Pearl.

"Who said my husband was comin'?" said Coral."

"Sisters, don't worry about it. If Shine and I are paying for this, there will be line dancing throughout the night."

"Good, 'cause I just learned the Baltimore Good Foot and I'll be dog-gone if I'm going to let that expertise go to waste." The ladies laughed as Ruby took the liberty of showing her and everyone around her new dance move.

"I love my cousins dearly, but that right there can be a piece of work," confessed Wednesday. "Now, guess which one I'm talking about?" They both laughed as they made their way to the dressing rooms.

Breeze stood gazing in the mirror staring at her reflection. She still could not believe she was doing this for the 10th time.

"Everything okay in there?" Blue asked.

"Put me out of my misery," she whispered cracking the door open. "I can't do this! Tell them the dress you gave me doesn't fit and you don't have any more samples. I cannot pretend to be a willing participant any longer, with that Black Angus of a bride! And what in the world is going on with the price on this tag?"

She barged in. "Listen, I picked out that dress especially for you! I don't know what is going on, but you will wear that dress with a great big smile!"

"Why? There won't be anyone of interest to see it! Didn't you hear her? She's making all the single chicks sit on the sidelines."

"Now, hush! Take a deep breath."

"I don't wanna take a deep breath!"

"Look, this needs to be your last bridesmaid dress. I wanted to send you off with some serious style. Now, put it on! The love of your life will thank me later."

"Please, not at this function if *she* has anything to say about it!"

"Breeze put on the ding dang dress and trust a sistah, okay?"

Breeze kicked her out of the dressing room and reluctantly tried it on. "*So far so good,*" she thought. "Can you zip me up, please?" she asked opening the door.

"Trust me," said Blue zipping her up. "Make sure Mrs. de Silva takes it in here, here, and here," she said pointing to the spots were alterations would be most needed. Breeze nodded her head in agreement. She also checked herself out in the mirror, along the way, as she joined the others on the critiquing circle.

"Ladies, you look absolutely beautiful," Mrs. Knight said glowingly. "Stand in order? Now turn around? Perfect. What do you think, Tuesday?"

"I have to admit, I'm just a tad bit jealous. Everyone looks really nice...excellent selection, Blue."

"I got a test," said Ruby. "Each of y'all do the Cha Cha slide." Everyone laughed except for Monday.

"Is this it?" Monday huffed. "Are we done now?"

"Yes, chile we're done. Honestly!"

Each of the bridesmaids retreated back to their dressing rooms. Breeze was relieved the rooms were spaced throughout. Although she did not care who overheard, she did not want to cause an unnecessary argument.

"Breeze, my dear?"

"Ma'am?"

"Here," Blue shoved the snow white strapless, organza laden gown into the dressing room.

"I thought you said I couldn't do strapless?"

"Not in the dress she picked out. Now hurry up. I bought you some time to try it on."

She looked at the organza, satin material, silhouette, neckline, and beading designed straight out of every girl's childhood dream. "This ain't from my dream," she mumbled to her reflection. "Blue, I just can't bring myself to--" Her thoughts were interrupted when she and anyone else within eyesight, noticed a bride wearing an absolutely wrong dress. "Girl, make her try this on, please," she said laughing, hugged her friend, and eventually joined the rest of the group.

"Ladies, I have your sizes recorded and the color will be 'Lipstick.' They should be ready in about 12 weeks."

"Great, now we can grab some lunch and go over the planning for my shower *and* bachelorette party," Tuesday said while clutching her planner.

"Daughter of mine, I am all for lunch, but we will not discuss any more wedding plans today."

"Well, I heard Breeze will not be planning my bachelorette party and I would at least like to know why."

"As I told your girls, they should be throwing your party. I'm already doing the work and the main bridal shower."

"Tuesday, you expect her to plan all the parties?" asked Mrs. Knight. "Sisters, let's go 'cause my chile dun lost her mind!"

"But mom..."

"Look, the bridesmaids can throw the shower while your friends can throw you the bachelorette party. And if they don't want to throw you one, then you won't have one. End of discussion. Ladies, chicken and waffles?" The aunts could not get up fast enough.

Breeze headed for the register when someone pulled her back.

"You startin' trouble again?"

"Mrs. Lyte. I didn't see you sitting with the rest of the group."

"Dat's because I was tryin' on *mah* dress. And jus' what were you doin' wit dat weddin' dress? You ain't de bride. Firs' you take someone else's dress. You took too long in de dressin' room, you have the noy've to try on a bridal gown and now you won't even throw a pahtay in Tuesday hon'ah?"

"Mrs. Lyte, with all due respect, I do not have to explain myself or the decisions that were made, to you. Why are you so concerned about me anyway?"

"Be-cause mah son's happiness is at stake and I don't want anythang tah ruin it, heah?"

"I hear you loud and clear, and I will make it my personal duty to ensure that your son marries that woman."

While paying for her dress, Breeze decided against going to lunch with the ladies. She had enough of anything related to bridal to last a lifetime. *"I knew her little funky friends were going to snitch. She better rely on them for a party, because if Monday has anything to do with it her lips will be stuck out long enough to wrap around I-495."* Mrs. Knight tapped her on the shoulder.

"We're going to head out and meet you at the restaurant because everyone is acting like their blood sugar levels are getting low."

"Thanks, but I'm going to head home. I really have to--"

"Come join us for lunch. I expect you in 10 minutes young lady." She gave her a hug. "It'll be all right my dear. As far as you are concerned the party issue has been officially squashed."

Breeze managed a smile and agreed to the invitation. *"God, please help your daughter get through this."*

Breeze was glad she joined the family for lunch. She was also thankful Wednesday saved her a seat away from Mrs. Lyte. Although her explanation was clear, she still could not understand the animosity towards her. *"If my presence was that much of a threat, why hasn't she said anything to her son?"* All of the day's events were a distant memory as Tuesday's aunts made her face hurt from laughing. The stories, jokes, and an attempt to show the group another line dance in the middle of the restaurant, brought hilarity to the table.

"Breeze, I have something to ask you," said Tuesday.

"Oh heavens, here it comes."

"I have an extra ticket to an ice hockey game tonight. Would you like to go?"

"What's this a peace offering," she thought. "Sure, I'm all for a good hockey game. Who's playing?"

"I have no idea. I just won the tickets and you are the only person I know that would want to go, especially on such short notice," Tuesday said while searching for the ticket in her purse.

"I see." Breeze decided against making any attempt to read into that last statement and graciously accepted the ticket. "Okay, ladies. Now I really have to head up the road before my lunch makes me sleepy."

"Breeze, Monday, and Wednesday? My house next month, on the 5th?" Mrs. Knight announced. "The community center will be available and we can see what can be done with the space."

"Sounds good."

"On my calendar."

"I guess so." They all shot Monday a look.

"Breeze, see you at 7?" asked Tuesday.

"I'll be there."

— ~

Breeze was amazed how close the seats were to the safe spot above the penalty box. She checked her watch and noticed that Tuesday was late, as usual. No matter. Nothing could ruin the mood she was in, relishing fabulous seats, and feeling great in her warm burnt orange sweater and chocolate suede blazer. Although she pulled a few front pieces back she wore her hair out and letting her natural curls fall all over the place.

She also noticed that she was the only person in her row. This did not matter when the game finally started. *"The Capitals act like they want to play to-day. Let's hope they keep up this momentum."* During a television time out, Tuesday and Spencer reached their seats. "Ah, good evening," she said trying to disguise her disbelief.

"Good evening to you, too," Spencer said responding first. "I wanted my boy to take the other ticket, but I see Tuesday gave it to you."

"So happy to disappoint." Breeze recognized his attempt at making a joke, but knew he was serious. "Tuesday, these seats are amazing. Thanks so much for my ticket."

The hockey game was in full swing. Breeze cheered and booed at the right places. She loved this game with its brawls and constant movement, especially live. Her phone was vibrating. It was her father. *"R U@ the Caps game?"*

"Yes," she replied.

"I C U w/an orange sweater & that hair"

"My dad can see me on T.V. When did he learn how to text?" They laughed. *"Call u back l8r,"* she replied. Breeze placed her phone back in her pocket and proceeded to enjoy the game again.

"This ain't the proper place to be using the phone young lady," said a deep voice towering over Breeze.

"Branford!"

"Gigi!"

"Now sit down so I can see the game," she said hugging him briefly. "We can have a teary eyed reunion during a time out."

"I see ain't nothing changed," he laughed returning the hug. "Aye, y'all."

"B-Ford!" The two men gave each other a hand slap and a half hug over Breeze's head while she still watched the game intensely. "Uh, Bran I think your seat is over here," said Spencer.

"Yeah, I'm 122."

"I'm 121," said Spencer. "Breeze, I need you to switch seats."

"But I'm seat 123," she said without taking her eyes off the game.

"Well, Bran and I want to see the game and I'm sure you and Tuesday have weddin' plans to discuss."

"Spence, why don't you and Tuesday just scoot down? According to my ticket, this is my seat," she said flinching over a player getting mashed by an opponent.

"Ooo, Gigi did you see that?" Branford asked also flinching.

"I know one thing, y'all won't be flapping your gums over us talking about all this weddin' nonsense!"

"No problem."

"So, are you going to move?"

She sighed, "Tuesday can sit over here and discuss whatever needs to be discussed, during a time out. There's a good game going on, with plenty of good fights, sittin' in these great seats. And I don't want to miss any of it or my dad seeing me on T.V. I hope he's recording this."

"Breeze, just change seats so we can all see the game in pea--"

She shot Spencer a look that made him slightly flinch out of his seat. The look also signaled the usher from the top of the stairs.

"Ms. Monsoon, is everything alright?"

"Is it?" she hissed keeping her eyes fixed on Spencer's face.

"Yeah, yeah everything's cool," he retreated. "Tuesday, just scoot down, dang!" Tuesday quickly obliged and Branford took his seat between him and Breeze.

"Can I get you anything, Ms. Monsoon?" the usher nervously asked.

"Thank you," Breeze said finally looking up. "Javier? Is that you?"

"Yes ma'am. Is there anything I can get for you and your guests?"

"I'll have a ginger ale. Would anyone else like something?"

"I'll have one, too," said Branford.

"Yes," said Tuesday happily. "I'll have..."

"No, we're fine thank you." Spencer declined the offer for the both them.

"It is so good to see you," Breeze said patting Branford on the leg while keeping her eyes on the game. Javier brought their sodas to them and asked to speak with her after the game. She thanked him and agreed. By then it was half time and the men excused themselves for a break. Breeze was glad Spencer's mood finally lifted. She did not mean to cause a spectacle. But this was her seat and she refused to be bullied.

"Breeze, what was that looked that you gave my fiancé?"

"What look?"

"The one you could have stopped a bullet with," said a woman from the row behind them. "I need to practice that. Maybe my husband would act right. I'm telling you, you put the fear of God in that man...and in me, too."

Breeze laughed, shaking off the sentiment.

"Well, anyway, I wanted to go over the music for the wedding."

"Tuesday, why don't you let this be a night out and a night off?"

"I need to have everything in place."

"It's eight months away."

"Please? You know me. Everything needs to be ready, like yesterday. Did you remember to choose a few classical pieces, like I asked you to?"

"Excuse me?"

"Remember, I asked you to choose some songs for me. You probably forgot, so I brought a list."

"I didn't forget. Just drop the 'like I asked you to.' I'm not a child. Now, let me see your list." Breeze looked at the laundry list of classical pieces. Her selection was good, but predictable. "Where's your program?"

"Why?"

"I need to see which songs best fit the order of the program. Do you want seven different songs for seven different moments?"

"What do you mean?"

"Before the wedding, the unity candle, the processional, your entrance, unless you want one song for both entrances."

"No, I want to come in on my own song."

"Okay, again. Take out your program and let's plan the songs accordingly."

"Breeze, just pick some tunes and I'll figure it out later," she huffed.

"This one is too pretentious. *Concerto in D Major* will put everyone to sleep. I absolutely love *Air from Suite No. 3*, very nice for an evening wedding. *Jesu, Joy of Man's Desiring*. Upbeat yet elegant. You can walk in to *Pachelbel's Canon in D*. Very pretty but a lot of folks play that for their wedding. *Trumpet Voluntary* is also a great choice. An instrumental version of *Ava Maria* would be great during the lighting of the unity candles. I really like *the Finale from Handel's Water Music Suite*.

"However, to keep it grounded yet elegant, you may want to consider a few selections from Jeff Majors. Anything with his harp will be more than enough for the entire ceremony. I also think you should incorporate Spence's request for a little hip hop. To keep it elegant, use the instrumental version of *All My Life*. I think there is a violin version. If not, see if you can get your D.J. to make a copy of that particular part of the song.

"Come to think of it, I think I have the perfect song. Since your wedding party is small, Michael Bublé's version of *You & I* would be perfect. It's a classic Stevie Wonder song, made timeless. Just be sure to get the D.J. to extend the song in certain places, so the time can accommodate your entrance."

"I still think I want to come in with my own song, so I may have to give that some thought. But this is good. We're on the right track. Thank you."

"Uh-huh, now get back to your seat before a riot starts."

Tuesday laughed, as she reclaimed her seat. The timing was perfect as Spencer and Branford arrived from their break with snacks.

"Branny, I don't mean to sound ungrateful, but I don't see any nachos in your hand."

"And risk you getting cheese on my pants...again? Not a chance." He leaned in, whispering to Breeze, "I was wondering if we could have dinner later."

"Rosa Mexicano?"

"Where else?"

"Word!"

The four watched, cheered, and celebrated the Capital's 2-0 victory over the Carolina Hurricanes. Breeze kept her promise and met Javier at the top of the stairs. "It's so good to see you and thank you for the soda."

"Yes, I saw that look on your face. And so did my coworker. It reminded me of that one time in class. When you had enough of one of my classmate's foolishness, you gave him that same look and the whole class got scared. None of us cut up after that."

All Breeze could do was laugh. She remembered that day and the student. "So what is going on? How did you finish at American?"

"Very well. I received my Masters in Economics. Now, I work for the State Department. This is just my part time job to help pay for my honeymoon."

"Javier, I'm so proud of you. Wait until I tell Mrs. Raab."

"Dang Breeze," Spencer laughed as the four walked outside. "Let me find out one of your *students* is getting married before you! Girl, you better step up your game, quick, 'cause time is runnin' out!"

"If this sorry, sack of--"

"Uh, Gigi! Let's go before the restaurant closes. Y'all have a good night!" Branford quickly escorted Breeze across the street leaving Tuesday and Spencer standing there bewildered.

"Nah, we ain't joinin' y'all," yelled Spencer across the street. "We got a weddin' to pay for. We'll hang out with y'all another time."

Branford acknowledged the offer with a head nod, making sure they were out of earshot. He massaged her shoulders, while whispering, "Gigi, shake it off. It'll be all right."

10

Spicy Sangria

"This is long overdue," he whispered pulling her back into an embrace.

"Branny, please get me out of this." Breeze was angry, fighting back tears, but returned the hug and melted under the embrace. *"Be careful Breeze. Pull away; this one is married and his oldest daughter has your first name,"* she thought. "I'm all right," she said reluctantly pulling away. "Now can we eat please? A sistah is starving!"

The two walked in the contemporary décor, dimly lit, yet busy restaurant and were extremely grateful being seated immediately by the towering, slender seating hostess clad in black with a sleek, styled ponytail.

"Ragan is letting you stay out this late?"

"Please, she couldn't wait for me to leave. It's all good, though." They ordered their drinks and dinner.

"Trouble in paradise?"

"No, we just have an understanding. We'll talk about that later."

"My question is how did you get away with naming your oldest after me?"

"It took some convincing. Then again, Ragan only knows you as 'Gigi.'"

"She doesn't know?"

"Not yet. I'll tell her before Spencer's wedding. Besides, technically, you're the one that got us together in the first place."

"I really need to get paid for my match making skills. But help me understand how. The way I see it, you two had science classes together, she asked you to the Red and White Ball, y'all hooked up, and the rest was history."

"Only because you didn't ask me and *she did*."

"What?" The arrival of their drinks, tortilla chips, and salsa interrupted the budding conversation.

"Gigi, it doesn't matter at this point. What does matter is that we've know each other almost twenty years. Can you believe it?"

"Our freshman year at Denton Hall desk. I was working a double shift; you caught me eating fried cheese sticks and drinking half of a milkshake from late night dining. And you were waiting for some chick from the eighth floor. You ended up staying my entire shift. Come to think of it, you ate the rest of my cheese sticks!"

"I made up for it, bringing you those cheese sticks every time you worked that late shift!"

"Not that I wasn't grateful for the trip. Crossing two quads to and from the dining hall was not an easy task. You even kept with tradition when we moved from the projects to South Hill. Now that was a hike. I gained 15 pounds."

"The chocolate chip cookies and cold milk after your aerobics class, helped too."

"Really," she laughed. "We had so much fun, sweating over exams… checking out the folks in both AASP classes…almost failing 00Dumb."

"Oh my goodness! Do you remember 00Dumb and 00Stupid? That math class was rough! I took trig in high school and still had to take 00Dumb. My roommate had to take 00Stupid, twice!"

"Yeah, yeah yeah. What I want to know is with all those pickins' from La Plata Hall, how did you end up drooling over some girl in Denton?"

"The fellas at Ellicott knew it was better to creep with the girls from Denton and Elkton. Your business was less likely to be in the street and less competition. Until y'all took AASP 100 and discovered a whole new world."

"Where did Ragan stay?"

"Cambridge and then I finally convinced her to move to South Hill."

"Are you going to tell me how I really got you two together?"

"You actually summed it up. But that ain't the story I had in mind tonight. I want to know how on earth you let it get this far with my boy. Do you know he asked me about your first name? When he called me the day y'all met and said, 'Gigi says hi,' my heart was on the floor!"

"What do you mean?"

Their appetizers arrived. Breeze was a little annoyed at the poor timing of the food arrival. She wanted to get to the bottom of Spencer's brand of inquisitions and attitude. She did manage to chuckle thinking about how Branford always called her Gigi. She loved that name. It was a special name he had just for her.

She looked at him, noticing the only thing that changed on her friend's face were the stray gray hairs on his neatly trimmed goatee. He was still thick, not fat. His pretty bald head was shaved clean. The confidence in his swagger made him appear tall. But he was tall enough for her. She was always entranced by his butterfly-like eyelashes; while his voice reminded her of taking a piece of rich dark chocolate and letting it melt on her tongue. Tonight, was no exception.

"I'll tell you everything, I promise. You need to tell me your side of the story about what happened that night."

"Fine. You bet'not leave nuttin' out! Picture it: A cute chubby, cream-in-your-coffee skinned girl, with unruly hair--"

"Why do you call yourself that," Branford interrupted. "You are not chubby. You do need to ease up on the sweet teas and glazed doughnuts, but you are far from chubby. And your hair is far from unruly. Okay, keep talking."

"Point taken. Anyway, we hadn't talked for months and I still haven't gotten over what he tried to pull at the concert. He called out of the blue, sayin' he needed a date. I kindly suggested he contact Ms. Stick Figure he took to the concert. He ignored what I said, and started talking about the function, and why he needed 'someone like me' to accompany him."

"Someone like you?"

"I'll get to that. Anyway, I hemmed and hawed, thought about this great dress I just purchased, and agreed. I allowed the invitation to be the perfect excuse to show it off and the results of my exercise class."

"Yeah, I heard about that bangin' blue dress."

"How did you know it was blue? How do you know it was bangin'? I know Spence didn't describe it to you that way?"

"Let's just say men do talk," he said smiling.

"Lemme find out...," she chuckled. "Anyway, he wanted to pick me up around 4 pm because the boat leaves promptly at 6:30. I told him to add thirty minutes because there was a big football game and I had to see my students play. He reluctantly compromised and arrived at 4:29 pm ready to go. I answered the door with a few rollers still in my hair and he was not happy. He complained that I straightened my hair instead of leaving it curly. I explained I was in no mood to have my hair looking like bush gardens by the end of the night!

"Then he thought my dress was too 'showy' for the occasion. I confirmed with him the party was, indeed, a 'black tie optional' event. And Branny, since when do I wear anything showy? I gave him the option of either me sticking with the dress or him going by himself. He sighed and finally approved. So, I removed the rest of my rollers, styled my hair, and off we went. He huffed and puffed that we were going be late during the entire drive. I told him, 'the way he drives, the ride to the waterfront will only take 45 minutes.' He made it in 30. I think I developed a patch of gray hair during that trip.

"We finally boarded the boat. Now I have to say, the set up was on point. From the table cloths to the gift bags, I've never seen the Odyssey that decked out. Your fraternity brothers know how to throw a party."

"Wait, why did Spencer need to get there so early?"

"You know how your boy is. By the way, I need to get the name of the D.J. I was itching to do the Cupid Shuffle when Spence gave me that look daring me to do so."

"I don't have his card on me, but he will be the D.J. at their reception."

"Hmm, I'll need it for another function, as Tuesday informed there will be no line dancing of any kind."

"Yeah, right. There will be if Ms. Ruby has anything to say about it," he chuckled.

"Mmm hmm. Anyway, he showed me around and introduced me to his fraternity brothers and their wives. He forgot I knew a lot of them from Maryland and because of you. He was not thrilled. When he introduced me to Cooper, who I hugged immediately, he asked if I slept with all his fraternity brothers, including Cooper."

"Lawd, help him," Branford said with his head in his hand. "Did you tell him who he was?"

"Hold that thought. But I will say this: you do not know how close your boy was about to be bait to whatever was at the bottom of the Potomac. At this point, I had enough and excused myself for moment, to 'check my makeup.' I let a few minutes pass and decided to give Spence a phone call. I asked him to meet me at the rear of the boat, in my sexiest voice, at least one that I can muster. He said he did not have time for games. I told him it would only take a minute. He reluctantly agreed.

"We stayed on the phone the whole time he was making his way outside. He asked where I was. I told him to look straight ahead. He said, 'he could only see the party going on inside and where we should be.' I told him to look the other way. He said there was nothing but cars. Then he finally saw me standing on the pier waving at him as the boat left the dock. I sent him a picture of me giving him the finger while holding the gift bag. I used my index, so I wouldn't go to jail and told him to never call me again."

"And of course that didn't stop Spencer."

"Of course not. If I understand it correctly, Spence hunted me down once the boat docked and all day Sunday. Once he finally caught up with me at my school on Monday, this nickel comes busting in my classroom with a 'Don't You Evah!' What stopped him dead in his tracks were three 210 pound linebackers with promising college football careers standing up like trees, ready to use him as a practice dummy. I cut their tutoring session short, sent them to football practice, and finally had it out with Spence."

"Okay, this is the part where he apologizes."

"Unfortunately, there were no apologies after this long agonizing scene." She paused with her head in hand. She, too, wondered how the relationship between her and Spencer got this far. Was she that needy of affection that she allowed herself to fall for a man that would treat her any 'ol kind of way?

She appreciated his approach. She was doing her thing *in church* when *he* started a conversation. Her family instilled a belief that when a man wants something, he goes after it. In her mind, Spencer did just that. The moment she finally agreed to meet him for breakfast, the relationship went downhill.

Their main course finally arrived. Her mood did not jade her taste for salmon, but she had to finish this episode once and for all.

"He did state the reasons why *he* was embarrassed, needing to explain why his date was no longer by his side. He claimed that I was disrespectful throughout the whole evening, knowing everyone on the ship before being introduced, including the wait staff. I was confused. If I was that disrespectful, why would anybody care where I was?"

Branford chuckled. "You knew the staff, too?"

"Two of the waiters were students of mine. Anyway, I let him ramble off his laundry list of what *I* did wrong that night. Here was the coup de grace: My disappearing act cost him his chance of becoming some 'imperial grand poohbah.'" Branford corrected her. "Like I care."

"I do. I love my boy dearly. But you just don't want anyone like him running your organization. By the way, dinner's on me just for that."

Breeze laughed and graciously accepted. Her pocketbook thanked him, too. "Okay, no more interruptions. I want to get this out before this spicy sangria takes effect. So apparently Cooper inquired my whereabouts, needing to speak with me. Spence told him that I left the boat before it pulled off. Cooper was not happy and told him my actions were a poor reflection of his words and decisions and told him to forget his... whatever you call your fraternity's head position. I informed him *my Uncle Cooper* does not tolerate blatant disrespect, especially in public. The facial expression on Spence's face was priceless. I thought that would stop his tirade. That only brought it to a slow crawl.

"He wanted to talk about what I did wrong in the relationship, like being a tease for instance. I told him that he being a jerk at every turn does not blow my skirt up. Nor did our numerous shouting matches count as foreplay. Now, I know I was wrong when I called him to wish him a Happy Mother's Day. But the messed up Valentine's Day, the concert, my birthday, his warped reasoning for not going on roller coasters, even trying to agree on a movie was drama that really wasn't necessary."

"Oh, so he didn't get the drawers?"

"Uh...ewe! Please don't tell me your boy said he and I got it on?"

"Not in so many words. Whatever y'all were doing kept him coming back."

"Indeed. You know Branny, I did see a drop of sincerity when he asked me if there was even the slightest chance for us. He *granted me permission* to use this moment to air out my regrets so that we could move on. I told him, 'I regret finally accepting your invitation to breakfast. I regret picking up the phone whenever you called. I regret letting you step even a toe into my life. And now I regret this conversation and whatever we had taking this long. I meant what I said, don't ever call me again.'"

Breeze paused. She felt tears welling up. Not tears over him, but the year and a half wasted on the hope that he could be the one sent by God. His actions clearly said that he was not. She believed when you meet a man in church that should be a good sign and give him a chance.

"Do you know what that hazel-eyed joker had the nerve to say next?"

"Yeah," he sighed. "But I want you to tell me."

"He wanted to know if I was finished with the 'Little Miss Independent' performance so I can be the girlfriend he *expects* me to be. Apparently, the look on my face made him fall over his chair. It also scared a coach and my three football players I dismissed earlier that were in the doorway. Coach Huntington gingerly asked if everything was okay. Without me removing my eyes from Spence, I said 'yes and our guest was just leaving.' He finally collected himself, smiled, and was *escorted* out."

"Spencer told me that's when he met Tuesday."

"I know."

"How could you possibly know that?"

"One of my students came back and told me, 'Ms. Knight made a date with your man and were leaving in a few minutes'," she mocked.

"Word spreads like mayonnaise. He told me about that look. He said he never wants to put that look on a woman's face again. He failed, because he saw it again, tonight."

The waiter came by to clear their plates. He asked if they wanted dessert. Breeze declined, but Branford insisted they share some milk cake. Being Breeze's favorite dessert, she agreed.

"He called me right after he finished his date with Tuesday," Branford continued. "He told me what happened between the two of you and meeting the love of his life on the same day. I suggested he do some serious praying and soul searching before pursuing yet another bad domineering relationship. He told me when he couldn't find you on Sunday, he prayed and went to your school to see if he could win you back. Apparently it was too late."

"I'm sure God did not tell him to bust in my classroom with his puffed up chest and start grilling *me* about *my* actions!"

"I understand, Gigi. He was trying to apologize."

"He was trying to justify his very own special blend of crap," she interrupted. "And he didn't even do that!"

He chuckled. "Gigi, can I finish please?" he asked trying to collect himself. "I'm not saying that he was right. In fact..." He paused, looking as if he did not know what to say next or how to say it. "I know my boy. Love 'em like a brother. But he insists on breaking down his girlfriends to their lowest level and makes an attempt to build them back up. Only, he said you could not and refused to be broken."

"I was not his girlfriend," she snapped.

"Yeah, you were. Anyway, the very first time he met you at the church he was visiting, he called to ask about you. He said he saw his future wife holding the prettiest baby girl. He said that he introduced himself to you, made small talk, and found out that you knew me.

"I tried to convince him that you were not his type and it would never work out. We argued about it and he even accused me of still having feelings for you. I told him that wasn't the case anymore. I just didn't want him trying the same thing on you, he would do to other women. But, he pursued you anyway. We didn't speak for years. Until he called the night you two had the last blow out and after he met Tuesday. Gigi, I ain't never seen him like this."

"Confused?"

"Remorseful. Although he said he wasn't finished with you, he felt at ease with Tuesday. I told him, if he was truly sorry for what he had done, then he would need to do right by you."

"A simple apology and a promise to leave me alone forever written in his blood would have sufficed. Making me a bridesmaid is the strangest way of making amends."

"You wouldn't let him apologize."

"For the love of lunch, Branny, the dude did not or has not apologized! And you know he ain't even gonna!"

"I know, I know. But something good will come out of this. You will be thanked in a way you won't be able to comprehend; because this offer was done in love. He did love you Gigi. He still does. It's just that Spencer has a very strange way of giving love and taking 'no' for an answer. And you do realize that God blesses you through people you don't even like."

"Well, He's about to bless me with a monsoon of blessings 'cause I can't stand him and I am at my wits end with that bride."

Branford smiled at her reassuringly. "Trust me on this. If not, trust Him to help you trust the outcome of this situation."

Breeze tried to listen. She tried to absorb what her friend said. It was hard to believe Spencer was capable of showing his sensitive side to anyone. Her thoughts were interrupted again when the dessert arrived. This was one time she felt she could not possibly stomach the milk cake. She wanted to know more about Spencer's reasoning and how he really felt about her. She was more intrigued about the word from her friend.

"Since when did you start trusting in the Lord?"

"Since my marriage was in serious trouble. You know why Ragan and I got married. And after five years, sharing a child together was no longer reason enough. We both cheated on each other emotionally, financially, and physically. Our marriage reached a point where one foot was in divorce court and the other in a jail house. But Cooper sat me down during my lowest point. I had to make a decision to save my marriage or lose my daughter forever. Cooper didn't preach at me. He listened as I poured my heart out. He, in turn, ministered to my soul. He really touched my spirit.

"Ragan and I found a great church home. We found an amazing counselor and vowed to work on our marriage. I eventually moved back in the house. The Lord helped us discover that our mistake after the Red and White dance, was no mistake at all. He had a plan. So, we are now marriage counselors at our church and we now have *two* beautiful daughters."

"Now that's a testimony. Just show me the video footage when you tell your story about how Ragan accepted your oldest daughter having my name."

"You know I always thought your name was cool. And like I said, your actions brought us together."

"Hmm. Would you have said 'yes' if I asked you to the Red and White dance?"

"Of course I would. I waited for you to ask me out ever since we met."

"What? I was never your type. The chicks you brought around were straight up hoochie. Except for Ragan. Ragan was little Miss Straight-laced Goodie Goodie. She acted like--"

"You. She reminded me of you. Good company, strong family background, amazing head on her shoulders, good taste in music. But she had this backyard--"

"Put your hands down. I get the idea," she said laughing. "So minus my backyard, are you saying you had a crush on me?"

"It was more than that Gigi. Besides, you were hanging around that skinny white guy. What was his name? Edward, Edwin, Elroy?"

"Elliott."

"That's him. Have you seen him?"

"We had a nosh and caught a flick last week. He's also how I got home from that tragic boat ride. And he would have called to warn me about Spence if he knew something wasn't right!"

"I'm still sorry for not contacting you directly. My fragile marriage couldn't take another distraction."

"So why tell me all this now, Branny?"

"Cause I didn't think we'd see each other again. And that was the other reason why I didn't want Spencer to call you that day. But that was another time and place. So are you seeing anyone special?"

"No. Listen, since feelings are out on the table, what did *you* really think of me?"

"This is a dangerous place to be, but if you insist. Picture it: A dark brown skinned, young man with a high top fade sees the cutest, curly headed, caramel coated young lady wearing green boxer shorts and a tight Mr. Yuck tee with a milkshake mustache that he is dying to lick off.

"He forgets the chick on the eighth floor, spending the most chilled evening with her. He even remembers the songs that played on her boom box that night. They learn, laugh, had great times in each other's single rooms, going to football and basketball games, eating mozzarella sticks, and share four and half years of memories that he still holds dear to this very day.

"Listen, I want you to find someone special, Gigi. You have a lot to offer and no, it was not wasted on Spencer. The love you gave him made him a better man. Unfortunately, it's being used for Tuesday. So, let's finish this milk cake and the rest of the spicy sangria with a toast. 'To my Gigi: trusting the one that God made especially for her, finds her.'"

"I so receive that," she said beaming and hugging her friend.

"And by the way…"

"What's that?"

"Stop being so stingy with it."

"I'm growin' real tired of folk tellin' me dat!"

11

Petty, Pretty, Plain

The traffic was at a standstill at the usual spot on I-95 South. She sighed, nibbled what was left of her cranberry muffin, and sipped the remainder of her sweet tea. She noticed the time was a little past 10 and decided to turn on the radio. WHUR's *Mr. C* of *The Time Tunnel* was in rare form, playing great old school hits.

She did her normal mirror check and spotted a welcomed sight. *"What is my Stealth doing on this side of 95 on a Saturday?"* She quickly checked for any signs of lipstick, reapplied, and hoped he would make his way to her car. *"Oh, someone has been working out. I see definition in those shoulders of his. He still has that look on his face. What on earth is he thinking? Wait, what's this? A smile? Oh thank God he has pretty teeth. Please make your way up, please!"* Her lane started to move again. "Dang it!" She looked back, checking him out one more time. She smiled when he laughed again. The smile stayed planted on her face all the way to the Knights.

"Here you go ladies, I thought you might like some snacks," Mrs. Knight offered as the bridal party gathered to plan the shower. "Later on, we can walk to the center where the shower will be. It's a lovely place and the rental fee is next to nothin'. So, Shine and I will take care of the cost of the fee. I'll leave you ladies to it," she said leaving the room while calling for her husband.

Breeze and Wednesday looked at Monday, ready to begin.

"Well, don't look at me! Breeze is the one with the shower planning experience."

"All righty then. Let's talk about a theme..."

"No, let's talk about a date," interrupted Monday. "Tuesday wants to have her shower at least a month before the wedding. But I cannot do Saturdays or Sundays. We'll just have to do a Friday night."

"Then you won't be able to go, because there is no away anyone can make it to Fredericksburg, on a Friday night, at a reasonable hour. There will be guests coming from Baltimore, Waldorf, and Southern Virginia. We'll be lucky to have anyone show up by 9. And that is no time for a shower."

"Listen, you have six months to plan your days off," Wednesday chimed in. "We need you to bend on this."

"I'm already bending, meeting y'all here on my Saturday."

"Hence..."

"Come to think of it Breeze, I'm stilling bending with that dress you stole."

"For the last time, Tuesday picked the ding dang dress! I had nothing to do with it. Now can we drop it please so that we can plan this event and go home?" Monday scoffed and sulked in her seat. "The month before is Memorial weekend. It will have to be the weekend after Mother's Day to accommodate already made plans. Does that Saturday or Sunday work for everyone, depending on the availability of the room?"

Wednesday agreed, Monday had other plans. "Wait, Breeze have you seen the guest list?"

"Yes, Tuesday gave me the list a while back."

"Why? I-am-the-maid-of-honor. That list should have been given to me!"

"Do you want it? I only need the work list."

"No, she gave it to you. I just want to know why."

"Then you need to ask *your* cousin about *her* decisions."

"Hmph! Well, since *Breeze* has decided on a date; let's discuss the theme, create the budget, and dole out the tasks, aw'right?"

"The good news is Tuesday already has the 'Double Happiness' theme for her wedding."

"That explains the red dresses instead of yellow," smiled Wednesday. "Thank goodness for that! The original color was ugly."

Breeze chuckled. "So, we'll take the derivative of that and make it a 'Chinese Takeout' themed shower. We can have fans and chopsticks as party favors, and place the prizes for the games in the takeout boxes. And we can serve Chinese food. How does that sound to everyone?" Breeze was relieved that both attendants agreed. "Okay, now we can talk about a budget for 65 guests."

"65? I didn't know Tuesday had 65 friends! Look, why don't we assign tasks and whoever has that task pays for it, okay? I'll do the food. Wednesday can do the favors? And Breeze can take care of the decorations."

Both agreed. "Oh wait, Tuesday did want a particular cake from Cakes Plus," said Breeze. "I can take care of that."

"Didn't I say I will take care of the food?"

"My apologies. The cake will cost $52 and a trip to Laurel, in addition to the cost of the catering. Have at it," Breeze snapped back.

Mrs. Knight walked in during the budding argument. "What's going on here?"

"Never mind, you can get the cake," Monday said storming out of the house.

"Why is this woman at my throat at every turn?" asked Breeze.

"Chile, no matter how well you plan, in every weddin' there always gotta be that one," Mrs. Knight said quietly. "C'mon y'all. Let's walk down to the center."

— ∽ —

"Evening ladies," Zenobia greeted her class and noticed she was missing a flower. "We have a full plate tonight, but I would like to wait for Tulip.

So, let's start out with an ice breaker: What is your least favorite...well, Tulip. So glad you could join us."

"Sorry ladies for being late," Tulip said breathlessly. "I was having the best conversation with my recently engaged coworker and I lost all track of time."

"Male or female?"

"Male."

"Another one bites the dust!"

"Yeah, but I learned something today. This time the situation was different and so was my disposition. This morning, the guy that I have what I call a 'suitable crush' on, announced he was getting married. We chatted about the details. And during the discussion, I kept thinking there goes my dream guy, having my dream wedding."

"A suitable crush?" asked Lily.

"He had what I look for in a guy plus a bit more. Decent height, weight, looks. He's not gorgeous, but nice looking. He's really good at his job and I know he's not broke. I like his work ethic and determination to succeed. My thing is if he's not likeable at work, imagine what he is like at home. I absolutely love his hair. He has this grade of hair that you could just wash, massage, and grease his scalp or play with for days. The bottom line is that he was just...suitable.

"All throughout the day, I was curious to find out why he decided to marry her. It's like what would make a man want to commit? What was that certain something that would make him say: 'that's the one I want to spend the rest of my life with'?"

Zenobia interjected, "Ladies, let us not lose our focus. We are here to examine what you are putting out, no pun intended, attracting either the wrong man or none at all. But since we are here, did you find out why?"

"Yep, finally. I think we as women internalize a little too much instead of just asking the brothah outright."

Everyone in the room nodded their heads in agreement.

"The first thing he mentioned is that their goals meshed. They both liked money, being the center of attention, and their views on kids and family. Even the type of house they wanted were in synch. The funny thing is during our whole conversation, he never described what she looked like. But his eyes and face lit up like a boy getting his first bike for Christmas talking about what *she* put on the table. The fact that she was intelligent, loves to travel, knows how to have fun, and their personalities complemented each other was all he needed. He liked what she had to say describing her five year goals. She knows where she is going and is actually making it happen. Here's what really got me. The true kicker was and I quote, 'she doesn't let me walk all over her with my mind.'"

"She's time enough for him, huh," said Rose.

"Pretty much. They planned to have a destination wedding in September. I wanted a destination wedding."

"And now you don't?" asked Breeze.

"I would if I was getting married. But the outlook ain't looking so good. I guess I can hang up that dream."

"Okay, stop right there," Zenobia interrupted. "I was with you when you finally mustered up the courage to ask him what he was looking for. But you came to a screeching halt when you started talking defeat! Do not think for one minute that you hang up your dreams because something you anticipated does not go your way."

"There are dreams and then there is reality," said Petunia. "I am facing reality. My philosophy is forget it, because it's not going to happen."

"My dear, you are here to change that crummy philosophy. That kind of mentality keeps you in mediocrity," said Zenobia. "Well, so much for the opening exercise I had planned today. Blessedly enough, Tulip's story touched on two things I want to discuss today. Though, before we get into that, I want to discuss what you bring to the table... financially. When God decides to bless you with a husband, I want you to know how to protect yourself and your assets, should things go wrong."

"If he was sent by Him, there shouldn't be a problem," said Lily.

"None of us are in heaven yet. Things happen. However, his mishaps should not cost you anything but your pride."

Zenobia rose from the table, patted Tulip on the shoulder, said something that made her laugh and motioned for the guest to come in. While waiting for the speaker to arrive, the table buzzed with congratulatory comments for Tulip's courage to ask. But all were in agreement with what Zenobia had to say about finding him.

"Ladies, this is a really good friend of mine: Star Moon. She is an attorney specializing in family matters."

"Good evening everyone," said the statuesque woman with reddish brown locs pulled into a simple bun. "I've heard so much about this class and the wonderful change that is going on in each of your lives. I'm extremely impressed as to how much you've got it going on: property, businesses, jobs, investments. However, it greatly distresses me that so many of you do not have someone to share it with. But when you do, I want you to keep a few things in mind. I am here to discuss how you *keep* what you bring to the relationship just in case things go wrong.

"Now, I am glad one of you was able to get out of your living arrangement with minimal drama. No, Zenobia did not tell me the details. What goes on in this class, stays in this class. The situation, however, prompted her to give me a call. Ladies, if you decide to have him shack up or once you get married and he is living in your house, here are a few things I need you to keep in mind..."

Without asking, the Flowers took out their notebooks and pens. For Breeze, shacking up was not an option. Forget about if the arrangement was *spiritually* wrong, there were just no guarantees. A roommate made sense. A significant other that may or may not want to get married, while living in your house for an indefinite period of time, did not.

"Ladies, do not be so quick to ask for a prenuptial agreement..."

"When did marriage become such a business transaction," Breeze thought as she listened to what Star had to say. *"If you had to go through all this, what would be the point?"*

"Please keep in mind the laws depend on the state. So if you move, make sure you know your rights. I am not presenting these ideas and necessities as a scare tactic. I just want each of you to be clear of what can happen and protect yourself when necessary. I also want you to go over your finances with a certified financial planner. Make sure you know your credit score, how to improve it, and remove as much debt as possible.

"Ladies, knowing the state of your finances keeps you in control and should be a crucial factor in your plan. And when he does find you, both of you should share your bill payment history and habits...at the appropriate time. Now I know you took notes, but I do have some cheat sheets of what we discussed, along with my number in case you need me before you say 'I do.'"

"Ladies, this will be a good time to break for dinner, which is being served in the room across the hall today," said Zenobia. "And Ms. Moon will be available if you have additional questions."

Everyone thanked her for her time and expertise. The Flowers left the room equipped with questions for their guest speaker. Breeze heard too many horror stories of love gone wrong and their hard earned cash and property along with it. She had mixed feelings regarding prenuptial agreements. They were indeed protection from those who are more in love with your money, rather than you. It also signaled this arrangement was temporary until they find someone better. That is where Breeze had the questions for herself and any other friend that needed to make a clean break.

After lunch was served and the questions were answered, the ladies came back to two sweet smelling confections in the middle of the table. One, decorated with whipped topping, sprinkled with toasted coconut flakes, giving an aroma of light and fluffy. The other, a golden brown Bundt looking oddly exposed.

"Ladies, I thought we would have some dessert before we get into designing your plan. I present you with tonight's major decision: Pretty vs. Plain. I need to step out for one more moment. Please, do not be shy and help yourselves."

"I'm going for the pretty," Violet said reaching for a slice.

"Surprise, Surprise," said Petunia. "Personally, I do not see why we have to choose. I think I'll have a piece of both."

"Surprise, Surprise," Violet retorted jokingly.

"You know, I've always been partial to a bald headed cake," Tulip chimed in.

"And no offense to Ms. Zenobia's cake but the pretty always let you down," said Iris. "I'm with Tulip. I, too, will go for the bald headed cake."

"I want to try something new," said Lily. "I've had my fill of plain cake from all of those Sunday dinners."

Rose was reluctant. "I think I will skip the sweets. At this point, I don't want what is not good for me."

"You know a good piece of cake now and then can be good *for* you as well as *to* you. A little indulgence keeps away the cravings for the wrong things. Live ya life Rosie, girl," Breeze said in a fake Jamaican accent, reaching for a piece of the plain cake.

"Both of these cakes look like a set up," Rose argued. "The caliber of plain looks plain, but could be richly satisfying. And the pretty could be as dry, boring and completely tasteless."

"Try downright nasty. But I do not mind taking this type of a risk," Daisy said with a mouth full of pretty cake.

Zenobia floated back into the room. "I see that everyone has made their decision and enjoying their dessert." She did not wait for the Flowers to respond. "In a few words or less, I want you to describe your experience. Then again, I can see some of your feelings on your faces."

"Um, Ms. Zenobia, this cake has a, uh, hair in it," said Tulip. "Hyacinth, Rose, would y'all care to escort me to the kitchen to get rid of this cake?" The two Flowers quickly agreed and started for the door.

"Stop! There is nothing wrong with that cake. You need to learn how to share."

"Was that cake that good that y'all stingy, greedy muffins didn't want to share?" asked Violet.

"Yep," Rose and Breeze said in unison with a mouth full of cake.

"Girl, you know how it is when you got something this good you want to keep it to yourself," Rose explained nibbling on her final decision. "Go on with y'all's pretty cake. This ain't no plain cake, this is 7Up quality!"

"Ms. Zenobia, no offense to your cake, but the taste of this cake proves the fine will let you down," said Violet.

"I have to disagree," said Lily. "The cake is gratifyingly fattening. If I had a couple of slices of this kind of cake growing up, maybe I would have had some curves."

"Okay, what was in that cake that gave Lily some bounce?"

"I will be more than happy to tell you," said Daisy.

"Ut oh, here it comes."

"No, no I will keep it light. The combination of flavors gives you a little lift. A hug. There is something sensual about the taste and texture. A little soft, a pinch of rough, something sweet, and a hint of bite with the pineapples. Ms. Zenobia, can I take a piece of this cake home with me?"

"Although, I will be more than happy to take a piece of *that* cake to go, I am enjoying this plain cake," said Iris. "Normally, I would overlook the plain when the pretty is presented, but shame on me if I didn't give it try."

"Well, I need the flavors of both the pretty and plain," said Petunia. "That is why I took both pieces so I can enjoy the best of both worlds."

"I think it is a privilege to be able to appreciate various styles of cake," said Breeze. "Can you cut me a slice of the pretty, please?"

"Oh, so now you want *us* to share?"

"Yep," she said with a mouth full of cake.

"Ladies, I guess I should have told you my *Better-Than-Sex* and *7-Up* cakes are normally used to describe your taste in men. Do you go for the pretty or the plain? The flashy and showy but *possibly* complete and utterly tasteless? Or, the ordinary yet overlooked, which has the potential to be extremely satisfying. Unfortunately, I experienced the former, first hand. But I was so blessed to experience the latter for the rest of my life."

"I'm growin' real tired of substituting food for what I ain't gettin'," Daisy said helping herself to a slice of the pretty cake."

Zenobia chuckled. "Let us discuss what you really want in a man. What qualities are you looking for in a husband? What do you think God wants you to have in a mate? This is your opportunity to say what you actually want. But first, let us do a quick exercise: Name some qualities you think God wants you to have in a husband?"

"At the top of the list, the brother must have a job. Better still, he needs to have a career. It would be a plus if he likes what he does for a living," said Violet. "Liking what you do eight to twelve hours a day makes for a more pleasant disposition."

"There needs to be mutual trust," offered Petunia. "If he is the head of my household, I need to trust him to take the lead and make the right decisions...with my input of course."

"The man needs to have his own space and know how to be on his own," said Rose. "He needs to be in his own condo, house, or townhouse. Depending on the circumstances, he can rent. But I prefer him to own something other than his car."

"Well, ladies, my ideal husband would need to be affectionate and have the ability to express himself *to me,* affection-ate-ly."

"Daisy, is this what God requires or what you want?" asked Lily.

"Both. How else are we to become one, be fruitful and increase in number?"

"Out of curiosity, if you and your soon-to-be-Mr. Right are in marriage counseling, and the pastor asks would you still be in love with him if he was bald, penniless, and impotent, what would you say?" asked Violet.

"I actually like the bald. And since we'll Tithe, we will not be penniless. The last time I checked, there is medication for impotence. And he would need to find some, quickly. Now if he doesn't *want* to do anything about his physical issue, then we have a problem. But my Mr. Right would already know I did not get married to be celibate. Once the Cha Cha slide is done, he will be slidin'--"

"Daisy, darling," Zenobia quickly interrupted. "Please, anybody else?"

"Personally, I think the fact that he needs to know and love the Lord for himself should be top of this list," said Lily still laughing. "Daisy made a great point. He needs to Tithe, know how to Tithe, and believe that God protects those Tithing pockets."

"Excellent point, Lily," said Zenobia. "And Flowers, I am sure everyone in this room is indeed Tithing."

"How else could I afford this class on a teacher's salary? He always manages to find a way," said Breeze. "Even if you really don't want Him to," she mumbled.

"I heard that," said Zenobia. "So Hyacinth, what would you place on this list?"

"We need to be comfortable with each other," said Breeze. "Not get in a state of complacency where we take each other for granted. I want him to want to come home, instead of sitting in the driveway dreading what awaits him. I would also say he needs to have a level of kindness and gentleness. He needs to view our relationship as a partnership. We need to be a team. Not one upping or competing to see who can have the last word."

"He needs to have goals and a vision, a plan for this life," said Iris. "If it is indeed to get married, have children, see the world, learn Spanish, finish school if he hasn't done so already, he needs to be already in the process of reaching that goal."

"Flowers, there are many qualities God wants you to have in a mate. However, do we agree on this working list as the core qualifications he must have: Knowing the Lord for himself, Tithing, gainfully employed, living on his own with his own means, mutual trust, intimacy, and goals? The items on *this* list should not be negotiated or compromised and everything else should be icing on the cake."

12

Interracial Icing

"So, what other ingredients do you want in your cake?" challenged Zenobia. "When you make your list of what you want, include everything. The Word says to write your revelation and make sure you make it plain, and know that you are not boxing Him in. The Word also says you do not have, because you do not ask. While making your list, keep in mind your wants and needs must be in line with what God needs for His daughter. He will not bless anything that is not in order.

"Consider the frosting, but do not set up camp here. You need to put down what qualities you can stand when those teeth are sitting on the nightstand. Or he needs you to massage his feet with the corns and bunions from wearing those tight shoes *you liked*. What will make you continue to smile when you pick up his stinky socks and gym shoes for the 50-11th time?

"And please, do not describe the current object of your desire. You do not know how he treated his past girlfriends, ex-wives, or mama. You may not be able to handle his situation, nor he yours. He may look good on the outside and got it going on, but be messed up from the ground up. And then you get married and his mess is now yours."

"Not unless you heed Ms. Moon's instructions," Lily added.

"Precisely," Zenobia chuckled. "Take a few minutes to think about the qualities, quirks, characteristics, and appearance. Write them down and be prepared to share."

"Ms. Zenobia, seriously, I've done this exercise before."

"I understand that a lot of you have created your list, and the request is still marinating within the Bible pages of your favorite scripture. However, please know that God is in the business of granting the desires of your heart. Just be careful of what you ask for. He will show you what you have prayed for and you may not like it. This is why I want you to do this list over again. Truly search your heart for what you actually need and then want."

"I need God to at least give me a peek, so that I know He is indeed listening," said Daisy. "Then I can properly tweak my list."

"Like Ms. Zenobia said, be careful of what you ask for," said Iris. "God gave me a peek of what I prayed for, and witnessed His wicked sense of humor. The peek revealed I needed to be specific. Case and point: I was on a cruise with my dad. We made our way to dinner, and on the last night we had an opportunity to sit by the window. My dad said, 'this whole entire cruise we've sat with folks and now you want to sit at an empty table?' I told him that I did not want to pass up a tremendous view of the ocean and a magnificent sunset.

"A few minutes later, the waiter escorted a mother and her son to the table. Y'all this brothah was adorable! It wasn't just his looks, although the man was very well put together. During dinner, I was going through my mental checklist: mid-thirties, lives in a townhouse, polite, goofy, a computer geek, loves his mamma, strong shoulders, interesting conversation, and the softest hands. We both owned Volkswagens and compared notes. We shared a love of music. He, too, had a filled iPod. I also found out that he appreciates the thick chick, by stating an interesting fact about Lane Bryant.

"Meanwhile, I'm smiling sharing the most pleasant meal both my dad and I experienced on the cruise, I am praying to God to confirm that He finally sent me my king on my all-time favorite cruise." Iris paused as she slumped in her chair smiling to herself.

"Did you get the room number, better yet, his email address?" asked Violet. "And how did you know his hands were soft?"

"I had to pass him the pepper. And there was no need for further contact. As I said before, God has a sense of humor. The Lane Bryant chick was his *fiancé* that bought him his iPod. He showed me what I asked for, but could not have, because the brother was already taken.

"Did his peek reveal that He needs me to choose something else because I can't have the one I want? Or the one that I need is out of my reach and out of His hands? Giving me that peek was a set up for great disappointment." Iris paused again, this time letting a few tears escape.

"I'm sick of this," she spat wiping away the hurt. "What would be the point in asking? I realize The Word says for us to ask, seek, and knock. I've *asked* so much I need a throat lozenge. I have been *seeking* so much that I need a new pair of glasses. And I need a cast on my hand for all that *knocking*. And He still ain't listening! If we are truly His daughters, then why is He making us wander around for 30, 40, even 50 years? And no, the promise land is not right in front of our faces!"

"Iris," Zenobia said softly, "He gave you a peek to see if you could handle what you prayed for. Did you storm off once you found out that he had a fiancé? Or did you keep the conversation pleasant, with a friendly tone?"

"The conversation was still good," Iris mumbled.

"Now take those qualities you told us about, add a few more to truly make it your own, go to Him with confidence, and continue to ask for what you need first and want second. We will also add 'he needs to be available, at all angles, for a relationship...with you' to the list. And yes, you are walking *in* your promise land for the moment. Enjoy it until He is ready to show you, your increased territory."

Zenobia rose from her chair and hugged Iris. She whispered something in her ear which Iris smiled and reluctantly started writing.

Each flower sat with their pens and tablets trying to brainstorm. Some looked for answers on the ceiling, while others just doodled. The list of what God wanted should have been a running start. Instead, the flow of what was wanted and needed, came to a halt.

"Would anyone be upset if I put non-black on my list?" asked Petunia breaking the ice.

"Albeit *your* list, are you trying to box God in?"

"Not if I'm asking him to be non-black. The Word commands us to ask. And looking at my list I'm asking the Lord for the impossible if I ask for a black man to meet my qualifications."

"It is a lot easier to talk to white men," Breeze chimed in. "I can be in my workout clothes, look a wreck, and they still make the time to chat. If a black man comes up and sees me looking his way, he would get a mild case of whip lash turning *away* from me."

"I hate that look," said Iris. "It's like they want to see anything but you. Or hope that you don't see them. If the dude doesn't want to talk to me, then don't! But then again, with these brothahs today, he won't."

"Ladies, ladies, if I may," interrupted Zenobia. "If a man is looking away from you, he is not your king. Let him look away...and stay away. Please continue."

"Um, receiving," said Daisy and a few others. "Why *is it* so hard to talk to black men?" Daisy challenged. "Like Hyacinth, if I'm not wearing the right outfit or hair style, it ain't happening. Eventually they'll talk to me, but that's after they get to know 'around' me."

"Interracial couples, whatever the makeup, have a tendency to stick together," said Petunia. "They have this bond, but they don't necessarily see color, they see the beauty in each other, what makes them wonderful, and ultimately fall in love. I want that."

"The black men, well at least the ones I want, are in it for the looks and worry about personality later," said Tulip. "You have to be no less than a runway model for the black men in my office to talk to you. All you need to do is look good."

"The problem with that type of man, when they realize they are with the wrong one, they get divorced *after* they have a couple of kids and the woman deservedly takes him to the cleaners. Then all he has to offer the next chick is half of his self-respect, a broken heart, and an eternal hand in his pocket. I want to be with a dude who wants to get it right the first time," said Petunia.

"...And stick with it," Rose added. "There's a reason why you got married. Now work it out and keep your eyeballs focused on what you got! But I want to go back to the interracial dating thing. Our black men are exercising their options. We need to start exercising ours."

"Indeed," said Lily. "But are men of other races willing participants? It's the *women* of other races cashing in on *their* options."

"I still have faith in my brothahs," said Violet.

"Well, I'm tired of hearing our brothahs, leaving our sistahs for anothah," said Tulip. "I'm also tired of him pushing me out of the way to get to snowflake. This phenomenon is getting old, fast."

"Okay, wait," cried Breeze. "Growing up in Columbia, I've grown to appreciate the interracial thing. I would be turning my back on my hometown if I didn't love all races. However, the one thing I have grown to know and understand, if the brothah is interested in white women, get out of his way. And ain't no amount of you workin' your neck is gonna change his mind! He does not want you! It ain't about your size, shape, what you look like, or your personality. Whatever he made fun of when we were kids, that's what he ended up dating or marrying. He-wants-white! And in some cases you *need* him to go to white or other, because we cannot or will not work with him. I think we need to learn from our Caucasian sisters as to how they can really work with a brothah. Through it all, through the mess, they stand by him."

"And we don't? I see too many a sistah sticking by the tired and trifling," Rose said. "Exhibit A," she said pointing to herself.

"And you eventually kicked dude out," said Breeze. "It's like what Ms. Zenobia said. It's who we are letting into our lives and letting them act any 'ol kind of way that makes us bitter towards the better brothah waiting for us! Oh, did I just say that?"

"I think Hyacinth just experienced a break through!"

The entire class clapped and cheered.

"It is always such a challenge with black men," whined Petunia. "They have a tendency to make everything so difficult, flocking to the ones that make life difficult. They head straight for the chaos with five kids from four different fathers. Add him and stir."

"Ladies, do you think black men are 'expressing' their desire to feel needed? Are you so caught up in what you have that he runs away to the one he can instinctively take care of?" Zenobia asked challenging the group.

"You know," Lily interjected. "You do not hear women from other races saying they do not *need* a man..."

"They don't have to," said Iris. "When they say there is someone out there for somebody, they weren't necessarily talking about us. They were talking about them...'them' with multiple choice options."

"Now, white folks will get married, have the wedding of their dreams and means, pump out two or three kids, then it's a storyline fit for a *Lifetime* drama," said Breeze.

"But there are other races of women that are in their 30's and 40's and still unmarried," said Violet. "A good friend of mine is Jewish, 36, and still single."

"Then she is doing something wrong," said Breeze. "She must have burned the Kugel or served some bad lox. If necessary, I can give you a website that specializes in hooking up Jewish singles with great results."

"I want the brothah who has not felt the need to repopulate the planet," stated Tulip. "One child I can understand. And if he was married, I can understand a few more. But if you have all of those kids, there is a reason why you made repeat trips to that well. Stay there. And multiple baby mamas is just downright sexually irresponsible. The last time I checked birth control, by any means necessary, was affordable and legal. That is why, I too, will need to go for the white guy. Although, if we do marry, I will be having my bi-racial child blessed with both worlds."

"Speaking of which, there is too much involved when it comes to sex," Iris said reaching for a piece of the pretty cake. "If I can't use it, why doesn't He just remove the desire? What is the point of having the desire if you cannot act upon it? Even then, you have to wait for an unspecified amount of time. But I have to say, this cake is making the wait a little easier."

"Three words: Man's free will," said Violet. "God's cruelest joke. You can act upon it, just be prepared to face the consequences."

"And that's what scares me the most," Iris whined. "There are so many consequences. What's the point?"

"Pleasure, love, intimacy, and ultimately the creation of life are the points," said Zenobia. "Shall we discuss the consequences and complications?"

"The biggest consequence is giving someone that is not your spouse a tie to your soul," said Violet. "When you have that connection with someone, you are giving that someone a soul tie. I date a lot. But when it comes to sex, I don't want a part of me being attached to someone I casually meet. I want to be connected with someone I love; and I know in my heart and mind that he loves me back. However, waiting is getting more difficult, especially when you get stopped by a sexy single cop and you are thinking of ways to arrange your way out of a speeding ticket."

"Uh, Violet, do you care to share?"

"I am pleading the fifth!"

"Speaking of complications, and before I say this with no pun intended, what is up with all of these performance pills, enhancers, and miracle grow?" asked Daisy. "Does every man have this problem or the increase in ads let the chosen few know that they are not alone?"

"All those products are some drug company's cash cow," said Rose. "Hopefully, they are using that ever growing profit base for research."

"My question is, what ever happened to good old fashion interest?" asked Iris. "Either you are or aren't."

"Ladies, the body plays tricks on you as you get older," interjected Zenobia. "The mind is ready but may not be sending signals to other parts like it used to. At least not fast enough as one would like. That is why God created brilliant scientists to develop those wonderful little blue pills."

"Uh, Ms. Zenobia..."

"Let us just say that I am empathic and most appreciative of the cause. Shall we move on?"

"I still say forget it," said Iris. "Sex seems entirely too complicated. First, I have to deal with the fact that he may or may not be interested, ready, or heavily medicated. Then I have to worry about him seeing me naked? I have 30 pounds to lose before I can even think about sex."

"30 pounds where?" asked Rose. "If you lost that much, someone would think you were going into bad health. At that point, sex would be the least of your worries."

"I mean the horror you feel when he has to see you naked. And then you're all self-conscious 'cause he's feeling your fat and seeing your imperfections up close. I don't think I can hold my stomach in for what? Two to five minutes? And above all else, what happens when the situations are, well...reversed? And I have to drive? I wouldn't want the brother to feel...*Shamu'd!*"

"Girl...," was all a few members of the class could muster as they all roared with laughter.

"Sweetie, there are plenty of men that can, um, handle being what you call, *Shamu'd*," Rose said finally. "And trust me, they will find you. Like we said at the beginning of this conversation, just be prepared to handle the consequences."

"Rose, would you care to enlighten the class of your own experience?"

"Just do not let the fat fool you," Rose said smoothing over her curves.

"That's not what I meant, dahlin'."

"I know," she chuckled. "Anyway, I'm sure the brother at the gym can appreciate that you are doing something about those so called 30 pounds. And if not, that's his loss."

"Ladies, I love that we can share what is on our hearts, whatever the case may be," Zenobia said still laughing. "However, I really want you to

create your list. And due to the time, you now have two homework assignments. Pray, praise, search your heart and mind, and create your list. For
some, this may be an ongoing assignment. You may want to tweak, add,
or delete a few attributes. But I urge you to make your list, make it plain,
and go to Him in confidence with what you need and want.

"Now, your second assignment, which I would like to be completed
by the next class, is this: Tulip mentioned the five to ten year plan. What
is *your* plan? What do you want to accomplish? And I am not just talking
about including him in your plan, at least not yet. What do you want to
do if God blesses you with blissful singleness for the rest of your life?
Married or not, you still need something to strive for.

"What are you doing to make your life count? Is it to see the world,
learn to Salsa dance, make the perfect omelet, or be a better whatever? I
need each of you to compose what some call an 'elevator speech'. Design
a 30 second discussion of your plan and how you are making it happen.
Details will not be necessary unless you feel the one you are sharing with
is worthy to hear it. You need to be prepared at every angle imaginable.
Of course, someone or some event will throw you a curve ball. But that
is what makes life and the journey so sweet. Hyacinth, will you close out
this awesome meeting with prayer?"

13

Words Hurt

"Lemme ask you a question," was all she heard. No 'hello', 'good morning', here's a doughnut'. She quickly refused, side stepped her gnome-like inquisitor, and retreated to her classroom. She felt her shoulders hunch to her ears when Hurricane Tuesday stormed her way in demanding an explanation of the bridal shower date. The conversation took an uglier turn when Breeze suggested she hire a wedding planner after she could no longer take hearing of the special dietary restrictions of the, yet again, revised guest list. Once the residue of a bride-beast left the room, the vertically challenged man determined to get his question answered, asked a basic question in the most outlandish way imaginable. The look she gave rendered the man speechless and like magic he was gone.

People were not on Breeze's menu tonight. She wanted peace and quiet. She wanted to go home, take a hot bath while sipping on something, and curl up with a good book. However, the stories shared in class were often better than the ones in her books. An unfamiliar wave of comfort consumed her as she realized that she actually needed her class.

She quickly gathered her belongings and headed out for her car, geared up for some serious discussion.

—~—

"Why is it so difficult to have what I want?" Iris pleaded storming in the conference room. "I asked with confidence for the guy in my gym class. I wanted to at least get the opportunity to find out what he was like. God abruptly put a stop to that! I actually took the opportunity to stand near him in class. This way, he could check out my progress and I could secretly drool over his pretty brown biceps.

"Well, apparently someone *else* was checking them out. And of course she was younger, thinner, and prettier. Her hair had the nerve to stay neat during our grueling workout. I'm melting and she's glistening. Little Miss Perfect decides to workout directly behind him, whispered something in his ear, making him smile like *The Cheshire Cat*. I also confirmed that he had nice teeth. Although he could use a whitening strip, they were straight, no gaps. But I digress. And the next thing I know, you could see the workout banter between the two. I mean where did she come from?

"The sad part is I looked at my melted reflection in the mirror, and wondered if I even had the slightest chance with dude in the first place. When I looked at him and I thought he was looking at me, I felt my hope coming back. That maybe I *can* have what I want. But once I saw the connection between them, the hope evaporated like my curls in that sweatbox of a gym class! I realized that it would take an act of God to land this guy.

"As usual, He snatches what I want away and makes me take *another* hard long look at myself. And what do I see? No amount of earrings, shiny legs, jiggle and bounce, or cute workout gear could compare to what she had to offer. I cannot continue to go on like this. How can I show my face again, feeling like the whole class knows and is laughing at me? How stupid was I to even remotely think I would have a chance?"

"Can you go to a different gym?" asked Lily. "I'm sure there are plenty of workout places in your area."

"Not an option! I finally worked my way up to the 'serious' section. The energy level is high and the music good. I'm really having a good time workin' off my weight, inches, and jiggly imperfections four days a week."

"Good," said Petunia. "Because there is no way you are changing gyms over your imagination!"

"I agree," Breeze interrupted. "But wait. You go to a gym that is virtually a sweatbox with an instructor called G?"

"Yeah," Iris said reluctantly. "Why?"

"Are you by chance talking about the gym behind Columbia Palace 9, called 'House of Results'?"

Iris hesitated, "Yeah, how on earth do you know about 'The House'? And whatchu know 'bout 'Palace 9'?"

"Because one, I thought you looked familiar. Two, there are not too many places around that you just described. And three, I know about the 'Palace' and the 'House.' I take the evening classes. And I think I know *who* you're talking about. Was he working out in the sadist section?"

Iris laughed, "Yeah, with the mirror hogs."

"Yes! No wonder you were melting. There is a reason why G calls the first two rows 'his kitchen'. Y'all, the man I think she is describing is kind of cute. And yes, the man does have some pretty brown biceps."

Breeze passed the box of tissues to Iris and said, "But Iris, hold your head up and dry your last tear my dear, 'cause I'll be doggone if you are going to cry over something that is already taken!"

"What on earth do you mean?"

"That same chick he was flirting with, is *his wife!*" Everyone at the table gasped, even Zenobia.

"Didn't you see a wedding ring while working out?" asked Violet.

"It's a bag class, so we wear gloves. And rings would pinch your skin. I never see a tan line when he takes them off. Come to think of it, he doesn't wear one during the regular classes, either."

"Okay, is it just me or does anyone else see something wrong with this picture?" asked Daisy. "If the man is married, why doesn't he wear a wedding ring? What is the problem with letting the world know that you are married, taken, not open for business?"

"My pastor told us during one of his sermons, to be aware of a man who refuses to wear a wedding ring," added Lily. "Of course, he said to be even more aware of the woman who doesn't take a man's last name."

"Gym dude is so out-of-order and out-of-uniform," said Tulip.

"A friend of mine wears a wedding ring and he is no more married than we are," Violet chimed in. "And he is still amazed how many women continue to approach him with it on, more so than when he's not wearing one. It's like what does that say about her pursuing a married man. And what does that say about him and his level of commitment behind that ring?"

"That their cheatin' behinds are made for each other," concluded Petunia. "Besides, I'm not surprised by this. My coworker does the same thing and swears by the results."

"Iris, are you all right?" asked Breeze.

"Yeah, just feeling a little silly. I'll just lay low in the 'starting out' section until things cool off."

"Dahlin', I'm sure he didn't even notice," said Breeze. "You will continue to take your rightful spot in the serious section. I'll even go with you to help you shake it off and move on, deal?"

Iris nodded her head and wiped the remaining tears away. Breeze mentally went through a few men that fit Iris' description. But the probable pair were indeed shameless flirts. They were cute and appeared to be in love. She liked that. Their scene gave a glimpse of hope and something else to add on the list of requirements.

"My week took an ugly turn, too," sighed Violet. "The source of my discontentment came from my own Bible study group. The pastor spoke about long engagements and not putting off marriage because we need the uh, *benefits* of marriage."

"What, like a better tax refund," Daisy joked.

"Physically, not fiscally," laughed Violet. "You of all people should know what I am talking about. Anyway, we were discussing his sermon, and a new wife said boastfully, 'well, I'm so glad that I am doing what I'm supposed to do', smiling her Joker-esque smile at me. At first I'm thinking how on earth would I respond to that statement, and that creepy smile? And then I realized, but kindly retorted, 'I am doing what I am supposed to do, with whom and when I want. Isn't God good?' and smiled back. I mean, this woman and that sneaky snake smile were just mean spirited. Why the hate?"

"Is it hate, jealousy, or missed opportunity?"

"Whatever it was, I didn't need to experience that noise during my time of Bible fellowship. Y'all know I'm a cussin' Christian!"

"Speaking of cussin', my aunt said someone was praying for me to find a husband," sighed Tulip. "I was so glad somebody on this earth had it on their heart to actually pray me a husband. I was happy that they recognized something in me that would take me to my desired level. Although, I hoped my desire to be married didn't appear too obvious.

"What drove me to cuss, was that my aunt had the nerve to tell this woman not to bother praying for me. She told her that I am not ready for marriage. How could this battle axe fix her lips to block someone else from praying for me? How dare she assess what I am not ready for! I cook, clean, take care of myself. What makes her think that I'm not ready? She got married young, how on earth did that make *her* ready? What would make someone want to block someone's blessing and prayer?

"I don't know what hurt me more, the fact that she told someone not to pray for me or when I confronted her with it, all she could say is, 'oh, I shouldn't have said anything.' It took everything in my being not to stomp that woman senseless."

"Here is my 'seniors attack' moment," said Daisy. "I am proud of my age, just sensitive. I'm knocking on 40's door with its aches, pains, and disappointments staring me in the face. The cutest baby boy and I were having a marvelous time when this woman asked me if I was the grand-mother. She knew she was wrong because she whispered it. My facial expression must have given her the green light to repeat the statement a few more times. I said, 'do I look that old to be a grandmother? If so, let me fire my hairdresser.' But here is what got me. *She* was *offended* that *I* took *offense*. What kind of sheep dip is that?" Daisy spat.

"Did the senior 'aints get together and have a hate conference?" asked Rose. "My mom's friend told me that I needed to beg my ex to come back to me. *He* did not leave. *I* kicked him out! Then she looks me up and down, implying that based on my age and appearance that I needed to take what I can get. Time was ticking; and I let a good thing go. This was the same woman giving me high–fives for the manner in which I threw him out." Rose slumped in her chair with her head in her hands. "Why do they have to be so mean?"

"I realize that one of the aspects of being single is dealing with people who feel it is their appointed duty to *tell* you about yourself," said Zenobia. "Thinking they can say any old thing that will feed you *their* truth and make *them* feel better. You can either do one of two things. Just say a short prayer before you do either, because you are going to need strength either way. One: smile and listen to their advice and comments. Let them get their own personal foolishness off their chest. This will give them something to brag about during their senior Bible study in the morning and Bridge in the afternoon.

"You, on the other hand, will let their venom laced unsolicited opinions roll off your back. What God has for you, is for you. Their timeline is stuck somewhere back in the 50's and 60's where marriage was a way to get out of their mama's house. You have and are exercising your options with endless possibilities."

"All except for one," someone murmured.

"I heard that! Which we are working on. Now, the other option is to let that old bird know how you feel in a way that is still respectful, but to the point. A few of them will disguise this as wisdom. Once you break it down to them, they will understand… eventually. And do not let them try to play the victim 'well, I was just trying to…,' especially when they do not apologize."

"Why don't they apologize?"

"They feel they have nothing to apologize for. They have been apologizing for the decisions they have made for years. They meant what they said whether their statement hurt your feelings or not. It will be up to you to let their words gnaw on your spirit."

"Speaking of which, my ministry leader never apologized," said Petunia. "I had to confront this broad who felt the need to ask everyone *but* me, about my relationship with this dude. The situation went from, 'Oh, I saw them at brunch' to 'Yeah, girl, they shackin' up!' It was just brunch! Several lovely brunches, actually. But it was just two people hanging out."

"Was he cute?"

"Really, really good looking."

"Was he *single*?"

"With no kids," Petunia nodded happily.

"Is he a prospect?"

"Forget all that," spat Lily. "What did the pastor say when you told him?"

"I should have, but I didn't. She's going to do this again. Only the next person won't be as sweet as me. That will be correction enough. Unfortunately, my friendship with dude will probably cool off, so no, he's not a prospect at this point. My involvement with this ministry *will be* cooling off as well."

"Ladies, Petunia's story brings me to my next point. Not everyone is looking out for your best interest," said Zenobia. "This is primarily why I designed this course. You are here to uplift and encourage one another. Yes, continue to feel free to pull up someone when their statements or actions are not in order. And The Word says to do this *privately*. But we do this in love, with love, and judging from this evening, a lot of humor."

"Well, I need encouragement right about now," Lily requested. "I attended the bridal shower of the woman who stole my blessing--"

"Stop right there," said Rose. "You mean the chick that *made room* for your blessing!"

"Agreed. But get this...oh wait, I brought a lovely fruit tray with the special dip that doubles as an ice breaker. I also took Hyacinth's gift suggestion befitting of the bride you didn't really care about. Thank you so much. The gift turned out to be a big hit among the sea of home improvement gift cards."

"Not one single piece of sexy knickers? No dessert toppings? No dips, chips, fuzzy handcuffs, or whips?" Breeze asked jokingly.

"Someone did bring the chips and its dip. However, this was a Christian shower. The hostess specified that 'gift cards are welcome' on the invitation."

"On the invitation?" Violet and Tulip asked in unison.

"And the last time I checked, Christians got a little freak in them, too," Rose chimed in.

"I have been to the most wholesome of bridal showers to the scandalous bachelorette parties. Sexy, yet tasteful lingerie was given at each one," Breeze added.

"Wait, before we get to Lily's story I want to hear more about this scandalous bachelorette party," said Daisy.

"Later, I really want to hear what happened at this hussy's shower that wilted Lily's blossoming spirit."

"Like I said my gift was a refreshing change. And someone did finally give her the prettiest lingerie set. She held up the top for everyone to admire it." She paused shaking her head. "She quietly confessed to a few within earshot that his last girlfriend would be too conservative and too frigid to wear anything like this. *Frigid?* His ig'nant behind dared me to even consider wearing something like that around our, would be, Christian home. Dude barely held my hand. And we won't even discuss the notion of him kissing me.

"Since when was kissing and hand holding among two consenting grown adults, a sin? Did I actually pray for this? He actually talked to her about *me* not wanting to be sexy for him and *only* him? I was 'Plain Jane' personified because he demanded me to be! That is what I had to do in order to be his wife. I wasted two and a half years of my hopes and dreams, only to find out *through her*, that I still was not good enough! It took everything I had to hold in my tears...and anger. And above it all, she has invited everyone to the wedding. Not the reception, mind you, just the ceremony. She wants all of us at the shower to witness her *special* day."

"Go, be nosey, take pictures, and be thankful that you won't have to waste any money for a wedding gift," cheered Daisy. "And at least you know that you are not going to the reception without getting your feelings hurt."

"My feelings were already hurt when I believed she stole my man. They were hurt even more when he threw *his* version of *my* business all over I-95! What cuts like a knife is that I wasted two and a half years trying to conform to this no count joker! I will *not* be a witness to this union!"

Lily placed her head back in her hands, crying. Expressions of anger, sadness, understanding, empathy, sympathy, disbelief, and anticipation of the next steps were painted on everyone's faces. Iris passed the box of tissues to Lily. During her moment, she reached in her handbag and pulled out a photo packet. "I almost forgot, I have visual aids of the scene of the crime." The mood and Lily's face lightened by her own statement. "That's the gift Hyacinth told me get. All of that for $20. They were having a really good sale."

"Lily, I need you to find a cute outfit and make an appointment to get your hair and nails done," Zenobia said finally. "And change the shade of your lipstick, because you are going to that wedding! Perhaps one of us could go with you if you think it would make the situation easier."

"I'll go," Petunia volunteered. "I really have to see this."

"I wanna go, too," Tulip whined.

"Why don't we make it a field trip," suggested Rose. "We can all blend in. I'm sure no one will notice."

"Uh, y'all may not have to go," Violet said staring at one of the pictures.

"Oh, it's no bother--"

"I know this chick," Violet interrupted. "And I just received my invitation."

"Can the world get any smaller today?" sighed Zenobia.

"The groom is my coworker. I met her at an office event this year. Lily, this woman did you a favor," Violet said shaking the picture. "Listen, I am allowed one guest and I am choosing you. This way you can go to the wedding *and* the reception without bringing a gift. I think he owes you a fine dinner and a Cupid Shuffle."

"Does this mean no field trip?"

"Nope, no field trip, 'cause we all can't hang out afterwards. But, I will be sure to take pictures, especially the one with the groom's face."

"Try to catch the bouquet, so you can be in the wedding pictures."

Lily smiled, soaking in all of the advice and gestures. She retrieved the last picture, placed the packet back in her purse and sighed heavily.

"It will be all right," Zenobia said reassuringly. "Okay, who has not shared their run in with satan's ambassadors this week? Hyacinth? You expressed some consoling words and I, too, want to hear about that bachelorette party. However, something must be on your mind."

"I'm actually okay."

"You are a real team player, Hyacinth," said Rose sarcastically.

"My story pales in comparison to what is on the table tonight. Listen, my issue is nothing that a session of cardio boxing couldn't cure." Everyone looked at her with disbelief with their arms folded for emphasis.

"Fine! My coworker asked me if my being single is by choice or personal disappointment."

"Ouch!" the class exclaimed. "How on earth could that residue of a horrible statement be cured with an exercise class?" asked Tulip.

"Picturing his face on that punching bag, while beating the mess out of it," she confessed. "I could have squashed that sawed off version of a man with my three inch heels. But I didn't want to get my Steve Madden's dirty. Besides, I did ask the same question about his height."

More smiles and comedic relief escaped the circle. Zenobia, too, expressed amusement; however her face was still stained with concern listening to her Flowers.

"Ladies, I can clearly see that satan is on his job," sighed Zenobia. "And he, too, is seeing your breakthrough. I need each of you to trust Him first, and not give in to any animosity the world lays at your feet.

"The good news is I see each of you making progress. And when the one God made especially for you *finds* you, a whole new set of problems, haters, and unsolicited opinions will surface. Only this time, you will have someone to share them with. He will be there to hold your hand, rub your shoulders, draw you a hot bubble bath, and just be there for you. And during the pampering hour, he may offer solutions to 'fix' your problems. Just smile, listen, and enjoy the attention. You may want him to just listen, but fixing things is his job."

"That's all well and good Ms. Zenobia, but he ain't here yet," spat Petunia. "The attitude I have in my heart and bad taste in my mouth can only be fixed with a martini! We can pray, fast, and twiddle our thumbs and toes *waiting* forever and a day for a breakthrough, but this sistah right heah, needs a martini!"

"Girl, I know a place that makes the best martinis," said Tulip. "At least 15 varieties."

"Ms. Zenobia can we have our class off site, or better still, cut class short?" suggested Violet.

"Well, I have not ordered dinner just yet. And the exercise I had planned for tonight can wait. First, let me give you your assignment. I want you to find 'your song.' The selection can be gospel, hip hop or a classical piece, whatever. Each of you needs a song in your heart to quickly remedy life's oppositions. By the end of this course, I want you to have your own personal upbeat soundtrack. Now that the assignment has been provided, we can close with prayer."

"Ladies, I don't drink, so I will see everyone next week," Lily said while gathering her things.

"Can you do a Shirley Temple?"

"I don't want to give the appearance of me drinking," she said fixated on her tasks.

"They make the best fish and chips in town."

"Now you're speaking my language," she said happily joining the circle of hands.

"Ladies, promise me only one drink. Order plenty of nibbles and water because the goal is to take the edge off, not drive off the edge of a cliff. All minds clear?" Zenobia said the closing prayer instead of volunteering someone.

14

Martinis & Wants

"I don't understand how you ladies can call yourselves Christians and drink like this," said Lily. "The Word says, 'do not get drunk with wine.'"

"First and foremost, this ain't wine," said Petunia. "Second, the goal tonight is not to get drunk. And The Word also says, 'everything is permissible but not everything is beneficial.' The fact that I'm grown makes it permissible and this," she took a sip of her drink and shivered, "mmm, makes it extremely beneficial!"

"Are we doing anything for Ms. Zenobia for Christmas?" asked Daisy.

"Can we get through October and November first?" Rose reminded sipping her drink.

"October is already here. And once we blink, it will be Black Friday. Let's all chip in and give her a spa day. I'm sure she could use it after listening to us for the past three months."

"I agree. There are eight of us. Would $40 a piece be okay?"

"Lynn's Day Spa has a wonderful package that includes lunch," Breeze suggested.

"Sounds good to me." They all agreed. "Ladies, I propose a toast to the woman who brought us together and taking each of us to a new level. To Zenobia Zee!" They all raised their glasses, clinked each one around the table, and sipped whatever was in their glass.

"Allow me to be Ms. Zenobia-esque for a moment," said Violet sipping her French kiss martini. "What do you really, really want? But I need you to be as *superficial* as possible. Lily, since your thoughts have not been befuddled over the first sips, you start."

"I want the clean shaven, fresh haircut, nice, church going guy looking amazing in a tank top. I love pectorals. Um, I guess I would like him to be my height with a pair of two inch heels. I want us to look cute together."

"That's what we all want! Well, mine would be four inch heels. But what do you *want*?"

"Hmm...I want him nerdy, with a nerdy job, so we can share nerdy jokes, and do nerdy things. And he should have dimpled chubby cheeks framing his freakishly white teeth with thick juicy lips. I like a sloppy kisser. That's what I want."

"Great start," said Violet. "Whatchu want, Tulip?"

"I need someone who can handle all of this," she said smoothing over her curves.

"Again, that's what we all want. I need y'all to take another sip and dig deep!"

Tulip took another sip of her apple martini and said, "I need a bald, chocolate, earring wearing, neatly trimmed goateed teddy bear with a gap between his teeth. And he must be able to cook his Gold Toe socks off. I want us to have a 'battle of the black iron skillet' to see who can cook the best dish."

"And I would like to be a judge during one of your contests," Violet cheered. "Okay, Daisy, I know you won't let me down."

"Wait, let me sip this before it gets warm." Daisy tasted her dirty martini and proceeded to confess. The Flowers sat motionless, bracing themselves to be floored, as she described what she wanted in a mate for life. Daisy did not disappoint.

"I do believe I can speak for every woman in this *tavern,* that is what we all, um, *need,*" Violet said breaking the silence. "But dang darlin', you may need some therapy!"

"Or a stripper."

"You wanted to know what was on a sistah's mind, so I told you," Daisy laughed.

"Mission partially accomplished…"

"Why do women need strippers at bridal showers?" Lily asked after taking a sip of her pineapple juice. "I can't imagine some baby oiled, muscle man gyrating and waving his imagination in my face."

"Depends on who you get," Breeze added while nibbling on the bits of the graham cracker from the rim of her key lime martini.

"I'm pretty partial to *Beep*," Petunia chimed in sipping on her vanilla bean martini. "That man has some serious skills."

"And that, my dear, *is not* his imagination," Breeze confessed.

"Girl, how on earth do you know?"

"I told y'all that bachelorette party was scandalous," she said sipping her drink.

"Okay, stop right there," Violet shouted. "Daisy, I ain't even finished with you, so be thinking 'bout whatcha want! Hyacinth, what went on at that party?"

"Picture it: we did the usual drinks, food, shower games, and gift giving…until the pole dancing teacher showed up." Breeze continued to tell the table about the weekend's antics. The ladies gasped, laughed, and asked for business cards for future use. "And then there was this goodie bag you left with to, uh, keep the party going. To this day, I still blush every time I peek in it."

"What was in the bag?"

"It isn't necessarily the Christian in me that can't say. It's the good girl that won't let me."

"Bump that good girl noise," exclaimed Rose. "You're still taking pole dancing classes with clear five inch heels, and you can't tell us what is in the bag? Heifah, please! There are drinks present! Git ta spillin'!"

Breeze was momentarily saved when the fish and chicken tender plat-ters arrived. She asked for extra barbecue sauce and water. One water request turned into eight, as the ladies made an attempt to absorb the martinis consumed. Finally, Breeze mustered up the courage to reveal the contents of the bag. A couple of ladies partially choked on their meal. The others wiped their hands, took out pen, and wrote the contents down on the nearest clean cocktail napkin.

"I have a bachelorette party of my own to attend. This is good stuff."

"I cannot keep this in my home any longer. All my friends worthy of this bag are married and have items of their own. The first one of us that gets married, gets the bag. Deal?" Everyone at the table, including Lily happily agreed. "Just be sure to check the expiration date on a few items. You don't want to get your feelings hurt with an unintended side effect."

"Girl, it is on," said Violet excitedly. "So Daisy, did you have time to think about what you want?"

"For starters, that gift bag! But I really want someone my age. I don't know what it is about me that continues to attract 'Mr. Otis' or 'Rahim'. I want a 'Gerald' or a 'Michael.'"

"With what you just described, you need 'Rahim' so that he can keep up with you," laughed Iris. "But the problem is the 'Gerald' and 'Michaels' of our time want something ending with 'isha' or 'ianna.'"

"I've come to the conclusion that 20 somethings have time to put up with the 30 something's foolishness," said Rose. "20 year olds can put up with the wait's, we'll see's, and maybe's. 35 and over females ain't got time for that."

"Daisy, I remember you talking about Mr. Otis. What's going on with Rahim?"

"Well, not so much as Rahim, more like Chad. I met this young white guy at a gas station, of all places. His approach was subtle, but I totally blew him off thinking it was just a sales pitch. I later realized this boy was serious. He looked 12, but his I.D. said 23. I brushed it off as fake, joked with him a few minutes, and went on my merry way. As I was driving, I wondered if he considered me a cougar or he just had a granny complex. As sexy as he was, maybe I should have accepted his offer.

"Again, we all want someone our age, young at heart, and a few other items you mentioned," said Violet. "What do *you* want?"

"Wait, you got another Mr. Otis story?" asked Rose. "How did he woo you?"

"With liquor, conversation, and compliments," Daisy said laughing to herself. "I met this older gentleman on a beach vacation. He offers me a drink, 'here, I think you need this.' I looked around uneasily, thinking this man spiked my drink. The bar tender reassured me it was okay. I took a sip. And y'all, it was the best daiquiri I've ever tasted! It was thick, smooth, and creamy. I'm trying to think of the actual flavor. The mixture of rum, ice, and vanilla was just outstanding. It was banana!

"Anyway, the gentleman offered me a seat and we chatted for a while. I really wanted to get in the crystal blue water, but that rum was getting in my way. The conversation was surprisingly pleasant. I eventually excused myself and changed into my bathing gear, found a spot on the beach, and stretched out. That rum was still doing a number on my head. The crystal blue water was inviting me and I happily accepted the invitation.

"When I got back to my beach chair, my gentleman friend was waiting with yet another drink. 'Try this one,' he said. Again, I accepted the drink. This time, the daiquiri was lemon. Not as good as the first, but very refreshing. So we talked some more and then he proceeds to compliment my legs. He said my legs made him hungry."

"Girl, you going on 'bout old dude and dem daiquiris is making me thirsty," cried Petunia. "Whatcha want?"

"Fine! I want him thin build, with a great smile, pretty feet, and strong hands with an amazing grip. He gets extra points if he's double jointed."

"Yep, Daisy, that is all yours," Violet laughed. "Rose? What about you?"

"I had my superficial type for six years. He was extremely good looking, strong, muscles everywhere. He was thick, had the skinniest legs that were smoother than mine. I would get lost in his everlasting eyelashes.

"So, I want what I had with thicker legs and he just needs to be good to me and for me. I know that is what we all want, just be careful what you ask for," she said finishing the last of her cosmopolitan. "On that note, are you sure we can't have another?"

"Unless you want one of us to drive you home and you leave your car here abandoned."

"The water will do for now."

"I want a tall drink of water myself," cried Petunia. "I want a tall, unmarried, no children, sports buff or better yet, sports newscaster with access to a whole lot of *beep*! The first thing out his mouth needs to be, 'I got tickets to…'"

"Minus the love for sports, we all want that."

"Speak for yourself. I would need my man to have access to some Ravens or Wizards tickets," Breeze added.

"This is hard," Petunia whined. "Well maybe not. I see what I want at the bar with the black Armani Exchange jeans and tight fitting tee shirt with snake skin boots nursing the beer and watching the sports highlights. And I'm hoping he's Italian…with blue eyes."

"Whatcha waitin' for?"

"I can't tell if he's wearing a ring," she said peering.

"How in the world can you see the brand of his clothes and not see some shiny thing on his finger?" asked Iris.

"We'll let you have the last fish finger if you go chat him up," said Violet. "And while Petunia is working up the nerve, you're up, Iris."

"Well," Iris said placing the remainder of her chocolate martini on the table. "It was Mr. Gym Class. Outwardly he was my type. I have no clue how he was on the inside."

"Doesn't matter. Whatchu want *now*?"

"He cannot be fine. I'm scared of 'fine.' I want pleasant to look at. Race does not matter. I want a glasses wearing, pretty teeth and long neck having with slim legs for days, movie and music fanatic. I give extra points if he's a DJ or a movie buff. Tulip, you want your 'battle of the black frying pan'? And I, too, would like to be a judge. I want the 'battle of the movie line or music lyric.'"

"Finally," cried Violet. "Claim it, own it, Iris! But I need some clarification. Where on earth do y'all workout that has a *sadist* section?"

"Forget that," interrupted Rose. "With the confession made in class that had everyone in comedic tears, you mean to tell me you've never done the Dance of the 20 Toes?"

"Well, I don't want to give it up to just anybody," Iris said sheepishly. "Unfortunately, a lot of time and waiting has caught up with me."

"Who else at this table has not done *the deed*?"

"Okay, Violet. That's a tad bit personal."

"That's two folks. Anyone else? It goes no further than this booth."

Two more hands admittedly went up. "Lily, of all people, I thought your hand would be raised."

"I wasn't born saved! I grew up in the country. Either you smoked the hay or took a roll in it."

"Are you happy now?" asked Iris.

"Um, yeah, yeah. All right, let's move on. Let's get back to the sadist section," she said in disbelief.

"That's what we call it," said Breeze. "There are four rows in our class: the row in the back is the 'Starting Out' section. You're either new to the class, determined G isn't going to kill you or you don't want to sweat your hair out. Then there's the 'Stepping it Up' section. You notice the pounds are coming off, slowly, so you 'step it up' a notch. Next is the 'Serious' section, better known as the entrance of G's Kitchen. Bring water, a towel, and ponytail holder, because it's about to get ugly. Last but far from least is the 'Sadist' section. You will feel every bit of your workout and every eye on you from the participants behind you. It's just you, the bag, your partner, the mirror, and their eyeballs from behind. And they take great delight in the pain. So, call us when y'all are ready to go."

"We're ready for you to tell us what you want! Although, I think we may need to take a special trip after the holidays."

"Y'all I am so far gone that I don't even know what I want any more. I was serious when I said I was done." She saw the 'girl please' and 'don't even try it,' sentiments expressed on each of their faces. "If you must know, I would like…"

"You would *like*? I would *like* another vanilla bean martini. Hyacinth, seriously?"

She sighed once again and confessed, "I want a roller coaster riding, soccer player legs having, glasses wearing, close haircut styling, goofball from Columbia. Race is unimportant. But I will give extra bonus points for that Dulce la Leche brother, whom I call Stealth, I'm drooling over during my commute. Is that good enough?"

"Yep, and I'll drink the rest of my water to that!"

"All right, Violet," said Daisy. "We had our moment of confession. We've shared, laughed, and embarrassed ourselves, especially if our booth neighbors overheard us. Now it is your turn."

"Honestly y'all, I really can't say." She shielded her face from the thrown crumpled napkins, straw wrappers, and harsh comments. "It would reveal too much! I would lose my diva status!"

"You're about to lose that wig of yours if you don't fess up!"

"This ain't a wig! I will be more than happy to give you the name of my Dominican hairdresser."

"You're going to need one as soon as I throw what's left in this glass," said Iris. "I can't believe you are punkin' out on us!"

"I can't have nobody call me a punk! But I will say this. I want a 5'8, skin smooth as Hershey bar, so black he's blue, prettier than me, sharing my secret passion. There, that should be enough!"

"Nah it ain't! What's your secret passion?"

"How about I pick up the tab, if I plead the fifth?" Her suggestion quieted the banter, name calling, and other objects that could be safely thrown. "One day, perhaps. I just cannot now." Everyone finally calmed down and agreed.

"Once the waiter comes to clear off the table, let's have our picture taken. This was certainly a night to remember." Again, everyone agreed to the idea. They still teased Violet of her non-confession, and all was forgiven when she actually did pay for their meal. The waiter finally cleared the table, processed the check, and refilled their water glasses. Petunia found the courage to ask the black shirt and jeans wearing gentlemen to take their picture. He happily obliged, as they noticed he was indeed, wearing a wedding ring.

"To Ms. Zenobia" they cheered as he snapped several group and individual pictures. They thanked him, purchased his next beer, and made their way out the door. "Is everyone okay to drive home?" everyone asked and reassured each other they were. Tulip promised to get the pictures developed before the next meeting, as they hugged their good-byes.

"Are we still on tomorrow, Hyacinth?"

"6:25, sharp!"

— —

"There you are," Iris said sounding relieved. "I started to go back home."

"I apologize. My students kept me longer than expected. Why would you go back home? This is your gym, too."

"This isn't my normal night and I didn't want to look obvious."

"You being here will not look obvious, because men are oblivious." The two laughed as they made their way into the gym. While Breeze purchased two bottled waters, Iris set out to find a bag they both could use. Breeze walked in and was relieved that Iris reclaimed her confidence, finding a spot in G's Kitchen. She did wonder if the spot was strategically chosen not to be seen by him.

After a few moments of warm up, the movements turned towards the part of the class Breeze loved the best: the bag. Not only were the punches giving her arms definition and upper body strength, she was about to work out a few issues of her own. "Come on, Come On, COME ON! Let's work!" She could hear the new level G was about take his class tonight. Such level came complete with a date with Epsom salt and an aspirin.

While working it out, Breeze saw the object of Iris' desire along with his wife. G commanded the class to do some push-ups. "Are you sure he's married?" Iris whispered.

"Yeah, I'm looking right at them."

"Where?"

"There, in the front row on the right with the red shorts, she's directly behind him."

"What? Girl, not him," Iris nodded in the opposite direction in the front of the class. "Him!"

"GIVE ME ONE LAP!"

"Oh, *those* pretty brown biceps! You need to go after that." The two made their way out the door to jog their lap.

"Yeah, but the competition is a little too thick in that corner."

"And a few members of the competition ain't out here runnin'. And if you can hold your own in this class, then you are truly a contender."

The girls gave their last ounces of strength left, finishing their lap around the building, only to come back to another round of sit ups, push-ups, and weight training. The phrase Breeze loved to hear the most, "I need eight more," was uttered and class finally came to an end. Before doing their stretches, Iris took their weights back to the rack. She noticed Iris smiling and saying a few words to Mr. Pretty Brown Biceps. She recognized the twinge of jealousy when the competition cheered their 'good-jobs', directly to him, too. They finally stretched, gave high-fives to each other and surrounding classmates and headed out.

"See you tomorrow at noon, G," Iris said as she gingerly made her way out.

"All right, Lyric. Looks like you're losing."

She smiled, thanked him, and confided to Breeze, "The only thing I'm losing is bra size and any remaining touch up." She took a few sips of her water. "This ain't cuttin' it. I'm officially hungry. Let's go to Bun Penny."

"Word!"

The aroma of her favorite shop's finest coffee blend smacked Breeze in the face, as she walked in. The Mall in Columbia roared with the center fountain on full blast. They ordered their sandwiches, UTZ chips, beverage, and found a seat in the shop's corner couch and chairs. Iris started to write her affection for Mr. Pretty Brown Biceps on the poetry/inspiration wall, but Breeze talked her out of it.

"Your name is Lyric?"

"Yeah, my parents are huge music lovers," she laughed.

"Breeze," the young man called from the counter motioning their sandwiches were ready. Breeze picked up both. "Family name," she said as she finally sat down to say grace. "By the way, I'm quite proud of you working out in the front row tonight."

"Thanks. Honestly, I was tired of seeing brown, pink, yellow, and tan rumps in my face. In the front, it's just me in the mirror and my own rump." They both laughed. "I don't think he's interested," Iris said finally.

"Does he even know that you are remotely interested?"

"Men are visual. And I have been putting it out there: the girls, hips, eye contact. I've even smiled at the man with my newly whitened teeth. So if he was interested, he would have done something by now."

"His focus may be elsewhere."

"Perhaps. Wouldn't it be nice to meet somebody while actually doing your normal routine? I never really paid much attention to him and I've been in that class for about two years."

"Why don't you turn that banter into a full discussion?"

"He runs off. I always wondered where he goes in such a rush."

"That could be your ice breaker. Or comment that his facial hair grows at an exponential rate."

"You noticed that, too?"

"His shaving takes years off his face, but he looks better with facial hair."

Lyric looked at Breeze questioningly, "Why haven't you checked him out?"

"First, my focus is to lose my 40 pounds. And second, I too, have seen the competition and I really don't have time for that."

"40 pounds where?"

"I was about to ask you about your 30. Anyway, this is the amount I need to lose in order to maintain an acceptable BMI rate. And the Linzer Torte I'm about to get will not help the cause."

"Did you notice the young couple on the bag next to us?"

"Yep. I've shared a bag a few times with them," said Breeze. "They're really nice. I'm actually surprised to see them on a Thursday night. What about 'em?"

"He's a runner, while she's a jogger/walker. So when G calls for a lap or two, she lets him run wild while she jogs her lap. What I love about him is that he goes *back* and jogs *with* her. He encourages her. I want that."

"You should have mentioned that last night."

"Mmm hmm. However, there is absolutely too much competition out here for the nice, supportive, encouraging, cutie pies, like Mr. Pretty Brown Biceps."

"First and foremost, I think it is a tad bit selfish of you to think there wouldn't be competition. Outwardly, this man is a catch: single, in good shape, has his own means of transportation, and I assume gainfully employed to maintain his membership payments. I realize that you are the reigning queen of Missed Opportunity, but you have enough in you to muster up the gumption and quietly ask him out for coffee. What's the worst that could happen?"

"Uh, he could say 'no,' and then I have to work out in the same class with the stench of rejection and sweat mixed in the room..."

"Lyric..." Breeze sighed.

"I cannot handle the word 'no.' If I know I can't get it, I don't ask. And what if he says no and share my intentions with other members of the class?"

"Okay, this ain't high school where your note gets passed around the class. Now G may call you out, but he does it quietly with encouragement.

And if dude is that much of a twit, then bullet dodged! I'm sure he's not. He seems really nice. You have to ask him out."

"I'll give it some thought," Iris dismissed. "Is this course helping you change your focus?"

Breeze could not answer her new friend's question. She shrugged her shoulders hoping it would suffice. "Tonight really isn't about me. This was for you. Lyric, maybe it's time you stop hiding. G is always telling us to stand up and be counted. This is God's way of putting feet to those prayers and encouragement. If he says no, it'll just make room for the better man."

"If he says no, the confidence I had left would be shot!"

"Once you ask, you'll know where you stand! Now, get that cute work-out outfit and work it out!"

"Easier said than done, Breeze."

"Since when is getting what you want ever easy?"

15

Favorite Things

Breeze walked in the office lobby to see her classmates gathered outside the conference room door. The look of worry and agitation escalated, as men draped in white coats bustled in and out of the conference room. The piped in classical music made a feeble attempt to calm the nerves of the concerned. "What's going on?" Breeze asked her classmates. "Is there something wrong with Ms. Zenobia?"

"We don't know," said Rose. "Lourdes told us to wait outside. We've been standing here for 20 minutes with no one telling us nothin'."

"Maybe we should pray," Lily suggested. The Flowers gathered for prayer as a steady stream of workers continued to make their way in and out. Tulip sidled up to join the last moments of prayer.

"Why are we saying grace out here?"

"Tulip, do you not see the stream of folks in their white coats," Violet said exhaustedly.

"Did y'all not see the catering trucks parked outside," Tulip spat back.

"I thought something smelled really good," Lily said with relief. "I was too busy with worry to notice. I wonder what's up the sleeve of our fearless leader tonight."

"I'm sure we will find out soon enough," said Rose. "Tulip, where is your watch?"

"There was a great 'One Day Only' sale at Pier 1," Tulip said shooing away the question. "I was not about to pass on the savings. I purchased enough wrapping paper, gifts for my Bible study group and found this beautiful dinnerware with a simple holiday motif. Now am I excused?"

"Only if there are gifts in the car for us."

"While we are waiting and hoping there are gifts for *us* in Tulip's car, I've got to tell you this story," said Petunia. "I won a set of football tickets for the Ravens-Colts game. One of the guys in the office congratulated me, made some small talk, and proceeded to make me a deal: If I gave him the tickets, he would arrange a date for me with his cousin."

"So when's the date," Daisy interrupted.

"Are you kidding me? I kept the tickets! Hyacinth, you down?"

"Word!"

"Let me get this straight," Violet interrupted. "You gave up a chance for happiness for some football tickets? Why don't you compromise and take the guy dude offered to the game? No offense, Hyacinth."

"I would pass up 'chance' for guaranteed happiness any day. And free football tickets never disappoint. Besides, that wasn't the deal. It was an 'if/then' transaction. Besides, I hope to run into my future happiness at the game wearing my cute Colts gear."

"I know one thing for sure, it had better be *Baltimore* Colts gear, 'cause if it ain't, them's fightin' words," Breeze said heatedly. "You are *not* stepping in *my house* with your Colts crud."

"Ladies, go enjoy your game," interrupted Violet. "Let's not rehash the great football debate once again."

"You know y'all 'crows' are gonna lose," Petunia whispered.

"Not," she said boastfully. "Five words: A whompin' and a stompin'! Ya'll coming into *our* house!"

Lourdes finally came out to provide tonight's instructions. "Good evening, ladies," she greeted closing one door behind her. "Thank you for being so patient. Ms. Zenobia is ready to receive you now. However, before you enter the conference room, please know that your seats are assigned tonight. So look for your name on the designated place card. Enjoy your evening," she said brightly smiling opening both doors in a grand manner.

The Flowers were frozen where they stood, overwhelmed with the spectacular transformation. Twinkling bright white lights, floating snowflakes, soft Christmas music, and a hint of apple, cinnamon and vanilla, beckoning them in. Unable to close their mouths, the Flowers slowly made their way in the recently created winter wonderland. Each ignored the previously said instructions, dumped their belongings in the nearest chair, never taking their eyes off of the holiday scene, and scattered in their own direction. Lourdes noticed the haphazard pile of belongings and started to say something. Zenobia quietly intercepted, allowing the ladies to absorb the fruits of her labor.

Breeze was immediately drawn to three highly decorated trees in back of the room, dusted in simulated snow, transfixed on the strategically placed ornaments. The first tree she reached was adorned completely in sparking silver and blue decorations. White lights that danced, dimmed, and then brightly shined hugged every inch of the tree, with crystal snowflakes and icicles to catch the light.

Miniature high heeled shoes, purses, wrapped gift boxes, toy dolls and soldiers, multicolored striped candy canes, neatly tied ribbons, among the twines of twinkling colored lights consumed every limb of the middle tree. "This must be a few of Ms. Zenobia's tree of favorite things," Breeze giggled. Her holiday daze was interrupted when a train came whizzing by her feet, through one of the tunnels amidst the draped snow covering the bottom of the trees. The last tree Breeze assumed was an 'Angel Tree' with harps, music notes, and singing angels of every color.

"Hey, this one has my name on it," Daisy squealed pointing to one of the ornaments on the Angel Tree. She noticed that all their names were on the tree. The rest of the Flowers stopped what they were admiring and rushed to the sight.

"Our names are on the presents, too," Lily said excitedly.

Before the entire class started to grab what was assigned, Zenobia softly suggested they find their seats. "This looks like the perfect time to start class. All will be explained, in due time." She gently removed the assigned items from their hands and placed them back strategically on and under the tree. "Come, let us find our seats."

Lourdes found their seats for them, placing their items in the assigned chairs. The Flowers were too busy to notice the beautifully decorated table with crisp white table linens, starched table napkins, place settings befitting a queen with sparking crystal goblets surrounding two silver, white, and pretty pink center pieces. At each setting, a present wrapped in pretty pink ribbon with a card set neatly on the silver charger. Zenobia noticed the smiles on her Flower's faces, all too eager to unwrap their gifts to pay attention. She again quietly suggested they keep the box on the table. She, too, could not stop smiling.

"Happy holidays ladies and welcome to my winter wonderland. Tonight's meeting will be slightly different. I know that each of you will have a lot on your plate dealing with holiday, work, and family obligations. I wanted us to get together before the hustle and bustle of the holiday season and the pre office party diets, begin. I have to admit, I love this season and all that it has to bring. The celebration of our Lord and Savior, Jesus Christ is first and foremost on my list of favorite things. However, what I love most about this time of the year are the lights: bright, twinkling, colorful or crisp beaming white lights. From a candlelight service to a neighbor who goes all out for a spectacular display; that light is shining bright. His light that is within you should shine even brighter.

"Before we get into tonight's class, I am going to ask Lily to bless the food; because I want us to eat first while the food is hot. I can predict our ice breaker alone will take about an hour to complete," she giggled.

Breeze was too enthralled with the Christmas tree decorations to notice the servers and chafing dishes in the front of the room. Lily blessed the food and each started on their way to the back. "No, no ladies. Tonight, you will be served."

A stream of servers marched in and presented the ladies with the first course: shrimp cocktail. Shrimps as big as baby shoes outlined the rim of the glass bowl with a circle of chilled cocktail sauce nestled in the center. A salad of mixed greens, chilled petite vegetables, and vinaigrette dressing followed. The main course finally arrived, presenting a plate of salmon with a lemon dill cream sauce, wild rice with mushrooms, and asparagus with almonds. A small dish of lemon sherbet was served, to cleanse the palate. The dessert was finally served. Breeze could not fathom dessert, let alone allow any room. Each Flower was presented with a vanilla soufflé sprinkled lightly with powdered sugar. The server gently cracked the top of each soufflé, gently drizzling in a warm Grand Marnier sauce. Breeze savored every last loving spoonful.

Zenobia started to speak, but Violet interrupted her, "I do not think words can be spoken, until after we finish this." Zenobia giggled and silently motioned for them to proceed.

When the last satisfied spoon clinked against the dessert glass, Zenobia motioned for the Flowers to join her in the back of the room. They sleepily made their way to where Zenobia was standing among the Christmas trees, the active train set, and a semicircle of eight chairs.

"I hope and trust you enjoyed your meal. By the satisfied look on your faces, mission number two was accomplished. The first mission was to wow you with my zeal for the holiday season. None of you said a word, but your faces lighting up like children on Christmas Day, truly warmed my heart, and assured me that my labor was not in vain. So, let us start with tonight's ice breaker: As a child, what was your favorite Christmas gift and why? I think we shall continue to go against the grain and start with Petunia."

"Okay, this one is easy," she said without hesitation. "My roller skates were stolen during a sock hop, at Skateland. Do Hyacinth and Iris know where that is?" They both nodded their heads. "My mother told me to put my name on the bottom of my skates. I refused, because I did not want to mess them up. When I came home skate-*less* with my cheeks burning with my tears, all my mother said was, 'that'll learn ya.' I was so hurt. I hadn't felt that dejected since my crush named Junior invited some other chick to go with him on 'couples only' skate right in front of me.

"Now, I started to add a new pair of skates to my Christmas list, but for some reason my sister warned me against it. To my surprise on Christmas morning, there was a huge box, wrapped in green paper with two belled white and brown frosted pom poms on the top with my name on it. Y'all I cried. I did not care what else I received that day. When I finished crying, I found a marker in my mom's kitchen junk drawer, and added my name to every inch of the bottom of my white booted skates with red wheels. I tried them out two weeks later at the next sock hop. I still have them. And I finally did get my chance to 'couple skate' with Junior."

"I will go next," Rose volunteered. "I grew up in a house full of boys where most of the toys catered to them. Balls, bats, helmets, even video games were for them. I could have all the girly toys I wanted, as long as I kept them in my room. I had every Little People and Weeble Wobbles figure and their house or store imaginable. But I always wanted the Little People Tree House. I did not get it, but received a Sesame Street town-house play set, instead. I loved it. It had all the figures I could want, plus a toy mail truck and a chalk board in the middle. Not only did I have *two* townhouses, I created a whole housing community, especially when I added an empty pencil box and my brother's Legos. And yes, I still have the town hidden in my attic."

"Speaking of doll houses, one year Santa Claus' knapsack blew up on our living room floor," confessed Violet. "Even though I never lacked for a Barbie, my then desire was for a Malibu Barbie. I remember one year, Santa Claus brought me this Christie Barbie Doll with serious eyelashes. She had this rooftop apartment that was decked out with a fire pit. I think I was too young to appreciate it. But I digress. Not only did I get *two* Malibu Barbie dolls, I got the dog, the car, the dream house, and the furniture. I felt I was unwrapping boxes for the entire day. That whole collection was my favorite Christmas gift. Incidentally, there was never a Ken doll.

"The good news is I, too, still have my dolls, the dog, the house, the car, and amazingly the fire pit from Christie's apartment. The better news is I have all of what I received that Christmas in real life and of course, I am the Christie Barbie doll with the serious eyelashes," she said batting her eyes. "Unfortunately, still no Ken."

"My favorite gift would have to be my Easy Bake Oven," Tulip chimed in. "I had a field day Christmas morning making everyone their own special treat. I think my mom knew I would try to use up all of the cake and frosting packets in one day, so she rationed out the extras as time progressed. Each year, I would get a full set of refills. My brothers would always burn their fingers messing with that little hot light bulb. I wore that oven out. That's when my mother introduced me to the life size version in the actual kitchen."

"I think Santa Claus added fuel to the fire of me enjoying my own company when he brought me my own television set," Breeze shared. "My mother and I never agreed on what television programs to watch. One Christmas morning, I found a brand new color television under the tree with my name on it. I was eight, and I honestly do not think I came out of my room for the entire winter break. I also think I watched too much when I still, to this day, know almost every cartoon, commercial, sitcom, and their theme song the seventies and eighties had to offer."

"I get my hearing checked each year due to my all-time favorite Christmas gift: my first Walkman," said Iris. "I came up during the time when rap and house music was getting serious. My dad could not stand someone ruining records while spittin' on mics, and bought me a Walkman. I loved it. To this day my father has always outfitted me with the latest gadgets. Now, I teach him on the latest and greatest. Even better, my Walkman taught me how to tune out the world. I put those earphones on, find a great tune, a book, and I am set for the entire afternoon...or the next distraction."

"Most of my friends had Cabbage Patch Kids," Lily said. "For two years I would look under the tree for mine, but it would never show up. The third year, I got tired of asking. And once I stopped, I ended up with a set of Cabbage Patch Twins. I squealed, tore open the box, made my family stop what they were unwrapping, and took the adoption oath right then and there. My parents agreed, took my picture, and encouraged me to open my other gifts. It was the clothes for the babies, extra diapers, and a stroller. I can still smell the baby powder. And yes, I still have and cherish my babies."

"I see we saved the best for last," Daisy said smiling. "My parents gave me a pink bicycle, with a white banana seat, a cute little basket with flowers on the front, and white tassels streaming from the handle bars. There was a doctor's kit with real first aid equipment in the basket. I did not get the connection until I tried out my bike, and did this little trick. Of course, I fell off. Fortunately, I remembered I had my first aid kit, fixed myself up, and away I went. And I didn't have to cry to or...interrupt my parents."

"So what was the favorite gift: the bike or the doctor's kit?"

"Both actually. I always wanted a doctor's kit. I loved playing doctor, and had a thriving practice. Fortunately, they gave me the transportation and the tools necessary to make house calls," she said with sly smile.

"Daisy, you never ever disappoint," Zenobia said laughing. "I hope this brief stroll down memory lane brought back some happy child-like excitement for the holidays. I want each of you to carry that feeling throughout this holiday season. However, let us not forget that you are still on an assignment. Now that the table is cleared and the gifts are placed in your assigned locations, let us go back to the table. The Flowers folded their chairs, stacked them against an empty spot on the wall, and reclaimed their designated place.

"Before we get to the assignment, let's get in this box!"

"Patience my dear, patience," Zenobia said calmly while regaining her spot at the middle of the table. "This holiday season, your assignment is to do the following: When you are holding that warm cup of whatever, I want your nails flawless. Make sure your hands are polished and chipped free...*at all times.*

"Also, whatever you wear to the mall, make sure it is fitting properly, showing off assets, camouflaging any flaws. Dress for the man that you want, not for the one you have."

"But we don't have a man," said Lily.

"Indeed...yet. Anyway, your shoes need to be clean, shined, and strategically matching your outfit. And please make sure they are comfortable. Walking like your feet hurt is not cute. But if you must take them off, make sure you are displaying well moisturized, chipped-free pretty feet or run free, no holes-socks.

"If you are between hair appointments, make sure your ponytail is fabulous. Make sure lipstick, lip gloss, or lightly tinted lip balm is on, displaying that bright pearly white smile. And please, do not leave the house without your earrings.

"Now that your outside is fabulous, make sure that your ride is, too. I want the car cleaned, free of debris on the seats, smelling good, rugs vacuumed, windows wiped, and tires sparkling, full of the proper amount of air. Your future happiness with the one made especially for you, could all start with a simple conversation in the parking lot. Also, a clean, item free car deters potential thieves. While shopping, please use cash for your purchases. Make sure your Tithes, bills, expenses, and savings account are paid first. We have already discussed your financial health and all of us could use a break from the charge and credit cards.

"Is your house in order? Be prepared for guests. Even if you will not have any, anticipate entertaining. Tulip mentioned earlier there was a sale on dinnerware. How many table settings did you purchase?"

"Since it's just me, I only bought one. I wanted a pretty set for the holidays."

"I need you to go back and get another setting. As a matter of fact, everyone needs to get a pretty set, complete with serving utensils. Ladies, I need each of you to welcome what this season and the seasons to come, has to offer. Just because you are single this Christmas, does not mean you will be forever. Expect that man to be there next Christmas. If you are entertaining, make sure you make a little extra for that young man that will be entering into your life. And know this: there is absolutely nothing wrong with making a man, *any man*, a plate.

"For your next assignment: I want you to write down all of the good things, deeds, and quotes you experienced this year. Bring those warm fuzzies with you into the New Year. Leave the rest. I need you to focus on what brought you joy, rather than what did not. Now, each of you has been given a box with an envelope on top. Do not open the envelope until you get home."

"Isn't it bad manners not to open up the card before the gift?" asked Daisy.

"Again, we are breaking with tradition tonight, so do not open the card until you get home. However, each envelope contains your third assignment. Each of you has been assigned an area to which you need to work on: confidence, a broken heart, humbleness, and restlessness. I believe these four challenges are hindering you from receiving your next steps.

"When you get home, I want you to open it. Think about why I said it, look up the scriptures on that card, meditate on His Word, and enjoy this moment. One caveat, if you are offended about what I suggest, please feel free to call me so that I can reassign you. All I ask is that you keep an open mind. All minds clear?" She waited for her class to agree. "Good. Let us get to the gifts!" she said excitedly.

Some of the Flowers tore into the pretty pink ribbon wrapped around the box. Others pulled the ribbon apart. Breeze took her time and carefully slipped off the ribbon and placed it neatly aside. She had every intention of putting it back once the contents were revealed and admired. Keeping her Christmas gifts under the tree until after the New Year was a tradition she did not want to break.

Each Flower gasped, as they found a single crystal champagne flute, surrounded by silver and pretty pink tissue paper. They each removed it from the box to admire it closely. "Ladies, among the few necessities you should have in your home, I feel that every woman should have a crystal champagne flute. There needs to be a special glass, designated to celebrate you.

"I am extremely proud of what each of you are accomplishing this year. You are taking a moment to rediscover yourselves and each of you should be in awe of what you see. I know I am. So, the last portion of your assignment is to raise a glass to the light that is shining within each of you, celebrate what you have accomplished, and anticipate the great things in store for the New Year."

The Flowers sat speechless, surveying the newly received gift and soaking in the assignments for the season. Lily and Tulip looked at each other and excused themselves from the able, while everyone else thanked Zenobia for her generosity. Discussion of their favorite Christmas gifts continued, as the class turned into a light holiday party. Lourdes brought in hot apple cider, cocoa, and cookies which kicked the holiday party up a notch.

As Lourdes was making her way out of the door, Lily and Tulip returned, encouraging her to stay. "Something told me to do this as soon as we discussed it," Lily said. Tulip moved one of the chairs beside Zenobia and gestured Lourdes to sit. "We cannot thank you enough for bringing us together, sharing your wisdom, listening to our thoughts, and taking the time to encourage our stubborn crushed hearts and minds. However, since you are taking the time to develop us, we want you both to take a moment to pamper yourselves. Merry Christmas, Ms. Zenobia. Merry Christmas, Lourdes." The class repeated the sentiment in unison. Lily and Tulip presented each with a card and two gifts apiece wrapped in silver paper covered in snowflakes.

"May I open this now?" Zenobia chucked. "Before I do, ladies, you did not have to do this. It is my honor, my pleasure, and my job to serve you and provide an outlet to reconstruct your crushed hearts and spirits. But I would be lying if I said I was not touched. I truly am. Thank you all, so very much."

"I certainly was not expecting any gifts, so I thank you, too," added Lourdes. "But the beverages are getting cold," she said getting up to serve the refreshments.

"You, sit, we'll serve," Rose commanded.

"Now, get to the gifts," Daisy said excitedly. Zenobia and Lourdes did as they were told. Once the gifts were open and admired, Zenobia and Lourdes hugged and thanked everyone personally. Someone increased the sound of the holiday music and elevated the class to full holiday festivities.

16

Pokeno & Pooh

Like most opinions, the holiday season is indeed the most wonderful time of the year. Family gatherings, holiday parties, unexpected giving and receiving presents, and her personal countdown to 10 days of time off, all make Breeze's season shine bright. However, the brightest star in this sky would not be allowed to even twinkle if her family's annual holiday Pokeno party filled with food, money taking, trash talking, and more food did not take place.

"Breezy – baby," a husky voice called.

"Yes, Birdie-Bee?"

"I see you brought dat cheese dip I like to mah party."

"Yes ma'am, it's almost ready," Breeze responded, while mentally preparing herself to answer her 95-year old great aunt's string of questions. Birdie insisted as long as she had breath, to host the holiday event. The women in her family happily obliged.

"Good. Are your freens coming by mah house dis e'nin' to play Pokenah wid' us?"

"Yes, ma'am, they are looking forward to it and your gumbo."

"Good. Did you tell dat gal not ta' brang no brown muneh, dirtyin' up mah change cup, back in mah house?"

"She knows, Birdie-Bee."

Birdie continued, "She bet'not! If she brangs dem thangs in my house, she won't wrap her lips 'round a spoonful of mah gumbo. If she has any sense in her head, she'd carry dem pennies to da bank and cash 'em in for silvah!" Her great aunt had a field day talking about her friend Spring who insisted that pennies were legal tender. *"Not in mah house,"* Birdie shot back and that is when the ribbing commenced. Knowing Spring, she would probably bring a bag full of pennies just to prove a point. And knowing Breeze's great aunt, she will be true to her word, and kick her out.

"Now go on 'n scoop me up a bowl and set'chit on da table," she smiled patting Breeze on the shoulder. She did what she was told while setting up the dip, with complementing condiments and tortilla chips in the middle of the playing table. She took a moment to grab her special Pokeno playing card when she finished.

Birdie's home buzzed with holiday greetings and the jingling bags of change. Holiday and hostess gifts for Birdie gathered under her Christmas tree. A stream of aunts, nieces, cousins, and friends of cousins all poured in as they hung up their coats, sat down their belongings, proceeding to either chose a card or make their way to the feast.

A spread of steroid-fed sized steamed shrimp, deviled eggs, a grilled chicken tender platter, a veggie tray with Birdie's creamy homemade dipping sauce, garden salad with every color of the rainbow represented, mashed potato salad, macaroni salad, a tribute to her great aunt's hometown deli platter, a tray of fruit which included her family's special sweet dipping sauce, and Liddy's prize winning *7 Up* cake, all circled around Birdie's signature seafood gumbo.

Breeze loved her aunts and cousins dearly, but she was elated to see her three friends through sick and sin arrive. She hugged her friend, Willow, who walked in first.

"Did you pick out my card?" Willow asked.

"Nope, 'cause if I pick the wrong card, you would blame me for the rest of the night."

Her friend Rayne from college was next. "I hope and trust that bag of something is for me," Breeze said peeking in Rayne's gift bag.

"I take great delight in dashing your hopes, 'cause it ain't," she said playfully snatching the bag away.

"Then it will be a greater delight taking your money tonight," Breeze said hugging her friend.

Pulling up the rear was another college friend, Spring. "Girl, why is that meat on that platter still mooing?" she asked while hugging Breeze.

"It's pastrami and corn beef," Breeze said exhaustedly. "It's supposed to look that way."

The annual Pokeno game started promptly at 7 with Birdie making a feeble attempt to shout, "$.05 a cup, ante up!" Every one grabbed their cup of something, a plate of nibbles, chose what was left of the cards, and took their place at the table. "Breezy-Baby, put mah muneh up for meh please." Birdie watched the color of the money gracing her cups like a hawk ready to pounce on its prey.

For the next intense hour, Breeze was the 'Belle of the Ball' calling a combination of corners, diagonals, and Pokeno, taking two of the biggest, well fed pots. The next round started with Breeze yelling, "Centers" after the second card was called. Everyone at the table rolled their eyes and groaned, as she danced in her seat, collecting her winnings.

"So, Breeze. How are the wedding plans coming along?" asked Spring.

"If this is your attempt to throw me off, it ain't gonna to work," Breeze said while her cousin Bella continued calling the cards.

"What weddin' plans? You finally gittin' married?"

"No, Birdie-Bee, I'm--"

"You in anothah weddin'?" Birdie asked while the card calling continued. "Hold on Bella-Bee!" She turned to Breeze. "Whose weddin' are you in dis time? Didn't you tell meh dat all your girlfreens is married?"

"Yes ma'am," Breeze answered not looking up. "Bella, continue please."

"Don't you dare call anothah card," Birdie boomed pointing her neatly groomed unpolished amazingly smooth finger at Bella and then back to Breeze. "Who-is-gittin'-married?"

"Spence."

"Who?" she asked looking around the table for the answer. "What does a man have ta do wit' you in a weddin' unless you're da bride, the mothah, or sistah?"

"Birdie-Bee, you remember Spencer, Breeze's ex-boyfriend," a voice volunteered.

"He was not my ex!"

"Well, whoever he was to you, he ain't now," Liddy added. "I keep telling her to check out this man from my church."

"Liddy-Bee, I know that man. And I do not feel the need to pull the sheets that bad!"

"And would probably be da bes' sheet pullin' you evah had," she snapped back without missing a beat, shocking everyone at the table. "And dahlin', the way you act..."

"Okay, ewww," Spring responded shockingly. "Why are we having this conversation with the elders at the table?"

"You thank you invented it?" Birdie asked. Breeze continued staring at her card as Birdie's eyes never left Breeze's face, waiting for the answer to the first question.

When it did not come from her great niece's mouth, Birdie motioned for Bella to continue. The next card was played and Breeze announced, "Four-of-A-Kind," in her best 'in-your-face' voice.

The groans and game continued and Willow yelled, "Pokeno! Finally. Now I can stay in the game." Birdie suggested the next game be a black out.

"I see keeping a secret is not this family's strongest virtue, is it?" Breeze asked while collecting her winnings.

"Not when it's a matter of the heart, dahlin'," Liddy responded.

The final game of the first round started with Breeze working on another sweep despite the interruptions. The next card was played.

"Breezy-Bee, when you gonna fin' you a boyfreen?" Birdie asked quietly while playing her two cards.

"He'll reveal himself to me soon enough," Breeze said quietly. "Corners," Breeze shouted. "And I do believe The Word says, '*he* who finds…,'"

"Yeah, but I need *you ta find* yourself a boyfreen at least fo' 15 minutes 'cause dat's how long dey would be able to stand to be wit' yo' sassy behind. 'Four-of-a Kind'," Birdie tried to shout with her raspy voice.

"He should be here by now as much as that class is costing me and for how long you've been in it," Liddy chimed in.

"Diagonals and Pokeno," shouted another cousin."

There were more groans. "What pot is left?"

"Who slept their 'Centers?'" asked Breeze's second cousin Kitty. "That and the Blackout are the only ones left."

"Neb' mind who slept what," Birdie spat. "You in school agin'?" The next card was played. "Every time I turn 'round you're in somebody's classroom," Birdie said studying her niece's face. "And you bettah ansah mah questions befo' you step a toe back in mah kitchen!"

"Birdie-Bee, do you want to win the 'Blackout' cup or not?"

Somebody finally called their 'Center' card. "I wanna find out 'bout dis class and why my niece didn't fix her lips tah tell meh." There were three cards left. The first syllable of 'Blackout' was on everybody's lips.

"Blackout," Liddy and a guest of another cousin shouted in unison.

"Good," Birdie said. "Breezy, get mah cup a money and come talk ta meh. The rest a y'all go git sumptin' ta eat," she said shooing away the losing members at the table all the while firing up a cigarette. "Tell meh 'bout dis class."

"For starters, it is not class in 'how to find a man' per se."

"Hurry up and divide the pot," Liddy ordered with one eye on the conversation and the other on her winnings. "My mouth's gotta get in this!"

"No it don't," Birdie and Breeze spat in unison. "I reckon yo' mouth has been in'nit long enough, 'specially not ta tell meh," Birdie added. "And Missy, you mind yo' manners. You got dem bress and dat fiery temper from yo' father side of the fam'leh, 'cause you ain't as sweet as us."

"Judging from the parade of opinions, I got my so called temper honestly from both sides," she retorted. Birdie changed her stance with one hand on her hip and a finger in Breeze's face ready to retaliate when Breeze interrupted the rebuttal. "I rest my case! Now, can I eat my gumbo in peace, please, before Spring eats it all?"

"Not 'til you tell meh what dis class is all 'bout!"

Breeze gave her and whoever was listening, the layout of the class. She finally admitted that she was enjoying what the class had to offer. If nothing comes of it, she at least made seven new friends.

"Just as long as they don't make you a bridesmaid. I don't think you could cram another dress in that closet," Willow added.

"'Bout time somebody is doin' somethin' to fin' you someone," said Birdie. 'Tell you da truth. Baby, I honestly don't know what you were thankin' datin' dat whatsitname, Spoons?"

"Spence, Birdie Bee," Breeze chuckled.

"Whatevah da boy's name is, I wouldn't give dat tired Negro da sweat from my armpit, let alone the key to mah heart. Wit everythang you were blessed wit, you choose to waste it on dat hot load a nuttin'!" She looked at Breeze sideways. "You and he didn't do da fatal thang, did jah?"

"No Birdie-Bee, the situation didn't get that far."

"Good. No use givin' him da milk and yo' cookies."

"Enough, Birdie-Bee, I am not seeing him anymore!"

"And what kinda spell did he cast tah make you wanna be in his weddin' anyway?"

"I really do not know."

"I know one thang," Liddy added. "That's why she's in this class now."

"Lis'en, aftah Breezy-Bee fixes meh a plate we'll be ready ta start anothah game, heah? So, get ready tah ante up, 'cuz it'll be $.10 a CUP!"

Three of the Flowers were enjoying their second session of Zenobia's gift. After four months of observation, Zenobia suggested Breeze, Petunia, and Daisy needed a quieter spirit. What better way to sooth the soul and focus on nothing but what the body is saying, than Power Yoga? Breeze was no stranger to a yoga class. However, time and circumstances contributed to major stiffness and greatly hindered certain poses.

The one pose she knew her body could handle was her beloved Savasana or corpse pose. Breeze allowed her mind, body, and spirit to melt into the mat. However, just as she entered in the state of bliss, three mobile phones started to ring. One of them belonged to Breeze. Too relaxed and too embarrassed, she tried her best to ignore it. Unfortunately, the caller was persistent. When class was finally over, Daisy, Petunia, and Breeze made their apologies and checked the message. It was Tulip. They gathered their belongings and made their way to the lobby to hear the message.

"I don't think I can take much more of this! It's a holiday tradition that I can't go through with. Someone should be buying my Winnie the Pooh Christmas doll for me. I'm sick of buying my own gifts! We've been in this class for five months now. Where is he? Y'all, I'll get myself together in a minute. Thanks for listening."

All three Flowers looked at each other and immediately started dialing. "Wait, I'll call and then I'll conference y'all in," Breeze said while dialing. "Tulip? Are you all right?"

"No, I can't take this *beep* any longer!"

"Hold on, let me conference in Daisy and Petunia."

"Okay. Rose and Lily are on the line, too."

"Hey, Tulip," Daisy said softly. "What is going on?"

"She's having a merry mini melt down," Lily chimed in.

"So not the time for jokes, but it is time for us to have a pow wow," said Rose. *"I have Violet reserving us a table now."*

"Well, somebody has to come get me, 'cause I have not moved from this spot for the last 15 minutes."

"Where are you?" Iris asked.

"I'm the new statue at the opening of the Disney Store at the Arundel Mills Mall."

"I'll get her," Breeze volunteered. "She's not that far from where we are now. Meet everyone in an hour?" The Flowers agreed.

"Have two apple martinis waiting for me," Tulip sobbed.

"No, stick with tradition. You will only have one," said Rose.

"Sticking with tradition is what got me in this mess in the first freakin' place!"

"She just had to have a meltdown during busiest shopping seasons of the year and on a Saturday," Breeze mumbled while finding a parking space. However, she understood. The smallest thing could set off the strongest among us. Whatever a person was lacking is magnified times 10 during the holidays. Personal obligations, commitments, and responsibilities are bound to take a back seat ensuring everyone else's happiness and never thinking of our own. While Breeze was in deep thought, she found an amazingly close spot. She thanked Him for favor, thanked the driver, and rushed to find her friend.

Tulip did not lie. She was standing right in front of the store, with on lookers staring as they walked by. "Tulip, are you still on the phone?" She started sobbing again.

"Yeah," she hugged her friend, while hanging up the phone. "I made Petunia stay with me on the phone until you got here. I didn't want anyone thinking I was crazy."

"Too late," Breeze thought to herself.

"I think I've officially lost my mind. I can't even get my legs to walk to that bench."

"Okay, Tulip, take a deep breath."

She went on without heeding any words of advice or encouragement. "I don't know what is worse: spending another Christmas with no one special to buy me the gift I really want or your family and friends stop asking about your love life? It's like they know there is no hope for me. No one asked me how my love life was going this Thanksgiving. No one cared if I was the next one to walk down the aisle. When I held my newest nephew, no one turned to me and asked when it was going to be my turn.

"I cannot take another year of this! All I want is some nice guy, with a nice smile, with a great job, and decent drama free life to buy me my *Christmas Pooh*. WITHOUT HAVING TO ASK! Then I can bring him home, show him off, and he can endure my crazy family with me."

"Come on, sit down," Breeze coaxed. "Come on, it will be all right," she said making an attempt to help her friend to the nearest bench. "Look, don't make me have to kick those legs. Come. That's it, one foot in front of the other."

"Believe it or not, this class is helping. I don't know whom I would call if it wasn't for this class. My friends would think I'm an idiot. And I really appreciate the Christmas class Ms. Zenobia gave me. I just wish I had someone to reap the benefits."

"Benefits? What on earth did she give you?"

"Pole dancing classes. She felt I needed confidence in my walk and stance. Iris and Lily are in the class, too. What are you doing?"

"Power yoga to quiet my restless spirit. Now y'all's class is a workout."

"You're telling me," Tulip said rubbing the top of her thighs.

"While I'm here, I need to pick up a few things for my godsons. Will you be okay sitting here?" Tulip nodded her head yes while wiping her remaining tears. Breeze got up from the bench to make her way in the Disney store, when Tulip interrupted her.

"And Hyacinth?" Breeze turned around. "Thanks."

"What are Flowers for," Breeze smiled. She made her way in the store noticing the variety of holiday plush dolls to choose from. She was thankful for the two-for-one sale and purchased eight. "One of us should have what they want for Christmas, at least once," she said handing Tulip a bag of two giant plush holiday themed Winnie the Pooh dolls and the miniature bean bag. "You will get the man, eventually. Tulip shot up to hug Hyacinth and started crying again. "It's gonna be all right, dahlin'," Breeze said reassuringly. "Come on, let's go. There is nothing worse than warm martinis and cold fish fingers. And by the way, you have seven friends who will bother you about your love life until it happens."

"What do you want for Christmas, Hyacinth?"

"I honestly have no idea. But for now, I will settle for a hot bath loaded with bubbles and Epsom salt. Our yoga instructor encouraged us to try a position no normal size human being should evah try!"

17

Cooking with Class

Breeze stole a quiet moment during her busy school day to check her messages for class assignments. In the past few months, Zenobia challenged each Flower to perform a grown up version of 'show and tell' based on the topic of the day, complete with an ice breaker and discussion questions. Like little pop quizzes. When she was questioned, Zenobia simply replied, "Do you know of a better way to be prepared at all times?"

Lily brought in the notes from a church service discussing dating vs. courting and the purposes of both. The following week, Daisy provided several arguments for this 'God created need.' Iris was tired of her box set of sad songs and challenged the class to create a top 10 list of love songs. Violet explored various heel styles and what to do if your date is shorter. Petunia brought in various samples of ice cream, revisiting the topic of dating other races. Tulip examined the necessity of making the first move and should it be done for our future goals. Rose tackled the dilemma the difficulty of completely breaking it off with your ex when his family loves you and you love them back. Lastly, Breeze presented 'How to

Feel Like a Million Bucks in your $10 Dress.' She provided reasons as to why the color and/or prints of a good supporting bra and panties should match with the class repeating, "From the granniest to the sexiest…"

Although a New Year, no one was assigned a topic, nor was there a class agenda. The lone message suggested wearing comfortable shoes and the directions to a remote place. *"Destination unknown,"* she thought as she printed out the information. *"Where is this woman taking us tonight?"*

✦ ✦

"Ladies, as I said before you will be prepared when the right one walks into your life…at every angle. This includes the kitchen…besides the ones in the back of your head!" Moans and groans of protest filled the room, which Zenobia completely ignored. "One of the biggest complaints from men and the mamas of men is that the only thing these gals can *make* today, is a reservation. You will not be one of those women!"

"If he wants a cook, he can go back to his mamma's house," Daisy said flippantly.

"Yes, he can go to his mama's house for dinner and then to his new girlfriend's house for dessert and a full breakfast…because she, too, can cook! However, this is not just a class to take care of him. This evening is about taking care of you. The Word says we are to treat our bodies as a temple. Dining out daily is not healthy for your body or your purse. I want you to enjoy the power, the control, and the satisfaction you achieve when you create your own meal. You know how the meal was prepared. You know your body will be able to handle the ingredients used. And you will also know if the chef washed their hands before touching your food. So tonight, we cook. My friend, Chef Piper will be here any moment to--"

"Excuse me," said a thick, clean shaven from head to neck, cocoa brown man wearing a chef's coat with black piping around the cuffs and collar, checkered pants, and a simple, yet sparkling diamond earring, as he walked in. "I'm Chef Smith Curry. Piper couldn't make it tonight.

She asked me to fill in and by the looks of this class, I need to call and thank her. Evening, ladies," he waved with a smile flashing a mouth full of pearly white teeth.

"Hi," the class sang dreamily in unison.

"Is she okay, I just spoke with her this afternoon," Zenobia said ignoring his sentiment and the stares of interest from the class.

"Did anyone else's panties fall to the floor when that fine brother walked in?" Breeze whispered to the gathered group. Each Flower snickered, as they nodded their heads in agreement.

"Girl, I thought you said you were done," Iris whispered while still laughing.

"I said I was *done*, not *dead!*" The giggling turned into chuckles.

The laughter placed Zenobia's concern on hold and attempted to regain control of the class with a glare. No such luck. The handsome gentlemen made his way to the center of the room. The swooning crowd tried to focus on his next words when Zenobia interrupted him and whispered something in his ear. He nodded and excused himself from the room, but not without offering a wink and a smile fit for a toothpaste commercial. Zenobia waited until he left and place her hands on her hips. "Like y'all ain't seen a man in years!"

"Not like that!"

"And he can cook, too?"

"I would gain so much weight with him," said Iris. "I would need to be in somebody's gym eight times a week."

"Girl, keep your gym! With a man like that, I know of a better way to work off dem pounds," snarked Daisy. The laughter filled the room as everyone agreed, high-fiving Daisy.

"Honestly," Zenobia said exasperated.

"And Ms. Zenobia? When did you start using words like 'y'all and ain't'?"

"Since *y'all* started acting like giggling school girls. But I *ain't* gonna lie, that man is fine," she confessed and starting laughing with the class. "I was not expecting that, at all." She regained her composure and signaled for her assistant. "Lourdes, can you bring them in, please." She addressed her class. "Ladies, before we begin, I have some gifts...and where on earth is my Tulip? She is never this late!"

"You may need to call her," Rose suggested. "She's slow to read her emails. I knew I should have called her this morning."

"Maybe you are right. Anyway, Lourdes is handing out little incentives for you to get in that kitchen." A pretty pink apron with the name and a design of their assigned flower embroidered on the bib was distributed. "With all kinds of stain fighters available, please do not be afraid to get them dirty," she said as the ladies assisted each other with their new uniforms. Two Flowers to a station, they took their place equipped with the necessary utensils, spices, and dry goods. Tonight's chef replacement walked back in, with a butter melting smile, noticing his students adorned in a sea of pretty pink ready for instruction.

"Is that extra one for me? Real men cook *and wear pink*."

"No," Zenobia sang. "We have one more student coming--Tulip!"

"Y'all, I am so sorry. I didn't read my messages until I got to the parking lot of our normal meeting place," she said breathlessly. Zenobia presented the last apron to her latest arrival, assisted with the strings and motioned for her to take the empty spot by Violet.

"Actually, I need an assistant," said Smith. "Her lateness qualifies as my new victim."

"That sounds good to me," said Zenobia. "Lourdes, would you like to take the empty spot by Violet?" Her assistant happily bounced from her seat, retrieved a spare apron supplied by the studio, and took her spot. With all her students and stations accounted for, Zenobia excused herself and stepped out of the room.

"Are you cooking impaired?" asked Smith addressing his newly appointed assistant.

"I was in the kitchen long before you were using the oven for *Shrinky Dinks*! 'Mattahfact, I will let you be *my* assistant while *I* teach the class. If I would have known we were meeting at a cooking studio, we could have had class in my kitchen and saved Ms. Zenobia a few bucks."

"Oh, you think you got skills?"

"Sweetie, I *know* I have skills." She addressed the class. "First--"

"Stop," he interrupted. "This is my class. I teach, you learn."

"Hmph, Teach!"

"Thank you." Smith shooed Tulip out of his way to address the class. "*First*, welcome to *my* kitchen. My job tonight is to not only help you prepare meals, but to make you feel comfortable in probably the most under-utilized room in your house."

"He can help utilize another room in mine," Daisy mumbled. Those stationed close by, giggled. Unfortunately, Smith was within hearing distance. He smiled sheepishly, ignoring the comment and continued.

"Growing up, the kitchen was the heart of our home. We had family meetings, entertained, and I received my worst whuppin' in the kitchen. Something always smelled good, waiting to be tasted with the aroma of whatever my parents cooked lingering throughout the house. And yes, both my parents and grandparents cooked. The men in my family actually cook, not just barbecued. Lovingly, the tradition of cooking was passed down to me and I decided to make a career out of it. So regarding the *Shrinky Dink* comment, I have been bakin', cookin', and creatin' before *Shrinky Dinks* evah came out!"

"Hmph, I didn't think you were that old," Tulip laughed.

"Hmm...and I see why you are still single," he sighed. The entire class straightened up with glares darting at the instructor.

"And just why is that?" Tulip spat. A few of the ladies took out the sharper utensils out of their canister waiting for him to clarify the statement to their satisfaction.

"Look, all I am trying to do is teach my class. First lesson: let a man lead sometimes."

"*Good point*," Breeze thought and placed her knife down, but kept it handy for a reminder. Tulip slightly bowed in agreement and motioned for him to continue. "So, are we cool? Can y'all put the guns on safety and place the knives back in the canister until further notice, please? We have to prepare five dinners for five nights in three hours."

"I thought it was three dinners," said Zenobia walking back in.

"I do not believe in leftovers. And ladies, lesson number two: please do not serve your man leftovers *for dinner*. You can use those for lunch the next day. I want to introduce you to the concept of making a freshly prepared meal, quickly. Besides eating the same thing can get boring and tempt you to seek unhealthy alternatives."

"But what if you're cooking a roast or a chicken?" asked Lily. "One or two people can't eat all that in one sitting."

"And please do not try, no matter how good the chicken is. I love roast beef sandwiches or chicken salad with crackers...for lunch."

"Does he expect me to cook every day?" asked Iris with the look of worry.

"Again, no," assured Smith. "Ladies, use this as an opportunity to set one of your standards. Designate a night or two a week when you go out to eat. If he can cook, ask him to share in the responsibility. We realize that you have jobs and lives to lead. But a man likes to feel catered to, from his woman in some way, at least once a day. And ladies if you are doing special things for your man and you know the effort is not being appreciated, move on. If you are genuinely 'doing for him,' a good brother will reciprocate. That is just my public service announcement. So, shall we get started?

"Oh, before we begin, I do know one of you ladies does not eat red meat. That's perfect because I have a ratatouille recipe that you would really like. Does this person at least eat seafood?"

"Mmm hmm and turkey, too," Petunia said while raising her hand. "So if the recipe calls for chicken, I just substitute it."

"Terrific! I also have some additional meatless recipes that I cannot wait for you to try," Smith said smiling his signature smile.

"Cool, bring it on!" Petunia encouraged.

Smith eagerly took his spot at the main cooking station centered in the front of the classroom, playfully bumping Tulip out of his way. "The microwave is good for heat and eat, but let's move away from prepackaged meals. Too many are full of sodium and preservatives we do not need.

Tonight we will prepare, taste, and cook. When you get home, you will have freshly prepared meals ready to freeze, for the next five days."

He did not waste time instructing the Flowers about menus, shopping lists, and the necessary utensils and ingredients that should be in the home of every grown up. A few members of the class looked insulted, while the others were painstakingly taking notes.

Breeze was somewhere in the middle with tonight's lesson. She knew of the mandatory ingredients and utensils and has most of them. She did make a mental note to check the expiration dates. However, not wanting to cook was not the issue. She did not need to cook. Picking up a prepared meal, healthy or not, was much easier and a lot less clean up at home. Dining out also eliminated the house smelling like whatever she cooked. Of course her waistline and ultimately her financial bottom line suffers.

However, working out four times a week and not spending money on upkeep for a date cancelled out the calories and the cost. *"There is no one to prepare for."* She winced at her last thought, but quickly shuttered it away with justification. *"Not having someone to prepare for keeps heartache at bay."*

"What about loneliness?"... *"Please! That's why I pay my cable and phone bill faithfully!"* She could not believe where the loneliness thought came from. Unfortunately, she did not realize the latter part of her mental discussion carried on outside.

"Hyacinth, what does cable have to do with chopping onions?" Iris overheard. "She takes one cooking lesson and now she thinks she's ready for her own show."

"I don't know, but I can chop the mess out of an onion without one tear drop."

"Chop not mince," Smith advised moving throughout the class. "I would hate to be the man you were thinking of when you pulverized that onion. Now take out that energy on some flank steak. You both are doing a fantastic job," he said patting both she and Iris on the shoulder. "Wait, don't I know you?" Smith asked while squinting at Breeze.

"Trust and believe, I would've remembered you. So, no I don't think we've met," she laughed.

Smith shrugged and moved from station to station monitoring the progress of his students. He complimented on their chopping ability. He provided cooking secrets to ease their time in the kitchen.

"I see he didn't waste any time snuggling back to his cooking companion," Rose observed.

"Those dimples are shining bright tonight," added Breeze. "She is really in her element."

"Ladies, I know that we, yeah including me, are watching our waist lines. But don't be so stingy with the butter," Smith instructed adding more ingredients to his sizzling sauce pan.

"I almost forgot the wine and music to go with this awesome experience," Zenobia said retrieving glasses from the closet in the back of the room. She rinsed the goblets, dried them, and set two at each station.

"And I will take care of the music. Chef Piper told me to pick out some jazz just for the occasion," Smith said smiling as he instructed Tulip to watch the pan while retrieving a few CDs from his bag. He walked over to the nook of the room that kept the classroom's sound system. George Benson's *Cruise Control* lightly filled the air waves taking the kitchen experience to a whole new level.

Zenobia presented the choice of liquid refreshment. "White or purple?" The Flowers looked at her strangely, still tending their creations. "Sparkling grape juice," she explained visiting each station, with decisions made based on their main entrée. The two additional touches elevated the class to full fledge frivolity with laughter, jokes, and arguing over the best prepared dish.

"The goal is to wilt the greens, not kill the vitamins," Smith announced as class moved to the side dish segment of the evening. Breeze was even more delighted adding a new twist to getting her green intake. She also realized the meals were surprisingly easy to assemble. And quick.

"I am so proud of these diva hands," Violet announced with her hands covered in tomatoes and scallions. "I may have to invite my mamma over to show her what I can do."

"Ms. Zenobia, did you bring a camera?" asked Daisy. "I would like proof that I did prepare my own meal sometime this year. I'm sad, but proud, our pretty aprons have sauce and spinach juice all over it." Zenobia happily obliged, capturing snapshots throughout the class.

Once the cooking was finished, their meals were neatly packaged in pretty pink reusable containers with labels marking its contents, the cleaning of their stations commenced. Breeze loved the cleaning part of cooking. She wiped down the countertop, shining it brighter than when she first arrived, removed her apron, spraying a little stain fighter where the bib was fed with every ingredient of the five dishes, folded it, and placed it beside her bag. Pleased with the way she tidied up her station, she joined the class ready to receive final instructions.

"I put together some additional menus and recipes to take home. If you follow what I have included in your packet, you will have a different meal each night for the next month," Smith stated as he handed each person a pretty pink folder. "Bon Appetite."

"Ladies, first let me start out by saying how truly impressed I am with your skills this evening," said Zenobia. "Let me stress again, this was not a class to cook for your man. Although, Smith has provided some valid reasons to do so. Therefore, your fasting assignment: no dining out. No restaurants, fast foods, vending machines, and Smith reminded me to add, 'refrain from using the microwave as a means to cook.' Heating is acceptable.

"Your homework assignment is to take what you have learned tonight and plan a dinner party. Instead of a girls-night-out, host a girls-night-in. Opening up your home to those you love and making them feel welcome is a part of letting your light shine and sharing the gifts He has blessed you with. Place your culinary gifts on an elegant setting and be the hostess with the most-ess. Are we all in agreement?"

The Flowers nodded their heads.

"Ladies, please help me thank our wonderful host and instructor Chef Smith Curry." The Flowers clapped and cheered for their instructor for the evening. Breeze immediately noticed the display of dimples consuming Tulip's face, as she brightly praised her cooking partner.

"Thank you, ladies, thank you. And I am pleased that you recognized Lesson#10: Show a man some appreciation."

"Did you also provide a list of your wisdom along with the menus?"

"No, but I can certainly send Ms. Zenobia a list," Smith said smiling.

"Smith, would you do the honors and close with prayer, please?"

"I'd be proud to. But first, can we thank Ms. Zenobia for putting this amazing event together?" The Flowers eagerly clapped, cheered, and thanked their instructor for the goodies and a memorable field trip. Zenobia graciously accepted the admiration with a huge smile and curtsied.

Although the evening air was cold and crisp, The Flowers stopped and took notice of every star in the sky waiting for them. Breeze looked up with wishful thinking, commenting the air smelled like snow. "That beef stew recipe will come in handy if that halo around the moon has anything to say about a possible day off."

"Somebody is praying for a good snow day," Rose giggled, as they all walked to their cars.

"I'd suggest we get a drink, but we have bags of food that need to be refrigerated," suggested Iris.

"As cold as it is," added Violet. "The car can act as a refrigerator. Let's go! Oh wait, where is that Tulip?"

"Chef Smith asked her to stay after class," teased Rose.

"Oh really?"

"Ms. Zenobia, will you be joining us?"

"No, tonight's class put me in the mood for something stronger. Like a good piece of apple pie...a la mode," Zenobia said quickly smiling at Violet. "However, I need to stick around to find out why my Tulip had to stay behind." She stood in the middle of the parking lot amidst the sea of frosted vehicles with her hands shoved in her pockets and eyes fixed on the entrance of the office.

"It should be obvious," Breeze chimed in joining the newly forming circle. "They were all over each other during the demonstration. I thought he was going to serve our Tulip on a silver platter. Speaking of silver, as in Silver Diner's pie a la mode?"

"Now, in their defense, they were fighting over which seasonings to use. If we are going to the Silver Diner, I'm getting a vanilla milkshake," Petunia added.

"Was all that passion over the food or each other?" Daisy challenged. "And I cannot believe anyone is thinking about a milkshake, as cold as it is tonight. But I can go for some warm cobbler...a la mode."

"Nevertheless, something was going on and I want to find out what it is. And yes, there is a Silver Diner not too far from here."

"Can we at least put our bags in the car while we wait," cried Lily. "My weeks' worth of dinner is getting heavy."

They agreed and went to their separate cars. Breeze situated her contents so nothing would fall over. While everyone reconvened, Zenobia never left her spot.

"Do you think they're, uh, waxing the floor?"

"Come on Daisy, not after the first meeting. Girlfriend ain't that hungry. You might be, but not our Tulip." They laughed as Rose gave Daisy a playful hug. "It has been at least 15 minutes. How long does it take to ask a question and respond, 'yes or no'?"

"I'm sure she said 'yes,' but you still need to know where to meet and when."

"There she is."

"Finally."

"What are y'all still doing here?"

"At first we were in the mood for a drink, but then Ms. Zenobia had a better idea for dessert. Then we noticed you weren't in the pack. And judging from yours and Chef Curry's demonstration, we had a little Q&A."

"Ms. Zenobia are you coming, too?"

"Yes, and now I have Silver Diner's entire dessert menu on the brain. But enough about me, Tulip, what did Smith want?"

"That obvious, huh," she responded looking embarrassed. "He wanted to know if I would be interested in watching a cooking competition he's entering next week."

"He did ask you on a date! Whatchu gonna wear?"

"I think she should wear that wrap dress she wore to class a couple of months ago."

"No, I think you need some color. Do you have anything orange or electric blue?"

"That purple dress she wore to the Christmas party would be perfect!"

"Ladies, ladies...I told him no. I'm not going."

"What?" the ladies cried disgustedly in unison.

"The chemistry between the two of you was stronger than the onion and garlic we chopped. Why on earth not?"

"Because, I realized this is my season to work on me and find out what I am doing wrong."

"For starters you said, 'no' to that fine young man that was obviously smitten with you," said Zenobia.

"I thought we couldn't date while we were taking this class."

"I did not tell you that," Zenobia spat. "I told you to shine your light and evidently you did. Question is, do you want to go with this young man to the competition?" Tulip nodded her head yes. "Phew, I thought you had sautéed what was left of your mind. Now go back and flash that dazzling dimply smile of yours and tell him you will be there!"

Tulip's face brightened as she agreed, and quickly tipped back to accept the offer. "And wear the purple dress," Zenobia shouted.

"Okay," she shouted trotting back.

"Are we still on for dessert," Rose shouted.

"Where are we going," Tulip shouted back. Rose shouted the place and location. "Okay, just have some hot chocolate waiting for me!"

"Play her cards right, she'll have some hot chocolate waiting for her in that classroom," said Daisy. The ladies, including Zenobia giggled. "I cannot wait to hear how this turns out." They started for their cars again, but noticed Zenobia still standing in the same spot with her same expression. "Ms. Zenobia, are you okay? I thought you said you were coming."

"Yes, I just want to wait for Tulip to come back out. Make sure she is okay."

"I'll wait with you," said Rose. They all decided to wait for their friend. "Can we all agree that Tulip performs the first ice breaker of the year?"

"Agreed," they said in unison.

"The title of her discussion will be: 'What did you wear on your very first date.'"

18

Pop Talk

"Aw shucks," Breeze's father said, as she made her way out of the bathroom. She decided changing her clothes for tonight's activities would be easier and closer to the restaurant from her father's house. "I hope you're meeting my future son-in-law or at least Mr. Right Now in that outfit."

"No dad, not this time," she said smiling. "My class is meeting at Maggiano's tonight. The instructions were to be 'First Date' ready," she mocked. "And for some reason, 'to use this time wisely.' Like we don't already." She giggled.

"Well, you certainly followed instructions tonight, baby girl," he said while Breeze hugged a 'thank you.' "What course are you taking now?"

"It is a really long story," she sighed.

"Shorten it."

"Liddy Bee and Willow convinced me into taking a Christian singles class after I agreed to be in Spence's wedding."

"Just what did you smoke to be in that boy's weddin'?" She started to answer, but he raised his hand to interject. "However, I would like to see you happy, at least for five minutes, so I'm all for that class."

"Why doesn't anyone understand that I am happy? If anything, you and mom should be happy for me, living the independent life you both wanted for me."

"Independent, not recluse. And come to think of it, there ain't nothing in your actions that say, 'happy' or 'content.' You act like you're just going through the motions. You know, whatchu call it? Complacent!" Breeze made another attempt to respond with no luck. "Now, go, have fun tonight and keep me posted on what happens." She quietly hugged and thanked him again, and made her way to the restaurant.

19

Calamari & Questions

The seating hostess suggested The Flowers meet in the bar area and wait for additional instructions. They were also instructed not to drink anything alcoholic. Breeze laughed, thinking Zenobia knows her class all too well. Her gussied up classmates, Petunia, Rose and Lily were among the first to arrive.

"Did anyone else notice those fine men under the awning?" inquired Iris walking in. "There were like, five of them! I'm glad I followed Ms. Zenobia's advice and wore this dress," she said twirling around.

"I must be numb or hungry because I was more interested in the calamari waitin' in here," said Petunia. "Has Mr. Gym Class seen you in that outfit?"

"If I can barely wear earrings to class, I'm certainly not going to wear this dress," Iris said smiling.

"Hey, what's going on with the *Ebony Man* convention gathered outside?" Tulip asked toting a shopping bag from Stein Mart.

"Hey ladies, are we still waiting for Ms. Zenobia? This sistah is ready to throw down on anything with an '—ini' in it," said Daisy strolling in.

D. M. CUFFIE

"Yes, we did and not exactly," Rose responded answering both questions. "The hostess instructed us to wait here. We just can't drink, so no *martini!*"

As if on cue, a handsome olive skinned gentleman with thick well styled hair, clothed in an impeccably tailored gray suit with red and silver accents, greeted the class. "Is everyone in the party present?" he asked huskily. The Flowers answered. "Excellent. Before I escort you to your table, your hostess would like a group picture. Please place your coats and belongings on the bench for a moment. And not that any of you need to, please check your hair and makeup."

The Flowers looked at the host strangely, then at each other, and finally obliged. "Excellent. Would everyone please meet at the foot of the stairs?" The host positioned the camera properly, made a few posing suggestions, paused looking at the vision and snapped five pictures of various poses. "Very nice ladies, very nice. Now, would everyone please follow me?" The Flowers gathered their belongings and followed the sharply dressed host up the staircase.

"Imma have to holla at him when this event is finished," Petunia whispered to Breeze.

"Not if I get to him first." Instead of the main seating area of the restaurant, the class was lead upstairs to the party rooms. *"A private room? The topic ought to be hot and heated tonight."*

"Ladies, it has been a pleasure. Please wait here until Mrs. Zee is ready for you," he said bowing and winking his good bye.

While Petunia's eyes followed him down the stairs, Lourdes appeared smiling. "Good evening ladies." She turned and looked in Petunia's direction, "Uh, he's married, happily with four children."

"I can still look," Petunia pouted jokingly.

"Everyone looks absolutely wonderful," Lourdes said looking over the class. "When you go in, please find your name among the seating arrangements. Yes, your seats are assigned again, tonight. Also, Ms. Zenobia wanted to remind you to use this time wisely. Trust me, you will not be disappointed. Have a good evening, ladies, and enjoy this moment," she said opening the double doors in her grand manner.

The Flowers walked in an L shaped dining room, exquisitely adorned with pristine glass and silverware. Two centerpieces filled with pretty pink and red rose arrangements were positioned at the head and foot of the table. A small silver gift box with a pretty pink or red ribbon was placed on top of the white charger.

That, however, is not what primarily greeted The Flowers. Seven handsome men in various shades of brown ranging from honey coated to rich dark chocolate with freckles, facial hair, or clean-shaven stood at attention, as they made an attempt to walk in. "Looks like Ms. Zenobia brought the *Ebony Man* convention to us," Tulip whispered to anyone within hearing range.

"Good evening, ladies," Zenobia said beaming. Her arm was linked with the seventh gentlemen with short silver gray curls and a neatly trimmed goatee. "Please come in, place your coats on the rack, and find your seats."

"Ms. Zenobia, I don't see a place c--"

Among the crystal, silverware and china, a pretty pink rose was neatly tucked in a starched white napkin, with black lettering, 'Made Especially for' and the name of the flower spelled out. As the ladies found their seats, the handsome men helped them with their chairs. Once the men's table companions on both sides were seated, they too, took their seats.

"Good evening," said the distinguished gentlemen still linked with Zenobia's arm. Various responses from the table answered back. "I am Linden Zee, husband of your lovely instructor, and I facilitate the men's class of 'While We Wait.' On behalf of me and my lovely wife, our thanks to each of you for coming out this evening. Ladies, you look absolutely lovely, tonight. And gentlemen, y'all are looking clean," he said laughing. "We felt the time was appropriate for the two classes to meet. We kept the other class a secret because the past seven months was to focus on 'you' and what 'you' bring to the table.

"But know this: every last one of you is in the same boat, looking for answers, solutions, or just some comfort to your current situation. My wife and I want each of you to express what is on your mind, ask questions, and be ready to receive insight. Because this is, indeed, your time," he closed smiling. "Wife, did I forget anything?"

"Oh and ladies," Linden added before she could answer. "Just one note: I am a science teacher. I gave my students the names of necessary elements. Because truth be told, men *are* necessary in your lives," he said smiling while making his way back to his seat.

"One caveat," Zenobia addressed the table, "We shall conduct our-selves in a civilized manner, while using this time wisely," Zenobia said still beaming. "Are there any questions?"

"I have one," offered Daisy. "Let me get this straight, the men at this table are over 35, never been married, no children, gainfully em-ployed, and actually *want* to get married? I didn't know they still made that model, especially in black." Everyone at the table laughed with relief. "Unfortunately, there are eight of us and six of them. Two or more of us would be without."

"Not necessarily," Rose added.

"As you can see, Daisy, they do," Zenobia interrupted. "However, we have a few minutes before dinner is served so, let us get to know each other with an ice breaker. Please state your flower or element and let us know if you prefer cookies, cake, or pie. Let us start with Hyacinth."

"Hello, my name is Hyacinth and I absolutely love warm chocolate chip cookies with ice cold milk," Breeze said smiling.

"Good evening, I'm Zinc and give me an oatmeal raisin cookie with *that* ice cold milk."

"I'm Violet, good evening. I will combine the likes of my classmate and neighbor and go with an oatmeal chocolate chip cookie."

"'Evening everyone. I'm Calcium and I love apple pie with a *little* slice of cheddar cheese."

"Good evening, all. My name is Lily and I go head over heels for strawberry shortcake. There's something about that combination of fresh fruit, cream and cake," she said enthusiastically.

"Hello everyone. My name is Oxygen. And your cake is too dressed up," he said turning to Lily. "Give me of piece pound cake and I'm happy."

"Good evening, I'm Rose. And I am anticipating some serious Tiramisu, tonight."

"I'm Linden, and I like anything my wife makes or offers. There is, however, a special emphasis to the 7 up cake."

"Hi everyone, I'm Iris," she said waving to the table. "I'd rather have cake. But, there's this almond cookie I flip for every time I go on my annual cruise. I always feel the need to box up a batch."

"You go on a cruise every year," Iris' neighbor turned to her. "Somebody's got bank."

"No, I just know how to budget my money," Iris said smiling politely. "And it's for a worthy cause."

"Huh," said Iris' neighbor. "Well, my name is Helium and give me some yellow cake with some thick rich chocolate icing. Oh, and a glass of ice cold milk," he said pointing down the table toward Breeze and Zinc.

"'Evening everybody. My name is Daisy and Ms. Zenobia's special confection got me hooked on cake."

"We heard about that cake. And I am hoping some young lady at this table knows how to make it. 'Cause you will make the brother that comes into your life real happy. By the way, I'm Lithium. And I love cake of all kinds."

"Hello everyone. My name is Tulip. We all got the recipe and well... never mind," she said smiling.

"Nah, don't leave us hangin'," said Lithium.

"Let me just say the cake is a crowd pleaser. But my preference would have to be a simple cupcake. I just love that small burst of flavor that you can either gobble up or savor."

"I'm Sodium," he said waving. "And I think pie is so underrated. Not everyone knows how to make it, but when it's made right and has a side of whipped cream, it is on!"

"Hello, nice to meet everyone. My name is Petunia and I'm going to have to bring it back to the warm chocolate chip cookies but with vanilla soy milk. To some of us, regular moo cow milk is our enemy." Everyone at the table laughed, some shaking their heads.

"Well, now that everyone has been introduced--"

"Wait, you didn't introduce yourself or share your preference."

"Where are my manners?" Zenobia asked with feigned surprise. "My name is Zenobia, wife of Linden. Although I am not much of a dessert eater, I have never been one to turn down a piece of pie. Granted I know who made it," she said shaking her own head at the last statement. "I see the staff is ready to serve dinner. So Husband, if you would please bless the table?"

Linden graciously accepted the honor and asked everyone to stand, join hands, and bow their heads in prayer. Once completed, everyone retreated to their seats and passed around the hand sanitizer. "I finally got my flu shot and I cannot risk catching a cold," said Lily.

"This late?" Oxygen asked motioning her to pass the bottle to him. "But, there's never an excuse needed to use hand sanitizer."

Background music was turned up just a notch to complement the meal and conversation. Everyone placed their neatly wrapped gift and rose at the head of their place setting, ready to receive their first course. The classes made their own icebreaker based on the choice of salad at the table. Lighthearted dinner conversation continued, with playful threats to who was eating the last of the calamari. Breeze always felt one could let their guard down when sharing a good meal. The moment was not about networking or who knew whom, just pleasant conversation. The entire table appeared to leave their troubles, egos, and hang ups at the door... for now.

After the tiramisu and pound cake confections were finished, the entire table declared the pound cake could only be made by a black senior saint from some southern Baptist church.

"The only way we know it ain't, 'cause there's all this stuff drowin' this pretty pound cake."

"Yup," said Oxygen. "This cake doesn't need friends. Well, maybe we can keep the scoop of vanilla ice cream. But, I am so glad I live alone, 'cause when this ice cream kicks in..."

"True confession: that is on my list," said Petunia. "I want some-one who understands when the lactose kicks in, and kicks my stomach, have the air freshener can at-the-ready," she commented finishing her point with a demonstration.

"Well, now that our guards are down officially," Zenobia said looking mildly embarrassed, "I see this as a lovely place to start." She giggled to herself while pulling out her pretty pink notebook with matching pen. "In a few words or less, what is the hardest part about being single and pleasing Him at the same time?" she finally asked as the last of the dessert plates were cleared. "Let us go around the room again, and this time let us start with Petunia."

"I would have to say, lack of choice. The pickins' get slim when you start adding Christian stipulations."

"Dealing with bitter women," Sodium added.

"So, you think we're all bitter?" asked Petunia

"If you take my *general* statement personally, I think the shoe fits."

"You can call us bitter if you want, but the actions of a few brothahs out here make us that way," added Iris.

"Maybe if y'all would let some stuff slide…," Helium added.

"How much and what do we have to let slide?" Iris asked chiming in again. "Should we just ignore all the side pieces, babies all over the place, blatant disrespect, not so much as having the basics? And just what in the world is so dag gone complicated? If you can't figure it out, stop seeking us out until you do!"

"All, please, this is an ice breaker," Zenobia finally interrupting the budding argument. "There will be time for discussion in a moment. Tulip?"

"Hmm?" she responded looking up from her iced tea. "Oh, um, I guess my issue would have to be finding someone who would be equally yoked, that's balanced. We need to serve Him and have a good time, at the same time."

"Can she also be fine and serve Him," Lithium added. "I want to find my wife in church, but the women in my church look worn out." Groans and rolled eyes could be heard and seen throughout the room from the Flowers. They retreated, respecting the 'do not start' look Zenobia flashed.

"I would have to say abstinence," Daisy said taking her turn. "He created it, so does He have to be so stingy with it, restricting the deed to married folks? I really do not understand why we have to wait during our stage of life. We're two grown folks. We can take the necessary precautions, as well as handle the consequences."

"I'm with her. Whatchu doin' tonight?" Helium asked slyly.

Daisy blushed. He scribbled something on a piece of paper and slid it to her. Everyone at the table laughed it off, as what appeared to be an act. "All jokes aside," she said reading it, smiling, and placing the note in her pocket. "It is just a natural part of being an adult. What is the big deal?"

"I think we all, well, some of us know," Rose interjected, "what the big deal is. The bottom line is you develop a soul tie with that other person. You don't want a soul tie with someone you barely know. And unless the other has fallen off the face of the earth, you are going to see that person again. I say just wait. It ain't all that anyway."

"Now, you had me up until the very last part," added Oxygen. "But for the sake of time and the company, I won't go there. Plus, it's not my turn yet," he said smiling. "Can we make sure we dog ear this conversation for later?"

"Maybe if y'all weren't so stingy with it--," Helium started, but retreated when he noticed Linden's stern face. "Anyway, I would have to agree with Ms. uh...," he said looking over at the name on the rose. "Daisy. We have the choice to do it, but the consequences are too great when you make the wrong decision."

"So, Helium, 'being stingy with it' is your response?" Linden asked.

"The hardest part would be waiting," said Helium. "The waiting can keep me guessing, just don't tease a brothah."

"Waiting patiently while trying to live a happy contented single life," said Iris. "It's discouraging talking to Him and getting nowhere.

I understand that His Word says, 'he who finds a wife...' I'm tired of waiting for him to find me. And is the dude even looking?"

"There are too many restrictions placed on us," said Rose. "I understand Believers have them for a reason. The situation, sometimes, was a lot better when I didn't care."

"I would have to also agree with Ms. Iced Tea over there," said Oxygen. "It is hard finding someone our age that you want to be equally yoked with. Now that I think of it, I can think of a few things we have to let slide in order to be married."

"I would have to say, wannabe matchmakers thinking the only thing he and I have in common is that we're both single and serve Him, is all that's needed for a match," said Lily. "I mean there's more to a relationship. What else would make him a good match...for me?"

"Don't you think that serving him would be a good place to start?" Calcium challenged. "For two people to be on equal footing and build upon that solid ground? They provided the foundation, now it's our turn to build the house that His love will build. Consequently, my response to the ice breaker would be all of the above. Finding someone to date, that's a Believer, and is up for a good concert is hard. The restrictions on who we should date and what we can do on that date gets a little too confining. And then she has got to be sweet enough to meet moms, but fine enough to show off to my boys."

"For starters, y'all drag your heels too much, for too long," Violet said flippantly. "The process should not take you five years of looking at me like I am something good to eat, before making your move. I feel as though I'm wasting my time waiting for you. And time is ticking if dude wants kids.

"And I do understand the purpose of corporate dating," she continued. "But how do you go from group dating to 'let's get married?' I want to get to know you as the individual you, not the 'friend of a friend' you. To add even more to this, the hardest part would be patience. How long do you have to corporately date before you make a decision?"

"I feel as long as it takes," Zinc responded. "Before you get on my case," he winced from Violet, "let me get to my answer of the icebreaker. Violet mentioned children. It is really hard to connect with a woman whose goals are compatible with mine, especially when you don't want kids."

"The hardest part about being single and serving Him would be the gratuitous use of the word 'submit,'" Breeze admitted. "Some men just want to take that word, too far."

"The Word does say, 'Wives submit yourselves to your husbands,'" Sodium added. "Y'all have instructions."

"You have instructions!" boomed a few of the Flowers.

"Men have a Ph.D. equivalent in studying that verse," said Breeze. "Have y'all even looked at what's before and after the verse?"

"This sounds like the perfect segue to the discussion portion of the evening," Zenobia interrupted. "Let me remind everyone this is indeed a *discussion*. All minds clear?" She paused until everyone agreed. "Good. Gentlemen, who would like to respond first?"

"First of all, yes, I've read it," said Sodium. "But there needs to be order in the household. I hope my wife will understand that I *will* have the final say."

Before the argument went to a new level, Rose spoke up. "You also understand that you will have to hear her point of view before making any final say."

"I guess, but I'm not one to deal with a woman with too much mouth, anyway, so...," he shrugged.

"Too much mouth...please," Rose spat. "If you did wrong, acted the wrong way, or said the wrong thing especially at the wrong time, a grown woman will let you know! I don't want *your* final say to mess up *my* money, *my* credit, *my* family relationships, or anything else I value."

"And a good woman would know when to do it," Violet chimed in. "We are not going to embarrass you in front of company, just as you should not embarrass us. Are we supposed to let you walk all over us because He made you first?"

"I just come across too many women who are attitudinal," Sodium said with a sly smile.

"Here we go," someone sighed.

"If that's what *you* come across, that's probably what you attract," Lily boomed surprising all the Flowers at the table.

Zenobia must have recognized the increased blood pressure and quickly defused the situation. "*Gentlemen*, does anyone else have any insight to Hyacinth's question?"

"Before the ladies get mad, I do agree with my brother...to an extent," said Lithium. "My job as a future husband is to protect my future wife and family. So, if I feel that she is spending too much time away from us, I will let her know. In all decisions, she will have a say, and we will discuss it. I will, however, have the *final* say. If it turns out to be the wrong decision, I will yield to her the next time. Is that fair?"

The Flowers agreed to the statement with head nods, Mmm hmms, and other verbal approvals.

"My question is," Helium sighed, "why are y'all in such a rush to establish a relationship? It's like y'all wanna move from date to wife in 60 seconds!"

"She was probably tired of the title: friend, baby's mama, or worse no acknowledgement of her place in his life until *he* felt it was convenient," said Petunia. "Men really need to be upfront with their intentions. If you want to just be friends and you ain't even thinking about getting married...*to me*... any time soon, say so."

"Look, all except one at this table is 35 and over," added Violet. "None of us here has the time to play games. If either party can accept the other's intentions, good. If not, keep it moving. But don't waste a chick's time, pump out two young'uns later, and now she is stuck with the seeds of a man who didn't want her in the first place. If you are perfectly content being a player, find yourself a willing playmate, and let the woman who wants and deserve a relationship to move on."

"What would make you go from 'date to *next*'?" asked Iris. "What are your deal breakers? The object of your desire has everything you want.

What is that one habit, trait, or quirk that makes you say, 'nope, I'm not going to able to do it'?"

"Girlfriend has got to know how to cook," said Calcium. "Our office had a potluck. And the young lady I had my eye on volunteered to make my favorite dish: mac-n-cheese. She was a really nice girl, carried herself well, educated, common sense, had a great sense of humor, and was stacked," he gestured. "She was everything I prayed for until she served the burned mac-n-cheese at the pot luck. How can you serve your man burned mac-n-cheese?"

"Was the top burned or the whole thing?" Tulip asked breaking away from her iced tea.

"Everybody else said underneath was bangin'. I just could not look her way no more when she served burned food."

"You do realize the operative portion of this equation was 'underneath was banging.' Does that mean anything to you?" Breeze asked feeling sorry for the young lady in question.

"Look, if she can make a mean mac-n-cheese, then she has my heart. And can she also cook something other than 'honey mustard,' 'lemon pepper,' or 'baked' whatever? And someone has got to fry me some chicken, please," he pleaded shaking his head.

"We are trying to keep *us* healthy. Don't you listen to the health concerns black folks have today?"

"Yeah, but don't you know that everything is fine...in moderation?"

"Who on earth wants the house smelling like fried meat?"

"*ME*," the men including Linden boomed in unison.

"I want to circle back to Ms. Mac-n-Cheese," said Daisy. "You didn't give her a chance to try again? She probably didn't want to disappoint the pot luck committee, showing up without a dish."

"While disappointing me in the process."

"Good grief," Breeze said in a huff. "Did she even know she disappointed you? Did she even know that you were checking her out? Listen, y'all just finished saying that *we* need to let some stuff slide; this is a prime example of what *you* need to let slide. Give the sistah a chance!"

"Weaves," stated Sodium changing the subject. "Why hide what He made you?"

"Even if it makes her feel good with the hair texture, style, sometimes color that she wants," added Rose.

"I respect all of that. She just would not be the woman for me."

"What if your wife loses all or sections of her hair?" asked Petunia.

"If it's out of need rather than want, I can definitely respect that."

"Chipped nails and ashy feet," confessed Oxygen. "I will take clear or unpolished nails over a woman trying to hold on to the remains of her French manicure. And I cannot stand a woman whose feet looks like she's been kickin' flour! There are plenty of products to win against the battle of the ash, find one. And if money's tight, bacon grease works wonders."

"Lemme find out we gotta country brothah at the table!"

"I have a low tolerance for nonsense," Zinc offered coolly.

"Drama or good ole fashion goofiness," Violet questioned.

"Both actually, I am a straight-laced guy. I do not like drama, nor do I tolerate excuses. And I also do not like--"

"Gee whiz, what do you like?" Daisy asked.

"You asked for deal breakers, I'm putting mine out there."

"With a vengeance," she said with annoyance. "And just how many women appreciate this 'no-nonsense' demeanor?"

"I'm in this class, just like you."

"Well, that leaves me out, 'cause I'm goofy as all get out," Petunia said flippantly.

"Actually, regarding your outside appearance, you are not my type," said Zinc coolly. "I like a curvy woman," he said looking over at Tulip. Petunia's eyes widened and mouthed to Breeze, '*Did you see that?*' Breeze slowly nodded. However, Tulip did not notice and kept to her iced tea.

"Finding a woman within my pedigree," said Helium. A chorus of 'what' was expressed throughout the room. "Listen, I find that influences, political views, and educational background are all just as important when we talk about being equally yoked. I feel the need to take it to another level."

"More like an *uppity* level," said Petunia.

"Actually, ladies, I understand what he is saying," Violet rescued. Helium thanked her, but she made a motion to continue. "However, a lot of men are asking us to lower our standards, just to be in a relationship. This sentiment should go both ways."

"All I'm saying is my brother married outside of his pedigree, and nothing came about the marriage except chaos."

"But men are always attracted to chaos," Iris added. "And what is up with this pedigree nonsense? What is she, a dog?"

"Both parties need to experience the same social class, upbringing, breeding," he said.

"You had me until you mentioned breeding part," said Breeze. "So, I guess you can't marry a crackhead, huh?"

"No, my wife-to-be would need to be able to speak at least three languages," said Helium. "That would be rather difficult while being a crackhead."

"Well, if she is to be a part of *your* pedigree, that would make her a cocaine user," she joked. Uneasy laughs, head shaking and a few of 'you ain't right, Hyacinth' spread across the room.

"Okay, let us move on," Zenobia suggested uneasily. "Lithium, I think you are the last one that still needs to respond," she said playfully pinching Breeze on the arm.

"A cussin' woman is a deal breaker for me. I can't handle four and five letter words flying out her mouth. I'm like 'how can you eat with that potty mouth'?"

"Would you end the relationship even if she said a few choice words at an, uh, opportune time?" asked Daisy.

"Now that would be something I would let slide. And ladies, I have to add this: I cannot stand a woman who cannot keep a clean car! I needed to take the bus one day, and this really nice young lady I worked with, offered me a ride. I saw her car and I was like 'no, that's all right.' Under my breath, I was like, 'just go wash your car.' I thank everyone at this table for listening to my public service announcement."

"Flowers?" Zenobia interrupted. "Exhibit A," she said pointing to Lithium's direction.

"So, ladies, what are your deal breakers?" Lithium asked.

"Too many to list," Lily quickly responded.

"We've bared our soul and y'all attacked," Calcium added. "Grant us the same courtesy."

"Ladies, I have this," Zenobia stated flipping the pages of her notebook. She ran down their list of deal breakers, as the men sat stunned at each response.

"Nappy chest hair?" asked Zinc. "Although I haven't received any complaints, some of us can't help that." The men, including Linden were shaking their heads in disbelief.

"Her arms must've been slathered in aloe before touchin' ya," laughed Petunia. "'Cuz you ain't cuttin' her with all that steel wool! On that note, I cannot believe you told them that, Ms. Zenobia."

"Men express their visual deal breakers on a regular basis. I find it only fitting that we express ours," Zenobia said calmly. "Next question?"

"My question is, how long would you wait to be intimate or are you willing to wait for marriage?" asked Daisy. "Or...what is your timeframe before you feel the need to start stepping out?" she asked gingerly.

"The game has got to be right," said Calcium.

"In other words, you try on the shoes before you buy them."

"You have to. I want the whole package. Not because it looks good, or is in style, or the price was right. It has to feel good and be comfortable."

"Okay, so, the game wasn't right. You refused to stick around to fix it," Iris recounted. "This is sounding like the macaroni and cheese dilemma. I cannot understand why you cannot give a girl a chance. Keep in mind gentlemen, if she is indeed within your *pedigree*, Ms. Intellectual will take a class to improve her skills and her efforts will be tried out on her next, the better, patient, worthy of another chance man."

"Well, she bettah brush up on her skills, 'cause if she won't, somebody else is willin'," said Helium.

"Please stop threatenin' and move on to that somebody else," snapped Rose.

"Let me ask this another way," suggested Daisy. "How long would *you* wait to be intimate?"

"After a suitable amount of time has passed," Zinc answered. "But we will have a discussion and understanding. And once we get to that point, it will be on."

"It would depend on where we are in our relationship," Oxygen added.

"Well," Sodium added. "I'm a believer and I assume that since we all serve Him at this table, we should all agree to wait until marriage."

"Okay, fine," said Rose. "If you are willing to wait for marriage, how long are you willing to date, court, and if she is indeed the one, ask for her hand?"

"As long as it takes," Sodium answered. "I do not want to jump into marriage. So if it takes one, two, six, or ten years, then fine. I've waited this long."

"One or two years I can understand, but six or ten?" asked Violet. "We could afford to wait when we were in our twenties. We would need to get off the pot, now that we are mid-thirties, forties...fifties."

"That's why I want a woman in her twenties that can afford to wait," added Helium.

"Ladies, I rest my case," Breeze said thumbing in Helium's direction.

"What do you mean by that?"

"Men in their thirties cannot 'get with' a woman in her thirties."

"That's because y'all are in such a heated rush to get the ring. Again, why can't y'all wait?"

"Wait-for-what?" Daisy asked with clinched teeth. "At a certain point, you know whether or not you want to marry this girl. Whatcha waitin' for?"

"I'm sorry," Iris said. "I need to get back to Helium's statement about marrying a chick in her twenties. They are a dime a dozen, waiting especially for someone like you. Why are you in this class? As far as I'm concerned, you could have saved your little money, go back downstairs, sit at the bar, flash the credit card, and the twenty somethings should flock to you."

"See fellas, this is what I was talking about," Helium bellowed. "Lemme ask you a question--"

"Everyone please, let's all calm down," Linden interrupted the brewing debate. "Everyone is here because all of us have been wounded or disillusioned in some way, shape, or form."

"Except him," Iris interrupted. "Sounds to me like he has the answer to his problems...and they're waitin' downstairs."

"The reason why we men can't get with a woman in her thirties is because y'all got too much mouth!"

"That's it!" Every Flower except Lily shot up from their chairs startling the rest of the table. Tulip quickly moved out of the way of the cross fire, taking her iced tea. Six different reasons explaining the need for necessary input was thrown at Sodium. Zenobia and Linden let the scene linger for only a moment, before making an attempt to control the situation.

"Ladies, please, let us all take our seats before Maggianno's calls the police," Zenobia said placing a guiding hand on their shoulders. "Iris, Petunia, Daisy please, remove your pretty manicured fingers from his handsome face."

Finally defusing the situation, everyone including Zenobia took their seats. "We expected tonight's discussion would be...lively," she said in a calm huff. "However, this is not *Thursday Night Smack Down!* If you have questions, please ask them. Tonight's goal is to gain insight on what the other is thinking. We understand completely the difficulty of meeting and dating. However, none of us get anywhere with a shouting match. Agreed? Ladies?" The Flowers mumbled their agreement.

"Gentlemen are we in agreement?" Linden asked sternly.

"She started it," Helium said playfully thumbing at Breeze.

"Watch me finish it," she responded playfully.

"I'm just playing...jokes," he said while trying to shield playful blows. The men finally agreed.

"Okay," Linden sighed. "Next question?"

"I've noticed a lot of married men are not wearing their rings," Iris stepped in. "If and when you do get married, will you wear one...and keep it on?"

"I believe in the tradition of a wedding ring, as long as she adheres to the tradition of taking my last name," answered Calcium. "There should be no reason why she wouldn't take my name, especially if she has brothers."

"So, if she has a problem taking your name?"

"Then she is not ready to get married...at least not to me. Don't get me wrong, I do understand there are some circumstances as to why she would hyphenate or use her surname as her middle name. But my last name needs to be in her title, somewhere. Actually, this is a discussion the couple really needs to have before they get married."

"And if her ring is bangin', mine needs to be bangin', too," added Helium with a sense of entitlement. "A simple band of gold, silver or platinum will not do." The ladies sat around the table staring at him in amazement. "What?" he asked. They shook their heads in unison and made a gesture for the next one, any one, to speak.

"I have a question. Why do women insist on trying to change a man?" Zinc asked. "Don't they know by now we are who we are? Love us or leave us alone."

"I'll take this one," Petunia volunteered. "On behalf of the ladies at this table, we know that a woman cannot and should not have to change a man." Streams of gratitude, praise, and 'that's what I'm talkin' 'bout' came from the men.

"Hold on now, if you are cheap, a player, a *beep*, or any other un- desirable quality you ain't willing to change, no woman should have to figure it out before too much time has been invested. You need to find someone that either matches that quality or has enough grace to put up with it happily. We promise to believe you, if you show us the real you. And if we don't like what we see, we are also strong enough to show you the door. So gentlemen, do you agree with our thought process?"

"I can agree if the same applies to women," stated Lithium.

"Of course it does."

"However," Iris decided to step in. "Men are going to try to make the relationship work if the outside package is fine, am I correct? Because you will put up with the madness or make an attempt to change, if she just looks good."

"You ladies really need to understand that it's more than that," added Calcium. A chorus of 'since when' came from women of the table. "Okay, I admit, being fine was the main requirement in my twenties. Y'all were just as shallow."

"But women grow out of that...for the most part," added Rose. "Men are visual."

"And we like what we like. I like a woman who is stacked, but I will find out if she's smart soon after."

"Does that *really* matter to you?"

"Absolutely," said Calcium proudly. "You don't want just anyone raising your children. And you ladies also need to understand that it's more than just looks, because if that were the case, every fine woman including yourselves at this table would be married." The Flowers actually sat smiling, taking in that last statement. Even Tulip paused from her iced tea.

"I see your lovely point," said Violet. "I truly do. But is the man with the tunnel vision actually pursuing their type, ready to get married? It seems as if most men are in eternal playa mode. Why can't you see and experience what you like, pick one, and stick with it? What is the problem?"

"Has it ever been that easy for you to find someone and stick around?" asked Lithium.

"First of all, I shouldn't be the one doing the finding," Daisy said flippantly. "Men are to *discern* and *find* while we are to *shine* and *be found*! *You* hunt, *we* are the prize. Let me make this last point clear: *we* are the prize, not *you*! That's just *my* public service announcement. Anyway, once the two find each other, it needs to be on. Now, if you are still on the hunt for something better, at least let a woman know. Do not waste her time getting her hopes up and passing up possible opportunities."

"But both parties have to be willing," sang Calcium.

"Okay, understood," Breeze interjected. "Picture it: she's exactly what you are looking for inside, as well as out. However, give or take a few attributes, we all agree to let a few things slide," the table agreed, laughing. "You can appreciate her flaws and she can deal with yours. A sufficient time has passed, depending on your comfort level, what do you do?"

"Wait, gentlemen, before you answer," Daisy interrupted. "What would be *your* timeframe?"

"Ladies, for the one hundredth time, it's gonna take as long as it's gonna take," Sodium said heatedly.

"And that right there *is* the problem," Rose said. "It is taking too long for a lot of men to make that decision. Maybe the question should be *what* would it take for you to make a decision?" The men at the table sat silent, appearing as if they were pondering the last statement. The Flowers waited patiently, appearing pleased with Rose's latest chess move.

"I think you know as well as we do, making a decision of this magnitude is difficult," Oxygen said finally. "No one at this table wants to make the same mistakes our friends, siblings, or some of our parents made. We all want to do this right, the first time."

"Agreed," the Flowers said in unison.

"You're still blowing over the point," Breeze said exhaustedly. "What would it take, what would make you want to take that trip down the aisle? Our parents, family, and friends made that decision, it's now your turn. And do you actually want it to be your turn?"

"I'm sure that is why all of us are in this class," said Zinc. "We are all here to actually sit down, take a moment, figure out what we want, and what to do next. And to answer your last question, I really don't know what it would take or make me want to say, 'I do.' I know you ladies are eager to be married, but..."

Objections were made from a few of the women at the table. "We have two that really want to be married, one that does not, and five of us are still undecided," Rose reported. "I'm sure the numbers may have changed after this event."

"I think it's honest that you don't know," Lily added. "However, if you are in a loving committed relationship that involves giving and taking, the 'waits' and 'we'll sees' just won't cut it anymore. And give reasons for those vague responses, because if you don't, someone is wasting their time."

"And whose fault is that," spat Helium. "She stayed in the relationship just so she could have a man!"

"You stayed in the relationship just so you could steadily get some," Lily shot back. Zenobia and the Flowers sat stunned at Lily's last statement.

"I just do not know why you women are so darn determined to get that ring and that title," he shrugged.

"Have you not listened to anything that was said at this table?"

"I heard a bunch of 'why wait' and what would 'trap' a brothah!"

"Trap?" Tulip asked finally chiming in. "It's funny that you cannot deal with bitter women, when you are the poster child for the bitter brothah."

"I do believe it was my boy Sodium who could not deal with bitter women," he said calmly. "I liked you better when you sat silently sipping your iced tea."

"And we would like *you* better, if you'd let grown folks talk," snapped Iris.

"I have a question for the ladies," said Zinc diffusing the next squabble. "What do *you* ladies, want? What would make you want to cook for a man? What would make you stay and deal with our flaws and all? And I especially want to hear from that quiet one nursing her iced tea. We haven't really heard her opinion, since the ice breaker." Tulip blushed. Her dimples attracted more attention, as she sheepishly smiled.

"We'll get to Ms. Tulip in a minute," said Violet. "I want to start by pointing out what we need. If we start here, then we can really express what we want. And don't get me wrong, this too, is not a lump need. Some women need more or unfortunately, less. But for starters, be a Christian. And we are not just talking about following a religion. You need to want to serve the Lord in and out of church. If you want to be lord of the house, you need to follow the Lord and listen to what He is saying to you.

"Now that's out of the way, we need you to have your 'stuff' together. That means financially, physically, and mentally before pursuing us. And yes, we still want to be pursued properly. Have a 401(k), savings account or a cushion to fall back on if you experience a minor setback *and* plan to retire.

"Have your house in order or at least work on it before I am in the picture. Because if we enter in the picture, helping you, as well as loving you, and you leave us for another, you just made a contribution to the 'bitter sister' surplus. We need you to be upfront with your feelings. If you don't want a commitment, kids, to be married or whatever, be upfront about it."

"It's not easy to discuss 'not wanting kids' during dates," said Zinc.

"Do you not want kids?" asked Daisy.

"No, and I don't want her to have them either."

"So, after an appropriate amount of time has passed, how do your dates react when you tell them about your vasectomy?" Petunia asked.

"Vasectomy?" Zinc asked disgustedly. "Even though that's a personal question, I never had a vasectomy. Why should I?"

"Because you just said you do not want kids. Why not seal the deal to be sure?"

"Can't a man can change his mind?"

"Sure he can," said Lily. "But make it clear that you do not want kids, period. Otherwise, you sound like you don't want kids...*with her.*"

"Unfortunately, that's what it sounds like, especially to the women within my desired age range. Like I said before, it is difficult to find and date a woman whose goals don't mesh with mine."

"My thing is, I don't want children now, nor do I want him to have kids, either," Iris chimed in. "Dealing with a man with kids means another woman's hands are rightfully and deservedly in my man's pocket. But I digress. Instead of saying, 'I don't want kids,' just say 'children are not mandatory.' If you are physically able, having children should be an *option*. Because if God wants that child to be born, He will make it happen. However, if you're that adamant about your decision, then you need to put your money where your mouth is," she said making scissor gestures.

"I think I'll just change my statement, thanks," he said crossing his legs.

"Is there anything else we need to add before we get to the wants, ladies?" asked Violet.

"Yes, one more thing," Rose added. "I need men to be men. There are certain times when we really need you to just 'man-up.'"

"At the same time ladies, we need you to *let* a man be a man. If we say we got your back, then we got you," said Lithium. "If there's a situation that needs to be handled, we need you to trust that we will handle it. There are times when we need you to take control of the wheel. But we still need you to make us feel like we are still the captain of the ship."

"Even when the ship is sinking?"

"Even more so," Zinc answered. "Anybody else? Dimples?" Tulip shook her head trying to hide her smile and dimples. She failed miserably.

"Ladies, I think it would be easier if we go around the room and state what we want in a few words or less," Zenobia suggested. "Tulip, you go first since you are in high demand this evening."

"I want someone who will be into the relationship, as much as I am," she said finally sitting down her glass. "He needs to be in the relationship whole heartedly."

"I want a relationship where we enhance each other," said Daisy. "We need to be better for each because we are together. But at the same time, he should take me as I am and I should accept him for who and where he is."

"It's the 'love me or leave me alone' syndrome," said Helium.

"Exactly," she responded. "Let us not forget, he must be willing to be down for a good time...eventually," she said slyly.

"Speaking of which, I want a man that I can have a good time with and has a sense of humor," Breeze added. "We need to want to relish each other's company. I want you to enjoy my company, over kicking it with your boys."

"We still gotta kick it with our boys, though," said Lithium. "Preferably in a man cave or the nearest sports bar."

"And trust me, we want you to," said Breeze. "We actually need you to still hang with your boys, just as we can still hang out with our girls. But when we are down to our last $5, cheering for the Ravens because they are beating the Steelers, when no one is in the mood, or we're snowed in, we need to be each other's preferred company."

"I still want to be pursued," said Lily. "That shows me you saw something within me that piqued your interest. They are too many of us having to do the pursuing. Aren't men supposed to be the hunters?"

"We are, but I actually wish *more* women would make the first move. I find that very attractive," said Lithium. "Don't even think Imma let you slide with that Ravens vs. the Steelers comment, uh, Hyacinth!"

"Please, go somewhere and wave your little yellow towel," Breeze said jokingly. "Anyway, your lot in life is to man up, hunt, and seek. Ours is to wait *patiently* and be found."

"Me and my yellow towel will *find* you *patient-leh*...after class," Lithium joked back.

"Well, I never had any problems with women coming to me," bragged Helium.

"Nowadays, we don't have to," Sodium chimed in. "Good brothahs like us are in high demand." The Flowers just sighed and shook their heads.

"Yeah, but y'all in this class, so, git-ta-huntin'," said Petunia. "Anyway, I'm looking for someone to do 'stuff' with. He has to want and be able to go to concerts, sports events, crab feasts, the movies, whatever. I can go with my girls, but I'd rather go with my man."

"This may sound odd at first. I want him to be the 'doer,'" said Iris. Everyone at the table looked at her curiously.

"Instead of being the 'do-ee?'" Calcium asked gingerly.

"What I mean is," she interrupted smiling sheepishly. "I have tendency to be a dreamer. I want someone to encourage us to the next level. If we're both dreamers, nothing will get done."

"I want someone who is willing to walk with me instead of eight steps ahead," said Rose. "Either you are with me or not. That act feels very arrogant to me. I don't need a bodyguard. I want a loving protector by my side.

"Now, that you heard our 'wants,' how prepared are you to be a husband and potentially a father?" asked Rose. "Did you learn or experience firsthand what it takes to be a good husband?"

"If I may interject here for a moment, Rose, that is an excellent question," said Linden. "One of the many reasons why my wife and I are here is to prepare and show you what makes for a successful relationship and union. As I said before, people are wounded. However, everyone here is doing something about these wounds, not just talking about it, but fixing it. You are striving for the next level, where ever the journey takes you. This is an excellent place to end the evening's discussion. In a few words or less, what qualities do you possess that makes you a good spouse? Rose, since you asked the question, let's start with you."

"I know how to treat my man without being his mama," she simply.

Oxygen started to speak, when Sodium interjected. "I think I can speak for all the men at this table that we are, each in our own way, good men. We have good jobs, never been married, have had some form of higher educational training, we do not live with our parents, and have a lot of love to give."

"That's fine and yes, you just described everyone at this table," Violet said. "However, you brought up the key point, 'each in our own way.' What makes *you* a good husband? What makes *me* a good wife? What makes you that someone she or he wouldn't want to live without? And not just what you are looking for. We already discussed that six ways from Sunday."

"My parents have an amazing relationship," Oxygen finally said. "They showed us kids, by example, the love and respect they have for each other. They know their role in the relationship. They played upon their strengths and accepted each other's quirks. My siblings and I find it odd, yet reassuring, that we still need to call first because we don't want to go into a mild state of hysterical blindness...again." The members of the table laughed. "My firsthand knowledge of a good marriage is what I bring to the table."

"Quite simply, I know my place as a willing helpmate," Lily said still laughing. "Hysterical blindness?"

"I recognize the need of taking care of home goes beyond bringing home a paycheck," Calcium said while finishing his laughter. "I'm an auto mechanic. So, my future bride will need to understand in order for me to pay for the date nights, trips, an occasional surprise bottle of Marc Jacobs, as well as the bills, there will be some long days and weekends at the auto shop. And since I am willing, ready, and able to take care of her, she will do the same, like having my bath ready with bubbles and *Lava* soap."

"I got your bubbles, soap, and a scrub brush," Violet laughed with the rest of the class. "I don't mean to sound arrogant, but look at me," Violet said. "What man would not want this as his wife?"

"Yeah, we see ya," said Lithium. "Too many brothahs get caught up chasing after fine."

Violet smiled and whispered a thank you. "But if the wife looks good, so does the husband, correct?" The men at the table nodded their heads in agreement.

"I'm learning how to compromise," admitted Zinc. "As an only child, compromising is a bit difficult."

"Zinc, I can really relate to the compromise and the 'only child' syndrome," said Breeze. "But I also bring balance to the relationship. It's very hard for me to do extremes. Among other things, I have a tendency to balance out those around me."

"Besides the fact that I have a great smile, a pretty pair of gams, a caring heart, and wicked sense of humor, I honestly do not know what qualifies me 'as a good wife' anymore because it's just not appreciated," Iris said solemnly. "Unfortunately, two of those qualities are constantly stepped on, and the rest are overlooked."

"Iris, you as well as every woman at this table, knows you have something to offer, sharing four of them," Zenobia added. Iris sighed, folded her arms and shook her head. "Helium, what do you bring to the table?"

"Not to cut you off, Helium, I want to get back to Iris," said Calcium. "Real men do not 'overlook' a great smile and certainly not a great pair of legs. You must not smile that often or wear pants too much."

"I smile when the occasion calls for it. I'm not going to walk around like some grinning idiot for someone like you to think I've totally lost it!"

"What do you mean 'someone like me?' You don't even know me."

"What are the chances that you or any other brothah would ever get to *know* me?"

"Personally, I think you have the wrong man."

"Unfortunately, I don't," she said quietly while getting up from the table. She excused herself and quickly walked out of the door. Breeze started to get up, but Zenobia stopped her.

"Everyone, please continue with the discussion," she said removing herself from the table after Iris.

"I'd give her the time of day, minus the drama. She's really cute. Just a little too close to the edge," Calcium said to the table. Breeze smiled and made a mental note to let Iris know. She suspected something other than tonight's discussion was troubling her.

"Let's just say I will take great pride keeping things interesting," Daisy said trying to lighten the mood.

"I am so intrigued," mumbled Helium. "Despite what I said tonight, I do have my priorities in the right place."

"Where did that statement come from?" Rose asked. "And where was this mentality during the entire evening?"

"I apologize if I offended anyone. And that's my second qualification. I am at the point where I want to be married. Therefore, I know how to *eventually* apologize to be happy and not just right...within reason of course."

"I put Him first in everything I do," said Lithium. "I know how to make good decisions that benefit me, as well as my future bride. I'm also willing and able to make decisions with her. And I'm proud to admit, I love to snuggle. Now, I will hold your hand in the summer because it's too hot for cuddlin'. But come fall and winter, it's on!"

"I respect my brother dearly," said Sodium. "I just cannot understand why that makes you a good husband."

Lithium started to answer, but a chorus of 'I can' came from every woman at the table. "I want to know why this man is still single," said Daisy. The Flowers agreed.

Tulip put her iced tea down ready to answer. "I know how to cook and entertain."

"Now that's a good answer," said Sodium to Tulip. "I love to go out and do things. Now, I can go places with my boys anytime. But I want to see the world with her."

"I have the gift of administration," Petunia answered. "My household will be organized. Even though, I will have the final say, I know how to make him *feel* like it was his decision."

"As soon as my wife returns, we can close in prayer," Linden said standing up. "It's about 10:30 pm and I am sure the staff wants to clean up. Thank you, everyone for brining your opinions and insight to the table. Yes, the discussions got a little intense. However, I hope that we provided a forum for you to express what was on your heart." As if on cue, Zenobia and Iris walked back in. Breeze strained her neck to see if Iris was okay. She believed she was, since she returned to the group. "Wife, I've thanked our classes for their insight this evening. Was there anything we need to add?"

"Yes, ladies, please remain in the room for few moments after prayer. Thank you gentlemen, for sharing your thoughts and providing answers to my Flower's questions," she said clapping and encouraged her Flowers to do the same. "And do not forget to take your belongings, rose, and gift. Husband, I do believe we are ready to close."

Linden said the closing prayer and the classes got up to gather their things and said their good byes. Tulip excused herself before meeting with Zenobia. "All that iced tea is starting to kick in," she whispered to anyone within earshot. Breeze noticed Calcium making a beeline to talk to Iris. She smiled and hugged him, before finally making his way out of the door.

The room looked emptier, much bigger once the men finally left. Tulip finally made her way back in and Zenobia instructed them all to sit in the closest chairs. "First of all, I am thanking you personally for sharing tonight. I hope you received a few moments of clarity to your questions and concerns that real men should be able to provide. Just be sure to keep it light, if you find yourself in this forum again." She paused, smiling to herself. "Ladies, tonight will be our last meeting together until May. The time has come to put feet to those prayers, petitions, and everything you've learned in and outside of class. I understand that some of you are sticking with the Christmas classes that I recommended, which is absolutely wonderful. If I am not mistaken, you are rotating the classes?" Zenobia laughed to herself and then continued.

"Please rely on your sisters within this room to help you get through those times when things get a little out of control. The Word does say, 'to not give up meeting with one another,' so make sure you continue to do so. I want each of you to shine extra bright these next couple of months, never forgetting that you have a purpose. Words cannot express how excited I am for each of you.

"Your assignment," Zenobia paused, appearing a little emotional, "I want you to live the life brimming with expectation, hope, and serious purposeful happiness. In addition to that radiant light that each of you are shinning, I want you to exude joy that no one can take away. And be sure not to let *an-y-one* take it away from you, do you understand?" she asked delicately wiping away her tears. "Now go, go bring momma back some good juicy stories," she said laughing over her remaining tears. "And we will reconvene in May."

The Flowers, wiping their own tears rose from their chairs to hug their instructor and each other. Another closing prayer was said and the Flowers gathered up their wrapped gifts, pretty pink roses, and belongings and made their way to the door.

"One thing, Ms. Zenobia?" Violet asked. "What *was* your type if that fine piece of silver gray haired man wasn't it?"

"Trust me, that was not what I went to school with," she said laughing.

"Ladies, I need to stop and get my niece a birthday gift," Lily said hurriedly, checking her watch.

"It's kind of late, do you want one of us to go with you," offered Daisy.

"No, no. I should be fine," she said making a bee line for the door.

"Well, ring the phone when you get home," said Rose. "Don't let me have to hunt you down."

"I won't," she yelled back.

"Hold it, a birthday gift? Where is she going to get a birthday gift at this hour?"

"Probably at Borders, to get her niece something educational."

"Or, she wants to get a little education on the benefits of a particular *element*," Daisy speculated.

"Are you serious?" Tulip asked.

"Are you blind," Violet questioned. "And where were you tonight? You were barely near the conversation."

"You mean the debate? Things are going really well with Smith," she responded happily. "The questions I have so far, he's already answered."

"Smith? Who's Smith?"

"You mean *Chef* Smith?"

Tulip nodded happily and the entire room squealed with happiness congratulating her. "My baby," Rose said in mocked tears while giving her a hug.

"I cannot wait to see what he has planned for Valentine's Day...*for me*," Tulip said shockingly. "Hence the dress," she said holding up the Stein Mart bag.

"And I assume everything else is in order?" Breeze asked.

"It may be a little granny, but my matching set is absolutely sexy," she said slyly. "However, we both feel it is too soon for the situation to even get to that point. So, if it peeks through, he'll be impressed and hopefully intrigued. But aren't we losing precious time? We need to see what is going on with Lily," Tulip said starting for the door. The Flowers agreed and started to follow.

"Wait, we cannot all go. I am sure whatever the reason, our Lily will be fine," Zenobia reassured. "But you know, Borders does make a great cup of coffee. And I sure could use a cup. Ladies, shall we take one more field trip?"

20

Sweet & Spicy Reggae

"Secret, did you bring the hula hoop?" Breeze asked while opening her trunk, realizing something was missing from her mental check list.

"Nope, she ain't apart of this," she spat with her hand on one hip, surveying the items for the party. "It is happily sitting in my garage waiting for you. And speaking of which, we need you to hurry up and find a husband, 'cause my nieces bypass the bikes and go straight to the hula hoop when they come over. It's getting a little weird."

"Tuesday is the next bride," she pleaded. "It's her turn."

"Her posse knows nothing about the hula hoop or would even begin to appreciate the significance behind it," said her friend Moshi. She and Moshie have been friends since they both started teaching. The petite, freckled faced, naturally styled redheaded English teacher was the first within her circle of coworker friends to get married. And that is where the passing of the hula hoop started. "The next one perfecting her skills and 'neck workin' with the hula hoop will be you. We ain't handin' down nothin' *to* her *ta*-day!"

"And I would like to point out for the record that you are wrong for introducing our little secret," added Breeze's other coworker sistah friend, Wren. Secret introduced the Caucasian gothic-like drama teacher with green cat-like eyes to Breeze after a night of much needed rum punch and reggae music. She, too, had her moment with the hula hoop.

"I do believe that I am giving them my own special spin on the scandalous tradition," Breeze said proudly. "My main concern is to keep tonight interesting...in a public place. Now if they want to, they could run with it. But Britt would be the last bride from that circle, so I do believe the tradition is safe...for now. Besides, they don't know what all went on or what was in that bag given at Secret's, um, shower," she said smiling. "Seriously, the Dollar Store is just down the street. Go get me one, please? I have to get the room set up."

"Breeze, we are standing our ground on this," said Secret. "The three of us are here to support you, be nosy, and of course to get some good Chinese food. The tradition of the hula hoop will remain within this circle. Passing on the hula hoop to someone not within our circle violates the sanctity of our 'Bride-Be-Ready' premise. We will let the rest of your little rendition slide, because we realize every bride should be ready," said Secret.

"At all times," her friends sang in unison.

"And once you are done with your unnecessary obligations," Secret continued, "you will be coming with us to the Crossroads for some serious reggae and rum punch. In the meantime, give me a box, my instructions, and let's get this party started." Breeze reluctantly smiled, handed Secret the box she was holding, gave out a few gift bags to the others, and instructed them on the seating and schedule.

"Girl, this party is going to be two hours, too long," Moshi ached.

Breeze and her friends walked in with boxes and bags and were greeted by the seating hostess. She smiled and showed them to the party room. Three large sized round tables of eight were waiting. She rearranged the seating for two of the tables to accommodate 10 people each. The third table was designated for the gifts for the bride, the cake, and seats for her and her three friends. Her seating plan made it so Tuesday was the focus of the evening, while Breeze's friends were out of earshot of any snide comments that were guaranteed to be made.

Satisfied with the scene, she immediately got to work. She instructed Moshie and Wren to place a red Chinese takeout box in the middle of the lazy Susan and surround it with the take home gifts for the guests. Secret busily worked on the gift and cake table according to Breeze's specifications.

"Girl, how much time and money did you spend on this?" Moshie asked while ensuring the gifts faced the way Breeze wanted it.

"Enough, but it pays to have friends in high places to keep the costs low," she said smiling as she placed the brightly colored name card and the order of the event at each setting.

At last, the room was ready to receive even the most finicky of guests. The first wave finally came in, and on time. She was grateful of that. Everyone greeted each other with hugs, dropped off the gifts for the bride, and made their way to their assigned seats. Small talk was shared about the place, time, distance, and theme of the event. Breeze promised all would be explained, once the shower begins. Finally, the bride and her tight knit few strolled in. Everyone got up and greeted each other happily.

"Breeze, everything looks wonderful," Tuesday praised. "Is there any reason for the assigned seats? I see your girls did not hesitate to claim theirs."

"Your seat and mine are specifically assigned. If necessary, everyone can sit where they want," she smiled. "Just make sure they take their place card with them."

"And just why is that?"

"Because I spent a lot of time working on those cards and I want them admired."

"Well, they do look nice. I think I just found another job for you to do," she said putting down the place card. "Oh and by the way, Breeze. Everyone keeps asking about my registry. Why wasn't that information on the invitation?"

"Because, that would just be plain tacky," she said officially ready to get this event over with.

"I know that's been a while since you've been in or to a wedding, Breeze," Tuesday said condescendingly. "But what we do *now* is--"

"Goes totally against etiquette and good taste. Now you have two choices: either bring this conversation to a close, so that we can start this event; or utter another word and I will pack up everything I put out, go home, and ya'll can fend for yourselves. Which is it going to be?"

"Everybody, find a seat let's get my party started," Tuesday said with a hint of defeat.

"Good evening ladies and thank you all for coming out to Tuesday's 'Sugar and Spice' event," Breeze opened while standing in the center of the room. "A couple of housekeeping items before we get started. The order of the evening can be found in your napkin. You will also see a blank white index card. There are three of us that are in the same 'single boat'--"

"I hardly think that you and I are in the same boat, Breeze," Tuesday scoffed.

"In the immortal words of your own aunt: 'you ain't married yet, chile!' As I was saying, there's a lot of wedded wisdom in this room. Throughout the evening, please write your marital advice and place it in the red Chinese takeout box in the middle of table.

"Now, for those who don't know what this evening is about, we celebrate up and coming nuptials in a slightly different way. It is supposed to be livelier than a traditional bridal shower and tamer than a bachelorette party. Our promise to the bride is to make sure she leaves blushing, with ideas to keep her marriage as sweet as sugar, as well as hot and spicy. *And* be ready for her husband." Breeze almost gagged on the last line.

"But first, Jez and Jas are ready to take our dinner order. So, while we wait to be served, let's start with a quick game, naming as many famous couples as you can. Whoever has the most by the time the orders are placed, wins a prize."

"Uh, Breeze, can we also name *infamous* couples," one of Tuesday's friends said snidely. "That is what we do at *other* bridal showers."

"Ladies, if you feel that you cannot come up with famous couples in a timely manner, then you are certainly welcome to use infamous couples, as she has pointed out," Breeze retorted with a smile she pulled from her reserve stash.

"Why you want my name," Breeze overheard another one of Tuesday's friends snapping at the waitress. Jez looked at Breeze, pleading for assistance. "Oh and one more thing, to make things easier, everyone will receive a separate check and an 18% tip will be included in your total," she smiled reassuringly. "Bon Appetite." Breeze looked at her girls with a 'see what I mean' look. Her girls gave the same look back.

After all the orders were placed, Breeze picked up a red goodie bag containing a small gift for the winner. She always kept a spare gift in case there was a tie. "Okay times up and pens down," she announced. The group agreed to use the first set of instructions to keep it an actual challenge. Tuesday's friend Britt was the winner citing 42 famous couples and everyone felt she earned whatever was in the bag.

"Congratulations Britt, you just won lunch or a down payment for dinner here at Hunan Manor," she said presenting the gift. "Now, let us get to the real business at hand, starting out with something sweet." She paused trying to think of a way to present the idea so that it would be well received. "On a cool afternoon in October, Tuesday was absolutely smitten with Spence when they met for the *second* time. They shared their very first meal in this very restaurant, hence the reason why we are here."

"Girl, I was smitten *the first time* I saw my Spencer," Tuesday laughed correcting Breeze and hi-fiving a neighbor. Breeze just smiled and looked at her girls briefly. True to fashion they gave her a look of support, with a hint of 'I told you so.'

"I know it may take a few extra minutes for some of you," Breeze continued. "In a few words or less, tell us about the first time you were smitten." There were no takers at first. A few looked up, pondering the question at hand. Others just looked at each other and rolled their eyes. "And you don't necessarily have to refer to your husband." The group laughed and relaxed a little with Britt giving her rendition of being hit by the thunderbolt.

For the next 20 minutes, the party shared their experiences. The stories appeared to bring members in the room closer with laughter and agreement of similar predicaments. Once the last story was told, Breeze announced that dinner was about to be served.

"Wait, Breeze," interrupted Tuesday. "Tell us a time when you were smitten."

"It ain't in my nature to share," she waved off. "Besides, I think Jes and Jaz are ready to serve us."

"We still have a few more minutes," Jez responded. "We want to hear your story, too."

"Oh, all right," Breeze said in huff. "Picture it: A cute curly headed 15 year old dressed head-to-ankle in the Limited's *Outback Red* fashions and Bass *Weejun* penny loafers, has a then, unshakable crush on a nerdy yet jockey blond blue eyed 16 year old. He would enter our typing class with this bouncy, self-assured stride. He would fluff his neatly parted hair in the middle, smile, and take his seat in front of me. He'd get himself situated at his desk, and then would spin in his chair to face me. Oh my goodness, the mere sight of his smile gave me goose bumps. Still does.

"To this day, I could not see how we learned to type with the amount of clowning we did in that class. Our typing teacher would say, 'someone's havin' a good time in here.' She wasn't kiddin'. We were having a blast. His presence was the highlight of my day."

The wait staff indicated they were finally ready to serve the food, as Breeze took her seat. "Where was all this passion during our confessional chat at my pajama party?" Secret asked.

"Please, she didn't even have this much passion talking about Spencer," Moshie added. The four laughed, but Breeze hoped no one heard that last comment.

"I knew you had a thing for brainy men," added Wren. "Is that why you won't give Coach Huntington the time of day?" Breeze cut her a look, while the other two looked surprised.

"Cool it, Wren," she hissed. "I hooked him up with Britt three years ago." They just sat and stared at her with disbelief. "I'll tell you the story, after this is over."

"Girl, who gives a kitty 'bout *their* story," Moshie spat. "When are you gonna hook yourself up?"

The mood and conversation was light during dinner. Tuesday, of course, had to inform everyone her order was the same she had on their first date. They momentarily marveled at the story, but happily went back to their own meal. Breeze kept her eye on the time, making sure she had plenty of time for gifts, cake, and clean up. She was pleased the evening was going well. She really wanted to just hang out with her girls.

"Ladies, I see the plates are being cleared," Breeze announced. "And judging how clean the plates are, I see everyone enjoyed their meal." She moved a chair from her table and centered it among the three tables with its back turned from the door. "Tuesday, if you would please...," she said gesturing her to the chair. "Now, I have been told by numerous friends, aunts, and my own mother that a bride should always be ready for her husband."

"At all times," a few members of the party cried out.

"Yes, and I honestly do not think I have ever blushed so much in my entire life, listening as to how. So Tuesday, get ready!" She was pleased with the party's reaction. Even Tuesday's hate squad laughed. "I found this lovely red Asian decorated box and felt it would fit neatly into to-night's theme and hold the contents of keeping her marriage sweet and spicy. So, let's get to the gifts!"

Breeze handed the gifts to Tuesday with her guests marveling at the slinky, edible, lacy lingerie, along with games, books, props, and dessert toppings. However, instead of the traditional ooo's and ahh's, she received: 'girrrl,' 'how on earth,' and 'now I've seen everything.' She was also glad that Secret took pictures and captured the point of the evening:

Tuesday blushing...miserably. "Was there a bra to go with this?" she questioned holding up a pair of 'what-is-the-point' sized thongs. "Spencer just loves how my bra and panties match."

After the last gift was revealed and admired, it was time to close the box. "I am so glad there are hooks for this lid," Breeze said struggling. "There's no more room left." She was finally able to close the box and presented it to Tuesday.

"Ladies, thank you for making this an interesting evening," Tuesday announced to the room. "I loved every one of my gifts and I cannot wait to show them to my Spencer. And I want to especially thank my hostess this evening, Breeze, for putting this event together." The members of the room clapped and gave shouts of approval. "Tonight was wonderful and everything was fabulous. I have one teensy question. Where is *my* gift from *you*?"

Breeze laughed in disbelief, hearing the chairs scrape from her girls. However, an unlikely person came to her rescue. "Tuesday, isn't it obvious the event, the decorations, and our parting gifts is the actual gift?" asked Mrs. Connor. "I've seen that same box and even on sale, it ain't cheap. There's your gift, dahlin'. Girl, wait 'til I tell your momma!"

Breeze mouthed a 'thank you' to Mrs. Connor and gave her friends the 'it's okay,' look. She actually *could* believe Tuesday would pull a stunt like this...in public. "Thank you, all for coming out," she managed to say. "I appreciate everyone participating in the theme and you did not disappoint. Please settle your bill with Jaz and Jes and don't forget to take my gift to you for making tonight a success," she said holding up a small decorated glass jar filled with cherry and cinnamon jelly beans. She motioned for Mrs. Connor to come up.

"Thanks again," she whispered.

"No, dear, thank you. This was better than hanging out with them in some seedy bar with strippers. You know that was their goal," she confided. She nodded, hugged her, and offered her the spare prize.

As the party disbanded, Tuesday made an announcement. "Based on Breeze's plan, we're all going to Silver Shadows tonight, if you'd like to join us." The group smiled and went back to talking amongst themselves. "Breeze, we're ready to go," she sang.

"Okay, the table is reserved under 'Tuesday Knight's Friday Night Out'," she smiled and went back to talking with her friends. "Oh, and have a good time," she said not turning around.

"Have a good time?" Tuesday questioned. "You're supposed to be coming with us! This is the first of my night out with the girls. We expect you to be there!"

"As far as you are concerned, my job is done," said Breeze. "I am going to The--"

"She'll be there," Secret said covering Breeze's mouth. "Y'all go on. We'll help her clean up and send her to the club once we're done. Go on, now," Secret commanded, shooing them away.

Tuesday and her friends finally left. Mrs. Connor gave one last round of hugs and left, too. She told the group that she was in no clubbing mood, plus she had a phone call to make. Breeze smiled, not believing that someone is going to actually tell on a grown woman. *"Yay, justice,"* she thought.

The party moved to the parking lot, polishing off the last of the cake. "It's gonna look extremely low budget, if you serve this last lonely section of cake in a club," Moshie said divvying the last of the dessert.

Secret reminded Breeze of the promise made and escorted her to her car. "You've gone this far, darlin', it's just the right thing to do at this point," she said smiling reassuring her friend. Breeze reluctantly got in the car. "I'm giving you one hour to make an appearance. Then you can come out and party with your real friends." She conjured up a smile and drove off.

Breeze finally made it to her destination and mustered up the energy to get out of the car. She made her way in, greeted the greeter, and searched for the party. They were not to be missed. Everyone wore a hot pink 'BFF of the Bride' sash. Breeze said hello and one of the guests informed her there were no more sashes left. "We didn't think you were coming," one of Tuesday's friends said feigning innocence... miserably.

"Okay, that's fine. Mine would actually say, '*Bridesmaid*'," she said looking for the nearest exit.

"Now that you're finally here, you can at least get a picture of us," Tuesday ordered wearing a white and pink satin sash that said, 'Bachelorette,' long satin white gloves, and a tiara.

"Sure," she sighed. "Where's the camera?"

"Where's yours?" Tuesday snapped. "I thought I saw you taking pictures at the restaurant. Why don't you just use that one?"

"That wasn't my camera, it was Secret's," she lied. Breeze was not about to waste anymore of her camera's memory space getting pictures of pettiness.

"Well, didn't you at least bring a camera?" Tuesday asked with frustration. "It is *my* party and *you* didn't..."

"Tuesday, among the nine friends you have here tonight, not one of you thought to even bring a camera to your function? Someone at least has a camera on their phone."

"You just insist on making things extremely difficult," Tuesday huffed.

"Don't even think about going there any further, tonight," Breeze hissed while giving her a look that would stop a hummingbird in midflight.

"Britt, can we use your camera?"

Britt finally pulled one out and gave it Breeze. She arranged the party in a couple of ways, taking a few extra pictures. Once the picture taking session settled, she made her way to the nearest bar stool.

"Where are you going now?" Tuesday whined.

"Grown folks business," she replied.

She resisted the urge to watch Tuesday huff again, making her way to other side of the club. She found a seat at the bar, strategically out of eye sight of the party. She ordered a Shirley Temple and watched Tuesday's friends get up and dance.

A few of them broke off and danced with handsome strangers. All except one. Britt was the unfortunate one on purse patrol. Out of all of Tuesday's friends, she was the only one Breeze could actually stand. For some reason she worshiped Tuesday and was amazingly tolerant to her cruddy ways. She honestly felt sorry for her sitting there. Almost enough to rescue the poor girl of her duties...almost. Breeze was in no mood to be on anyone's purse patrol tonight. She also noticed the party occasionally looking around to see if they could find her. She smiled sipping on her Shirley Temple feeling safe in her inconspicuous spot.

"I thought I felt a cool breeze," said a warm-tea-with-honey voice, making her spot not so inconspicuous.

"Lincoln," Breeze squealed. "How on earth are you?" she asked giving a handsome man with sparkling green eyes and an amazingly wide white smile, a warm hug. "Omigoodness, it is so awesome to see you!"

She and Lincoln were good friends in college after her friendship with Branford cooled off. They met while Breeze was pulling a double shift at South Hill's resident desk. She was in pajamas with a head full of rollers. He was in tattered lounge pants, tank top, and taped soda bottle eye glasses. While he came out to the lobby for a study break, the newest restaurant ran a promotion on their pizzas, asked how many people were at her location, and delivered three pizzas to the hall. Other students from the study room joined in, the music was cranked, sodas were purchased, and the arrival of the pizzas led to an instant party. The others went back to studying, as soon as the pizzas were polished off. He, however, stayed the rest of her shift.

What should have been a romance, became a friendship. And Breeze was quite happy with that. She felt he was nice enough, and extremely good looking. They took each other to some great parties, and it was nice to have a buddy. However, she never could take him seriously, with him constantly in between girlfriends. And the ones he did choose were either high maintenance, or just plain certified crazy. She felt she was neither, and did not want to be labeled as such. She also realized that was just an excuse. She did not want go through the disappointment she felt when Branford finally found himself with an actual girlfriend.

"So, what brings you to my neck of the woods?"

"I live in the Fort Meade area and I wanted to check out tonight's D.J. for a party I'm throwing," he said smiling. "I see you're still in Columbia."

"But of course," she said batting her eyes. "My hometown is very hard to leave." She allowed herself to get lost in the 'catching up' banter, laughing and smiling, being totally carefree with the conversation. It had been a while since she had the opportunity to act like this. She liked how she felt and would later confess she missed feeling this way.

"I think I hear the start of house music," he sang. "Shall we," he suggested offering his arm which she gladly accepted. *This is just good fun and just a dance. Enjoy it,* she thought making her way to the dance floor. And she did. She felt Lincoln tugging her towards him as the tempo increased. Time seemed to stand still as she and Lincoln got lost in the hypnotic house beat.

"BREEZE," someone shouted breaking her happy trance. "Where have you been? We've been looking all over for you!"

"Lincoln, give me five minutes." He reluctantly agreed and slowly walked back to the bar.

"Well, while y'all hash this out, I'm about to dance with that handsome piece of man Breeze left on the dance floor," said one of Tuesday's friends. She would reclaim her dancing partner, as soon as she finished making short work of this showdown.

"Tuesday is furious with you!"

"Like I care at this point," she responded flippantly. Tuesday finally made her way to the spot where Breeze was standing. She also noticed the one trying to steal her dance partner, made her way back.

"You are ruining everything," she ranted. "You are supposed to be with us! Poor Britt had to sit all by herself, to watch purses!"

"Couldn't one of you relieve her?" Breeze asked trying to stifle a laugh.

"That is why you are here tonight, Breeze," Tuesday hissed.

"To watch purses," she concluded. "I see. And on that note, have good evening ladies," she said waving making her way back to her dance partner.

"You and your funky attitude are *out* of my wedding," Tuesday shouted.

Breeze clapped her hands with enthusiasm. "Sounds good to me, but I will be sending you a bill for tonight's expense."

Tuesday stopped her. "You didn't get me a gift! Then you got all sneaky, separating the checks, and then you refused to throw me a bachelorette party! Mrs. Connor is now against me! Now we're at this lame dance club, and we gotta pay for our own drinks, with no strippers! And I couldn't dance with *all* of my girls all because of you! I don't owe you *beep*!"

"Let me get this straight," Breeze said laughing with disbelief. "You are losing it because I made sure your minions paid their fair share of their own ding dang bill, no man will buy y'all drinks, and I won't be on purse patrol? I am so glad your nerve is not in my tooth!"

"Nerve?" she asked. "I'll show nerve! Not only are you not in my wedding, I want *my* real friend to have *your* bridesmaid dress!"

"As soon as you send me the cash for tonight's festivities and $164.17 also *in cash,* I will be more than happy to give you *my* dress. Until then, have a good one." She left Tuesday shouting streams of obscenities, as she finally made her way back to Lincoln.

"What on earth was that," he inquired offering a glass of what appeared to be water. Not knowing what it was, she declined.

"Forget that. Listen, would you like to go with me to the Crossroads?"

"I haven't been there in years," he responded. "Dance Hall reggae, Jamaican Beef patties, and rum punch? It's on," he said offering his arm again. She took it, threw up 'deuces' to Tuesday and her crew, and left.

Breeze and Lincoln made their way to the *Crossroads* night club, staying on the phone the entire trip. Once they were in, they met up with her friends, and proceeded to dance her cares away...and not a clunky purse to watch, in sight.

"Why didn't you recommend the Crossroads in the first place," Secret shouted over the music.

"It was the only way I could get them to dress decently and you know Silver Shadows doesn't tolerate stank," she laughed. "They let them in anyway, so I guess the club lowered its standards."

They all made their way breathlessly back to an empty table. Lincoln excused himself, and the friends could not wait to fire up the questions. "Okay, Breeze, what is going on with that sexy beast, with them pretty eyes, and those nibbly ears?" Moshie asked. "And did I see some freckles?"

"Lincoln's a friend from undergrad whom I have not seen since we walked across the stage," she responded unable to wipe the smile from her face if she tried. "And I must admit, milk did a body real good. But I am keeping this friendly." She noticed the looks her friends gave her. "I just mean there was a reason why I didn't take that trip to the promise land, eighteen years ago. I am too old to find out the hard way now."

"I know you're too old to keep talkin' that nonsense," spat Secret. "You need to shake things up. And he looks very capable of doing so."

"Your lack of a love life is getting old," Wren chimed in. "Make this an opportunity for something new."

"What am I going to do with my dress," she ignored. "I know Tuesday won't pony up the cash, so I gotta find something to do with it."

"Wear it on *your* wedding day," Wren offered.

"It's red, drama queen."

"Then wear it to *your* reception. Every bride should make an entrance. And if the dress is all that you say it is, your mission will be accomplished."

Lincoln finally made his way back with a plate of Jamaican beef patties, meatballs, and a pitcher of rum fruit punch. "Y'all mind if I steal Breeze away for a minute?" he asked. The ladies excitedly agreed, and the pair made their way to a quiet corner. "I'm going to have to call it a night. My soon to be ex-wife just walked in the door with her friends. I do not want this to turn into a scene. Right now, she is getting only half of my money. If she sees me with another woman and a group of them at that,

I won't be able to keep what I have left or my self-respect by being cussed out in public."

"Please don't tell me the D.J. is for your divorce."

"You always managed to figure me out," he said sheepishly with his smile that Breeze could never get enough of. "Do you think I could, uh, spend some time trying to figure *you* out?"

"As soon as the ink dries on the divorce papers...give me a call."

"At least come to my party."

"I look forward to my invitation," she said hugging her heavenly scented friend for an extended period of time. She finally broke free, wished him well, and rejoined her friends.

"Where is Mr. Spark that will ignite Breeze's flame?"

"Ignite what?" Breeze asked perplexed. The music was too loud to comprehend one of Wren's statements. "He had to leave. His wife just walked in and didn't want to share the same space unless it involved a courtroom."

"Girl, one thing I can say about you: black, white, or whatever, you know how to pick 'em," said Moshie. "That's who you should've been talking about at the restaurant! C'mon, tell us. Did you give him some in college?"

Breeze sighed with a mix of embarrassment and annoyance, "I did say he was friend."

"Not from what we saw on that dance floor," said Secret. "Dude look like a friend with bed rockin' benefits! And what is going on with you and this exhausting 'friend' zone?"

"Listen, I am perfectly happy with the 'keep-the-legs-closed' zone I own, thank you very much. However, I was invited to his 'the divorce is final' party."

"Very good, you can seal the deal then," said Moshie.

"I'll think about it...if and when he calls. But right now, I want to celebrate the 'I'm no longer in this beast wench's wedding,' anymore!"

"I'll put a straw in the rest of this pitcher of rum punch to that," said Moshie.

"Not so fast," Secret interrupted. "We'll celebrate once this wedding nonsense is over. You know, as well I as do, Doomsday will use some kind of mind trick to con our Breeze back into the wedding."

"Whatever," Breeze dismissed. "Right now, I hear a Buju Banton beat, and I'm ready to shake my hips," she said jumping up. "But I can't thank y'all enough for hanging in there with me," she smiled. "Wait, did y'all heifahs leave me at least one beef patty?"

21

Clarification & Consequences

Breeze was amazed that she could wake up bright eyed and bushy tailed from last night's reggae fest, crawling in around 4 am. After a good power nap, her body was ready for gym class. Sufficiently exhausted once class was done, she high-fived Iris and her classmates, downed the rest of her water, and headed out for a bran muffin and an unsweetened tea. On her way home, she made a mental note to do some cleaning...after a nap. Or so she thought.

"Tuesday, you have five seconds to either move that car from my driveway, or a tow truck will be on its way to do it for you," she announced.

"We need to talk," Tuesday shouted not moving from where she stood.

"One."

"I cannot believe you--"

"Two"

"You embarrassed me in front--"

"Three," she said opening her phone.

"You are such a--"

"Four," she said speed dialing for the tow truck. She needed to have it ready at all times, being a board member of her condo association.

"Wait a minute," she said finally getting in her car. She backed out in a huff, almost hitting another parked car on the street. Breeze finally closed her phone, got back in her car, and pulled into her garage. Tuesday returned to the driveway behind her.

Breeze closed the garage door, entered her condo, peeled off her drenched clothes, and proceeded to take a shower. She took her time showering, shampooing, shaving, and exfoliating. Once done and dried, she took a moment to pluck any gray hairs from her eyebrows. She never could figure out how so many made their way in the strangest of places.

Her morning beauty routine was interrupted by a phone call, and was thankful for caller I.D. *"Who's the lunatic banging on your door?"* asked one of her neighbors. *"Do you need me to call the cops?"* She smiled at the vision of Tuesday being hauled away in handcuffs. Then, she quickly remembered that her car would still remain in the driveway, causing more drama of getting it removed.

"No, I'll take care of it, thanks." She grabbed a pair of gray yoga pants and a matching top, lotioned up exposed areas, tied her wet hair in a towel, and made her way to the door.

"You know you are *dead wrong* for making me wait out here for 45 minutes!"

"And the 'Big Dummy Award' goes to: 'Tuesday, for waiting out here and causing a scene in my quiet neighborhood for 45 minutes.' Now, what is the point of your existence on my doorstep?"

"Well, for starters, you owe me and my friends an apology!"

Breeze made a dismissive tone and gesture, while shutting the door.

"Breeze, stop," Tuesday commanded while trying to stop the door with her arm. "This is my wedding and I want--"

"Stop right there! I am vehemently aware of whose wedding it is! But I am not your enemy, or problem you make me out to be. If you need to vent your frustrations, take it out in an exercise class. Now, *last night*, was the *last time* you will ever flip out on me again. I have done everything possible except kiss your rump! And if that's what you are after, you and Spence can kiss mine first!"

"For the last time, it's Spencer, *Spencer,* repeat after me...Spencer! How many times do I have to tell you he does not like nick names?"

"Probably the same amount of times I have to tell you to check that tone. I am very much aware of how to pronounce his name."

"Well, anyway, I expect my bridal party to do things for me," she hissed.

"What haven't I done, Tuesday?" she asked exhaustedly. "Please, stop all this poutin' and shoutin' and tell me what we haven't done!"

"I can't think--"

"And that right there, is the problem! You do not think, especially before shootin' off your mouth! But you know what? Your mouth is no longer my problem, since I am no longer in your wedding," she said shutting the door.

"Will you wait a minute?" Tuesday shouted stopping the door. "After telling my mom about the scene *you* made last night...Breeze, stop!" Tuesday shook her head. "After telling my mom about what went down last night, she told me to let you back into my wedding."

"*Let*?" Slowly she hissed an expletive, while shutting the door closed.

Tuesday's rants could be heard through the door, with the doorbell ringing as if her finger was stuck to it. "First and foremost, get your finger off my doorbell!" Breeze demanded finally opening the door. "And don't even think about lying on your mother like that! What did she actually tell you to do?"

"She told me to ask you if you would be my bridesmaid again," she said reluctantly.

"Now that I can believe," she said leaning on the doorway. "I'm sure there was a 'please' and an apology in there, somewhere."

"I am not begging anyone. And I have nothing to be sorry for," Tuesday said proudly.

"Then you see yourself with one less bridesmaid," she said closing her door.

Tuesday caught the door. "We need to hash this out."

"I said all I was going to say. If I don't hear a 'please' and an apology from you, right now, you are going to find yourself with four less fingers. I had to put up with too much of your snide comments, and spent too much of my money, only to have seen too much of your behind, to be your bridesmaid!"

"Why can't you just graciously accept the honor of being my bridesmaid?"

"You know...I let you get away with that raggedy statement the first time. What makes you think it would be an honor *for me*?"

"Look at how many people you beat out for this honor."

"Whatever. But I will not accept it unless there is a 'please,' and an apology coming from that mouth."

"Fine, I apologize for the scene last night and will you please be my bridesmaid again?"

"We'll see," Breeze hissed.

"What kind of answer is that?" she asked waiting for a response. When none came, "Well, can I come in?" she asked in huff. "I'm tired of carrying on this conversation outside."

"Be sure you check that tone and attitude at the door," Breeze said reluctantly letting her in. "I have plenty of insurance to throw you out from the nearest window, making it look like an accident." When they both made their way up the stairs, Breeze turned to Tuesday, "And I also want an apology in front of your friends in the teacher's lounge."

"Why must you make everything so difficult?" Tuesday asked in a huff. "The drama all started with you not giving me your full name, to the fiasco last night. All I wanted was a drama free engagement. I have enough drama dealing with Spencer and his crazy mama."

"Tuesday, once again, I am not your enemy," Breeze said trying to stifle a laugh, realizing the end of Tuesday's statement.

"I just want everything perfect on my day...my way," she said quietly almost in tears.

"And I'm sure it will be," she said ignoring the budding tears, while finding a spot on the couch, getting comfortable. "I did not have to be in your wedding. My existence and certainly my attendance are not mandatory on your day. Why did you choose *me* to be a bridesmaid? Why didn't you choose a few from your circle of sash wearin' friends?"

"I knew you would get mad at that," Tuesday said smiling slyly.

"Please. My point is, I find it very odd that you did not choose at least one of them to be your bridesmaid. None of them showed up at the tea parties, favor assembly, or any other function that required an extra pair of hands. They're not hostesses, gift monitors, bouncers, or anything. Are they even invited?"

"Breeze, admit it. That was a sneaky thing you did at the restaurant and club."

"What? Make them pay for their share of the bill and made sure I did not get stuck with a bar tab? No, that wasn't sneaky, that was necessary. Your friends are notorious for not tipping or skipping out on a bill."

"It was still sneaky. Smart, but sneaky."

"The bill for the dinner was paid and the staff was properly tipped. And I did not have to come out of my pocket more so than I already did for the cake, shower, your dinner bill, and the upcoming main shower. Now back to my question. Why am I a bridesmaid?"

"I think you just answered it. I can't trust the seven of them to throw me a Frisbee, let alone a shower. Britt would, unfortunately, nothing would get done if I left things in her hands. I chose you because of what you did for Secret. I know last night was based upon it. I wanted that same special attention for my day. I may get that from Britt, but not of this magnitude. I have to admit, the Sweet and Spicy theme was extremely entertaining. I cannot wait until all the dust settles and show Spencer what is in that box.

"And you stick up for me. Remember that day in the teacher's lounge I came in saying, 'you know what I need,' and you said a better bra because I had too much, what did you call it, 'pop and fresh action' going on, under my shirt. And the conversation turned to your insistence of a good bra with matching undies. You said from the 'granniest to the sexist,' they still must match. I was like 'they'll just end up on the floor anyway.'

"Well, I rearranged the girls, took your advice, and went to the nearest department store. Yes Breeze, I do listen. I bought the better bra and panties to match. And that better bra led me to the better man. And Spencer cannot get enough of seeing me in my matching sets. At that point, I blew half my paycheck buying every matching set, in every color, in my size, I could find.

"I thought I owed you for the piece of advice, and for reconnecting me with Spencer. He was coming to see you about the trouble his nephew was having in one of your classes..."

"So, that's how he managed to connect all the dots without a tongue lashing," Breeze thought. *"If I tell her the truth this could be my actual ticket out of this wedding. No, that would just be mean. I see a spark of sincerity in those eyes."*

Tuesday continued pouring out her heart, while Breeze sat and listened. She almost felt sorry for her, especially the part about her friends. *"I could have made some arrangements for those who could not pay. That would be just plain wrong, leaving them out,"* she thought as she heard the doorbell ring. She excused herself and made her way to the door. *"Then again, lack of money is no excuse for the cruddy way they acted last night. That noise could have stayed home."*

"What are you doing here, Spence?"

"We need to talk about your funky attitude! But first, why is my bride's car parked outside?" he asked brushing by her and making his way up the steps. "Tuesday!" he shouted. "Whatchu doing here?"

"It is a long, drawn out story," Tuesday sighed.

"Well, if you don't mind, I would like to speak to Breeze...alone. Please?"

"Darling, I love you dearly. If you think I am going to leave my man alone, in a single woman's house, you are sadly mistaken. And what are *you* doing here; and just how do *you* know where Breeze lives anyway?"

He sighed and collected himself. "Tuesday, I do not have time for the questions and I will deal with your disobedience later." He turned to Breeze. "Why did you feel the--"

"Whatchu say?" Tuesday interrupted. "You'll *deal* with my what?" she asked heatedly while getting into Spencer's face. "Right 'bout now, Imma 'bout five hot seconds from puttin' foot in my *beep*'s disobedient *beep*!"

From that moment on, Breeze witnessed the most spectacular verbal butt whippin' she has ever seen. "Don't cuss at me, Tuesday...Look, I'm sorry... I know...wrong choice...words...I said please...wait...will you just...let me...Tuesday, please... dang girl...look, I said I was sorry...okay, okay...all right...Lemme just... Baby, okay...I didn't mean it...C'mon, now... I apologize...Seriously, I apologize...please..."

"Tell me some *beep* like that again, heah?" she boomed finally removing her finger from his face. "Now, handle your business!" she spat finding the nearest chair.

He finally pulled himself together. He rubbed his face and let out a sigh looking as if he did not know what to do next. "...No, I need to get this straightened out. Why did you lie to my mother about us?"

"What on earth do you mean?"

"She asked you if you were my former girlfriend at the tea party and you said, 'no.'"

"I told her that we went out a few times. But I would hardly label myself as your girlfriend."

"Really, Breeze?"

"The way you treated me? Really! As far as I was concerned, we dated off and on for one long year...of which we spent arguing over your inflated ego."

"It wasn't all bad, Breeze."

"There were too many fights, arguments, and you missing in action to even think about the good. I thought I made it perfectly clear when I said I never should have accepted your invitation to breakfast. If I didn't, none of this would have been an issue, except you would not have met your future wife. So, we both got what we really wanted: you found the love of your life; I finally got some serious peace and quiet...until now."

Breeze and Spencer were too wrapped up in their own conversation to notice Tuesday sitting in a chair, seething. She did not say a word. Her head, however, went back and forth like she was watching a heated tennis match, with her eyes as big as tea cup saucers soaking up what was being said. Spencer finally looked her way, immediately noticing her disposition.

"Tuesday, it was not a secret that Breeze and I were together. You and I met for the first time while, she and I were on a date."

"I-am-trying-to-wrap-my-mind-'round—the-fact that *you* insisted on an ex-girlfriend *in...our...*wedding."

"First of all, *you* insisted! And, we went over this--"

"You failed to mention that you actually considered her your girl-friend! How does one remotely think this is acceptable?"

"Look, the both of us had an explanation as to why Breeze should be a part of our day," Spencer said. Breeze recognized this tone as his method of defusing a situation. She could not wait to hear the actual justification.

"I do realize that I treated a wonderful, lovely woman, badly. In the past, I had my own process of how to treat my girlfriends or how to 'groom' them for that status. After talking with Breeze, I realize I had to put a stop to all the game playing if I wanted a wife. That's when I ran into you."

"All this time, I thought you were seeing Breeze about your neph-ew's grades, you were trying to get back with her," she said looking at Spencer with disbelief. "That's why you looked like someone jacked up your Mercedes."

"Let's just say that Breeze is no one to mess with. When I left her class-room, I wanted some time to figure out how to eventually make things right. But you came along, we shared a great meal, and had a really good time that night. We've been having such a good time ever since. It was just never the right time to tell you the real reason I was there. Since I couldn't, I just decided that I wouldn't put you through what I did in my past rela-tionships. All the things I did and said to Breeze, I wouldn't do with you."

"I just wished you could have told me all of this a lot sooner," Tuesday finally said. "Are you the reason why Spencer doesn't use nicknames? I had the nerve to call him 'Spence' one day and he flipped out." The only thing Breeze could do was shrug and suppress a smile. "I'll look like an idiot with my groom's ex-girlfriend in my bridal party."

"If it makes you feel better, I was never his girlfriend," Breeze interjected. "If not, does this mean I get my $164.17 back plus the cost of what I put into last night and the shower?"

"Not so fast, Breeze," Tuesday said. "In more ways than one, you are still the reason why we are at this point. I just need a moment to process all of this," she said making her way downstairs. "By the way, how did you know when we had our first date? And where?"

"Someone told me," she said with a smirk.

"That daggone Keisha! Breeze, are we okay?"

"I'm sure we will be," Breeze managed to say. "I still would have settled for a gift certificate to Lynn's Day Spa as a 'thank you' for all of this happiness. However, I do want to be sure that you two will be okay. I did promise Spence's mother, that I would personally see to it that the two of you make it down that aisle, June 21st. Please don't make a liar out of me. Now, you two, go home!"

"Tuesday, are we okay?" Spencer asked gingerly following her.

"I honestly don't know," she said walking down the steps.

"Tuesday, you corrected me that you were smitten the *first time* you met Spence, not the second. Think about that while you make a decision on the next steps to take," she said giving her a slight smile. She smiled back and left with who Breeze hoped was still her fiancé. "*Otherwise, I really would have to find use for this dress,*" she mumbled while hearing the phone ring.

"You always know the right time to call. You would not believe who just left my house," she said breathlessly.

"*I could only imagine,*" Willow said with disinterest. "*Why are you breathing so hard? I told you not answer the phone if you're--*"

"Cut it out," Breeze spat. "Spence and Tuesday were here. I just sent them out the door. So, get this..."

"Girl, seriously. Imma need you to get some business of your own. When am I going to see a return on my investment?"

"Finding the one made especially for me takes time...in His time."

"Is that what she's been feedin' y'all for the past nine months? I coulda told you that for free. Well, at least you could look good while doing it. Meet me at my house for lunch and lipstick hunting. One hour." Before Breeze could respond, she hung up.

22

Smiles & Parasols

"**G**irl, you will not believe who is inching their way on this highway on my left," Breeze said finding herself along with a gazillion other cars practically parked on I-95 South. She decided to roll down the windows, put on the emergency break, and gave Willow a call, needing a distraction from mentally reviewing her checklist for the umpteenth time.

"Please tell me it's Stealth so that we can finally put some real purpose in this party."

"It is," she said excitedly while checking her mirror. "Dang it, not a trace of lipstick on and none within reach." There was no need, he already reached the car. Not knowing what to do she stayed on the phone while Willow scolded her for not being ready. "Oh my gosh! I know this guy!"

"What? What do you mean--"

"It's his laugh! I remember that weird laugh!" She heard Willow say something, as she held the phone down. "Excuse me! You-Who," she sang grateful that she got her nails done. She got his attention. "Do you re-member a girl named Willow?

"Yeah, yeah I do remember Willow," he shouted after a few moments of thought. "She was my date for the senior prom."

"Forest, right?"

"Yeah, how did you--"

Breeze excitedly got back on the phone with Willow. "Do you remember you went to a prom with a guy named Forest?"

"Yeah, I remember him. I remember his friend a whole lot better." She and Breeze went into teenage mode reminiscing about a complicated evening of twists and turns that Breeze recalled with ease, even though she herself was not there for the dance portion of the evening.

"Excuse me," Breeze heard him say.

"Oh, I'm sorry. Willow is married," she said over her shoulder wanting to get back to the conversation.

"I know she is," he shouted back. "She and Reach invited me, but I was called out of town."

"Oh," was the only thing she could say to him. "Let me find out that you invited Stealth to your wedding," she hissed on the phone. Before she could hear a response, he called for her again, this time getting her attention using *her* name. Her *first* name.

"You remembered," she said smiling finally facing him.

"Yeah, I remembered," he said smiling back. "Do you remember Kings Dominion?"

"Uh, Willow, Imma hafta call you back," she said trying to hang up the phone.

"Girl, get the digits! Get the digits!"

She could not help but feel her whole face smile, thinking about that day. "Are you kidding me? I got punished for a whole month fooling with y'all. But it was so worth it!"

—– —–

"Don't fo'get ta send meh back a plate," said Mr. Fellows, the security guard. She smiled, agreed, and waved as she made her way, admiring the beautifully manicured landscaping and slightly swaying oak trees along the way. She wanted to run through the lush green grass with her bare feet while doing a couple of cartwheels and back flips. She snapped herself out of her trance when she arrived at the glass and brick, yet angularly designed, community center.

Breeze bounced in, hugged Tuesday's family, and greeted the helpers for the shower. She directed a few to unload the rest of the car, gave instructions to remaining hands as to what else needed to be done, and got to work. She felt light hearted and a little light headed, thinking about her conversation with Forest. She needed some music. She chose a 'house cleaning' CD filled with old school hits, and immediately got to work.

The tunes put everyone in the room in an uplifting mood, snapping their fingers, doing a two-step, or stopping to dance with an elder. Breeze was bouncing to a James Brown beat while spreading a black tablecloth, when she suddenly felt a tap on the shoulder.

"Girl, if you called me one more time, I would have kicked you out of the wedding, myself," Wednesday said smiling.

"I knew I should have made that one last phone call that was on my mind and saved the time and expense," Breeze said hugging her.

"Well, speaking of *wasted* time and expense, you should've seen that bachelorette party. It was not pretty."

"I am so glad someone threw her one. Who hosted it?"

"Monday gave in. And where were you by the way?"

"Thankfully, I was not invited," she said spreading out the last red tablecloth.

"I wished you would have invited me to the other one, because Tuesday's hungry hellions could not stop talking about it. You made some enemies among the family, too!"

"It was for work. And I do believe this shower is for the family and her close friends. Now, lemme see whatcha got." Breeze admired the gifts and prizes for the guests. She was pleased with the selection, especially the gifts for Tuesday's elders. She instructed where to set up the gifts and continued decorating the tables...and thinking about Forest.

"I love my cousin dearly, but I am so ready for this day to be over with. This is more pressure than the actual day," Wednesday said gathering her items and making her way to her designated tables. Breeze laughed and agreed.

"BREEZE!" Mrs. Knight boomed storming in frantically. "PLEASE TELL ME THAT YOU BROUGHT THE CAKE!"

"Yep, the cake and the fruit are here. Why?"

"WELL... my, the room looks absolutely lovely," Mrs. Knight stole a moment to admire the set up. "You all did a wonderful job." She stopped to look at the flowers. "Are these real?" she asked smelling them.

"What's going on, Mrs. Knight?" Breeze demanded.

"Chile, I have no idea," she said plopping herself in the nearest chair. "I called the center's office to make sure the caterers set up in a certain place. The receptionist said they haven't arrived yet. That was at 1 o'clock. It's now 2:45 and there's still no caterer. I made a phone call to Monday. Found out she and Tuesday had a falling out over sumptin' silly. And that heifah cancelled the caterer! We ain't got no food! All we're gonna eat is some snack mix, fruit, cake, and punch. We do have sumptin' to drink, right?"

"Yes, Aunt Opal. The beverages are here," responded Wednesday. "I told you that party was ugly," she mumbled to Breeze.

"Wednesday, what on earth could've happened at that party to cause all this mess?" Mrs. Knight asked exhaustedly.

"Mrs. Knight," Breeze interrupted. "We do not have time to find out who shot John and why. I need to know how much money we can collect and find the nearest, cheapest, tastiest, and most reputable Chinese food place. Oh, is there a party store nearby?"

"I think I know where you're going with this. I know just the place."

"I have $32 you can use towards the cost," Breeze said going for her purse.

"Put your money away. Y'all spent enough. I'll get my money back from my sister or out of my crazy niece's behind! Make a list of what you want from the party store. I'll go get the menu," she said mumbling a stream of obscenities all the way to the lobby.

Everyone else the room just looked at each other while Breeze got to work on her list. This did not surprise her at all. She was always skeptical as to why Monday insisted on handling the food arrangements. However, she placed skepticism aside, and constructed her list. Once Breeze received the menu, she chose possible menu items that could stretch, and gave the list to Mrs. Knight.

"Is this gonna be enough? I cannot have my table lookin' chintzy," Mrs. Knight said looking over the list one last time. "I wanna make sure that everybody has sumptin' to eat."

"When we get the egg and spring rolls, cut them in half, diagonally. Not only does it make the menu stretch, it's visually appealing. This will be plenty. Now go, I have to finish decorating."

"What else is left to do?" Mrs. Knight asked.

"We got whatever is left to do! I need you to git ta gittin' before your daughter comes in with her mouth stuck out, 'cause her guests ain't got no dinner!"

Mrs. Knight nodded her head looking at the list a final time. "You're right. Knowing my tight-fisted niece, I'm sure this would've been more than what she had in mind. Come on, Pearl, let's go."

"Wednesday, can you go the party store for us, please?" Pearl asked her daughter. "I'm sure you know Breeze's specifications."

Breeze watched them leave, gave additional instructions to the remainder of the group, turned the CD player back on, and allowed herself to get lost in her work. She was determined not to let Monday's antics ruin her good mood. "Stealth is Forest! Forest is Stealth," she sang to herself. Her thoughts were interrupted when James Brown's 'Doin' It to Death' came on, and someone tapped her on the shoulder.

"You got skills ta do the Electric Slide ta this?" Tuesday's Aunt Ruby asked.

"Please, a friend of mine taught me one better! Lemme show you." Breeze took this opportunity to work off some of this joy, dropped what she was doing, and counted off: "5-6-7-8..."

"I thought y'all were supposed to be busy decorating," Wednesday said walking in with her purchases. She and Ruby were so engrossed in a new line dance, they lost tract of time. Wednesday dropped her bags and tried her best to join in.

Once the song was done, Breeze announced, "Okay, okay let's get crackin' so we can get this party started."

As if on cue, Mrs. Knight came back with the food...loads of it. "To keep up appearances, don't let nobody in this kitchen, understand?" She held up a black square serving platter. "Good thinking, Breeze. We can use this to replenish the buffet. And thank you Wednesday for pickin' up the servin' items." She stopped for a moment. "Really, I thank all of you for pitchin' in and savin' my baby's day," she said emotionally walking in the kitchen.

Everyone provided their assistance with cleaning the warming trays, setting up the buffet table, and started filling the trays with food. Mrs. Knight managed to pull herself together long enough to handle a knife and brought out a tray of egg and spring rolls cut exactly how Breeze suggested.

As the last piece of foil paper was placed on the last tray, the guests started rolling in. Wednesday was the designated hostess, so she got to her spot, and performed her job.

Breeze stole a few moments to freshen up. Mrs. Knight came in a few minutes later. "Whew, Lawd! I tell ya, I am glad I'll only have to do this once," she said washing her face and hands. "Listen, are you gonna tell me why you're beamin' like a star on a Christmas tree; or do I have to beat it out of you with one of those lovely parasols? Nice touch, by the way."

"It's a long story Mrs. Knight," she said trying to not smile. She failed miserably. "And how did you find out about the parasol?"

"Pearl told me about the table y'all were setting up for Tuesday. I took a peek, once the food was on the buffet table. I wanna parasol, too."

"Ah, then you did not look hard enough," she said walking out with her.

The room buzzed with small talk, hugs, and guests wanting a peek at the gift bags...and food trays. Breeze changed the CD to fit the mood and greeted the guests. Tuesday finally danced in announcing her arrival. "Let's get my party started!" Breeze also noticed the game face Tuesday wore, looking as if nothing was wrong. Even though everything was finally taken care of, she could not figure out why Tuesday did not say a thing about her tiff with Monday.

"Ladies," Breeze announced while ringing a small silver bell. "We can officially begin, now that our guest of honor has arrived. Our first game involves some movement while getting to know your neighbor. Now listen up for the rules. You know how y'all get when there's a prize involved…"

Breeze left the ladies happily chatting, taking a moment to check on the arrangements on the buffet table one last time. A basket for the utensils and napkins started the table following the plates. Four warming trays lined up like soldiers. Mounds of sesame chicken, beef and broccoli, shrimp fried rice, egg and spring rolls, and a dish of white rice made for a fabulous 'Double Happiness' feast.

She also noticed everyone except for Wednesday, Mrs. Knight and her sister Pearl found their seat ready to enjoy the fruits of their labor. Breeze told the plotting pair to sit down and rest. But they refused, and continued thinking of ways to get back at Monday, and ensuring no one goes in that kitchen.

"Breeze, let's start serving the food, before it burns up. Get Ruby to say the blessing. And while they are eating, we'll grab a plate and you can tell me about that *long* story," Mrs. Knight winked.

Breeze smiled and made her way to the center of the floor. She felt a few introductions were in order before the food was served, which lead to Ruby blessing the food. The helpers made the plates and served Tuesday and the elders. Once served, the rest of the guests were free to serve themselves. "Ladies, please feel free to use both sides of the table," Breeze said noticing a long queue of hungry guests forming.

A few more of the helpers replenished a few items, as guests made their way back to the buffet for seconds…thirds. She motioned for Wednesday to do the next game. "Ladies, this will be a group game and Tuesday will be the judge of the best group."

"What's in the bag?" asked one of the guests. "I want to play a game that wins the bag."

"Patience my dear, patience. Now this side of the room will be one group, the middle, another group. And the other side, the other group. And yes, you can take your plates," Wednesday instructed. "First, I need you to choose a team captain. Next: choose, discuss, and prove..."

Happy the guests willingly received the challenge, Breeze made a plate for Wednesday. "Are you going to be okay by yourself?"

"Thank you," Wednesday said taking an egg roll of the plate before it was even served. "Yep, this should be good."

"Okay, let me know if you need me," she said making her way back to the buffet. Once her plate was made, she walked back to where Mrs. Knight and her sister were still plotting.

"Okay, we're waitin'," Mrs. Knight said eating the last spoonful of beef and broccoli on her plate.

"We?"

"Yes ma'am," said Pearl. "For a moment, I thought you were the bride, the way you were glowing."

"To make a long story short, the guy I've been checking out on my way to and from work, turns out to be an acquaintance from high school. And we had a lovely 10 minute chat in traffic, on the way here."

"That's it?" Mrs. Knight asked while eating an egg roll. "They'll be in that room debatin' for days. Come on girl, give us the story."

"Alright, picture it: A cute brown skinned girl with a head full of cascading curls gets a phone call from a half black-half Filipino girl with equal amounts of '80's heavy metal band' hair, needing a fourth to go to Kings Dominion."

"You know we're only 30 minutes away," Mrs. Knight interrupted.

"Very much aware. Anyway..."

Mrs. Knight's sister, Jade strolls in...without Monday. "Sorry I'm late y'all," she said breathlessly. "Everything looks lovely. There's a certain mood to it. It's simple, yet sophisticated. Monday finally took her job seriously and whipped this party into shape! Where is she anyway?"

Mrs. Knight's hand went up before anyone could say a word. "Whatdidjah just say, Breeze? 'Picture it?' A beautiful salt and pepper gray haired woman, with skin as smooth and dark like a chocolate bar, makes a phone call to a...mmm. That heifah got my pressure up so bad, I can't even think straight," she said frustrated as she rushed her sister into the kitchen.

"Aunt Opal, we're going to need some more eggrolls," one of the helpers said following her.

"They'll have to wait," Mrs. Knight snapped, slamming the door in the helper's face. A few minutes later, a tray of eggrolls and hands were held out of the door.

"Wednesday, please don't put us through this madness when it's your turn," Jade shouted walking out with a take-home plate of food in her hand.

"Now that's all settled," Mrs. Knight walked out of the kitchen with a satisfied smirk on her face. "Pearl, here is Wednesday's share of what's owed. I'll get the rest from Jade, later. Breeze, let's get started on the gifts. Looking at that mountain of presents, we'll be here 'till midnight if we wait any longer."

Breeze gave Wednesday the cue, as she retrieved the prizes for the winners of the debate. "Tuesday, please take your special seat," Wednesday said trying to calm the ladies down from the previous challenge. Breeze gave out midsize Burma fans with red, gold or black ribbons to the winners. Britt came forward and offered to write down the gifts and the names, to provide them a break. Breeze and Wednesday were most appreciative.

"Before Tuesday gets into her gifts, allow me to tell you how to win that red or black bag on the table..."

After the last scandalous, yet tasteful gift, Tuesday expressed her gratitude and made a few light hearted remarks. She especially thanked Breeze, Wednesday and the rest of the shower crew for assembling her day. Breeze noticed she did not say a word about Monday, good or bad. Convinced that Tuesday was acting like a decent human being, she and Wednesday presented her with a ruby red parasol with an Asian motif. They also presented Tuesday's elders with white ones. Everyone loved the look and the group picture taking commenced.

"Before we leave, the person sitting in the marked seat is the winner of the floral centerpiece." Guests frantically turned over their chairs, hoping. "If you did not win, that's fine. You still have your 'thank you for coming' gift waiting for you," Breeze said smiling. The guests continued mingling and snapping pictures with the bride and each other, while packing up their winnings, shower favors, and take-home plates.

"Don't fo'get ta make me a plate ta take to dat fine Mr. Fellows," Ruby whispered slyly to Breeze. "It may be warm, tah-day. But it's gonna be hot tah-night," she said laughing. "Opal," Ruby shouted. "How long do we have dis room fo'?"

"For about two more hours. Why? What are you 'bout to do now?"

"Can we git some line dancin' in? I mean dis is a party, ain't it?"

"Yes, I suppose so," Tuesday answered for her mother. "But get it in now, Aunt Ruby, because Spencer and I are standing our ground with no line dancing at the reception."

"Whatchu mean we ain't line dancin'?" asked one of Tuesday's friends.

"Look y'all, we discussed this. We feel line dancing is just played out, and you should be dancing with your husband or date."

"That's messed up," her friends stood around her with their hands on their hips, objecting. "*We* discussed it and declared your day, 'Girl's Night Out.'" Her friends continued to express their opinions.

"Aw'right y'all," she said in huff giving in. "I'll talk to Spencer and the D.J. about a selection of line dancing music. In the meantime, y'all ain't got no music."

"Breeze...," called Aunt Ruby.

"I'm on it," she said finding just the right CD.

———

The yummy night air encouraged Breeze to put her take-home plate, bags and boxes, in the trunk and drop the top. She pulled her hair in a ponytail and started off. Just in case, she stopped and checked her phone for messages. She noticed five missed calls from Willow. She decided not to call at such a late hour, in fear of waking up her godsons. The phone rang anyway.

"*Girl, I thought they kidnapped you,*" Willow said not waiting for a greeting.

"We've been cleaning, line dancing, and schlepping the gifts from the center to Mrs. Knight's house. Y'all, let me tell you what went down this time--"

"*We are confident that you put on a stellar performance of Little Ms. Happy Shower Hostess fixing whatever got jacked up and er'rybody had a good time. What we want to know is, what happened with you and Forest!*"

"But there was drama, suspense, chopsticks. And just what do you mean by '*we?*' Who else is on the phone at this hour?"

"*Everyone that matters are on the line,*" said Rayne. "*Now, what say you?*"

"Forest and I are having lunch, tomorrow at two." Breeze had to adjust her earpiece hearing all the congratulatory squeals.

"*So, are you excited?*" asked Spring. "*I mean are you really, really excited? Because I know I am excited for you!*"

"I am very excited! I could not stop thinking about him all day. Even the drama of the day could not get me down. I planned the time, so that I could take an 'after church nap' and get myself together. But I know I'll just be too giddy to sleep."

"*So my girl got the date and the digits,*" said Rayne. Breeze was silent. "*Breeze, you did get his number, correct?*"

"I forgot the digits," Breeze finally said gingerly, bracing herself for the next reaction. "I didn't have time, because the traffic was moving."

"*No excuse,*" snapped Rayne among the groans and obscenities. "*What do we always tell you to do?*"

"I know, I know. We're meeting at two. We'll exchange numbers then. I promise."

"*Wait, wait! You never told us where y'all are meeting,*" said Spring.

"And have an audience? I can't risk y'all staring and pulling me in the bathroom when I do something wrong...again. I will call everyone once I get home."

"*Please don't let us have to call you,*" scolded Willow. "*We are so excited for you dahlin'!*"

"Thanks. I'm excited for me, too!"

The word 'excited' would not be strong enough to describe how she was feeling. Instantly, she woke up at 4:30 in the morning, with Forest and what to wear on her mind. She willed herself to sleep around six, almost waking up late for church. When she got there, everyone asked about this glow she was wearing. Not wanting to give any details, her smile and coy response continued to pique everyone's curiosity. She tried to take notes on the Sermon, but just could not concentrate. She purchased the CD because she really needed to hear the topic. She just could not receive it. She went home, forfeiting her nap, going through five outfits. Finally choosing her first pick, she fixed her hair and makeup and floated her way to Pei Wei.

Too excited, she arrived a little early. She walked in, making sure he was not waiting inside. There was no sign of him. She made her way outside, sitting on the nearest bench enjoying the beautiful spring weather, going over what to say in her head, and thinking about her perfect day at Kings Dominion. Breeze thought about their 14 hours of coasters and conversation with a little Waffle House at the end. Forest insisted that she sit next to him at the restaurant, and Breeze happily obliged. They did however, debate over grits vs. home fries. Home fries won because there was nothing to doctor up. She also thought about the longest punishment she ever received, when she finally made it home. The last hug she received from him was worth every tongue lashing, stern looks, and nothingness she experienced for an entire month.

Deep in her own bouncy thoughts, she lost track of time. It was now 2:45 pm and still no sign of Forest. At this point, she was sorry she did not get his number. She continued to wait. However, with each minute she started beating herself up, feeling more like a fool watching people come and go. Soon, she felt the word 'idiot' being etched across her forehead.

Finally, she picked up whatever was left of her dignity, ordered a mandarin orange tea and edamame and left, struggling to hide her tears. As soon as she got in the car, none came out. She shook her head in disbelief. She rested her head on the steering wheel trying to figure out what to do next, wishing her boxing class opened on Sundays. Although she could not think or see straight, she made her way home feeling completely and utterly defeated.

23

Fried Fish & Empathy

For the entire day, she found herself on autopilot teaching her classes, answering questions, and trying her best to keep a stiff upper lip and mind off of her recently discovered mixed match shoes. She ditched an invitation to go to happy hour with Secret, Wren, Moshie, and Thaddeus in fear that she may wash away her troubles with the entire contents of the bar.

While making an attempt to grab some lunch, she kept hearing her name being called. "Ms. Monsoon..." Not being in the mood to be sociable, she shrugged off the squeaky voice demanding her attention. "Ms. Monsoon..." Feeling like she would probably wear whatever she put in her mouth, she instead grabbed a bottle of water and went back to her class room. "Ms. Monsoon..." She tried her best to ignore it, and quickened her pace. The squeak turned into a squawk, "BREEZE!"

"What?" she shouted spinning around to the source.

"Breeze, I've been yelling your name for the past half hour," squeaked Britt. "Didn't you hear me calling you?"

"Apparently not," she lied. "Please, whatcha want?"

"Just the name and number of y'all's seamstress, sheesh!"

"Britt, I'm sorry. You did not deserve that. C'mon, I have her card in my classroom."

"Tuesday told me you recommended the seamstress, and she altered the dresses for the entire wedding party, her mother and aunts. With those recommendations, I plan to keep her busy for the whole summer," she said following her down the hall. When Breeze did not respond, she continued. "Did Tuesday tell you that I will be taking Monday's place in the wedding?" She did not wait for a response. "I'm taking her dress and having it altered since Monday never paid for it." When Breeze still did not respond she asked, "Are you feeling all right?"

"Just peachy," was all she could muster while searching for the card in her planner. "Good. At least most of the maid of honor responsibilities are out of the way. All that's left is your toast," she said with a fake smile and handed her the business card of the seamstress.

"Oh no, didn't she tell you?" Britt asked looking at the card and then putting it in her purse. "Not only am I not the maid of honor, she and Spencer are getting you to do the toast." Breeze just stood there in total disbelief. "Oops, I guess I should have kept my mouth shut." Breeze nodded her head in agreement. "Well, I'm sure they will be asking you shortly. Are you sure you're feeling okay? You've been walking around like a zombie for the past two days. Just this past Saturday you were glowing like it was your day."

Breeze snapped out of her disbelief. "For a moment, it was."

— ~

She called in sick for the next three days. She was sick of seeing people... sick of trying to appear all right...sick of crying with no tears coming out...sick of dodging questions she did not want to answer...sick of hearing new developments and duties of the wedding. She was totally sick of the mountain of mess she got herself in, finding solace on her couch. No music. No lights. No television. No phones. Just transporting herself from the bed to the couch with an occasional trip to the bathroom. She could not even look at herself in the mirror. She was just sick and disgusted with what she allowed to happen. She felt all she had to do was just graciously decline Forest's offer, once the mystery was solved, and kept it moving. "But oh, no. I just had to bat my eyes. I just had to flash my smile. I just had to agree to lunch. Stupid, stupid, stupid girl!" she yelled to herself and plopped back on the couch.

— —

"Breezy, what are you doing home?" her father asked waking her up.

"Hi, dad. I'm just not feeling well," she responded not moving staying under the throw.

"Yeah? Sorry to hear that. Whatchu takin' for that cold?"

"Whatever is in my medicine cabinet, dad."

"Now, you know I taught you to drink some orange juice and take a laxative. Knock that cold right on out!"

"I don't have either, dad."

"Oh, okay. Lemme just run over to--"

"I'm all right, dad. It will work itself out. No pun intended."

"Aw'right then. Did you get the Sunday paper?"

"Yes, it's sitting on the counter."

Breeze was relieved the questions finally stopped. She could hear her father picking up the paper, sigh as he sat himself down, and started reading. Normally, she would sit with him and discuss current events. She just could not bring herself to face anybody, at least not for the next 100 years. "Why do I smell Chinese food?" She could hear him getting up to find the source.

"'Cause that's what I had this weekend."

"Ooo, spring rolls," he said rifling through the contents of her refrigerator. "That's all you got in here 'cept for some yogurt cups and water. Maybe that's why you ain't feeling well. You ain't eatin'!"

"Dad, the Chinese food has been in there since Saturday. I really don't think you should eat it. And I am in no position to visit you in the hospital today...PUT IT DOWN, DAD!" she demanded knowing good and well he ignored her warnings. "DAD! Step your old rump away from the old Chinese food!"

She heard him slam the containers down. "Fine, but Ima need you to take your behind to the grocery sto', 'cause I'm hearin' my own echo in this ice box! I will take a few of these waters, though."

"Take the lot if you wish. Just put the Chinese food in the trash can. I'll go to the store tomorrow."

"Take the what? You really need to stop watchin' dem Britcoms," he said opening a bottle. "You know, uh, baby girl, it'll help if you just talk about it."

"No, it wo-- I'm just not feeling well, dad," she lied.

"Good Golly, Miss Molly! Is this another weddin' invitation?" he asked while taking a swig of water.

"It's probably just Tuesday's official invitation."

"You told me that girl's name is Knight and that good-for-nothin' boy's name is Lyte. This invitation said B. Greene."

Breeze's eyes popped open in sheer fright staring at her cream colored couch realizing what Britt meant by keeping the seamstress busy. She and Coach Huntington are finally tying the knot. She sighed and closed her eyes tighter. "Lawd ham mercy," was all she could muster.

"Listen, since you won't talk to me or let me go to the store for you, do you want me to call Willow?" he asked while picking up his mail. "Or how 'bout that Elliott?"

"NO!" she boomed. "Dad, please do not call Willow or Elliott. I will be fine. I promise."

"Well," he said quietly. "I'm here if you need me." She felt him ruffle her ponytail sticking out from under the blanket.

"I know dad. I appreciate that."

"I hope you also know that he's not worth it if he makes you feel this way."

"Yeah...I know."

"You sure you don't wanna talk about my potential son-in-law?" When no answer came, he made his way to the door. "I'll just leave you to your thoughts. Are we still on for Sunday?"

"Of course."

"Good. Don't be late! Oh, thanks for the Chinese food," he said shutting the door.

Breeze heard him lock the door and let out another sigh, "Hard headed, booger."

— ◆ —

Breeze mumbled an expletive when she heard Willow sing, "Breezy-Bee," from the front door.

"Come on, she's okay if she's cussin'," she heard Willow whisper with several footsteps making their way into her home. They walked up the steps and noticed the scene on the couch. "Girl, what on earth happened *heah*?"

"Do I dare ask about the date, seeing as you didn't call any of us back," said Rayne. Breeze did not answer. "Will you get up, please?" When Breeze still did not move, Rayne took matters into her own hands. "I-am-'bout-sick-a-dis-whiney-wench...," yanking off the throw only to reveal Breeze wearing a tank top, panties, and socks. "Please tell me those aren't the drawers you had on since last Sunday!"

"Would it make you leave if I say they were?" she asked snatching back her throw.

"With a quickness, but I know you ain't that depressed. And you could use a moment at the spa. You look as if you're smuggling your aunt's mink stole."

"You know what? I may not want to lose our friendship over what I really want to say at this point," Breeze said trying to resume her sulky state.

"Since when was this a friendship? This is a sistahhood! You stuck with us dahlin'!"

"Aren't I blessed?" Breeze mumbled sarcastically under the throw.

"I heard that!" Willow snapped.

"The skivvies are cute," said Secret still laughing. "And I see they match the tank top. Once you get the waxing done, wear them on your vacation with what's his name...Elliott. You know...to finally get things cooking."

"Secret, what on earth are you doing here?" Breeze asked trying to situate herself under the throw.

"Well, for starters you declined happy hour. Then Mrs. Tingle said you didn't even look at the box of glazed doughnuts she had waiting just for you. Those at the bridal shower said you looked more radiant than the bride. And for the past two days, you looked like you lost your best friend. Even your favorite student, Keisha, snitched. You wouldn't answer my calls, so we all had to take matters into our own hands. I can't believe this is all over a date-gone-wrong. I guess the good news is we finally know that Mr. Nibbly Ears' divorce is final. "

"Yoo-hoo, is it safe to come up?" Spring sang from the door. "Is she all right?"

"Yeah, she's fine. Half naked but fine," said Rayne.

"Please cover it up so the food won't spoil. And did someone say something about a man with nibbly ears?" she asked marching up the steps. "Hey Secret, you made it! You must be talking about that fine freckled face Lincoln...what in the world--?" she said finally noticing the scene on the couch. "If this is how you act...and look when a date goes wrong, I'm gonna need you to take some time to just 'do you'!"

"That's the best advice I've heard all day," said Breeze.

"That's the *worst* advice we've heard all day," said Rayne. "She's been doing for self, for too long!"

"We really need somebody *to do her*," said Secret. "How on earth have you held out so long?"

"I keep dating *beep*, so I won't feel the need."

"That's just completely jacked up," Spring said making her way to the kitchen.

"Wait, Lincoln didn't seem like a bad guy," said Secret.

"Lincoln and Branford were oblivious of Breeze's intentions," said Rayne.

"Speaking of which, let me tell you about her and that fine high-yallah Lincoln, while Breeze is out of swinging reach." While Spring dished the dirt, Breeze just sighed. "Wait, I thought the date was with some dude named Forest, not Lincoln."

"It *was* with Forest," said Rayne. "Let me find out you had a run in with Lincoln."

"Ta-Da," said Breeze.

"Now the puzzle pieces all fit," said Secret. "Walking down the aisle with Branford, running into Lincoln, being in an ex's wedding, and who is this Forest character? I'd take a sabbatical, too with your 'Rated G' past crashing down. Again, what is going on with you and this 'friend' zone? You didn't seal the deal with at least one of 'em?" She waited around for an answer. When none came, she continued. "Do we at least have a picture of this man that has Breeze looking like a sloppily wrapped burrito?"

"I figured somebody would ask," Willow said pulling out a picture of Forest and filling in Secret on the details.

"Oh my, he puts Lincoln to shame," said Secret. "I see our Breeze has a *type*."

"Can we please eat first before we get into specifics and the solution?" Spring interrupted. "I don't want the food to get cold. And what's worse is that wonderful little sandwich shop, what was it called, Henny Penny, Money Penny or Little Bunny Foo Foo, was closed. By the way, I do believe that Spencer and Branford destroy that 'type' theory."

"What do you mean, Spring? *Bun Penny* doesn't close until the mall closes," Willow said walking to the kitchen. Everyone else followed rummaging through Breeze's kitchen for plates and utensils. "You're right, though. Spencer and Branford were the opposite of Lincoln and Forest, at least in the appearance department."

"The one thing all of them definitely had in common was 'fine brothah,'" said Spring. "Anyway, whatever you called the store, it was closed permanently. But I remembered that fish place, Chick 'N Friends that Breeze got those tasty wings and fish things from. I hope he put some extra tartar sauce in the bag, like I asked him to. Rayne, please take this nasty hot sauce. You know, I've been meaning to find out if the owner's son is single…you know for Breeze. I mean, he *looks* like her type. By the way, I got us a couple slices of that wonderful homemade lemon cake. You know, with the bits and pieces of lemon…"

"Spring, will you please shut up about the ding dang cake and the cute Republican!" Breeze boomed. "I was trying to have a nice quiet week, doin' me and…wait, wait, WAIT! WHAT THE *beep* DO YOU MEAN THEY CLOSED DOWN BUN PENNY?"

"What is going on with the language, Breeze?"

"Listen, if none of y'all heifahs cannot handle what is coming out of my mouth, then pack up your stuff, grab a chicken box, and leave! I am in absolutely no condition to be morally correct, today! What is in my heart, will be coming out of this mouth!"

"I only got one chicken box. The rest is fish. And I thought you were supposed to be saved?"

"We all gotta be delivered from something," she said getting back to her spot under the throw, whimpering.

"Did we ever confirm dude was indeed a Republican?" asked Secret. "Either way, that bet'not be a deal breaker… Good granny this fish is pipin' hot. Can you hand me a fork?"

"Can you all just leave, please and let me wallow in my disappointment in peace?"

"For crying out loud," Willow said exhaustedly. "Every woman on the planet has been stood up, at least once. We finally get to celebrate, while consoling you during your rite of passage… Can I have some more tartar sauce?"

"At this point, I'm not sad about that. I'm sad because my beloved Bun Penny is gone. And I never had a chance to say good bye. No more chicken salad. No more thick slices of Applewood smoked bacon. No more Ann Arbor sandwiches. No more of that lovely honey cup mustard that would clear up the cloggiest of sinuses. No pungent aroma of freshly ground coffee that would have you craving a cup, even if you didn't drink the stuff. No more sexy five o'clock shadowed, muscly 20 year old sandwich makers slyly asking if you wanted your buns buttered. And that particular day, I ordered a salad."

"I still think you should have accepted his offer," said Willow. "All I saw were teenaged girls working the counter. There was that one who refused to tuck in her hair. Some guy probably told her, wispy tendrils were 'cute.' To the person wanting a sandwich, hair sticking out all over the place makes a person nervous... These fries have been cooked to perfection. Did you taste yours?"

"I've seen her," said Breeze. "I also leave when she's there or hope she's helping someone else if I really want my good sandwich fix." She sighed. "First they took away the poinsettia tree and now my beloved Bun Penny. But I'll be all right...eventually. If I could just get a moment to myself, by myself--"

"Ain't happin', Breeze," said Rayne. "Let's get back to the real subject at hand. Personally, I really need you to shake this off. I mean, he's not the only single man left on the planet... Please say there's a corn muffin to go with my chicken!"

"The only one that's black, never been married, with no kids, a good job, within my age group, and seemed interested in me, not you, not my cousin, me. Yes, yes he is," she said while still under the throw. "And he likes roller coasters. I just cannot understand why this is such a difficult qualification to meet," she said mumbling her last statement to no one in particular. "And...and...and he, too, could appreciate a good Bun Penny sandwich! Dang it! Why did they have close down Bun Penny?"

"How in the world did you get all of that and still manage not to get the digits? ...Spring, check and see if Breeze has a soda in the fridge."

"She's right about the single man with a good job, though," said Willow. "I'm just not sure about the 'no kids' part. It's been years since Cypress or Reach talked to him... Breeze never has soda. But I'm sure there are some juice boxes. Spring, check on the left side of the fridge."

"Juice boxes? What is she, five?"

"By the looks of her on that couch, I'd say she is mentally," responded Secret. "Throw me one, too, please."

"Y'all, listen! I totally have had enough! Y'all got five seconds before I call the cops for breaking, entering, and stealing what's left of my juice boxes."

"No, Breeze, you listen--"

Breeze pulled the phone out from under the throw, trying to convey she meant business.

Willow shot up across the dining room and snatched the phone away holding it gingerly. "I hope this was not on vibrate." Everyone in the house, including Breeze roared. "First of all, I have a key. So this would not be considered a crime," Willow said after the laughter finally subsided. "Let me call Cypress. I'm sure he still has Forest's number, so we can get to the bottom of his disappearing act."

"NO," Breeze boomed again sitting straight up. "DO-NOT-CALL-CYPRESS! There's no need getting your big mouth brother involved, only to have him use my situation as his next anecdote at this year's family cookout."

"Maybe he could use that same anecdote at your wedding," said Willow.

Breeze made a dismissive tone and retreated under the throw. "And don't even think about telling Reach either. No one else needs to be involved. I will deal with this my way, in my time."

"Which is what, moping around the house wearing a pair of fancy drawers?"

"For the last freakin' deakin' time, get out! I was hurting no one until everybody started showing up!"

"We need you to hurry up and find somebody so that we can give you the 'serving' plate," Spring ignored. "I'm growing real tired of catching my husband using that plate when we're out of clean ones. And I sure don't want him serving my fried chicken on that plate... Girl, when y'all try this cake..."

"Does he not remember how he used the plate when you and he got married? And, what is the plate doing in your kitchen, anyway? I can smell the lemon from here. Break me a piece of it will ya?"

"Where else should I keep it? It's a plate--"

"Wrapped up and tucked away with the other keepsakes you plan to pass down," said Rayne. "When you get home, please wash the plate, bundle it up in protective wrapping, and put it away until Breeze says, 'I do.' You've had it twice, so you should know better.... Girl, this cake is off the chain!"

"Yeah, that sounds like a good idea," said Breeze. "Go home right now and wash, no, disinfect the plate. Go home and wrap up the plate. Go home and keep it safe. Go home now, before you forget. Are you receiving the common denominator of this message? Do I need to isolate the variables in these sentences?"

"You ain't getting rid of us that easily, dahlin'!"

"I just realized something," Spring said nibbling on a piece of fish. "You got a lot of 'quit' in you. If something doesn't go your way, you just run and hide. This one and I do mean miniscule set back should be a lessoned learned... Did y'all leave me *any* tartar sauce?"

"Yeah, like get dude's number," Rayne added while giving Spring two tartar sauce packets. "This is the first and last thing we tell you to do."

Breeze sighed heavily as she kept her back to her friends and stayed buried under the throw. "Well let's prove Spring's statement to be true. She says I have a lot of quit in me. How about we quit this conversation? I think that proves it."

"I thought you needed at least two proofs for a statement to be true?" inquired Secret. "But this cake right here, needs no proof!"

"I kept my back turned away and trying my best to kick y'all out. That should be proof enough."

"I just cannot believe what I am seeing," said Secret. "Maybe a moment by yourself will actually do you some good. So, I am going to let you get yourself together because this crappy disposition ain't like you at all. I do, however, expect a complete change of attitude come Monday. I'll take the rest of my fish tenders and a sliver more of that heavenly scented cake to go, please," she said to Spring. "Was there a corn muffin left?"

"I'm with you on that one," said Rayne. "Besides, my husband is planning date night and I'm praying that he doesn't burn the house down with those cheap candles he purchased. But Breeze, I really think you should reconsider using your resources to get to the bottom of this... Does anyone else want the rest of the hot sauce?"

"I am standing my ground not allowing anyone to call motor mouth Cypress! Just make sure I get a piece of that cake. That lemon is soundin' off."

"At least she's willing to eat something," said Rayne. "Spring, dish out her portion of the food, put it in the fridge, and let's go."

"We're just getting started. We gotta come up with some kind of solution." When no one responded, she reluctantly fixed a plate for Breeze. They cleaned up in silence and all but one headed for the door. "Aren't you coming with us?"

"No, not yet," Willow said shaking her head.

They pulled down the throw just enough to expose Breeze's cheek, kissed it, and jokingly pulled on her hair. "A complete change of attitude...and drawers," Secret said finally heading for the stairs. "At least you could say bye!"

"A-M-F!"

"Breeze!"

"Adios, My Friends. And thanks for caring about me," she finally admitted. "Now get the *beep* out and take Willow with ya!"

She shook her head, waved goodbye to the girls, nibbled on a piece of fish, then a French fry. She grabbed a bottle of water and the remaining takeout container contents, and made her way to the living room. "All right Breezy-Bee, it's just you and me," she said setting her food and water on the coffee table. "Why does Forest have such a hold on you?" Breeze did not answer. "Don't even think about giving me the silent treatment."

"I don't want to talk, because y'all refuse to just shut up and listen," she said still under the throw. "I do not need you or everyone else's two cents adding fuel to the fire."

"Well, you know I'm gonna give you my opinion, if you ask for it or not."

"And that is just it," she exclaimed finally sitting up. "I'm not asking for it. I'll figure it out...my way," she said retreating under the throw.

"Fine. I'll shut up and listen," Willow mocked. "But you have to admit, you're never like this when you stop dating someone. You certainly didn't show any interest in Forest after Kings Dominion. And I don't think I've ever seen you sulk like this over a man. As a matter of fact, this is the first time I've actually seen you finally giving a kitty about any man."

Breeze finally turned around to face her. She paused for moment, wondering if it was worth the effort. She looked at her friend's concerned face and finally started talking. "First of all, the date never got started. Secondly, each of you found the love of your lives doing your thing. Spring dumped the wrong one, found the right one at a conference, and now they are trying their best to start a tribe. Rayne found hers coordinating someone else's family trip. Not only did she plan the trip, she got an extra discount, a free room, used it, and eventually married one of the cousins. And you, Ms. Flirty Mc Hot Tail. I take you to Elliott's fraternity party. You chatted up and fell in love with the only raisin in the bowl full of peanuts."

"Uh, excuse me, he chatted *me* up. And what does all this have to do with the price of cheese?"

"That story will be etched in pencil for corrections when I tell Reach what you said," Breeze retorted. "The point I was trying to make is that each of you was doing your thing. I was doing my thing, at the time, when I met Forest, helping out a friend at an amusement park. Now he's back in the picture again, while I'm doing my thing: being bridesmaid. And while I'm doing my thing, I reconnected with the 'like' of my life.

"One of my best days of my life was spent with Forest. There was great conversation, heated debates, laughter that made my entire face hurt, and our zeal to pick the perfect spot on the roller coaster car. I loved the fact that he didn't mind driving, and I experienced his good taste in music, while riding shot gun in his car.

"It was my one perfect day...at the time. It ought to be because I got the worst punishment of my life. Mom was so mad that I didn't directly ask her permission to go. Their bedroom door was closed, so the only thing I could do was leave a note. I mean, I couldn't open the door and get my feelings hurt...again. I think the last time I opened that closed door, I was scarred for life."

"I keep telling you that part was optional," Willow interrupted. "But you need to try it when the time comes."

"Uh...ewww," Breeze said shuttering the thought out of her head. "Anyway, mom asked if my disappearing act was worth the punishment I was about to receive. I apologized for the profanity in advance. I thought about the butterflies fluttering in my stomach the entire day. I could still feel that hug he gave me, after he walked me to my door. I looked her straight in the eye and said, '*beep* yeah,' and went to bed. I decided to wait for the exact details of my punishment, until I was better rested. Eventually my mom understood my reasoning, so she lessened the sentence to a month.

"I think I'm still waiting for a day like that to come again. Now don't get me wrong. I'm having some rockin' good times with Elliott. But no date or so called relationship I ever had could compare to the giggly, giddiness and mutual interest during that one great day. Or so I thought. Anyway, that one day showed me what I wanted in a guy."

"You were only 15. How on earth could you know your standards?"

"Something inside me clicked and said, 'he's the one.' I've never felt that way with anyone else."

"Not even with Spencer? I mean, you were with dude for an entire year. And what about Elliott?"

"Definitely not with Spence. I was *supposed* to like Spence because I met him in church. He approached me first. And he was persistent. Unfortunately, I appreciated that a little too much and got caught up with the so called proper order of things. And again, Elliott and I are just friends. He doesn't feel that way about me and I already told you how

I feel about him." Her mind quickly turned back to that day at Kings Dominion. The scowl she had was replaced with a huge smile.

"Wait, did I see a smile? I see that pretty smile. Tell me what's behind it."

"Do you think it's kind of pervy that my first kiss was in *Smurf Mountain*?"

"Just a bit. There was nothing else to do or care about in that old dark converted *Haunted Mountain*, but make out. And--hold the heck on! Whatchu you mean your first kiss was in *Smurf Mountain*? And with *my Prom date*?"

"See, that's exactly why I didn't say anything," she said excitedly jumping up from the couch. "I knew you had feelings for him! I knew it, knew it, knew it!"

"No, not at all. I just wanted to get you off of the couch. But his friend, however... That's probably why I never noticed what was going on between you two. I guess that turned out to be a great day for the both of us."

"Mmm," Breeze said. "Incidentally, wasn't dude your first? And I don't mean *kiss*."

"Okay, this conversation ain't about me! Today we are focusing on you. And for starters, you lied to me. You told me your first kiss was on your Prom night!"

"As far as you were concerned it was," she said settling back on the couch. "I just didn't have the heart to tell you about Forest," she said lying down at the sound of his name. "The saddest part of this story is I won't have the fantasy anymore. Now I have to find a different route to work."

"You can still keep the 4 o'clock fantasy and please keep your five-light route. Just leave earlier... So, how was it?"

"How was what?"

"The kiss. Did the boy have skills or what? Then again, he must have since you're sulking on this couch." Breeze smiled but, did not answer. "Please don't tell me you did other things besides kissing in Smurf Mountain." She still did not answer. She felt there were some things, some memories you keep to yourself. "Heifah, you and your couch are about to wear this bottle of water!"

"Cool it. Things did not get that far. And how could they, I was only 15 and at an amusement park?"

"Well, just as long as he didn't use you for his own personal amusement...at least not then, anyway. By the way, don't you think it's time you open up for business?"

"Oh, Willow, really," she said exhaustedly while situating herself under the throw again.

"I know that you're a Christian. But you're 38. I truly feel sorry for the brothah's back once you do or say, 'I do'...and then do. I hope you put 'strong back,' 'extra limber,' and perhaps, 'double jointed' on your list of preferences. And make sure you add--"

"Just write it down somewhere. I'll save the information for a rainy day."

"All right, I honestly believe this madness goes deeper than just one perfect day." She did not respond. "You know, Secret brought up a really good point. This friend zone you seem to find yourself in. And by the way, why didn't you tell me about the run in with Lincoln?"

"Oops," was all Breeze could muster.

"Oops, my foot! We will be getting to the bottom of that, later. Anyway, could this 'friend zone' stem from your parents being friends instead of lovers?"

"My parents did love each other," she said still under the throw. "They just couldn't live together. They realized they needed their own space after they got married."

"How did it make you feel?"

"It took me a long time to understand their arrangement. Once I did, I was okay with it."

"They must have known their divorce affected you in some way. You have a habit of keeping men at bay. I'm sure your mom noticed it when you barely brought any guys home."

She thought about Willow's statement and finally sat up to face her. "Mom was concerned. Dad doesn't care, as long as I'm happy. I just couldn't ignore the hollering and screaming over something stupid every night to the eventual peace, quiet, and civility that finally took place when they divorced. What I finally saw, is how I live. 'It's real nice to see you...now go home.'"

"Breeze you can't possibly live your life that way."

"I can and I will! Look what happens every time I let my guard down. Nothing but chaos, confusion..."

"Don't forget cussin'," Willow added.

"Look, I need you and the rest of the crew to just let me stew over this, take a nice hot bath, go to the gym, and wear out that punching bag. I promise, I'll be fine."

"We'll see. Breeze...have you prayed over this?"

"What makes you think I haven't?"

"This scene on the couch, the cussin', the poutin', the lack of bounce back..."

"What else am I supposed to do when I'm frustrated with the situation, and God's special time-release blessings and breakthroughs ain't coming fast enough?"

"Scratch your rump and just get glad, that's what!"

"Listen," Breeze paused but chuckled. "I'm just feeling pretty stupid and downright vexed for letting this happen to me again. And I am entirely too old for being disappointed repeatedly. Nothing ever gets started. I know He'll work it out. But in His time. That is entirely too long for me right now. I need to just take a quiet moment to stew, wallow, and eventually figure this all out, so I won't end up this way again."

"Girl, do you still keep your laxatives in the fridge?"

"Yeah, but I'm out. Why?

"Well, you need to get some, 'cause are you are just-so-full-of-crap!"

24

Robes & Repercussions

The voice inside her head was loud and clear, *"Get Up!"* The voice may have sounded determined and motivating, but it did not make her feel any better. *"It's not supposed to make you feel better!"* She shuffled to her bathroom and took a hard look at herself in the mirror and was less motivated. *"How about a moment at the gym? You'll get to hit something."* That was inspiration enough. She shuffled to the shower, washed off three days of thoughts, disappointment, and unsolicited advice. She did however keep the good natured-ness of her dad and friends close to her heart. She also decided to send them a 'thank you' note...later. Realizing she only had 15 minutes, she lotioned up, got dressed and made a bee line to class. She was amazed how quickly she could get ready seeing as though it was only an hour ago that she never wanted to leave her couch ever again.

"Hey Breeze," Lyric said greeting her with a big hug. "I got a spot right here waiting for ya! Missed ya last week. Did the shower go okay?" Breeze nodded her head yes. She almost forgot that Lyric would be an hour long reminder that class was to meet and share today. She was still not ready to face anyone let alone share, especially with her classmates. Lyric continued, "Listen, I have to leave early to get my hair done so I won't be late for class. I still can't even believe this will be our last class. I'm curious as to what she has in store for us today since she said we have to be sure to get our nails done, wear pretty undies, and flip flops." She noticed Breeze's distant facial expression. "Hey, are you feeling all right?"

"I will once I start hitting the bag," she said mustering up a smile.

"Well, make sure you hit *the bag* and not me. I don't want to leave for my cruise with a black eye," she laughed and headed toward the back for some weights.

Breeze noticed Lyric making progress with Mr. Gym class, smiling, laughing, and making small talk. She could not wait to hear the story behind that smile she was flashing him. Lyric came back with weights for the both of them. "I am so ready for this bag therapy," she said. "I think we both need to wear this bag out!"

Once class was finished, she high-fived the remaining classmates, and glanced at her watch to see how much time she had left before class. She had plenty and decided to get a manicure and pedicure. "That will put me in an even better mood," she cheered plopping herself in the car. But as soon as she inserted the key in the ignition, she realized that she got her hands and feet done just last week. "Seems like a year ago," she sighed. In lieu of the shower, she decided to settle for a hot bath and a good book.

— ⁓ —

"Good afternoon, Hyacinth. So wonderful to see you again," Lourdes said greeting Breeze with warm hug in the middle of the lobby. "I hope and trust that you had an eventful three months with great results to share." Breeze just smiled and headed towards the conference room. "Oh no, there's a slight change in plans today. For the next hour you will be in room 'four.' Once you go in, make a right, and you will receive further instructions." Breeze thanked her, but could not hide the confused facial expression. "Trust me, you are going to enjoy this," Lourdes reassured.

As she entered room number four, she was greeted by a white partition with an Asian motif. She headed right as instructed and was welcomed by a handsome caramel coated stranger with sandy brown dreadlocks, wearing a crisp fitted white tee shirt, white pants, and flip flops. Breeze noticed his hands and feet were just as pretty as he was.

"Good afternoon, Hyacinth. I will be performing your massage for the next hour. Please undress to your comfort level, but remove your bra. Once you are ready, place yourself faced down under the covers. I will be back in five minutes to begin," he smiled flashing a neat pearly white row of teeth. Breeze momentarily speechless, nodded her head to indicate she understood.

"Now *this* is what the doctor really ordered," she said getting undressed. She looked at the massage table covered in pretty pink towels, a spread, and sheets. "I am so glad I followed Ms. Zenobia's instructions," she said to no one in particular while settling herself under the covers as much as she could.

The masseuse walked in and gently asked if there were any areas that needed special attention. "*If you only knew,*" she thought to herself smiling. "Not really, just my shoulders and upper back."

"Very well. Let's get started." Soft meditation music was turned on while she heard him pick up a bottle of whatever was about to be used. He started with her back and immediately got to work. And for the next hour Breeze got lost in the heavenly scented massage oil, soft music, and strong hands. "What is going on in your life with your shoulders so tense?" he said softly. Breeze just smiled and sighed as he continued to work out the physical kinks of her life.

He gently drummed his fingers to the beat of the final violin strings from the top of her temples to the sides of her arms. "Hyacinth, your experience has ended." She whimpered. "How do you feel?" he asked gently.

"Like I could stay here for the rest of the day," she said not moving from her spot. "Seriously, I have money…"

"I can see that I performed well," he said laughing softly. "But all good things must come to an end. When you are ready, please sit up slowly, and slip on the item on the hanger. I will be back in a few minutes with some water," he said bowing.

"Like he wasn't a tall glass of water, already," she mumbled while getting up. She stretched and shuffled to see what was actually on the hanger. A pretty pink envelope was attached.

"I hope you enjoyed your massage. Please slip this on and join me and your classmates in the conference room. And do not forget to give your masseuse the $14. I am sure he earned it. Z."

Breeze smiled, nodded, and pulled out a $20. She stretched again, yawned, and put on a fluffy pretty pink bathrobe with her specific flower embroidered into the lapel.

"Hyacinth?" her masseuse asked softly. She told him to come in. "Again, I hope you are feeling okay," he said offering her a glass of water with a ribbon sliver of lemon.

"Spectacular, really. Thank you so much," presenting him with his tip. He thanked her and gave her a small bottle of muscle soak for relaxation purposes. She thanked him again and headed out the door. She met Rose, Violet, and Daisy in the lobby, nodding their acknowledgements, as they all shuffled contentedly in the conference room. Iris and Lily were already seated with the same relaxed facial expression.

Zenobia sat in the middle of the table with a grand smile on her face, not saying a word, as her Flowers walked in. Breeze finally took a sip of what was no ordinary water. She could taste a blend of lemon and cucumbers that felt absolutely refreshing. Everyone silently took their seats, still sipping their water, melting into the coziness of their chair and robe. Petunia and Tulip were the last to come in with looks of extreme tranquility, resuming their usual spot and snuggled into their chairs, contentedly.

Zenobia smiled again, retrieving two pitchers from the rear of the conference room, and placed them on the mid-size squared cork coasters in the center of the table. Everyone looked at the sweating pitchers, then looked at their glasses, and retreated deeper into their chairs.

"Ladies, we have to get started sometime today," she said softly. Eventually everyone sat up, trying to support themselves upright. "Judging from the limp noodleness, everyone enjoyed their massages." No one responded, at least not verbally. The only feedback she received were contented sighs and smiles. "Do I dare serve the refreshments?" The mention of food seemed to be the operative word to perk up the class, while still saying nothing. "Very well. This will be a working lunch due to today's discussion and presentation." Lourdes came with fancy boxed meals consisting of a choice of tuna or chicken wrap, orzo pasta, a strawberry and spinach salad, with chocolate covered strawberries for dessert.

"Ms. Zenobia?" asked Daisy finally breaking the contented silence. "I want to go to the spa that employs that Nubian statue, you call a masseuse! I don't know how much you paid for him to make house calls, but he was worth more than the tip you suggested!"

"I gave him $20," one said. "I gave mine $25," said another. "I gave him a 20 *and* my phone number!"

"I am glad everyone enjoyed their session. And you all are going to spoil them rotten. They are actually students at a massage therapy school, a few doors down. They graduate in two weeks and I will be sure to provide you with their future work assignments.

"Now that the ice has officially been broken, let us get started," she said taking her usual spot at the middle of the classroom. "I thought the best way to end class would be to show you, instead of telling you, to be careful of the power of touch. Judging from the size of the tips you provided, everyone was seduced. I do believe that each of you will find the right one made especially for you. Just keep the emotions in check when the hugs and hand holding commence.

"Next, let me remind you to take time for yourselves. When life and circumstances get out of control, you need to be able to take a step back, get a better perspective, and take the necessary next steps. Now getting a massage every time you have an issue, could be quite pricey. But every once in a while, treat yourself to something with longer lasting effects... other than shoes, a purse, or another article of clothing you probably do not need or already have.

"The spa robe I provided is my second gift I have for you tonight. When you take time out for you, make sure you examine *whose* you are, who you are, and be content where you are. Besides, how do you expect your light to shine bright, if you are not comfortable in your own skin? Lastly, a good massage, lounging in a comfy robe with your sister friends, help loosen the lips. So, let us discuss how you were able to let that beautiful light shine bright these last few months. First, take a moment to describe your newest chapter in a few words or less. Then, write the title on the card in front you. Once everyone is finished, we shall start with Violet."

All too familiar with the drill, the Flowers busily got to work on their final class assignment. Again, they scribbled and crossed out ideas on a spare piece of paper. A few comedic comments were shared, as they finalized their decision. Once everyone was satisfied of their chapter title, the sharing commenced.

Violet flipped over her card to reveal: **'NERVOUSLY BLESSED.'** A friend of mine invited me to an all-you-can-stand 'pizza, root beer, and bowling' night hosted by her church's single ministry. Pizza and bowling? I could not resist. By the way, I can now comfortably confess, that my secret passion is bowling."

"Not with those fingernails," said Petunia.

"Girl, years of practice," she said wiggling her fingers. "This diva knows how to work a bowling ball. I get there and she has a spot waiting for me on a lane. They gathered in prayer and not a moment later, the pastor asked if the team members within the two lanes were here for fellowship or competition. I was there to rock and roll, yet remain humble. So, I told him both. Thankfully, I accomplished my goal beating the pastor and a few others within our lane. But there was this one that was clearly there for the competition. We bowled and trash talked for the entire two and a half hours. We had ours and the nearby lanes cracking up. I did manage to beat him by two pins.

"Everyone was preparing to leave, I'm putting my ball and shoes back in my bag, and the trash talker challenges me to a rematch. I told him that would be fine, just let me know when. He said how about now, and suggested the loser takes the winner to dinner. I am always up for a challenge. Long story short, we closed the place with him owing me three dates.

"We finally leave and he walks me to my car, takes my keys, opens the trunk, and places my bowling bag in it. Then he unlocks my car door, opens it, sees that I'm all buckled in, and closes the door. At this point, I am so glad I got my car detailed. I started my car, and rolled my window down to thank him. He shooed my 'thank you' away, mentioned he was hungry, and asked if I would be interested in some pancakes. This diva knows there's always room for pancakes and I did not mind cashing in one of my prizes. We talked and laughed so much over French toast and pancakes that we didn't notice the sun was up...and a fight broke out. And we have been seeing each other ever since. His name is Duncan and I am nervously meeting his family next Saturday."

"So why are you so nervous?" asked Rose. "I'm sure you've met dozens of parents before."

"Oh, did I mention that Duncan is Filipino?" Jaws dropped and gleeful gasps could be heard throughout the room. "He admitted that his parents are a little old school. I was like, 'wait until you meet my dad,' who was under the impression that I was holding out for my 'BMW.' My mom knows, and is ecstatic that I found someone to love.

"I have everything I could possibly want in a man, just wrapped up in a different package. A very nicely dressed, permanently tanned, looks rockin' in a tank top, but can rock a suit better than any *GQ* model. His looks do not compare to how he treats me. Spoiled, pampered, loved, cared for, and...liked!

"He doesn't just love me, he likes me. We like each other and cannot wait to be in each other's company. However, we do respect the need for space. And, he can dance! He loves the fact that I let him lead. And he makes it so easy to follow...on and off the dance floor. So, shouts out to Ms. Zenobia for the dance lessons!"

"This is awesome news, Violet! See what I mean, ladies? Keep that car cleaned."

"Because it can all start with a conversation in the parking lot," said the class in unison.

"Precisely. Iris, would you like to go next?"

"If I must. I do have good and not so good news to report," she said holding up card saying: **'NEW FOCUS.'**

"Please tell us the good news is that you made some head way with Mr. Gym class," Petunia pleaded.

"Well, that would be considered part of the bad news. Long story short, no I did not. Anyway--"

"You were making so much progress," said Breeze. "Y'all should have seen the smile she flashed him this morning."

"The bottom line with Pretty Brown Biceps is that he's a flirt, silly of me to get caught up."

"That smile he flashed *back* this morning and the statement you just made are not congruent."

"I said he was a flirt."

"So that's it?" asked Rose. "Are we putting the idea of, what did you call him, 'Pretty Brown Biceps' to bed?"

"Speaking of which, I cannot deny wishing I was under him while he was doing this morning's push-ups. But yes, I am officially done." The entire class gave her a questioning look. "What y'all? In the immortal words of Hyacinth, I said I was done, not dead. I was able to examine my problem during the last couple of months--"

"Hold on Iris," Daisy interrupted. May we ask what happened at the Valentine's Day eve dinner? You ran out after a brief rant that had all of us worried."

"I took a chance with a blind date who reminded me of a piece of dried up turkey sausage, with the dude insisting all throughout the evening that I was not *his type*. But I don't wanna talk about that," she said with a little tone of frustration. "I wanna talk about the dance classes."

"Wait, wait," Rose said while she and the class roared with laughter. "He looked like what?"

"You know, the kind of sausage that's all dried up and wrinkly from a microwave. And he's five years younger," Iris said chuckling to herself. She waited until the laughter subsided to continue.

"Anyway, in addition to *my* special dance class you recommended, Rose and Violet convinced me to take their hand dancing class. Apparently, they were tired of seeing me dancing all by myself. This, is after I took y'all to my line dancing party. And I have to admit, that I have been dancing all by myself for so long, that I've forgotten how to dance with someone else. My dance partner told me that I have the moves of a stiff white woman. And he was white. I couldn't even get the basic steps. I thought about giving up, because it was just so hard. He was really patient with me. He never gave up until I was able to dance in a straight line, turning on beat, really making the moves look cohesive."

"Ah, somebody got a little taste of the Topper experience," said Violet. Rose nodded her head in agreement, smiling.

"I did," Iris said with a big smile. "I am beyond excited about the hand dancing soiree he's taking a group of us to, when I get back from my cruise. I just hope I can remember my dance moves."

"You can practice and shine that dancing light on the cruise."

"I can practice my new line dances, but not my hand dancing. Finding someone to dance with is difficult when you are a 'Mary Ann' on a boat full of 'Gingers.'" The entire table looked at her with disbelief.

"Look, I'm just being honest. And above all I'm being honest with myself. I realize He only places you in situations you can handle. I had to examine my past and present, and concluded that I can handle new dance moves, just not a relationship."

"Yet," the Flowers said in unison.

"I guess," she said dismissively. "Anyway, I'm placing my relationship issues and the lack thereof, in His hands and happily leaving it there. I'm just glad that I can finally scratch 'how to hand dance' off my 'to-do' list. I am back on course, enjoying what life has to bring without worrying, obsessing, or losing my hair stressing over him finding me. It's a weight off my back; I feel as though I lost 10 more pesky pounds. I feel incredible." The table was still speechless. "What are y'all staring at?"

"Iris, listen to me," Zenobia said breaking the silence of disbelief. "He gave you your special light so you can be the best line and hand dancing Mary Ann where ever you are! I gave you those pole dancing classes so you can feel like a Ginger and continue to be a Mary Ann! So, all those in favor of hearing about Iris shaking a tail feather on her cruise, complete with pictures say, 'I.'" Everyone agreed. "Good. Now think of a Saturday for all of us to meet. And do not forget to pack that pink dress for speed dating."

"I can't find...wait, how did you know about the speed dating? And how on earth do you know about the pink dress?"

"I have my ways, darling. Tulip would you like to go next?"

"I would, but I need to know if Iris is indeed okay," said Tulip looking at Iris with concern. The whole room was looking at Iris noticing something was not right.

"This revelation has to come from something deeper than Mr. Turkey Sausage," said Breeze with a slight chuckle. "What happened?"

She paused for a moment and then smiled. "For one special moment in time, I thought I did everything right. My being the supportive, encouraging friend to a really great guy was about to pay off. I listened, laughed, and found myself spiritually open yet accountable. We had so much fun. Good laughs, amazing conversations over great meals. We even had the best arguments where I'm laughing in between making my points. Oh, and those late night phone calls, talking about the strangest topics.

"For the first time in my life, I felt like a giddy teenager. Laughed like one, too. I enjoyed myself with him. Even his belly button faced me when we talked...for hours. I liked who I was, when I was with him. I *liked* him. I do believe that he *liked* me. And I could *stand* him, which is a factor I really need to add on my list. I honestly believed what I wanted, what I prayed for in a husband was finally within reach, and I was able to hug what I wanted on a regular.

"BUT... reality kicked in. He didn't flat out tell me, but he showed me, we can be friends, nothing more. Just as I was getting used to this theme of not being some guy's type. This one comes along, looks my way, smiles, and eventually hurts me to my core."

"Dahlin', I'm listening to you," said Violet. "I really don't think he's ready for you."

"On the bright side, he has shown me if he wants something, he'll go for it. If he's interested, he will not hesitate, as Hyacinth puts it, to chat someone up. Unfortunately, he's not chatting *me* up."

"Iris, unless 'disrespectful' is on your list of 'must haves,' this one has got to go straight to the trash with Mr. Turkey Sausage," said Rose. "None of us here are going to let you toss away your hopes over this."

"Listen y'all, I appreciate the encouragement. I came to the conclusion that I was just not enough. That if we were to be in a relationship, he would always be on the lookout for something better, more exciting, more...experienced. I make no apologies for being the 'good girl.' So what, that I'm so...innocent? So what, if I haven't been around the block more times than an ice cream truck? I'm not a prude! So--"

"Girl," was the only thing the group could muster up between the laughter.

Iris also laughed at her own statement, while wiping away a few tears. "Anyway, I would like to know what the Lord wants me to learn from this. I'm too tired to wait another 40 years for an answer, only to get hurt... yet again.

"Now, I am focusing on what I do best: attending some rockin' concerts, experience some laugh-until-my-face-hurt comedians, see some old friends, make a few new ones, parading around in the best costumes, take some pics with a few select celebrities, try a new martini...or three, and shake my hips until the DJ gets tired for the next seven days. I refuse to bring 'anger and bitterness' on my very expensive cruise; nor do I want them waiting for me when I get back."

"I see," was all Zenobia could muster holding up her hand before anyone else could offer sentiments. "If you believe deep in your heart that he was meant for you, set up a time for clarification, *privately,* with this young man *once* he finishes vying for 'Player of the Year.' For now, have a good time on your cruise and find that pink dress! Tulip, if you would please?"

"Ms. Zenobia, I have to confess. In Iris' defense, a few of us got together and admitted some of us are just not going to get married or at least get what we want. Having faith while waiting for him to find us, can become a hopeless situation. That 'in due' time, instead of 'you time' could and has stretched into years. At that point, we resolved that we cannot have everything, and one big part of being an adult will not be met. Personally, that is what I used to think until Smith came into my life.

"What I want to know is how one loses a pink dress?" she asked lightening up the tone in the room, again. "Actually, don't answer that. I'm known to lose a pair of shoes in my own house, so I feel your pain. In more ways than one, dahlin'," she said hugging Iris. Violet joined in on the hug.

"Enough about me and the pink dress that disappeared into thin air," Iris said shooing the Flowers away. "I want to hear what is going on with Mr. Cooking class."

"I cannot thank each of you enough for encouraging me to go with Smith to his cooking competition," Tulip said while turning up a card to reveal a '**SMILEY FACE**' as big as the one she was wearing.

"Did he win?"

"No, but two of his recipes are featured in a few local restaurants. Anyway, these past five months have been the happiest of my life. I finally have someone made especially for me to try out my recipes, do things, or do absolutely nothing with. Good gracious, did He really get it right this time," Tulip said beaming with her deep dimples.

"But hunnah," Tulip said shaking her head. "All of this upkeep is hurtin' a sistah's wallet! Dating is expensive! I am so glad that he has seen me at my less than best. Gone are the days where I could skip a hair, nail, or wax appointment." She noticed the looks on the faces around the room. "The face y'all! I'm talking about my brows, lip, and chin. I can't strut around town with Smith with Wolfman Jack's goatee. If I miss one appointment, my 5 o'clock shadow will be more like 10 o'clock." Tulip paused to chuckle to herself. The class laughed, too, while nodding their heads in agreement. "I hired a cleaning service three times to make sure my house was spotless. I purchased four new sheet sets. I have three sets of plates just for dates. I bought five new sleep bonnets and painstakingly ensured my hair smells nice."

"Your hair needs to smell nice?" asked Lily. "I never would have thought about that."

"Smith is a snuggler and my head always falls under this chin. I found out it is the little details such as keeping the hair smelling nice, that keeps him close. Speaking of which, I even had to revamp my underwear drawer. I mean, I have to keep 'em pretty and yes, matching."

"From the 'granniest to the sexiest,'" the entire table said in unison.

"Hold on, let me ask you something," Rose interrupted. "New bed sheets and upgrading the lingerie? Has this relationship, um, progressed?"

"No," Tulip said coyly, while batting her eyes. "The awesome thing is I finally have someone to be my best for. It's one thing to be your best for yourself. Now I have someone thinking of me, phoning me just because. I cannot believe that I finally have someone care if my back is ashy, puts lotion on it, and zips up the back of my dress. And he has really great hands. Last week he gave me a foot massage that sent my senses through the roof! Lawd, I can still feel it!

"Woo, anyway, I'm meeting his family next month at a wedding. I still cannot believe there's someone just for me. I did not realize I could be this happy. Until..."

"Until, what?" a few members of the table gasped in unison.

"Oh good gracious, here it comes," Petunia sighed.

"Please don't tell me the Steve Madden heel is about to drop?" sighed Breeze.

"Hold on y'all," Tulip said trying to ease the situation. "I didn't know I could be this happy until I met Zinc, um, Graham. Remember the guy who sat between Hyacinth and Violet?"

"You mean short, light, and handsome that was into no nonsense curvy girls?" asked Petunia.

"And could not get enough of our Miss Iced Tea," added Violet.

"Yes, and I can see why," Tulip answered. "His family is full of all types of curvy women, from the shapely to 'oh sweetie, those are not curves.' Walking around looking like Capital B's." Once the laughter died down, Tulip continued. "Representing various letters of the alphabet aside, he comes from a great family complete with parents, aunts, uncles, and cousins who spoil him rotten." Tulip paused again. "I just can't believe that I am dating two guys! *Me!*"

"Do they know about each other?" asked Petunia.

"Yeah," she sighed. "They do. Smith understands the dating thing is new to me and he is being really patient. He does want me to make a decision before I meet with his family and young son. I have a month to think about it. I really want to go this wedding. The drama behind the members of the bridal party would be too good to miss." Tulip looked up pausing, as if she was trying to recall the details. "Let's see...the groom used to date one of the bridesmaids--"

Breeze suddenly snapped her fingers startling everyone in the room. "Sorry. I forgot to pick up my dry cleaning."

"No, worries," Tulip said. "And another groomsman wanted to date the same chick. I really need to see how all of this unfolds...live."

"Talk about a triangle," said Lily.

"What on earth was this bridesmaid thinking?" asked Rose. "I mean a bridesmaid is supposed to be one of your girls, not the groom's."

"And what does that say about the groom, dating his boy's crush?" asked Daisy. "Don't they have a code, too?"

Breeze just sat in her chair squirming on the inside, while hopefully displaying her, 'I'm listening' face.

"Hyacinth, do you have anything to add before we continue?" Zenobia asked politely.

"I'm sure the bridesmaid is probably wondering why she is still in this mess to begin with," Breeze added. "There is always a reason and we are all on assignment."

"My dear, I'm sure this was not the exact assignment He had in mind for His daughter," Zenobia replied. "However, He does place us in the strangest of circumstances. Daisy, would you like to go next?"

"Speaking of strange circumstances, Violet, remember you said your cousin found her husband in the weirdest way after taking this course?" Violet nodded. "Ladies, I found mine in a party store parking lot!"

"What do you mean *your husband*?" asked Rose. "Aren't we being a wee bit presumptuous?"

Daisy used her right hand to hold her card: '**HE LISTENED!**' with 'sort of' written in small letters. While her left hand shot straight up. "I'm getting married November 7th," she said excitedly.

Everyone at the table squealed, shot up from their chairs to hug her, and check out the ring. After the congratulatory remarks and sentiments finally died down, the questions commenced. "How did it happen? What does he look like? What does his credit look like? When is the bachelorette party?" However, the voice of reason could not be ignored. "Daisy, albeit exciting, this is quite sudden," said Zenobia. "Are you and this young man sure about this life changing decision?"

"I understand your concern, but let me tell the story first!"

"Please tell me you are not pregnant," said Petunia. "I'm ready for a bachelorette party, not a baby shower. Not yet, at least."

"No, I am not pregnant. I will get to the sneaky freaky part, shortly. "Anyway, I had to realize that my faith in Him gives me the strength to endure my season of drought. I decided enough was enough, stop going against the grain, and just be the 'supportive, genuinely happy for the other' friend that I know how to be. God must have heard me loud and clear, because no sooner than I made the decision, a friend called needing me to pick up some balloons for a baby shower. I agreed, but only after spending quality time in a nail salon. If I'm going to spread around all of this awesomeness, I will have pretty hands and feet.

"Now, I must have been under the trance of a rockin' leg massage to agree to this request, as I had nowhere to put three sets of balloon bouquets in my two-seater car. I called my friend to send reinforcements. She had the nerve to reluctantly agree to send her brother.

"While I'm waiting, providing onlookers with comedy hour, I see her brother drive up in a black SUV. I'm waving him down, thankful that he didn't take too long. He turns, pulls up to my car, and I'm ready to give him the biggest hug. Only it wasn't my friend's brother. Just a handsome man, so black he's blue, with the prettiest set of white gapped teeth wanting a burrito."

"Sounds like a great dude, already."

"I knew you would approve of his taste, Hyacinth. We had a good laugh over my dilemma, accepting a challenge under the influence. He told me my toes turned out nice. Y'all, I still had the separators between my toes. I blushed and continued with the conversation with him offering to take the balloons, if I agree to go with him later to get that burrito. That was an offer, I happily accepted.

"He stayed the entire time, setting up and breaking down the tables and chairs, bonding with the other gentlemen that were in attendance. The elders fed him royally. When we finally left, we were too full to eat anything else. He walked me to my car, pulled up in his, and we just talked and talked and been talking ever since."

"Okay, Daisy," said Violet. "You got the good brothah with good taste, great manners, and pretty gapped teeth. Let's get to the real subject at hand."

"I'm getting to that. I really need to tell you what led to the proposal. As I said, we've been having a glorious time hanging out, being a couple. He belongs to a men's singles group at his church, and his mentor noticed how close we were getting in such a short amount of time. I found out that he couldn't stop talking about me," she paused to giggle. "Anyway, his mentor recommended that we take a premarital counseling course to see if we were on the same page and the right track. I asked, 'what if were not?' He said, 'first of all he wasn't going anywhere and we'll work on what needs to be worked out, during the process.'

"Y'all, this class gets all up in it! Few, if any, stones are left unturned. We did the readings, sweated through the assigned homework, and memorized scriptures. We not only grew as a couple, but as individuals. Admittedly, there are some things we still need to tweak and we still have some moments of intense fellowship. But, we realized that we do actually love, as well as, like each other, and know one another intimately. During the season of counseling, we met each other's family and friends, having a marvelous time. We passed the class, making some new supportive friends in the process.

"During our own quiet celebratory dinner, he told me he lied when he said he wasn't going anywhere. At first, I didn't know how to take his confession. My old instincts wanted to wipe away three months of pure bliss and I almost let him have it...almost. He saw my brewing anger, calmed me down, and told me that he wanted to move forward...with me. At that point, that's all I heard, because I started screaming and crying when I saw the little black velvet box, and him getting down on one knee! I'm not even sure if I even said, 'yes.'" Daisy paused just beaming. "Hmmm, he did a good job, huh?" she asked wiggling the fingers on her left hand.

"He sure did," said Rose. The entire room agreed. "You do know that we have to circle back to the sneaky freaky part."

"The good news is he made it quite clear that he is, indeed, ready for takeoff," she said beaming brightly. "However, the better news is we are on the same page with the waiting. It helps that the men within his circle agree to wait until marriage. They, too, realized that sex can complicate a good, strong, Godly relationship. The making up after intense fellowship and keeping it Christian is pretty tough. One thing shall not lead to the other. So, there will be no sneaky freaky until November 7th at 7:32 pm."

"7:32?" asked Lily. "Why so specific?"

"The reception should end around 7:30, and it should only take about two minutes for us to get to our suite."

"I'll feel right sorry for that man at 7:33," said Violet. Once again, the entire room happily agreed.

"So, what is the name of this young man?" asked Zenobia.

"Slayton," she said brightly. "And by the way, Iris, you will be coming with me to his church's annual cookout to meet some of the other brothers."

"What made you feel he was the one?" asked Petunia.

"Besides him being a man of God, employed, single, with no kids, a registered voter, and a genuinely good guy? He met a very odd, yet nonnegotiable item on my list. We were on a dinner cruise and I asked him what he wanted from the dessert buffet. He said to surprise him. I made him a sampler plate. He not only took his time with each dessert, he savored every morsel with such sensuality, that I couldn't help but hope that I was next."

"Don't get me wrong, I see your point," said Violet. "Is that actually on your list?"

"For a man not treating his dining experience like a race, yes. Because in my opinion, if he's in a heated rush to finish now, what happens when--"

"Daisy," was all Zenobia could muster at the moment. "We will reconvene with the girl talk when you and Slayton come back from your honeymoon," she said still laughing. "Rose..."

"And try to top that?" she asked. "I think we can end the class right here and get this party started!"

"Spill it, Rose!"

"Yes, Miss Daisy," teased Rose. "Okay, it took a while for me to wrap my mind around this statement," she said flipping over her card: 'I **LET HIM LEAD.**' "Knucklehead's mama asked me to drive her to a family reunion dinner for her other son's in laws. Even after the break up, we still remained close. Anyway, we had a great time laughing, talking, and line dancing. And thanks to Iris, I was able to keep up with six of those line dances. One of the cousins, named Owen, asked me if I could hand dance. I confessed that I was learning, but ready to put lessons four and five into practice. We danced until my cute hair style fell to the floor.

"The evening was getting late, and I really had to get up early in the morning. So, Owen offered to drive the mama home so she could stay a while longer. I am so glad I had my car cleaned because he walked me to my car. We chatted for a while, he tucked me into my car seat, and asked me out. Even though I was all for it, I told him I was uncomfortable with the idea of dating someone so close to the family, again. Come to find out, he already asked the mama if he could date me during one of those mini line dance marathons. *She* was all for it.

"Our first date was a hand dancing party at one of the local lodges. We had a ball and the music was on point. Unfortunately, Knucklehead showed up. We gave a polite hello, and made our way to the buffet line. All of that dancing made us hungry. Being the lady that I am, I made us both a plate. I turn around to ask if he wanted some greens, Owen and Knucklehead were gone.

"Owen comes back looking a little miffed. He thanked me for making him a plate, gave both our plates to another couple, and announced that he wanted seafood instead. I really wanted to get some more dancing in; plus, I wanted to throw down on those chicken legs and greens. He promised to tell me the story at dinner, only we needed to leave.

"Y'all we didn't go to my favorite, Red Lobster. We went to McCormick & Schmick's. Come to find out, Owen forgot that it was Knucklehead who told him about the place. I didn't even know Knucklehead was capable of a two-step, let alone a Chicago eight-count. Owen let him have this place, while we found plenty of other places. So much so, that you can check out our rug cuttin' skills on a local cable channel."

"Let me find out we got a celebrity in the house," Zenobia said laughing. "And that Topper was on point with that advice!"

"He was," said Rose. "Letting *him* lead, really does make *us both* look good!"

"I just absolutely love it when the plan all comes together," said Zenobia. "Speaking of which, what is going on with Mr. Oxygen, Ms. Lily?"

"I do believe everyone here knows that I have been seeing Harper since the ambush at Borders," Lily laughed. "First," she said flipping over her card: '**THE LIST WORKS.**' "About two weeks ago, Harper dropped by unannounced to break up with me, feeling the need to do so face-to-face. I respected him for that. He *felt* he was not the man for me. At this point, I told him if he wanted to date someone else, just free himself. He stated that was not the case. This conversation concerned me, but I told him to wait right there and let me show him whom I prayed for. I presented him with the list I made in class. It took him what seemed like, 10 minutes, to digest what was on my list. 'What's up with the boxers,' was all he could say. I told him that eventually I wanted children and tighty whiteys constrict. He told me they constrict for a reason. We ended up laughing about the contents on my list, of which he meets all but two."

"Is he willing to change to the boxers?" asked Rose.

"Like thongs, I really don't see the point," said Daisy. "If the boys are going to be all over the place, why wear 'em?"

"He said he would happily switch when the time comes," she said still laughing at Daisy's comment.

"Are you the woman on his list?" asked Violet.

"He had his list in the car, within his Bible. I meet all, but four, on this list. He says he would overlook a few; I just needed to learn how to be…a little spicy. So, I reached into my shopping bag that I forgot to put away, and asked would my pole dancing shoes be a good place to start? I had just purchased them for next week's class. Maybe now I can reach the floor. Needless to say, mission accomplished, especially when I actually modeled the shoes. I'm so glad I got that pedicure. I am happy to report, we are still together."

"Again, I just absolutely love it, when His plan comes together. And I will be sure to thank my husband for the strategic seating arrangements," Zenobia said smiling brightly. "Share please, Hyacinth?"

Breeze flipped over her card: 'COUNTING DOWN.' "The bottom line is, everything is fine in Hyacinth's land. I only have 30 days until summer vacation. 36 days until my duties as a doting bridesmaid are over. Actually, the bride monster is acting like she got some sense, so life is much easier. Most importantly, my dress looks fabulous, and I look even more fabulous in it. And a week after the wedding, I go on a 10 day vacation loaded with beach, beverages, and a trusty BFF. So, things are good."

"That's it? No stories of testing your faith?" asked Rose.

"Did you at least check out who you are walking down the aisle with?" asked Lily.

"Yes, he's married."

"At least tell us that you have a date lined up?" Daisy said chiming in. "Do I need to invite you to that cookout, as well?"

"No, I don't have a date. And I'm always up for a good grilled hot dog," she said. "Besides, the bride will only allow spouses and significant others as guests of guests. In her words, 'This is a wedding, not date night'," she mocked. "And since there is no line dancing, all the single ladies will be sitting down. Oh, wait she changed that. We will be line dancing after all. And thanks to Iris, I learned a few new ones."

"Is there anything else you care to share with the group, Hyacinth," Zenobia urged peering over her glasses.

"No, ma'am. Everything is all good."

'No it ain't,' was the look Zenobia shot back. "Last but not least, Petunia if you would please?"

"Before I go into the sordid details," Petunia said holding up her card reading: **'BAD vs. WRONG DECSION.'** "Iris, it would be a shame to throw away your confidence and keep that cute pinup," Petunia said smiling. "We've seen such a glow, especially on that dance floor. You do know someone is waiting for your smile, perhaps that guy you were talking about."

"Excuse me, excuse me," Zenobia interrupted. "You are stealing my closing statements. We are currently focusing our attention on you."

Petunia laughed and apologized. "I said all that to say that I, too, am at a crossroad at this point. I don't really know if I want to get married; and I'm totally undecided if I want children. I can't get along with the ones without kids. The divorced daddies I meet offer so much, yet expect too much, too soon. And they don't want any more children. I may not want them either, but I would like some wiggle room of choice in case my biological clock explodes. Can I have a healthy, abundant balance of what I want and need, at least once?"

"Do we dare ask what you want and need?" asked Lily.

"Do ya really wanna know?" she asked peering over her glasses. The entire class, including Zenobia eagerly nodded their head 'yes.'

"All right," she sighed. "First, I am having really good time with two guys. I met Guy A at an after work happy hour, through a friend. We talked well after happy hour was over. I gave him my 30 second spiel about my goals. He simply asked 'where would he fit in,' which intrigued me.

"I was trash talking with Guy B at a football game, and I finally asked him a simple question: 'Do you wanna piece of me?' He simply answered, 'yes, yes I do.' And that's where my madness with him, started.

"Guy A provides me with what I finally admitted to myself that I needed: affection, listening, conversation, hand holding…and a handyman. He really cares for me. One day, I had a really bad cold. He nursed me with healthy doses of laughter and this chicken soup that his mother used to make for him. What I could taste, was incredible. And whatever was in it, worked. I made him bottle up some of that for future use…and for Tulip to let me know what was in it."

"I can only imagine what Guy B provides," said Daisy.

"Plenty, along with some great season club level seats for both The Ravens and The Orioles. And that would be pretty much it. I'm not too proud of what I let fester with this, um, relationship, but it's what I need at the moment."

"Do you really need to make a decision now?" asked Iris. "It's just fun and dating."

"Guy A wants me to meet his kids, now that I found room in my life for him. If I move forward with Guy A, I know I would be in a loving relationship…and possibly thrust into motherhood. His kids range from 'snotty nose' to 'smart mouth.' I don't think I'm ready for that level of drama. I also know there is absolutely no future with Guy B. The kind of drama he brings can be fun and exciting, at first. Too many feelings get hurt in the process, especially mine."

"Does Guy B have kids?" asked Violet.

"He, too, has three kids. Two are grown and one is still in high school."

"Maybe I missed something," said Lily. "Is Guy B actually available for you to even worry about this decision?"

"I really don't know how to put this…"

"Actually Petunia, I do," interrupted Zenobia. "And I think this is a good place to close. But first, you need to ask yourself if this piece of fun, excitement, and physical activity you *need* that Guy B is letting you *borrow*, will be enough." Petunia started to answer, but Zenobia continued. "I need you to really think about your response while you are at your crossroads, my dear.

"Flowers, I asked you to bring back stories, and you brought me breakthroughs. Words cannot express how proud, overjoyed, and quite frankly, in awe I am of your progress. I know the pole dancing classes were not the most Christian. However, every woman, especially His daughters, should exude confidence. The Word says that we are not to throw away our confidence. A lot of you did just that when you first came to my class, but certainly not now. And if I am seeing it correctly, some of you are receiving a great workout, with even greater results.

"I wanted a few of you to quiet your mind and focus on His Word, what He wants for you, your own breathing, and just be still. I am beyond glad that you are recognizing that need. As you continue with the yoga class, focus now on His next steps for your new chapter. Just do not forget to sit and listen, especially after you have prayed.

"Topper once shared with me, women take the lead 23 hours of the day. Let him take the lead and let him make us both look good at least for one hour. I wanted you to feel comfortable and show the benefits of yielding to a man's direction. Chef Smith touched on it, while Topper demonstrated this nugget of wisdom.

"With that said, I am extremely proud of the awesome transformation of minds, hearts, and spirits of the women in this room. The confidence, the answered prayers, the restored hope, and expectancy is really paying off. A few of you are at a crossroad, but know that you are equipped with His encouraging Word, good friends who understand, and a desire for the new and exciting next steps whatever the case may be. I am proud of you for stepping out of your comfort zone, taking chances, and now experiencing bumper crops.

"You have a lot to give. And each of you give a lot. However, I need some of you to change your focus as to whom you give your time, attention, talents, and self to. He lets mess happen for a reason. He also provides a way out. You just need to receive His direction to make the right choice.

"Enjoy your time of courtship. Getting to the altar is not a race. Your turn is within His time, there is no need to rush it. However, Ms. Daisy?" Zenobia asked smiling while shaking her head and resting her hands on Daisy's shoulder. "Meeting a man by accident, dating him for three months, and getting married in six? I know that's right! Because sometimes you just know when the love of your life, walks into your life!

"However, ensure your conclusion of your next steps are in line with His will. The more you go against the grain, the more you get irritated. Taking a break and having a different focus is healthy and necessary. I hope and trust this class and the lessons learned has taught you to pray, ask for Divine direction, and actually go for what you want in your renewed love life, budding, or otherwise.

"Ladies, I have one last gift for you. It is just a small token of what I want for each of you. It is the reason why we spent eight months examining ourselves, making friendships, and establishing an absolutely necessary support system that will sustain before, during, and after whatever the case may be."

Lourdes quickly came in with four large pink shopping bags filled with medium sized white boxes tied with a pretty pink satin ribbon. The Flowers excitedly cleaned off their surrounding area and sanitized their hands, ready to receive.

"I just want to know how she could top that massage."

"And this plush bathrobe," said Lily. "I can stay in this, the entire weekend."

"My hope is a box full of those mutant chocolate covered strawberries," said Petunia. "I think I just found my next relationship in those things." Lourdes laughed, shaking her head no.

"She placed a gift box in front of each Flower. They knew instinctively to wait until all were served before touching the box. However, the anticipation did not stop them from eyeballing the box, giddily, and doing a dance in their chairs. Once all the boxes were placed, Zenobia simply nodded and the Flowers untied the pretty pink satin ribbon, removed the box lid to reveal the matching crystal champagne flute.

"As I said to you before ladies, I want each of you to always remember to take a moment to celebrate you. My prayer, my wish, my hope is for each of you to find someone as extra special as that toasting flute, to share the celebration.

"Ladies, our journey within this conference room has ended. I personally have enjoyed listening, sharing, and scrutinizing your experiences. I hope and trust the lessons, instructions, and obviously the friendships made were worth your while."

"And then some," a few Flowers said in unison. The others just smiled and nodded.

"You know we had to get you and Lourdes a little something," said Rose. Lily reached from the bottom of her chair and presented Zenobia and her assistant a pretty pink paper bag containing a spa gift certificate and designer bath products. One by one, the Flowers rose from their chairs to give each other, Zenobia and Lourdes hugs, expressions of thanks, words of encouragement, and a few side jokes.

However, gazing at Daisy's ring was the main item on the agenda. "Daisy, your card said 'sort of.' What's going on with that?" asked Breeze.

"Girl, Slayton does not have what we call taco meat. He has shag carpeting for chest hair! I make him put a shirt on before he eats a snack because crumbs would get caught. It's soft, though."

"Oh, so we felt his chest," teased Rose.

"Yeah, but the first time was by accident. He could have fed a small country with the amount of potato chip bits he left in his chest hair."

Whatever attempt any of them made to leave the room was thwarted, as they fell back in their chairs from laughter.

"Okay, I'll bring the bag and *a rake* to Iris' picture party," Breeze said with air quotes still laughing.

"What bag?" asked Zenobia. "And why was I not invited to the line dancing party?"

"We're sorry," said Petunia. "I think the next one is the second week in June." Iris nodded yes. "Just bring two bottles of cold water, an extra tee shirt, and a personal fan. We'll fill you in on the bag later."

The ladies laughed again while nodding their heads in agreement. They gathered their belongings, and causally headed out the door. "Iris, have you finished packing?" asked Rose finally heading out of the conference room.

"No, my living room is my closet for the past week with my outfits, costumes, and undies all over the place."

"Costumes?" asked Lily. "What kind of cruise is this?"

"Seriously, a cruise like no other. And am I just now noticing that you are on crutches?" asked Iris. The other Flowers noticing, as well.

"Yeah, I forgot to mention while modeling my new shoes, I tripped on my carpet, and twisted my ankle," said Lily. "Harper has been quite the nurse. He's picking me up after class. I better make the call, now."

"Hold that call, we need a pre-picture party at Iris'," said Petunia. "All in favor of a packing party at Iris' say, 'I.'" All but one agreed.

"If you don't mind, I'm going to sit this one out. Iris, do not forget to pack that pink dress to go with that confidence," Breeze said trying to smile. She made her way for the door determined to go home before any more questions regarding her state of mind could be asked. Besides, she already previewed the outfits and costumes, making a small mental note to try to go on the cruise next year.

They all made their way for the lobby behind Breeze, when Zenobia called her back. "Hyacinth, may I see you for moment?"

"Ms. Zenobia, really, I'm fine," she said in a huff.

"I need to see you in my office...now."

"Really, thank you for--"

"Get your narrow behind in this office this instant before I snatch you bald headed!" Zenobia boomed.

All the Flowers stood still, stunned. However, Breeze kept it moving. "I left my mama at the cemetery!" she snapped turning towards the front door. As quick as she could blink, Zenobia grabbed a clump of Breeze's hair and dragged her into the office.

25

Whines & Wants

"Spare me the 'it's all good' speech, when clearly it ain't," Zenobia said practically throwing Breeze in her office and slamming the door. "First and foremost, have a seat." Breeze did not budge from where she landed, with her arms folded. "PARK IT!" Reluctantly she slumped herself in one of the shiny black leather and wood chairs nearest the door. "Now tell me what the devil is going on with you?" Breeze did not answer and instead slid further down in her chair and stewed. "Fine. Let me make this easier for you. Tell me, Breeze, what do you want?"

"I want to go home," she said finally. "I just want some peace, so I can at least function until my vacation starts."

"First, never ask for peace. That is what we all want, but go through hell to get it! But let me get this straight: you want to go home, sulk, and spend what's left of the weekend trying to figure out where it all went wrong?"

"I am very much aware as to where it all went wrong, Ms. Zenobia. I've created a lifestyle of just dealing with it. And I was doing quite well, until I was thrown into this class!"

"If that were true, you would have left the first night. So here is a better question: Where do you *believe* it all went wrong?"

"We both do not have time to rehash 25 years of nonsense tonight."

"Agreed. Just give me the *Cliff Notes*," Zenobia said making herself comfortable reaching under her desk.

"I cannot believe I'm admitting this out loud..."

"That is what this time and this class is for," she said opening a can of orange soda. "Say it!"

"For starters, I was never good enough."

"Oh, honestly," Zenobia sighed sipping her soda.

"You said you wanted to know, and now I'm telling you," Breeze said straightening up in her chair. "I realized this noise came to a head in high school. I was never white enough for the black guys or not black enough for the white boys."

"I think that should be the other way around."

"No, I'm from Columbia. I meant what I said. In college, I was always too fat for the guys to even consider me and too skinny for the chubby chasers. A couple of guys in college gave me the best, yet the worst compliment: 'You have the qualities I want in a wife.' But they did not want *me* as a wife. And that has been the extent of my love life ever since. I've always wondered what it was about me that I could never seal the deal."

"If I understand this correctly, you were placed in this class because you are in an ex's wedding. You have had dates."

"*Dates* and not *boyfriends*. I've always had a string of friends that are men, and that was the extent. Spence was not my ex. We dated. He even tried to change me and for one moment of weakness, I tried to change. I resolved in my mind that if I wanted to keep a man, especially one that found me in church, that I would have to change. Then I didn't like what I was becoming. So, I changed all right."

"I see. You do realize all of this is just a season."

"For 25 years? You mean I have to wander around in my loveless wilderness for another 15 to make *anything* happen?"

"Have you asked Him for what you want?"

"Repeatedly! His Word says for us to ask. But when you constantly ask and never, *ever* receive, only in this one area, you just stop asking."

"Ah, did you believe you were going to receive what you prayed for?"

She started to answer, but paused for a moment. She realized hope for a loving relationship was always there. Sometimes she could reach out and touch it. "At one point in my life I could," she finally answered. "Not now, though. Not after what I just experienced."

"Maybe it is time that you start again, my dear. And that is why your aunt and friend signed you up for this class. They recognized your suppressed hope. I do believe you are getting it back. You just need to wait patiently on Him to make it happen. However long it takes. So, let us discuss this fresh start and back to my original question. I want to know what you want for your love life. Use this moment to speak to the universe what you really want."

"I-don't-know! Someone in the group has to be single and satisfied, and I came to the conclusion it was going to be me. My life *showed* I didn't care that I was 38, single, with no prospects...and enjoying the lack. Then I let my guard down for one brief moment." She paused for a moment, shaking her head. "All I wanted was to share a nice lunch, with a potentially nice man, having a nice pleasant conversation. Once again...I guess this is a prime example as to why The Word says to 'guard your heart.'"

"Yes, you are to guard your heart. But you cannot hide from *Him*," Zenobia shook her head. "Breeze, you must understand that He wants His children to be happy."

"DO I LOOK HAPPY TO YOU?" she bellowed. "For the past week, I've looked and felt miserable, and acted miserably. My friends are worried. My dad is at a loss as to what to do or say. My aunt was under the delusion this class would help. Because the results aren't coming fast enough, she gave up. At this point, I am now drained and frustrated.

"I have to admit though, I loved how I felt after speaking with Forest. I think I was actually floating for a good 24 hours. I felt that He finally had something just for me, at least once. And then, whatever I thought I had, was gone like puff a smoke. He gave and He snatched away.

"Then again, all this may not have been in His plan in the first place. But you know what? I am really sick of this guessing game!" She heard her phone's ring. She ignored it. "And I really don't want to play this game, His game, or their games anymore!"

"Games? More like trials as His way of getting our attention. He wants something you and He can talk about." .

"I talk to Him plenty."

"Perhaps. However, you really need to ask Him how He wants to use you and possibly take you to your next level."

"Actually, I'm quite comfortable where I am, thank you. Besides, *new level* requires *more* work."

"I see," Zenobia sighed. "Now we get to the root of the problem: You are not comfortable or content. You are downright complacent and quite out of order. So, lesson number one: Let's get it right, this time. Lesson number two: You need to use the resources He's given you." Breeze's phone rang again. "Are you going to get that?" Zenobia asked annoyed.

"Hey, can I call you back?"

"*Where have you been? I've been trying to reach you all day? And no, just be ready by six.*"

"What? I can't--"

"*Yes you can! I got tickets to the Battle of the DJs and I want to get some dinner before we go.*"

"I am in no mood to stand up for three hours, behind a couple of love crazed twenty somethings getting it on, while some stringy headed blond whips her hair back and forth *in my face* to her own beat!"

"*We're not--*"

"She *said* she could not go," Zenobia boomed snatching the phone away heatedly. "Who is this?" She looked bewildered. "This is a man. You did not tell me this was man," she whispered to Breeze.

"Ms. Zenobia, meet my friend Elliott. Elliott meet Ms. Zenobia," she said a little louder.

"Is this the one who stood you up?" Zenobia tried to say discreetly.

"No and why does everyone keep saying that?"

"Because that is what happened. Now it is up to you to find out why." Zenobia turned her attention back to the phone. "Listen, I am having a conversation with Breeze, so...yes, she is okay and will explain later... okay...okay she will be home and ready to go by *seven*. Nice to meet you, Elliott," she said finally ending the call. "What is going on with that?" she asked turning the phone off and placing it on her side of the desk.

"We've been friends for years--"

"Once again, you want to go home and pout, instead of dinner and a concert with a friend? Lesson number three I am sure He wants you to master: Lean on your friends."

"I just don't want to be around people right now."

"You'll recover faster with some laughter, good food, and music... with a friend you say?" Zenobia inquired peering over her glasses. Breeze nodded her head. "You know good friends, make great husbands." She gave Zenobia a look as if to say, *'Don't-even-go-there-at-this-point.'* "Anyway, I understand you need time to grieve. Do not think for one minute He is going to let you stay there. Lesson number four: No matter the circumstance, He is going to pull you through. The operative word is 'through,' not set up camp in your misery.

"Go to the concert, have a good time, flip *your* pretty natural curls in someone else's face, and see if you do not perk back up. Actually, you might want to flip your pretty hair in this, uh, Elliott's face, while you are at it." Breeze gave her a look. "Anyway, lesson number five: Lighten up! I sent you to those yoga classes for a reason. You need to relax and let that positive energy flow through you, again. And the last lesson: Give the man a chance."

"Who are you talking about, Ms. Zenobia?"

"I will leave that to you to decide, my dear," she said reaching for hug. Breeze was reluctant at first, still pondering that last lesson, and reciprocated the hug. She had not felt that warm of a hug since her mom passed away. "It will be all right, I promise." The hug and the sentiment was all she needed to hear and she finally broke down.

—　—

"And just where do you think you're going?" Iris asked. The Flowers were all standing outside the conference room door still in their bathrobes. "Before you waltz out of this office, you are gonna spill what's ailing you after we bared our souls and cried on *your* shoulder," Iris demanded.

"For starters Ms. Thing, you didn't tell me that Bun Penny closed," snapped Breeze.

"What the devil do you mean *THEY CLOSED DOWN BUNNY*?" Iris roared. "We were just there--"

"Last year. They closed in December. And don't you have some packing left?"

"Girl, the packing can wait! What is going on?"

"It's a long story. And I really have to--"

"Sit your nonexistent behind down and tell us what's wrong. That is what you have to do," interrupted Petunia. "By the way, Lourdes is warming up two slices of your favorite pizza for you."

"Pizza? We just had lunch."

"Please, y'all were in there for at least an hour. We got hungry and the remaining chocolate strawberries Lourdes stashed away weren't cuttin' it," said Petunia. "By the way, we decided to meet every first Tuesday of the month, except for November. That's when we'll vote and usher in that fine young senator from Illinois as president...and allow Daisy to get ready for her wedding."

"Come on dahlin', tell us what's wrong," said Violet softly.

Breeze finally sighed, knowing she could not get out of telling the story, but not about the wedding shenanigans. She was not ready to accept her 'Big Dummy' award just yet. "All right y'all, picture it..."

26

Dancing & Discovery

"You are officially checked in, Ms. Monsoon," said the perky, petite, polished hotel receptionist. "Here is your room key, welcome kit, and the itinerary which will start promptly at 7pm. As a member of the bridal party, you are to check in with the bride by 4:30." She thought she smiled politely. Her facial expression must have said otherwise. "The good news," the receptionist continued, "your roommate has not yet checked in. So, you have a few extra minutes to enjoy your amazing suite overlooking a breathtaking view of the courtyard."

Breeze finally felt herself genuinely brightening up, as she accepted her key and made her way to a tall golden arched filled-to-capacity valet cart. She was extra thankful for valet parking, as she and a handsome, stocky valet transported the load from car to cart. Her luggage, dress, three boxes of programs, favors, ceremony and reception accoutrements lined up like soldiers ready for battle. She made the initial struggle to move the cart to the elevator when interruptions commenced.

"*That's* why you snapped your fingers, startling the whole class," a voice whispered sassily from behind. Breeze turned around to see Tulip glowing with her warm dimply smile. "Forgotten dry cleaning, my pedicured foot! You do realize if the class knew the recipient of the 'Dumb Dumb' award was you, we would have talked you out of this wedding," Tulip stated while giving Breeze a warm welcoming, supportive hug.

"I know," said Breeze smiling reassuringly. "It really is all good."

"No it ain't! We need to talk."

"Tulip, I assure you, I've heard it all. No stone has been left unturned. Well, maybe one, but I can't worry about that right now. Besides, you do realize I was forced into our class because I said 'yes' to this mess."

Before Tulip could even respond, the interruptions continued. "I told Saffy I knew you from somewhere," Smith said giving Breeze a bear hug.

"You must've hid your face in Mr. Knight's spectacular barbecue pit," she said returning the hug.

"Before I forget," Smith said releasing Breeze and giving Tulip a peck on the cheek. "We're meeting in the main room at 6 pm sharp instead of 7 like the itinerary says. And Tuesday is on the warpath, so please don't forget to check in with her by 4:30." Breeze sighed, nodded, and looked at her watch feeling the time ticking away. "Oh and Saffy, change of plans. I volunteered your services in case the wedding planner doesn't show in time. Breeze, I trust you have all the things for the ceremony?" She smiled and nodded. "Phew, okay," he sighed. "Thank you. Oh one more thing, Saffy, you are coming to the rehearsal dinner with us. I got some folks that can't wait to meet you.

"Ladies, I need to check on my cousin and a few last minute details, so I will leave you two. Saffy, please don't tell *too much*," Smith smiled, kissed Tulip again, and made his way into a newly formed crowd.

While making another attempt for the elevator, Breeze noticed Tulip and her dimples beaming brighter than the lobby lights. She could not help but just smile for her friend.

"What?" Tulip asked noticing the smile.

"I see you made your decision."

"Well," she said coyly, "I haven't. But this weekend, meeting his family and friends, and just spending good quality time with him is making the decision a lot easier. I'm still seeing Graham, just not as much. I need to schedule a call, just to make a date. When we do get together, it's wonderful, the way I imagined it should be when you are dating. While Graham is fun, Smith is real. He makes it easy for me to find the time to spend with him, like I'm Smith's priority. It does require some work and patience. We even had a few moments of intense fellowship. I know there will be more, but the good outweighs the bad. His son is such a sweetheart, an absolutely lovable kid." Tulip paused for a minute while Breeze called for the elevator. "I guess I just made my decision, huh?"

"Breeze, BREEZE!" Tuesday shouted in a panic. "Where you have been? The clerk told me you checked in 15 minutes ago! I left specific instructions for the bridal party to check in with me *once* you arrived. I cannot--"

"Tuesday, I have been making every attempt to get from the desk to the elevator with not much luck. You are the third, and I must admit the most unpleasant interruption, I've had since making my way from A to B. Since ya found me, I'm checking in."

"Are you the sitter my mom hired?" Tuesday inquired turning the wrath elsewhere. "Because if you are, I really need you to be where you are supposed to be, which is watching--"

"No, dear, I'm Saffron. Smith's plus one."

"Oh, I am so sorry. Everything is in shambles, no one is where they should be! Britt is still with the seamstress, and all y'all just refuse to check in! Breeze, can you at least call the sitter and find out where she is before those kids drive me bonkers?"

"First of all, ask your mom to call the sitter. Next, have your wedding planner check the whereabouts of the rest of the bridal party--"

"That's just it. She ain't here! I told her to be here by three. It's almost five."

"Tuesday, please relax. Traffic is heavy around this time. She will be here. Besides, according to the itinerary, we are meeting at six. That gives her plenty of time to come, unload her things, and dote on you and your schedule."

"Oh, so you at least know the schedule," she sighed in relief. "Please say you have the music for the ceremony in that box."

"Yes, Tuesday, I do."

"And the order of service, you know, just in case the planner doesn't show up in time?"

"Girl, you are twenty feet from the bar. Find yourself a stool, say a quick prayer, and knock two back! Everything will be all right."

"It bettah be," Tuesday sighed finally. She smiled, giggled, and actually took her advice while throwing her hands in the air.

"Okay, I see Smith did not exaggerate," Tulip said calling for the elevator. Breeze just smiled while collecting her own thoughts on the matter. "I really cannot wait to tell you what really went down."

"What, more than what I went through just now or for almost an entire year? I honestly do not believe I could stand anymore at this point."

"Yeah, you can stand this. For starters--"

"Hey, Breeze? Yoo-hoo, roomie," Wednesday sang from a far. "Girl, why didn't you tell me my cousin was on the warpath?"

"We just crossed it. Wednesday, this is Tul, um, Saffron, Smith's significant other." The two started to shake hands, but hugged instead. Breeze called for the elevator one more time, while Wednesday tried to find some room for her belongings on the valet cart.

The elevator doors finally opened, welcoming them in. Wednesday pulled the cart in first, while Breeze steered. "Ladies, I'll let you get settled," said Tulip. "And Breeze, we'll talk later. I gotta phone call to make."

"Please don't tell nobody 'bout this!"

"That's my second phone call. The first one ain't even 'bout chu!" She smiled and waved as the elevator doors finally closed.

"Girl, I cannot wait until this madness is ovah," sighed Wednesday. Breeze agreed wearily nodding her head.

— —

Breeze and Wednesday arrived in the lobby promptly at six, fresh and refreshed, ready to join the rest of the bridal party, friends, and family. However, the party was not found at the ceremony site. A crowd formed a circle, cheering on two sets of well-seasoned hand dancers, swinging to a catchy tune a jazz trio was playing. Breeze did not recognize one of the couples, but noticed the Knights putting on a specular show. Their eight-counts were so tight, they floated, making their dance moves look effortless. A tall, statuesque woman with smooth caramel coated skin with reddish-brown dreadlocks made an attempt to bring the crowd back to the subject at hand. Breeze noticed the clipboard in her hand, and assumed she was the planner that finally arrived.

"Everyone, please, the bride is wait--," the woman commanded only to be swept off her feet by an older gentlemen looking like the spitting image of Mr. Knight. They, too, were swept up by the moment and hand danced for a couple of minutes. The assumed planner kept up with her dance partner, letting him lead, despite the major height disparity.

Twenty-five minutes into the frivolity outside of the ceremony site, appeared to be beyond enough for the bride. "Can y'all please get my rehearsal started?" Tuesday pleaded with the crowd. Her father released Mrs. Knight to grab his daughter's hand. "Daddy, we have to be outta here by seven," she whined but she, too, could not resist the music. Realizing this was indeed a celebration, other couples paired off to dance. One older gentleman asked Breeze to dance. Not too confident with her new skills, she declined. He did not take 'no' for an answer and told her to follow his lead.

"Okay, everyone, we really need to get started," the planner said thanking and breaking away from her dance partner. The crowd laughed, clapped, and made their way to the mouth of the ceremony site. "First, let me introduce myself. My name is Hope Wells, and I am the wedding coordinator for the weekend. The site has been set up to give you a feel as to where you will sit or stand depending on your role in the wedding. So, if are not in the wedding, please make your way in and have a seat on either side of the aisle." She waited until the intimate crowd made their way in. "Now, I will need Pastor Clary, the groom, and the best man to make their way inside. I will show you where to stand."

The men in question did what they were told, only in their own way. Spencer and Branford clowned their way down the make shift aisle to the beat of whatever the jazz trio was playing, while Pastor Clary gave the wedding planner a few more twirls. Outside the site, the other couple said their goodbyes and wished the bride all the best. "So nice to meet you and congratulations," Mrs. Knight said to the couple. "They're celebrating 40 years of marriage tomorrow night with a huge party in the other ballroom," she said to anyone within hearing range.

"Now then, if we can have everyone line up, with the mothers and their escorts in the front." Hope positioned them, instructing what to do, where, and when to sit. Next, the junior bridesmaid and groomsman were paired up. Breeze was finally able to see Branford's oldest daughter, looking like a good cross between him and Ragan. Then it was the bridesmaids turn to be matched up with their groomsmen. Due to the change in plans, Breeze will walk alone. She was a little relieved, not having to walk down the aisle with Branford, at least within proximity of his wife Ragan. She was not ready for that stone to be unturned tonight. Her mood really lifted seeing Branford's youngest daughter, as the flower girl and Smith's son, the ring bearer, comfortably linking arms and smiling their snaggle tooth smiles.

"Tuesday, you will be with your father, just not during rehearsal. So, if I could have, um, Saffron take Tuesday's place, please? Tuesday, you can make your way in, so that you can see the arrangement and make changes if necessary. And Saffron will need your practice bouquet." Hope made sure all were spaced, linked and straight. "I think we can get three practice runs in before we need to leave. Ragan, can you get the music for me, please? On my signal, play track number three. When Michael Bublé starts singin', mamas start walkin'!"

— ᔈ —

"It's been so long, Gigi," said Ragan. "May I call you Gigi? I mean it's only natural that I call you Gigi since Branford always called you Gigi. Why did he call you Gigi anyway? I swear, my husband must have had the biggest crush on you in college, 'cause he could never stop talking about Gigi."

"Breeze is fine," she interrupted nervously. Although she was actually having a good time mingling with the family members, she made a mental note to avoid Ragan. Breeze noticed her "spread of time" with a few slight worry wrinkles. Her neatly styled haircut framed her flawless complexion she maintained since college, allowed her to own her look.

"Well, Breeze it is, then. Wow, it's been, like, 17 years since I last saw you. You look so good."

"Why, thank--"

"And I am so glad you kept your pretty hair, long. Will you be wearing it down for the wedding? I still don't know what to do with the girls' hair. I'll just wait until tomorrow to see what Tuesday wants. Mmm, still no husband I see," Ragan said holding up Breeze's left hand with her boulder laden left hand. "I thought someone, anyone, would have snatched you up by now. Do you at least have a date for the wedding?"

"Well, --"

"I mean you were dateless for our wedding. I'm sure you could have found someone by now. I'm surprised you didn't marry someone from our college days. What about that light skinned freckle faced guy you were lappin' around for a while? Him or oh, that white guy. Now he was really nice and you two were inseparable. No worries, you'll find someone very soon. As a matter of fact, I'm going to pray over it. I will pray for someone wonderful to come into your life and you'll be dating in no time."

"Ragan," Breeze finally said. "Although I'm finally finding myself in a good place, thank you for praying for me, and I will certainly pray for you."

"Pray for me about what? I already have a man. A good handsome man, two beautiful girls, a mini mansion, two award winning dogs, and minus the cruise Branford refuses to take, I am living quite the charmed life."

"My prayer is for you to one, go on that cruise and two, cherish every minute of what God has blessed you with," Breeze said finally making an exit to anywhere. "Talk to you soon, Ragan."

Breeze gingerly made her way to the buffet table after freeing herself from the mouth almighty prying pest. She knew Ragan meant well and appreciated someone praying for her circumstance. She also remembered why should could not stand to be in her company longer than five minutes. She surveyed the buffet items seeing her healthy, yet favorite foods. Grilled salmon, chicken, and vegetables found their way on her plate. She smiled at the thought of not gaining unnecessary weight tonight. The reception will be another story.

"You need ta put some mo' collards on dat plate ta balance out all dat protein, don't cha' thank?" Mrs. Lyte asked grabbing Breeze's arm almost knocking the plate out of her hand.

"Really? All righty then, be a dear and go get me some more of those greens," she snapped moving her plate, regaining her arm, and finding a seat.

"Young ladeh, I will have you know--," she said with her finger in Breeze's face.

"Mrs. Lyte, please don't start this mess tonight," she retorted quietly so that the brewing discussion was between them. "Everyone is having a wonderful time, I've held up my end of the promise I made to you…so far. And whatever you have against me, please pray about it, and let it go. I am not yours, nor your son's enemy. And I wish you would stop treating me as such!"

"I see," she said straightening up. "I jus' wanted ta apolahgize fo' the way I acted."

"Go on…"

"I spoke wit' mah son aftah dat bachelorette party mess. I still say you shoulda done what Tuesday asked you ta do. I mean you a bridesmaid and all. You supposed ta do fo' da bride."

"Now I finally see the family resemblance between you and your son. When are you getting to the apology part?"

"You smart mouth littah--"

Breeze quickly rose up from her chair, took her protein laden plate, and tried to make her way elsewhere.

"Hold on, hold on, hold on now, chile," Mrs. Lyte retreated. "I'm sorray fo' the way I acted. I apolahgize. Spencah told me how he treated you. And he had no right ta call you his gurhfriend, 'specially since we nevah met. Please, please accept mah apolahgy."

"Apology accepted," she said hoping that was the end so that she can get back to her plate before the food gets cold.

"And thank you fo' seein' to it dat mah son and Tuesday werked out dey problems. I thank it brought 'em closah, don't you thank?"

"Yes, ma'am I do."

Spencer and Smith playfully grabbed, hugged, and escorted Mrs. Lyte to the front of the room for presentations, toasts, and gifts before she could say anymore. Breeze was relieved, but her food was indeed, now cold.

— ~

"Good evening, I'm the bride's mother, Opal," Mrs. Knight said shaking the hands of the small crowd of four. "Breeze, dahlin', I hate to pull you away. Shine and I arranged a little something for the bridal party, so that we could spend some quality time with the hors d'oeuvres we paid for." Breeze was having a marvelous time talking to Thaddeus, Secret, and Secret's husband. The intimate crowd laughed, as they both excused themselves. "Chile, please tell me the one with the plaits was the same one you were beamin' about at the bridal shower."

"No, that's Thaddeus," Breeze sighed. "He's one of the History teachers at our school. I am beyond excited that Tuesday invited him. Now I have someone to dance with."

"Have you seen anything interesting, while working this room with that smile, hair, and red dress? You know most of the folks in this crowd better than I do."

"Now you know, Mrs. Knight, everything here is either coupled or married. My job tonight is to smile, laugh, and look good for the pictures." And that she did. She allowed herself to enjoy the best part about her position as a bridesmaid. Hugging family members she met over the past few months, while laughing with her work colleagues and acquaintances from college. Her crowd remarked on the loveliness of the ceremony, the radiance of the bride, and how each one of the dresses were made especially for each bridesmaid.

"Gurl, lemme take ya outside so we can stop some traffic," said Mr. Fellows during one of her promenades throughout cocktail hour. "If Ruby will let meh, save meh a dance durin' da reception, heah?" Breeze graciously agreed.

After the bridal party finished their refreshments, they checked their teeth and snapped behind-the-scene pictures of each other in their finest. Hope announced the guests were making their way into the reception room and suggested the party to start forming the line, ready to be introduced. Breeze relished the opportunity to finally be on Branford's arm, and snapped a couple of pictures to preserve the moment. "Hold on let me get a picture of the two of you," said Ragan. "And now my girls with their father." Breeze graciously moved out of the way, making conversation with Wednesday and Britt.

"GENTLE," a tall handsome dulce la leche coated man wearing a tuxedo shouted from the bottom of the stairs. Unfortunately, not one but two specific heads turned to face the source, now making his way up the steps.

"Say, bruh?" intercepted Branford. "How do you know my--"

"Um, Branny?" was all Breeze could muster while stopping him.

"Is *that* why you call her Gigi?" snapped Ragan. "And this is how you came up with our daughter's name? Kids, your father will be taking us on that Disney cruise...this summer! Ladies, be sure to thank your, um, Auntie Breeze."

"Thank you, Auntie Breeze," cheered their daughter Grace.

"Thank you for my name," the oldest daughter said. "Everybody loves it."

Breeze smiled wanting to get back to the subject at hand. "Hold that thought" she said to the young man. "Oh Ragan, I believe my prayer worked."

"Hope mine works for you, too," she said finally smiling, nodding in the direction of the young man, and made her way back to the reception room.

"I am so glad to see you," said the sharply dressed man. "You look amazing in that dress! I can't believe I recognized you with your hair up. But, I could see that smile from across the room."

Breeze found herself smiling and blushing but asked, "Forest, what are you doing here?"

"My parents are celebrating their 40th wedding anniversary in the other room."

"So, you're the young man they were talking about," said Mrs. Knight. "Breeze, he's single," she said whispering.

"I know. This is the Bridal Shower guy. Forest meet..."

"Yes, my parents talked about last night's hand dance marathon," he said shaking a few hands. "Evening, everyone." He gently pulled Breeze to the side. "Um, can we talk alone for a minute?"

"The reception is about to start. We're getting ready to walk in."

"Y'all got time," said Mrs. Knight. "The bride and groom are probably somewhere still working out their insatiability issues. Go, on baby."

Breeze reluctantly excused herself from the line. She felt like this was all a dream, but her gold sling backs pinched her back to reality with every step. "It's so good to see you again," grabbing both her hands once he found a quiet spot. "You look absolutely amazing."

She started to reciprocate the compliment, but blurted out, "Why didn't you show up for our date?"

"Wow, straight to the chase," he said slowly letting go of her hands. "I had a family matter to take care of, and could not make it in time. I really apologize, and hope that you enjoyed your edamame and mandarin tea. So, let's exchange numbers this time, you know, for future dates," he said reaching for her hands again. Only this time, Breeze stopped him.

"Forest, it is really good to see you and I hope you were able to take care of the matter you spoke of. It's just that these past seven weeks allowed me to examine myself and I realized that I cannot handle getting hurt. And I won't let anyone hurt me again."

"I don't make it my business to hurt anyone. If we just exchange numbers..."

"Forest, thanks. I am so glad the mystery has finally been solved...But I'm done," Breeze said looking at him one more time, turned around, and quickly rejoined the bridal party. Before anyone could start asking anything, she held up her hand and simply stated, "I'm fine."

"What did we miss?" Tuesday asked breathlessly.

"For starters, Breeze's first name."

"Finally," Spencer said exhaustedly. "What is it?"

"Long story, bruh," sighed Branford. "If you really wanna know, ask your Goddaughter."

"Tuesday, what do you have on?" asked Mrs. Knight. "I thought we agreed on one dress, especially because of that price tag."

"Mom, if I was going to do the Electric Slide, I might as well come out in something shocking. BAM," she boomed twirling around in her silk halter sheath dress dripping with rhinestones.

"It is lovely. You could have at least waited until after dinner."

"Everyone, the guests have calmed themselves down and are finally seated," said Hope. "Let's start the second act of the show with the mamas and their escorts..."

"You aw'right, Gigi?" Branford whispered.

"Yeah, I'm fine," she lied feeling her entire demeanor change a little too quickly. She found herself on autopilot, while getting in line with Branford. She, too, felt his demeanor change after the revealing. She playfully tugged him, asking if he was all right. "I told you to let her know."

"Yeah, yeah, I know. Just don't be surprised when I need to borrow your couch," they both laughed. "I think you need to make things right with dude over there. He seems like a good guy."

"Branny...," was all she could say. She did look back to the spot where she and Forest shared a conversation, seeing him still standing there. She sighed, found some muscles to form a great big smile, and did a two-step to a Michael Jackson tune into the reception as they were being introduced. Once the party was in, they formed a soul train line to welcome the newlyweds.

However, there was a slight delay with the introduction of the bride and groom. Breeze assumed Tuesday was making Spencer practice their grand entrance one last time. The DJ took the initiative, playing a few James Brown tunes to keep the fingers poppin' and the hips swayin'. Once the cue was given, the DJ mixed the music back to the designated song and introduced the new Mr. and Mrs. Spencer Lyte. The newlyweds entered grooving through their soul train line, dancing their way to their sweetheart table.

The groomsmen escorted the bridesmaids to their seats once the song was finally finished and the frivolity subsided. Breeze was ecstatic seeing her personal support group seated at her table. "What's wrong?" Thaddeus and Secret demanded in unison as they shared a group hug.

"Is it that obvious?" she asked while trying to hold it together. "Forest is here. He's in another party across the room."

"Girl, what does he look like?" inquired Thaddeus.

"Forget that," snapped Secret. "Did you get to the bottom of his--," Secret started but was interrupted when the DJ called Breeze's name for the toast.

She immediately forgot the change in the order of the reception, totally missing Branford's speech. "Good evening," she said while taking the microphone. "I know that everyone is ready to make a 'soul train' line to the buffet, so I shall make this brief. I had the privilege to witness two individuals excitedly plan for just this one day, to a God favored couple ready and equipped to start their new lives together. Spencer and Tuesday: please continue to love each other, like each other, do for one another, and continue to keep God first in your life. I said it 10 months ago, and I still mean it today. You both deserve each other's love. To the new Mr. & Mrs. Lyte." Everyone raised their glass to the new couple as the DJ played LTD's 'We Both Deserve Each Other's Love' for their first dance as husband and wife.

Breeze stood smiling, watching the newlyweds make their way to the dance floor when Tuesday startled her. "This is especially for you," Tuesday said tossing her a miniature replica of her bouquet. "We'll explain later," the couple said in unison making their way to the dance floor.

Breeze assumed the bridal party would dance with each other. Instead, the members of the party danced with their spouses or significant others. She was happy to see Wednesday dance with a nice looking young man that appeared to be about her age. Tulip was beaming those dimples, dancing with Smith. She was also relieved to see Branford and Ragan smiling, laughing, and dancing with each other. While making her way to her seat, Thaddeus stopped her, asking for a dance. She graciously accepted the offer and the two made their own way to the dance floor.

"You do realize that I am so glad that you and Secret are here." The DJ invited other couples to share the floor. "Where's Thurston?"

"You know this crowd ain't ready for me and Thurston. Besides, he sends his love and best to you. He's also making me bring him back two pieces of cake and a picture of you and this dress." She smiled and twirled to the beat. "Ah, someone has been taking lessons."

"I have, so hush. I'm trying to concentrate."

"Breezy, what are you going to do?"

"It's done. I'm done. I will only get hurt again, if I see him again."

"Do you really believe that, 'cause you ain't convincing me. Did he give you an explanation?" She nodded her head yes. "Accept it and move forward."

Breeze was thankful the music and dancing came to end for the moment, not wanting to hear any more of the advice she was not ready to accept. Thaddeus escorted her back to her seat when the newlyweds intercepted Breeze, and pulled her to the side.

"Hope filled us in on the brothah standing in the lobby staring at you," said Spencer. "We talked to him a bit and...I gotta say this. Breeze, on behalf of every man that messes up, give him another chance. We are gonna mess up, but you got to work with us. Anytime a man notices you all the way from the other side of the lobby, walks up, and pleads his case in front of strangers is worthy of another chance."

"Read the tab on my bouquet," said Tuesday.

"Meet me in the lobby at 11 tonight."

"It really is your turn, Breeze. So, don't be late for that date." The newlyweds smiled made their way back to the table ready to enjoy the rest of their reception.

"Yay, the salads arrived," she said sashaying back to the table.

"Forget the salad," said Thaddeus and Secret in unison. "What say you?"

"Pass the rolls before they get cold," Breeze sighed. "And apparently, I have a date with Forest at 11 pm tonight."

27

Pictures & Plates

"Tuesday told me you have a date with that dashing young man in the tuxedo tonight," Mrs. Knight said relishing a moment of peace.

"Yes," Breeze sighed. "Before I go, is there anything else that needs doing that would require me to stall and think about it some more?"

"Yeah, you can wait right here while one a 'dem waitresses brings back a plate," said Mr. Knight massaging his wife's foot. "I told you, if you have a man waitin', make sho' you bring him a plate," he said reaching for the other foot. "Bunny told me he put a smile on your face so bright, everyone at the shower needed shades. Seems like a good man, though. Nice famileh. Give 'em a chance."

As if on cue, a waitress brought a plate of a few sample goodies, with silverware wrapped in a red cloth napkin. She put the plate down and hugged them both tightly. "Have fun baby. Oh, come by and see us the next time you are on your way to Kings Dominion."

"I will," she said picking up the plate and bouquets, scurrying off to the lobby.

"Just call first," shouted Mr. Knight.

— —

"Hey," she said.

"Hey yourself," he responded standing up with his hands in his pockets. "I thought maybe you decided not to come."

"It was a thought. I had to wait for your little care package," she said setting down the covered plate in front of him. "I also realized you knew what I ordered from Pei Wei. So, when did you finally arrive?"

"Actually, I called Pei Wei to let you know I was running late, to give me 15 more minutes, and have you order anything you wanted plus my order because I was hungry. I described you and the guy who answered told me you were there 30 minutes ago, ordered, and left. He said you were cute. So, if this doesn't work out, give him a call."

She laughed but could not picture who the admirer could be. Forest offered her a seat, while he peeked at what the late night snack included. He wasted no time digging in, but offered her some of the food, first. "Why didn't you call Cypress to get my number?" she asked using a spoon to scoop up some fried rice.

"Cypress and Reach called me first," he said nibbling on a spring roll. "He said if I dare call, proceed with caution. Judging from our scene earlier, they were correct. So I gotta ask, who hurt you? Wait, don't answer that, Spencer filled me in."

"Listen, I am not *that* guy and I would love to see how this turns out. Unfortunately, I've been down this road before, and almost married her. If you have some unresolved feelings for that guy Spencer or any other issues that would keep you from moving forward, give me a call once you figure things out."

"First of all, if you ain't that guy, stop acting like that guy! Next, I have absolutely no feelings for Spence! You should have figured that out after y'all's discussion. Now, *you* should have manned up, threw caution to the wind, and called! As far as I was concerned, you didn't show up! I am not the bittah sistah, but it is actions like that, and mess like this, that makes us bitter! So, you give *me* a call when *you* can handle this," she spat getting up in disgust.

"Wait, wait. I didn't mean it that way."

"How else was I supposed to take it, Forest?"

"Yeah, yeah, I should have called," he smiled sheepishly. "Sit down, please." She reluctantly sat down still feeling a little steamed. "I was unable to call during the time of our date. And I should have called when I got the number from Cypress. I apologize for not calling. Forgive me."

"We'll see," she said smiling finally.

"Do you have your phone in that red pouch?" She nodded. "Good, let's exchange numbers," he said reaching into his pocket. He also pulled out his wallet. "Hope this will speed up the forgiving process," he said giving her an old picture of the two of them at Kings Dominion.

"Oh my gosh, *The Shockwave*, right?" she asked grinning from ear to ear. He nodded. "We kept riding until we got that picture right! Please don't tell me you've kept this in your wallet, all this time."

"Would you forgive me quicker if I said, 'yes'?"

"You would score some major brownie points."

"Actually, I found this on the day of our date, while I was over my parents' house. I was going to make a bigger copy and bring it."

"Can you make me a copy?"

"Can you forgive me?"

"This is a very good start."

"Let's see if we can snap a few pics, better than this one," he suggested. Her smile was brighter than the camera's flash.

The two stayed up talking and laughing about the years that went by. They debated over the changes that were going on with their beloved Columbia. He, too, was disappointed about the Poinsettia Tree. He was also furious over the closing of Bun Penny, both were glad that it was not the designated place for their first date. Roller coasters, friends, best places to eat, movies watched, stories of bad dates, and a spontaneous foot rub made them lose all track of time. Breeze saw Tuesday and Spencer checkout at the front desk, most likely making their way to the airport to start their honeymoon. They all smiled and waved. Breeze mouthed a 'thank you,' they both mouthed it back.

"Good granny, is it really 5:15?" Breeze asked finally looking at a nearby clock. "I gotta get some sleep."

"Agreed," he said getting up stiffly. "Hold on...," he said kissing her. "Yeah, I remembered that," he said finally.

"Smurf Mountain," she said softly wanting another reminder. She got one.

"We can go there tomorrow, I mean today," he offered. "Have a little Waffle House..."

"Now that's an offer I can't refuse."

They slowly strolled to Breeze's room hand in hand, smiling at each other. She could not believe what she was feeling at this moment. Thankfully her shoes were in his hands, so they could not pinch her into reality. She reached in her pouch for her room key. She started to use it, when Forest stopped her for another kiss. Only this kiss resulted with shoes, bags, jackets, bouquets, and what was left of Breeze's inhibitions falling to the floor. Kisses moving from her lips to her trigger points, caused Breeze's back to make contact with the door with a loud thud. *"Don't wake up the roommate! Don't wake up the roommate,"* she thought giving into the moment deeply. What she felt next, could not happen.

"Um...okay," she said breathlessly breaking away from the entanglement. "Uh...10 o'clock...breakfast?"

"Uh...yeah...yeah...10 o'clock," he managed to say while busying himself picking up the items off the floor. He handed the items to her, used the key to open the door, and gave her one last kiss, but on the cheek.

"Oh wait, I don't want to wake up my roommate. Can you unzip the back of my dress?"

"And then what?" he whispered slyly with his lips dangerously near her neck.

"Just down to here," she managed to say with her hand on her back. He unzipped a little lower. "I...can manage from here, thank you."

"Let me know if you need anything else tonight," he said giving her one last kiss. "My number's now in your phone." He slowly walked away still looking at her. Breeze stayed in the doorway, until he was out of sight.

*"Breeze, I'm staying with my boyfriend tonight. You have the room all to yourself.
Enjoy and thanks for everything,"* said the note left by Wednesday.

"P.S. Saffron left you a little something."

"I would not be what I am right now, if I knew this a few minutes earlier," she giggled to the universe. Before she could get to the white box with a pretty pink ribbon, she let the dress fall to the floor, freeing herself. She stretched while searching for her phone, momentarily forgetting the box. She found her phone, but curiosity got the best of her.

*"I think this is what you said you wanted for Christmas. I think you need this now.
Thanks for all of your support. See you at the picture party! Love, Tulip.
P.S. You know I wanted that bouquet!"*

She untied the pretty pink ribbon and opened the box to reveal lavender scented bubble bath and a small container of Epsom salt.

"I am going to wear this out tomorrow night when I get home from Kings Dominion... with Forest." She smiled wanting to call somebody. She looked at her phone, saw a number she did not recognize, and immediately thought of Forest. She also noticed three missed calls and a text from Elliott.

"Call me, doesn't matter what time."

"Hey," she said panicking. "What's wrong? Are you all right?"

"Yeah," he said groggily. *"What time is it?"*

"You said the time didn't matter."

"So I did," he said still trying to wake up. *"I must have been under the influence of that pic of you in that red dress, you sent."*

"Elliott, are you under the influence of sumptin' else?"

"Yeah, much needed sleep. So, did you have a good time?"

"I did," she said wanting to tell him about Forest, but wanted to wait until they were face to face.

"Did you catch the bouquet?"

"In a matter of speaking."

"I guess that means you did. So, is all of this behind you?"

"Yeah, why? What is going on, Elliott?"

"Don't you think it's your turn?"

"I would like to think so," she said looking at the bouquet and thinking about Forest.

"I think you are ready for a real relationship…with me. We'll talk more once we're on the plane. For now, I need some more sleep. Love you!"

"Love you, too," she said standing bewildered, slightly miffed, and now wide awake.

It's In His Word

Matthew 5:16 (NIV) In the same way, let your light shine before others, that they may see your good deeds and glorify your Father in heaven.

Philippians 4:11 (NIV): ...for I have learned to be content whatever the circumstances.

Proverbs 4:23 (NLT): Guard your heart above all else, for it determines the course of your life.

2 Timothy 1:6 (AKJV): Why I put you in remembrance that you stir up the gift of God, which is in you by the putting on of my hands.

Esther 2:12 (NIV): ...she had to complete twelve months of beauty treatments prescribed for the women...

Psalm 37:4 (ESV): Delight yourself in the LORD, and he will give you the desires of your heart.

Psalm37:7 (NIV): Be still before the LORD and wait patiently for him...

Ephesians 5:22, 25 (NIV): Wives, submit yourselves to your own husbands as you do to the Lord; (25) Husbands, love your wives, just as Christ loved the church and gave himself up for her...

Habakkuk 2:2 (NIV): Then the LORD replied: "Write down the revelation and make it plain on tablets so that a herald may run with it.

James 4:2 (NIV): ...You do not have because you do not ask God.

Matthew 7:7 & **Luke 11:9** (NLT): And so I tell you, keep on asking, and you will receive what you ask for. Keep on seeking, and you will find. Keep on knocking, and the door will be opened to you.

John 14:13 (ESV): Whatever you ask in my name, this I will do, that the Father may be glorified in the Son.

Matthew 18:15 (NLT): If another believer sins against you, go privately and point out the offense...

Ephesians 5:18 (NIV): Do not get drunk on wine, which leads to debauchery. Instead, be filled with the Spirit...

I Corinthians 10:23 (NIV): "I have the right to do anything," you say--but not everything is beneficial. "I have the right to do anything"--but not everything is constructive.

Proverbs 18:22 (NASB): He who finds a wife finds a good thing and obtains favor from the LORD.

I Corinthians 6:19 (NIV): Do you not know that your bodies are temples of the Holy Spirit, who is in you, whom you have received from God? You are not your own...

Hebrews 10:25(NIV): do not giving up meeting together, as some are in the habit of doing, but encouraging one another...

Hebrews 10:35 (NIV): So do not throw away your confidence; it will be richly rewarded.

Ephesians 2:10 (NLT): For we are God's masterpiece.

Psalm 139:14 (NIV): I praise you because I am fearfully and wonderfully made; your works are wonderful, I know that full well.

Made in the USA
Middletown, DE
21 June 2017